Incursion!

They pushed through the crowds, and made their way outside. They lost Governor Turnball in the crush, and hopped into the first taxi they saw.

"Admiralty Headquarters and don't spare the gees," Rob said.

"Right you are," the driver said, and the taxi went vertical to clear local traffic.

Fischer grunted as the acceleration shoved him into his seat. He stared out of his window and saw contrails forming as shuttles raced for orbit. He shivered. There were dozens leaving. All at once.

"Faster," he muttered. "Go faster. I'll pay your fines."

The driver nodded. The taxi's drive howled as he pushed the throttle to the floor. The city turned to a blur beneath them.

Also available from Impulse Books UK

The Devan Chronicles

The God Decrees
The Power That Binds
The Warrior Within
Dragon Dawn
Destiny's Pawn*

The Merkiaari Wars

Hard Duty
What Price Honour
Operation Oracle
Operation Breakout
Incursion
Countermeasures*
Resurgence*
No Mercy*

The Shifter Legacies

Way of the Wolf
Wolf's Revenge
Wolf's Justice*
Wolf War*

The Rune Gate Cycle
Rune Gate
Chosen

* Forthcoming from Impulse Books UK

These and other titles available from Impulse Books UK
http://www.impulsebooks.co.uk

Incursion

by

Mark E. Cooper

Published by Impulse Books UK

Published by Impulse Books UK December 2016
http://www.impulsebooks.co.uk

PUBLISHER'S NOTE
The characters and events in this book are fictitious. Any similarity to real persons living or dead, business establishments, events, or locales is entirely coincidental and not intended by the author.

Books are available at quantity discounts. For more information please write to Impulse Books UK, 18 Lampits Hill Avenue, Corringham, Essex SS177NY, United Kingdom.

Cover design: Tom Edwards http://tomedwardsdesign.com

A CIP catalogue record for this book
is available from the British Library.

ISBN: 978-1-905380-67-1

Printed and bound in Great Britain
Impulse Books UK

Acknowledgments

Special thanks go to Colin Jubb, Tristan Parker and all my other friends over at the Snakeholme Facebook group.

Also thanks to Angela Swain Jackson, Dave Milne, Robert Begg, John Bradley, and Lcdr Craig Holoboski for all their help in making this series better than any one person could alone.

Thanks for everything.

A word on language and pronunciation

These books were written and produced in the United Kingdom and use British English language conventions. For example the use of 'ou' in the words colour and honour instead of the American spellings: color, honor. Another example would be the interchangeable use of ize and ise in words such as realise or realize.

The Shan are an alien species with their own verbal and written language, but for story purposes all Shan dialogue is translated into English. However, names of characters remain as close as is possible to the actual alien name. See examples below for pronunciation:

Shima = Shee-muh
Tei'Varyk = Tie-va-rick
Kajetan = Kah-jet-an
Fuentez = Foo-en-tez
Evrei Xabat = Ev-rye Za-bot
Parcae = Pah-k-eye
Kisa = Key-sah
Merki = Mer-key
Merkiaari = Mer-key-ah-ree
Orbit = year
Cycle = day
Seg = hour

1 ~ Do Not Go Gentle

Aboard ASN Odyssey, Faragut orbit.

"Kill that," Captain Jane Powell said, highlighting a Merkiaari ship on the main viewer with her control wand.

Odyssey bucked and rolled as Merki cap ship missiles repeatedly slammed her from all sides. They were hammering her into scrap despite her dreadnought armour and shields. She held station on the planet and soaked up the punishment, not out of choice, but out of necessity. Her drives and aft section had been reduced to slag. Despite that she was still a powerful unit, and one in a much better condition than the rest of her squadron. The dead hulks of Faragut's picket force drifting throughout the system attested to that. Odyssey was the only ship left in any condition to fight.

Powell sat at her ease with legs crossed and her control wand in hand. Her crew were working at their stations with precision and skill like an extension of her will. She ignored the burning remains of Odyssey's comms shack; the acrid smoke pouring from it and the engineering console dedicated to monitoring the drives, did little to break her concentration. The tactical situation on the main screen and its duplicate on her number one monitor, held her full attention as she evaluated and discarded targets. She pointed her wand at a heavy cruiser and highlighted it. Battle damage appeared beside the flashing icon, and she nodded her approval. The earlier battle had already degraded its armour and shields by a significant amount.

"Kill that," she said and dismissed the cruiser from her mind to inspect another target.

Obedient to the order, Odyssey's gargantuan particle cannons and grazers swivelled on their mounts, locked on, and spoke. The ravening energy poured into the hull of the Merki ship and smashed on through. Deck after deck after deck succumbed to the massive outpouring of energy. The beams speared the ship clean through and hammered another ship on its far side. Both ships blew apart in a spectacular display of fusion pyrotechnics.

Powell noted the destruction and highlighted another ship. "Kill that."

Commander Stevenson, Odyssey's XO, looked up from his place at scan. "The cruisers are withdrawing, Skipper. Shame we can't pursue."

"Yes. Shame," Powell said and highlighted a cruiser lagging behind its fleeing brethren. "Give that a broadside, tubes one through twenty."

"Aye, ma'am. Target locked. Firing," Lieutenant Sinclair said. He was more than happy to oblige.

Twenty missiles raced into the void; each had a fifty megatonne nominal yield. One and then two more missiles failed for one reason or another. They lost lock and were left behind by their speeding brothers. Half were decoyed off track and wasted themselves on destroying a multi-tonne decoy, but that left eight unwilling to be shaken off.

All eight struck.

"Target destroyed, Skip!" Sinclair said happily, but then with a dejected sigh he said, "No targets in range, Skipper."

"New contacts!" Commander Stevenson announced. "Multiple contacts incoming. Merkiaari assault ships with dreadnoughts and escorts."

"How many?" Powell demanded, already knowing that even one assault ship was too many for Odyssey in her current condition.

"Five assault ships and fifty dreadnoughts plus the escorts, Skipper," Stevenson said grimly. "And you remember that formation holding back on the edge of the zone?"

She nodded. "What about it?"

"It's advancing. Marauder class transports plus escorts."

Five dreadnought squadrons paired with Marauders and escorts. They had a full-scale incursion on their hands, not a raiding force as earlier assumed. The Red One Alert had suggested it might happen. Everyone knew it could happen somewhere in Alliance space, but it was happening to her right here at home. A Merki cleansing fleet was loose in Alliance space and no one outside of the system knew it. She was witnessing the start of the second Merki War and she couldn't tell anyone. She eyed the still smoking comms shack bitterly.

It didn't matter.

She was dead, and so was her ship. All that mattered now was making the Merki pay dearly. Sector HQ would receive Faragut's drones posthumously. She knew at least one had reached foldspace before the squadron was blown away. The information it carried was incomplete, and she regretted that, but there was enough for Admiral Fischer to put it together.

He would avenge Odyssey and her crew.

"More for us to kill," Powell said, trying to sound confident for the crew's sake. "Target the assault ship in the central formation." She highlighted the huge ship with her wand. With luck the Merkiaari's First Claw would be in that unit. They usually did use assault ships for command and control. He could be in any of the five they'd brought, but the central ship seemed most likely. "When it's dead take targets of opportunity."

"Aye aye skipper," Sinclair said and programmed his fire control computers. He hesitated for a moment afterwards, but then he activated a program he'd prepared called Doomsday. "Target locked."

"Helm! Can you give me a barrel roll?" It would enable both of Odyssey's ravaged broadsides to bear on the target.

Lieutenant Glenn turned toward her. "I haven't got much left, Skipper, but I'll try."

"Do your best."

"Aye aye."

Glenn used his few remaining thrusters to push the ship into a spin on her longitudinal axis. It took time but they had a while for the Merki to come back into range. Odyssey began rolling in place, sweeping space around her with targeting sensors.

"Here they come!" Glenn whispered.

"Target in range. Firing!" Sinclair snarled.

Every weapon on Odyssey's port side opened up and went to rapid fire. The roll brought her starboard broadside to bear and she slashed at the Merki with laser, grazer, and particle beams. Missiles raced into the void adding their destructiveness to that heaped upon the approaching ships. Two full broadsides slammed the Merki, and then Odyssey's portside weapons came to bear again.

They spoke like the breath of God unleashed.

Merkiaari decoys and point defence could never hope to stop all the fire aimed their way, but they tried. Tried and failed. Perhaps a third of the missiles reached their target and space erupted. Merki shield generators howled, taking the load. In one case, notably Sinclair's original target, the generators failed and the assault ship added its own magazines to the fury boiling in space. Two dreadnoughts joined the ship in death amid the chaos.

"*Excellent* shooting, Weps," Powell said. An assault ship and a pair of dreadnoughts dead in one salvo was remarkably good luck. Lucky or not, it proved the Merkiaari's shield tech hadn't improved significantly. Shame she couldn't tell anyone. "Continue action."

"Aye aye," Sinclair said, but he didn't need to intervene in the attack. His computers had their targets already. He simply held down a key marked timeout override and let his computers fight the ship.

As the range closed the Merki began firing. Odyssey returned fire but it wasn't enough. Merki cap ship missiles sleeted in and detonated. Odyssey writhed at the heart of a sun. Her titanic shield generators howled and began to fail. A grazer beam strong enough to destroy a city breached engineering, and Odyssey's already useless drives along with her entire engineering staff were wiped away. Every single boat bay was ripped open to space a moment later, and small craft spilled into the void to burn up as they entered Faragut's atmosphere.

Odyssey continued her roll presenting her port shields to the Merki fire. On the bridge all was quiet until a Merki particle cannon slashed open the compartment. One moment Sinclair was at his station, the next he was gone leaving an empty chair contrasted starkly by the star speckled blackness of the void. Atmosphere blasted through the hole in the bulkhead behind his station, but he was the only casualty on the bridge. Everyone had their helmets on and sealed.

Odyssey's computer noted the timeout override suddenly begin counting toward zero and followed its programmed instructions. The magazines of an Alliance dreadnought contained thousands of nuclear missiles, something a tactical officer like Sinclair had known intimately well. As the counter reached one hundred Odyssey ignored the sudden consternation on the bridge and jettisoned every nuclear device in her magazines. Her fire was suddenly cut in half as her launch rails ran dry, leaving only her energy mounts to rage at the Merkiaari.

"What—" Powell began to say.

In the eternity between words, Odyssey had plenty of time to activate her already scattering munitions—almost nine hundred milliseconds-worth of time, in which every missile the ship had carried uploaded Sinclair's program.

Odyssey rolled on and her failing starboard shields again presented themselves to the attack. Environmental was destroyed and with it CIC. Magazines one through four were obliterated and her energy fire suddenly became erratic as targeting sensors shut down or were destroyed. Power runs fused and energy mounts locked as their data feeds cut them off from the firing circuit.

Marines in battle armour took over and continued the fight in local control, firing the huge guns as the Merki ships entered their engagement envelopes.

Odyssey turned, soaking up damage and her starboard shields failed disastrously. The Merki beams peeled away her armour devastating an area reaching from her drive tubes all the way forward to the gaping hole that used to be CIC. Her entire starboard broadside was gutted.

"—is happening?" Powell said. Her ship bucked and yawed end over end.

Odyssey gave her next command and thousands of missile drives roared to life. Like a pack of wolves the unguided missiles began hunting. Milli-seconds later they found the Merki and raced to the attack.

"We're—" Commander Stevenson began to report.

The Merkiaari lasers and grazers slashed in and smashed through Odyssey's unprotected starboard side. Captain Powell smiled goodbye to Stevenson and her ship's fusion containment failed.

A miniature sun was born and Odyssey began her final journey, burning and breaking up as she entered Faragut's atmosphere. Less than a minute later Sinclair's last present to the Merki arrived. Four assault ships had been his target, all four ships survived.

* * *

2 ~ Into That Good Night

The Cradle, Duchy of Kentmere, Faragut.

"It feels damn good to get out of the palace for a while," Nicholas said as he gazed up at Mount Cho. "That suffocating pile will kill me one day, you see if it doesn't."

"No one ever died of boredom, your Highness. Climbing accidents now, they're pretty common."

"Nonsense. The conditions are perfect."

"Accidents happen."

He shot her an irritated glare but Major Eleanor Hutton had fielded worse. She was his aide and bodyguard in one pretty package. She'd witnessed all his moods. His father had assigned her to him when he left Faragut to attend the Naval Academy on Earth. They'd served together for more than a decade since then on various ships.

"I'm sorry, Ellie."

She shrugged. "Not your fault, your Highness."

He winced. "Do you have to be so formal, even up here? You used to call me Nicky."

"That was a long time ago. You're my prince not my boyfriend."

"I want to be more than either. We're a good match."

"Not good enough. Letting you marry me gives no advantage to your father."

That was true. Earl Peckforton's stranglehold on the upper house meant more to the king than his heir's happiness. It had to. Unfairness didn't enter into it, and even Nicholas understood that. Richard Windsor loved his son, but in public his alter ego, King Richard, loved nothing but power. He couldn't afford to, lest it be used against him. Everything he did he did for Faragut; even if it sentenced his heir to a loveless marriage.

"The king can be reasoned with. Help me do that."

"Renouncing the throne isn't a reasonable tactic. It's idiotic."

"It won't come to that. Just work with me, Ellie. *Help* me!"

"I *am* helping you, you idiot."

"By abandoning me?"

"By stepping aside. I won't make you choose between me and your father's throne. Disowning you would break his heart."

"And you're breaking *mine!*"

The hoods of their coats and the high altitude masks they both wore hid their expressions from one another. Frostbite was a real danger at this altitude. He didn't need to see her face to know the expression she wore. The hurt and accusation must surely be there. He'd promised. On his honour he had promised to ask his father to reconsider his betrothal upon their return to Faragut, but he hadn't bargained for his father's eagerness to cement an alliance with Earl Peckforton. To his horror they'd arrived home to find the Palace had leaked his betrothal, and the newsies were already broadcasting it all over the system. He wondered what Lady Charlotte thought. Not that it mattered. Like him she hadn't been consulted, and like him, she was expected to marry her father's choice.

"We need to get going, your Highness."

Ellie carefully probed the way ahead with the long handle of her axe and left him behind without a glance. Her spiked boots made the snow creak with every step she took.

Her impersonal tone hurt. She was already putting distance between them in anticipation of his wedding. It would be all he ever heard from her in future if he didn't do something. He would be HRH Prince Nicholas to her, or Commander Windsor. Her principal. Someone to guard not love. Never again just Nicky. He watched her go for a space, and then followed before the rope linking them ran out of slack.

The trek to base camp gave him time to consider and discard various plans. In the end it came down to one of two options. Marry Charlotte or defy his father. No choice at all he realised, and felt his spirits lighten. He would defy his father and if pushed to it he'd renounce the throne in favour of his little brother. William was still in school but only barely. He'd make a fine king… in twenty years. He sighed glumly knowing it for truth, but maybe that would work in his favour. Their father knew it too. It might help his case. It would certainly add some pressure.

They were still an hour or so out from base camp when his plans fell apart. Ellie looked back over her shoulder and paused. She did that a lot, and not because of the location. It was part of her training. His too in a way. Royal bodyguards had to keep their primary in view at all times, and as the body being guarded, he had to make it easy for her to do that. Not a hardship in his case. He loved her. Their private times together were a pleasure.

Ellie thrust her axe into the snow and raised her goggles onto her forehead. She shielded her eyes against the glare. He smiled before he realised she was studying the horizon not looking at him. He turned to look but saw nothing of interest. Just more snow. It was a pretty view and he was about to say that, but something was wrong. She was coiling the rope and hurrying back towards him. She'd left her axe stuck in the ice as a guide back to the last safe ground she'd tested. That was his Ellie, always thinking.

"Turn around!" she yelled on the way to him.

"What, why?"

She didn't explain but spun him roughly around to attack his backpack.

"Hey, go easy!"

She found what she wanted and stepped in front of him to raise the binos. The Magnatec auto zoom field glasses were one of a pair they'd brought with them. He wanted to grab hers from her pack but didn't dare disturb her. Something had her seriously rattled.

"What is it?" he whispered to her stiff back.

As answer she offered the glasses to him.

He pushed his goggles up and raised the binos, using the controls to zoom beyond the snowbound Cradle to scan the horizon. He panned them slowly left and right but all he saw was emptiness. He didn't get it, and said so.

"Where's the tether?" Ellie said tightly.

He lowered the glasses and frowned at her.

"We should be able to see it from here. High altitude, clear sky. Perfect conditions like you said. Where is it?"

He raised the binos again. This time he did a methodical search. The Cradle resort was far too close but he used it as his guide. He selected wide angle to get his bearings and found the airport that served the resort. He frowned, noting the lack of activity there. Not too surprising he supposed. It wasn't as if it served the el. The space elevator had its own port facility for transhipping cargo. There was warehousing and other stuff there for maintenance and refuelling. Still, the lack of any air traffic on the field was a bit odd.

"The airport is quiet," he murmured as he searched.

"The tether?"

"Still looking."

"It should be obvious, your Highness. Is it there or not?"

"Of course it's there. I just have to find it. What, you think it evaporated?"

She didn't answer and he continued his sweep.

The Magnatec range of field optics were one of Faragut's exports to the various Alliance militaries. The Marines wouldn't be seen dead using anything but Faragut scopes and binos. Ellie was Faragut special forces. She liked to use the best toys available. The binos had more than enough magnifying power to find the blasted tether, only…

"I can't find it," he whispered and lowered the glasses, more perplexed than worried. "Check me. I'm looking south-east of the resort, right?"

"Yes."

He raised the glasses again. The spaceport was over the horizon, and he wouldn't be able to see it even at high altitude like this. He'd need a comp and uplink to a satellite, but the tether was just short of 50,000km long. It was the largest structure on the planet. Even at this range it should be visible to the naked eye as a black line on the horizon.

"It's down," he said lowering the glasses. "It must be. I can't find it and what else is there?"

"Nothing I can think of, your Highness."

He handed the glasses back to her but she didn't bother to use them. She stowed them in his pack and picked up the coil of rope before starting back toward her axe, paying out the line as she went as if nothing had happened.

"Wouldn't we have, I don't know, heard it maybe?" he called. He lost her in the glare from the snow. He pulled his goggles back down. "Ellie? We would have heard it."

"I don't think so. Too far," she yelled and tugged her axe free.

The Duchy of Kentmere was the perfect location for the space elevator. It was part of a landmass on the equator with ocean to the west and a relatively low population within the impact zone. If the el ever collapsed, considered impossible but still, the tether would fall from east to west. Losing the tether, the physical connection between the surface and Terminus Station in orbit, would be a disaster. Such a cataclysm would cause it to drag west and splash down in the ocean.

That was the theory.

In reality the tether's built in failsafe architecture ensured a controlled collapse. Meaning no drag. No drag was a good thing, fabulous even, but a collapse guaranteed lives lost. There must have been hundreds of passengers aboard the climbers on their way up or down, and anyone at the port would be in danger from debris.

What of Terminus Station in orbit? The loss of the tether would destabilise its orbit. Would it come down as well? Probably, but maybe there would be time enough for evac. Maybe, and maybe not too. There must be thousands of travellers passing through the station, and thousands more working there. It was a big one.

The rope jerked him off his feet. "What the hell!"

"Keep up, your Highness. We need to move fast."

He climbed back to his feet and followed her, keeping the slack in the line to a minimum. "Shouldn't we go back?"

"That will take days. Base camp is closer and they'll have comms there."

"Point."

Ellie wasn't kidding about moving fast. Nicholas kept up but he was panting by the time the camp came into sight. If she hadn't needed to test the ice ahead for hidden crevasses or weak points she would've made him sprint all the way. He wasn't her equal in this environment. He was a naval officer not a ground pounder of any stripe. She was special forces and one of the elite royal bodyguards. Few could match her on Faragut.

"Stop here," Ellie said and stepped behind him. "Let's not

walk in like green recruits." She retrieved the binos and knelt in the snow to study the situation.

Nicholas went to one knee to get his breath back. He could see people moving between the tents. They weren't being stealthy. All were wearing brightly-coloured gear similar to his and they carried no weapons that he could see.

"You're thinking… what? Terrorists took down the el?"

"Maybe," Ellie said. "Maybe not."

"But?"

"But I'm not walking in there with you and getting famous."

Nicholas smiled. "Famous?"

"For being the first royal bodyguard to lose her primary on Faragut."

He noted the *on Faragut* part. She wouldn't be the first to lose a royal. That dubious honour was already taken. His cousin had fallen to an insurrectionist plot on Terminus Station, but it hadn't been the fault of his bodyguard. His entire detail, five men and one woman, had died to give him a chance. Nicholas didn't remember much about it. He'd been a child but he remembered the aftermath. His father had gone to war over it.

"Wouldn't want that," he muttered.

"It looks clear."

Nicholas nodded and started to rise, but a hand descended on his shoulder.

"I said it *looks* clear," Ellie stressed. "You'll wait here for me."

He didn't argue. She wasn't beyond knocking him unconscious if that's what it took to complete the mission. He nodded and took charge of her pack when she shrugged out of its straps. She gave him the binos and claimed her pulser from her pack.

"You wouldn't have another one in there would you?" he said, a little wistfully. He hadn't seen the need to add more weight to his pack. It was a climbing trip, dammit. "No I didn't bring one before you say anything."

"I didn't ask. Here," she said and handed him the pulser and two spare mags. She rummaged around in her pack and brought out an even more impressive pulser.

"Yours is bigger," he said, trying for whiny to lighten the mood. He sounded worried to his own ears.

"Your… *weapon* is big enough, your Highness. I know you know how to use it," she said with a smirk, and stuffed her spare mags in various pockets. "Keep watch. If I go down wait for night and slip away. Then frag the bastards."

He nodded. "Count on it."

She moved out confidently, testing her footing with her axe.

Ellie did everything confidently, and he loved that about her. She hadn't meant for him to fight. She would expect him to exfil back to the resort not risk himself to take out her killers. If he died to avenge her she would consider it a loss not a win. The only win she cared about was keeping him alive. His cousin's detail had felt the same about him, he was sure.

Nicholas watched Ellie approach the camp and promised her he'd survive. No one in camp would if they hurt her. If it took an air-strike called in from the safety of the resort then so be it. He wouldn't waste her sacrifice on heroics.

Maybe he had that in common with his father. King Richard had gone to war to avenge the death of one of his family. Thousands had died before the end. He vowed he would do no less for Ellie.

* * *

3 ~ Rage Against The Dying

The Cradle, Duchy of Kentmere, Faragut.

Nicholas watched through the binos as Ellie entered the camp, and prayed her paranoia was just training. The alternative didn't bear thinking about. The loss of the tether could be the start of another insurrection, and who was the only available representative of the evil-doing Windsor dynasty to kill up here? Why, HRH Nicholas Windsor himself of course.

He scowled.

His ego urged him to follow and protect her, but Ellie would probably shoot him herself if he tried that. Her skills and her place in the Royal Guard were the only things she took pride in. She wasn't like other aristocrats on Faragut. Her family name wasn't everything to her as it was to most of their friends. Honour meant more. The oaths she'd sworn held real meaning, as they should to all of the ruling class, but rarely did.

He tensed when she strolled straight into the camp without a care. He immediately lost her among the tents. Minutes passed before she reappeared. She stood in the open and gestured come ahead. If there'd been someone with her, he might have hesitated, but just then her right hand patted the air as if calming a stray dog. It meant ease down, safety on, or any number of other things that meant don't kill anyone.

He tucked his gun and the binos away, hefted both packs, and went to join her.

People in colourful high-altitude gear similar to his, emerged from the camp to greet him. They obviously recognised him. One stepped forward to take the packs, and Nicholas nodded his thanks before joining Ellie.

"Your Highness, this is Dave Westerman. He's senior guide for the expedition," Ellie said.

Westerman offered his hand and Nicholas shook it.

"It's an honour to meet you, Your Highness. I was looking forward to the climb, but under the circumstances," he broke off with a shrug.

"Circumstances?" Nicholas said, looking to Ellie for his answer.

"Unclear at the moment, Your Highness. The tether is down. Dave's people are trying to reach someone at the airport. No answer yet."

Westerman nodded. "It's really crazy over there. Lots of chatter, but none of it makes sense. I'm trying to arrange for a shuttle to pick us up. If we don't get an answer before morning I'll lead you down the way you came up. The south-eastern trek is the safest route. I'll have you back at the hotel safe and sound in a few days, Your Highness."

Nicholas nodded. "Do we have net access up here?"

Ellie shook her head. "That was the second thing I asked about, and that's really bad news."

"Why?"

"Because my wristcomp should have access anywhere on the planet and it doesn't right now."

Nicholas pulled off his gloves and pushed his sleeve up to reveal his own wristcomp. He tried a few commands, but fared no better. That was more than a little worrying; it was terrifying. Ellie's wristcomp was military grade like his, but although hers had been issued by the Palace and had special permissions, it didn't have full access to all levels of the system like his. As heir to the throne he shouldn't ever be locked out of Faragut's net. It meant the system had crashed, or someone had managed to take out the satellites. He couldn't waste time up a mountain waiting to learn which it was.

"I need to contact someone at the palace," he said.

Westerman led the way to the comms tent and then hurried off to supervise the rest of their group. Everyone was packing in anticipation of evacuation by air. Nicholas held the tent flap for Ellie and followed her inside.

"I'll take over," Ellie said to the comms operator. "You need to get your gear ready."

The man's eyes widened at the sight of Nicholas entering behind her. He nodded and fled.

"That face of yours comes in handy sometimes."

"I'm attached to it," Nicholas said dryly.

"So am I, Your Highness." She removed her coat and found the port she needed in the back of the comm. Without a hardwired connection to her wristcomp she wouldn't be able to use the encrypted guard channel. "I hope someone's listening."

"So do I."

"White-Knight, White-Knight, this is Shepherd-2 over," Ellie said.

Nicholas held his breath but there was no reply. The guard channel was never left unmonitored, but he didn't know if the local relay satellite was up or not. They might not have the range without it.

"White-Knight, White-Knight, this is Shepherd-2, over."

"It could be a satellite malfunction. Just a stupid glitch."

Ellie looked at him. "And the tether?"

He had no answer.

"White-Knight, White-Knight, this is Shepherd-2, over."

"Shepherd-2, White-Knight," a voice replied. He sounded grim as death. "Phoenix. I say again *Phoenix*. Authenticate Lima-Alpha-Six-Foxtrot-Echo-November—"

"*God no,*" Ellie hissed, shock choking her words.

Nicholas paled. "It's a mistake. Tell them it's a bloody mistake! I want to talk to someone at the palace. *Tell them!*"

She shook her head knowing it would do no good. "Break-break. White-Knight, Shepherd-2. I do *not* copy."

"Shepherd-2, White-Knight. Phoenix is confirmed. I say again *Phoenix*. Authenticate Lima-Alpha-Six-Foxtrot-Echo-November-Niner-Niner, over."

This time Ellie entered the code-string into her wristcomp, and read back the result. "Code is Sunflower. I say again, Sunflower."

"Affirmative. How many souls?"

Ellie hesitated, and looked to Nicholas for an answer.

He knew what she was thinking. Her duty was to him alone. Westerman and the others would make it back on foot in a few days if a storm-front didn't move in. If his life had been at stake she wouldn't hesitate to ditch them, but it wasn't.

Not yet.

"All of us. None left behind," he said firmly.

He didn't know how many had already died today, or how many would die in the days to come, but he wouldn't help that number grow.

Ellie nodded. "Fifteen, I say again one-five for evac."

"Copy fifteen. Coordinates follow," White-Knight said and reeled off a string of numbers. "White-Knight clear."

Ellie punched in the coordinates and frowned at something her wristcomp displayed. She shook her head, punched in something else, and nodded in satisfaction. She saved the route.

"Roger. Shepherd-2 out," Ellie said, unplugging the patch cable and letting it retract into her wristcomp. She selected a random channel on the comms to disguise the settings she'd used. "I'm sorry, Your Majesty."

Nicholas flinched. "He's not dead."

Ellie remained silent.

He spun on his heel and left the tent unwilling to confront her surety.

Nicholas spent the time before departure thinking about his father, and watching the other climbers getting ready. Ellie didn't emerge from the comms tent; she probably wanted to listen for news. He couldn't believe this was happening. When they'd left the palace a few days ago everything was fine. The security briefing that morning had been routine. He couldn't believe this was happening. He wasn't ready to be king; not that it mattered now. Ready or not, phoenix meant he *was* the king.

"The king is dead, long live the king," he said bitterly.

How could it happen? Had an assassin penetrated the palace? How and why? The capital had been safe even at the height of the Separatist War. How could security fail so disastrously, and why now? His upcoming wedding was the biggest change on the horizon. Could that unwanted event have caused this? He couldn't see how.

He frowned as he considered plots and reasons. Another noble house's ambitions *could've* been threatened by his betrothal to Lady Charlotte; their marriage would close that avenue to the throne for another generation or two. It might be enough to cause some unrest, but the security services would have detected anything like that. And they hadn't.

His mind buzzed with unanswered questions.

Ellie joined him when the time came to move out. She helped him with his pack and he did the same for her, but both of them wore their weapons in holsters now. Neither of them knew what dangers they might face, but they would be ready.

Before leaving, Westerman ordered most of the equipment stowed in the tents for protection against the weather. They didn't need it on the descent. Base-camp was a semi-permanent feature of Mount Cho's south-eastern trek. It was a popular staging area. Nothing would be wasted. Nicholas wondered if he'd ever come back to use any of it. Probably not. He'd be a prisoner for the rest of his life. Once crowned he'd never be allowed to go anywhere without a heavy security presence.

Westerman conferred with Ellie before leading the way down the mountain to the rendezvous point. It was only a few hours away, chosen to minimise the risk of avalanche when the shuttle arrived. They were all experienced climbers and were able to make good time. Roped together but moving rapidly they were soon at the rendezvous waiting for the shuttle.

Ellie gave Westerman one pair of the binos they'd brought and asked him to help keep watch. Nicholas didn't protest. She had rightly diagnosed his mood. Relying upon him for anything right now wasn't a good idea. He couldn't concentrate. He kept seeing the last time he'd spoken with his father in his rooms at the palace. They'd argued about his betrothal. The Privy Council had funnelled the information to the media, and the king had sanctioned it. The so-called leak hadn't been hard to figure out. Politics 101 Faragut style.

Nicholas regretted that meeting more than he could say. He could still see the hurt on his father's face when he'd accused him of loving nothing but power. He should never have invoked his mother's name. He knew very well that his father still mourned her. He shouldn't have done it. Hurtful, spiteful, empty words were the last spoken between them. His memories would be forever tainted by them. He hated himself for that.

The shuttle took forever to arrive, but it did eventually show up. Evening was coming on when Ellie pointed it out in the distance. It was approaching fast and low escorted by a wing of Nighthawk fighters. That seemed like overkill to Nicholas, but maybe not to General Sir Peter Carter, current Chief of the General Staff. Carter would have questions to answer. If those answers weren't satisfactory he would be looking for another job, and Nicholas would need a new CGS over at the Ministry of Defence.

Carter was the top man at the MOD, and directly responsible for all of Faragut's forces. In truth Nicholas preferred the way the Alliance subordinated air and land forces to the navy. He was navy himself and biased, but that didn't mean he was wrong. His father had been army all the way. Depending upon what he heard in the next few hours it might be time for a change over at the Ministry.

"*Take cover!*" Ellie yelled as she charged Nicholas. She slammed him off his feet. "Don't move!" she hissed from atop him. "Incoming."

Incoming? Of course there was bloody incoming! They'd called for evac. He managed to catch a glimpse of the fighters peeling off in pursuit of something he couldn't see. One was trailing smoke and falling behind his wing-mates.

What the hell sort of rescue was this?

"Get off me, dammit! That's a bloody order!"

Ellie ignored him but he'd regained his breath and was able to roll out from beneath her. She gave in to the inevitable and let him sit up. With weapon in hand she scanned the sky for threat. What she thought she was going to do with a pulser, even one like her cannon, he didn't know.

"Get them up," Nicholas said. Everyone was still hugging the snow watching the sky. The shuttle was coming in fast for a hot landing. "They're really hauling ass."

"But *why* are they hauling ass, Sire?"

"I don't know, and don't call me that!"

"Maybe you're safer down here. Westerman can get us to the resort on foot. I can't protect you up there."

"Don't be ridiculous. We're taking that damn shuttle straight to the capital. I want to know what's happening. If I'm your bloody king now obey my orders!"

Ellie straightened to attention. She didn't salute but she did give him a courtly bow. "As you command, Sire."

Nicholas watched her organising things and knew he was going to lose her. That little bow was only a gesture but it felt like more. She'd been putting distance between them ever since their return to Faragut and now she was bowing to him. Strangers bowed to their king. Not friends.

The shuttle landed and the Nighthawks returned. There were only three left and one of them was trailing smoke. He assumed it was the same one he'd seen earlier, but he couldn't be certain. Two missing. He hoped the pilots had ejected safely.

What the hell was going on? How could rebels get their hands on fighters and training simulators? Procuring them would take serious backing from the nobles. Who had his father upset enough for this level of reaction? Someone other than him didn't like his betrothal to Earl Peckforton's daughter; that was his guess. His father's alliance had been a serious error in retrospect. It seemed increasingly certain that Nicholas's reign would be heralded by civil war.

The shuttle landed with its cargo ramp already partway down. The pilot was in a serious hurry. His ship was a military HLV not a civilian craft designed for mountain rescue. Heavy lift vehicles were essentially atmospheric tugs. Powerful yes, but not very aerodynamic. They were designed to support ground troops by airlifting artillery into a war zone, not personnel. It would be a hellishly slow and uncomfortable ride.

The ramp landed in the snow and well-armed troops descended. Nicholas froze in disbelief as Ellie's paranoia kicked in and caused her to face down a dozen men. They were in the correct uniform and armed with rifles, but in her mind that didn't mean they were friendlies.

"*Code!*" Ellie shouted over the roar of the shuttle's engines. "*Weapons down!*" she yelled as the fighters screamed by overhead again. "*Down down down, I said! Gimme the damn code or die!*"

Nicholas pulled his own pistol to back her up.

"Sunflower!" one of the men shouted and waved urgently for them to enter the cargo hold. He anxiously scanned the sky as the fighters screamed by again. "Sunflower! Are you fucking nuts? *We have to go!*"

Ellie holstered her weapon and waved everyone into the HLV. She was the last to enter. They took off with the ramp still closing.

* * *

4 ~ The Dying of the Light

Aboard HLV, Duchy of Kentmere, Faragut.

There were no seats within the cargo area. Westerman and the others were sitting on the deck clutching the cargo netting to anchor themselves against the HLV's acceleration. The pilot was pouring on the power, boosting so hard that Nicholas guessed their destination to be one of the stations in orbit. He didn't want to rely upon guesses; he needed to confirm it and learn the situation at the capital.

He carefully made his way forward using the netting and many respectful hands to prevent a fall. He glanced back, but Ellie wasn't following. She was clinging tightly to a take-hold near the ramp and talking to one of the rescue squad. He could've done the same but he wanted a direct line to the palace. He prayed the Code Phoenix was a mistake.

What a horrible misnomer that code was. A phoenix rising from the ashes should conjure a feeling of joy and hope. He felt no joy at his father's death, and no hope for himself. The king is dead, long live the king, he thought bitterly.

God, make it not so.

Nicholas reached the airlock separating the cargo hold

from the crew spaces and cycled through into a short passageway that led to the various crew stations. If he climbed the ladder on the right and headed back, he'd find engineering and the main drives. HLVs were very simple ships. A hollow box that could be pressurised with a ramp at one end plus a drive module and cockpit package bolted on top. That was about it. The stubby wings and tilt jet engines of the flight module allowed atmospheric flight and V-TOL landings, while the magneto-plasma rockets of the main drive section allowed limited spaceflight capability. HLVs had limited fuel bunkerage. The design sacrificed range in favour of cargo capacity, but that design also limited speed. They weren't very aerodynamically efficient and relied upon brute force to get anywhere.

Nicholas made his way forward to the end of the passageway and climbed the ladder that led to the cockpit. He undogged the deck hatch at the top of the ladder and swung it up to enter the flight deck. His training made him close and lock it again before he addressed the crew. Safety first. His instructors would approve. HLVs normally ran with a crew of four; two pilots, a flight engineer who doubled as the nav and astrogator, plus a supercargo who doubled as the drive specialist. If Nicholas had needed further evidence that things were far from normal, what awaited him on the flight deck would have set alarm bells ringing.

The pilot was a civilian, and he was alone.

"I need to contact the palace," Nicholas said and the pilot darted a surprised look his way. "May I?" The pilot nodded, and Nicholas took the co-pilot's seat. "Nicholas Windsor, and you?"

"Tim Donovan, Your Majesty. I was all they could scrape up. Sorry."

"Good to meet you, Tim. No need to be sorry. I'm grateful for the rescue I assure you, but why is a civilian piloting one of our HLVs?"

"I only know my own story, Sire. I have no idea what really happened up top, but from the panic down here it must have been pretty bad. I do know that the capital is gone."

"Gone?" Nicholas said, puzzled. "How gone? Captured or just off the air? Did the rebels attack the palace too?"

Donovan gaped. "You haven't heard?"

"I've been up a bloody mountain. What do you know?"

"I don't know much. The Merkiaari took out our ships and stations—"

Shock made Nicholas lose focus. In one small way it was a relief to hear his own people wouldn't be trying to kill him, but the Merki didn't play favourites. The enemy had changed not the danger.

"Wait," Nicholas said, trying to catch up. "Have they made landings? What about the capital?"

"The capital is gone. I heard rumours it was hit from orbit but someone at the port said it was an accident. Something about one of our dreadnoughts coming down. I don't know for sure. Everything up there is gone. They blew away Terminus; did you know?"

Nicholas shook his head in disbelief. "I knew something bad had happened, but not this. We couldn't see the tether."

"Well that's one thing that went right. The tether's self-destruct worked like a charm. I was at the port when the collapse started. The nanos took it apart like magic. The debris took out my boat. She was a sweet little in-system runner. I owned her free and clear of the bank too." Donovan shook his head sadly. "When the tether came down I thought I was dead for sure, but Stinger grabbed me to fly this junk. He's a supercargo not a pilot." Donovan grinned. "I guess we sort of stole it, technically at least."

"I'll pardon both of you," Nicholas muttered.

"That's nice of you. I don't suppose you could see your way clear to signing her over to me? She's a piece of junk but she's better than nothing. Maybe I can sell her and get enough for a stake. I'm a bit old to start over but what else have I got to do?"

Nicholas nodded, not really listening.

The Red One alert hadn't been rescinded but the excitement it caused when first announced had faded from most people's awareness. Not from his though, or his father's of course. Their forces had been on high alert for more than a year.

Faragut like all members of the Alliance tithed to maintain the navy and the Alliance's ground forces, but it was a matter of pride for Faragut to protect its own system. The Red One had changed that. Admiral Rawlins had insisted upon assigning extra squadrons to Faragut. The idea had been to station reinforced task forces in key systems throughout Alliance space. Any Merkiaari activity would attract notice and a quicker response. A system attacked by the Merkiaari had to hold long enough for a relief force to arrive. That was his job now. Holding out.

The destruction of Terminus Station and the capital were terrible blows. The loss of life must have climbed into the millions already. *And my father! My father!* Nicholas screamed in the silence of his mind. The Alliance would feel the loss of Faragut's industry more than the loss of life. It was a key system in the production of arms. Most notably capital ship missiles and point defence laser clusters for use in the new Washington class heavy cruisers. The Merkiaari didn't need reasons to cleanse planets, but taking out Faragut would be an impressive gain for them.

"Where are we going?" Nicholas said, struggling to wrap his mind around the calamity. He had to hold out long enough for help to arrive. "The port?"

"Afraid not. There's not much left."

"Where then?"

"Silver Bay. It hasn't been hit and if we have to ditch there's a great big ocean out that way."

Donovan grinned.

Nicholas tried to think of something he could do, but all of his high level contacts must be dead. He felt the weight of responsibility settle upon his shoulders. Crowned or not there was no doubt he was king. He needed to set up a semblance of command and control. Silver Bay was as good a place as any to begin. The castle there wouldn't stand against the Merki; all such fortifications on Faragut were built for historical authenticity not defence. The castle itself wasn't important but Silver Bay was the ancestral seat of the Earl of Longthorpe, and General (ret.) Sir Harry Longthorpe had been CGS before the now presumably deceased General Carter.

"Do we have a comms link with Silver Bay?" Nicholas said.

"Faragut-1, Dragon-3. Go for the deck!" the voice of a frantic Nighthawk pilot said over the comm. "Merki interceptors vectoring for attack. I have two on scope inbound."

"Roger Dragon-3. Good luck, and thanks," Donovan replied. "You had better strap in, Sire. This might get a little rough. This piece of junk isn't exactly what you'd call nimble."

Nicholas was already strapping in, but his fears were for Ellie and the others. They didn't have crash couches. He snatched up the co-pilot's headset and selected a channel to the cargo hold.

"High-speed manoeuvres!" Nicholas gasped as Donovan went to max thrust. "Ellie!" he cried as the ground rushed to meet them.

"Don't worry, I'm pretty good at this... *oh crap!*" Donovan swerved to miss a rocky outcropping. "See?"

Nicholas opened his eyes.

"Watch our six would you?" Donovan said.

Nicholas reached for the controls. He *was* navy but not a navy pilot. He'd never flown an HLV or anything close, but there were a few similarities to civilian shuttles. He found the external cameras and radar scope in time to see the Nighthawk pilots die for him.

"We're on our own. One interceptor left."

Donovan nodded. "We're royally screwed then. No pun intended, Sire. I'll hug the dirt as best I can but at this speed he'll catch us easy. Hell, one missile up our asses is all he needs."

Nicholas grimaced as the Merki pilot did exactly as predicted and launched on them. "Your call-sign wouldn't be Oracle would it? Missile incoming. Countermeasures?"

"They're automatic on these clunkers."

Flares and decoys popped free of their bays, but they weren't very effective at such low altitude. The flares barely had time to deploy before they disappeared into trees or behind hills. The terrain played havoc with the decoy's ECM emissions. Instead of blanketing the sky with ghostly images meant to confuse a missile, the hills shielded them or bounced their signals back at the HLV unpredictably.

The missile ignored them all.

"I have one more trick," Donovan said grimly. "It will probably kill us."

"And the missile won't?"

"Exactly."

"Do I want to know what it is?"

"I don't think so. It was nice knowing you," Donovan said and fired up the mains.

The ship leapt ahead, its acceleration enough to reach orbit. HLVs were powerful tugs meant to carry extremely heavy and bulky loads. Lighting off the plasma drive to outrun a missile was madness. The ship reacted like an empty can kicked along the road.

"Crash," Donovan said between gritted teeth as he dodged between a pair of hills. "My call-sign I mean."

"Great," Nicholas said sourly. "Do it a lot do you?"

“I survive them. That’s how I earned it.”

Barely under control the HLV hugged the terrain, and the missile fell behind. Donovan saw an opportunity and took it. He sent the ship heading toward a gorge. He nearly made it. The shuttle clipped the ridge at full power and cartwheeled. The stubby wings and engines broke off flying crazily away from the ship. They slammed into the sparse trees and exploded. The missile was finally decoyed and added its destructiveness to the fireball.

The broken ship, nothing but a crushed box containing a few fragile humans, cartwheeled through the trees crushing and smashing them into kindling. Its main drive roared with power but there was no one left on the flight deck to shut it down. A fuel line finally ruptured causing the automatic safeties to engage. The drive shut down and the HLV came to rest.

A shocked silence descended over the valley until one final indignity occurred. A gigantic tree slowly toppled to slam down atop the wreckage, as if to shield the horror with its branches.

A lone Merkiaari interceptor flew slowly over the crash-site to scan for survivors, but the fires satisfied the pilot. She wasn’t willing to waste another missile on dead vermin.

The interceptor accelerated hard into the distance.

* * *

5 ~ Scavenger

Zuleika, Child of Harmony, Shan System

"*Tei...*" the voice sighed and faded away.

"Merrick, no!" Shima cried, startling herself awake.

She reached with the Harmonies to find Chailen. Two sleeping mind glows reassured her that all was well, and tension drained away. She rolled off her sleeping mat and onto four feet to pad through the silent house. She wouldn't find sleep again this night. She decided to use her dream of Merrick to get some work done.

She ate a quick meal of cold Shkai'ra washed down with water. She remembered the Human drink called coffee. It was a bitter brew that curled the tongue, but it did have the effect of waking one up. Coffee was a stimulant in Shan, just as it was in Humans. Tired as she felt, a cup of the disgusting stuff would be very welcome. Ah well, her life on Snakeholme was a distant thing. She was home now, and needed to make the best of things.

Back in her room, she chose her oldest harness to wear. It had been her favourite once. Tahar had given it to her one nameday, and she'd worn it many times on the hunt, but it was a sad remnant of better times now. It had been mended so many times, stubbornness was all that held it together. It had served her well through the war, but it was so shabby now that she only wore it when out with Sharn on a salvage run. She pulled it on and tightened the buckles. It still fit her like a second pelt.

Outside, the sun had yet to appear over the roofs, and Shima paused to feel the night. The Harmonies promised that all was well. Chailen and Sharn were safe in Tahar's house behind her, sleeping. She sampled their mind glows and knew they dreamed of pleasant things. They were happy. It made her smile knowing they were content, but her own mood intruded to spoil the feeling. Her sib had no future here. Sharn was barely able to feed them despite working hard, and all of their hopes were feeble things. The Harmonies recoiled, pulling away from her dark thoughts.

It was time to take charge and fix things.

Shima hefted the sack, and on two legs headed for the market. It was a long way, and four legs would've been faster, but she needed her hands. The sack contained tools and a few trade goods she'd been saving. Food chits were too precious to trade, and money had been worthless since the war. Despite everything the Humans were doing to help, the Harmony of Shan had turned into a pitiful thing. Scraps of pre-war technology were the only currency in the shattered remains of the city. That wouldn't always be so. Better times lay ahead, but harder times lay between. The scraps Chailen and Sharn needed to survive were running out.

The streets were empty and the houses silent. Many of them remained abandoned despite the war being long over; their owners dead or fled. Some still lived within the keeps, but many had chosen to join remnants of family and clan on Harmony. The exodus to homeworld had slowed, but it hadn't stopped altogether. The Human fleet spent much of its time ferrying people and supplies between the twin worlds of

Harmony.

She understood her people's need to consolidate their clans and families on one world or the other. The Merkiaari had driven many family lines to extinction, while others were in perilous need of new blood or they too would vanish. There was a steady flow of people in both directions to satisfy this need. Once done, the clan elders would reassess things, and choose a new path for their clans.

Shima left her district behind, following the road into a bombed out district. The Harmonies warned her before she saw the feral eyes watching her pass by. She didn't stop, and didn't try to coax the younglings out of hiding. She had nothing for them, and no words of comfort would help. They were the leftovers; feral younglings without family or clan to care for them. She didn't stop, and for their love of Chailen, they let her pass through their territory unmolested.

The market was no such thing in reality. It was simply a cleared patch in the rubble where items were traded. Shima zeroed in upon what she'd come for. A working vehicle. A few early risers were already setting out their meagre offerings as she walked by. She noted the lack of power cells. Those were coveted, and the means to recharge them also. Normally that would be bad news; everyone needed the things to power the tools they used in their salvaging work, but here and now it was very good news. It increased the value of what her sack held, and she badly needed a car. Working vehicles were rare in the city. They had never been numerous to begin with, and the Merkiaari had taken a positive delight in blowing the things up when they found them. There were far fewer in Zuleika now.

"The Blind Hunter honours me," Hamal said, performing her bow before offering a hand. "What do you need?"

Shima's ears went back. She couldn't prevent the involuntary flinch, but she said nothing about it. Her mission was too important. She briefly touched Hamal's palm.

"Trade," Shima said, and shook her sack.

Hamal's ears flicked in agreement. "Of course, let me see what you have."

Shima handed the sack over, and Hamal rummaged around inside. She pulled out the tools and offered them back, correctly assuming they weren't part of the trade. Shima used the Harmonies to watch the trader, trying to get a read on her chances. Hamal's ears stayed up. She was interested. The sack held all of Shima's precious power cells for the beamers she no longer owned, plus an equal amount she'd saved from her runs with Sharn. She'd been planning this trip for a long time, and had saved up a stash.

"Well," Hamal began and Shima's ears wilted. The Harmonies were clear. The sack wasn't worthy. "Do you have anything more to offer? I can hold a car for you if you need to fetch it?"

"I have nothing else."

"Perhaps your mini-computer. It's a Human device is it not? There's a good market for anything alien."

Shima knew there was. The market for Merki technology had always been lively, but such things were all traded soon after the war ended. There wasn't much left to find. Human tech was also coveted, but very rare.

She indicated her wristcomp. "I cannot trade this. It's linked to the little machines inside me."

Hamal's ears pricked at hearing that. "I've heard of the invisible machines. In future, Harmonies willing, all shall be blessed as you have been." She peered into the sack again, and her tail rose to gesture a shrug. "I would like to help, but…"

Shima swallowed her pride. Thinking of Chailen and Sharn, she bowed very low to Hamal. "Honoured Hamal. I beg your indulgence." She glanced up, and then back at the ground in supplication. Hamal's ears were down and her eyes wide in dismay. "My sib and her mate have great need. I… I *beg*…"

"Don't!" Hamal gasped. To see a *hero* reduced to begging was shocking. It was shameful, and reflected as badly upon her as much as Shima. "Please. You must not. Someone will see."

Shima had never considered herself a hero, but most did, including Hamal. The Harmonies revealed her wavering, but not enough to take the trade. Shima swallowed the last of her dignity and let her knees hit the ground. She heard the shocked oath from behind her, and knew her humiliation would sweep through the market. Well, too late now to take it back. She went all out, and bowed from her position, kissing dirt.

That did it.

Hamal pulled her onto her feet. Her ears were hard back, and her eyes white-rimmed in a kind of shocked panic. People were gathering around, and muttering about the shameful display. Shima began to feel sorry for her, but by the Harmonies she needed a car. *Needed* it. She would make it up to Hamal later, but for now she would take all the sympathy she could get.

In no time at all, Shima was airborne and flying out of the city. The car Hamal supplied was a wreck, but it was just about airworthy, and hers for the entire cycle. Its canopy was missing, and all of its interior had been scrapped to increase its cargo capacity. Her destination was the Centre for Agricultural Research; her old workplace. If she was right, no one had looted it yet. It was too far from the city to reach easily, and surrounded by empty countryside.

Hundreds of heikke blurred beneath her as she flew the familiar route, and memories arose. The Merkiaari had killed her father, and millions of others, the last time she'd been this way. It seemed like another world now, like a dream. She wondered where Adonia was, and their colleagues. If she'd survived, she was probably living in a keep somewhere. As far as she knew, Adonia's family were all on Child of Harmony, not on homeworld.

Shima landed in her usual spot outside the main administration building. The parking apron was weed choked, but otherwise empty. She could tell no one had visited in a long time. She climbed out of her car and listened to the sighing of the wind. Her ears swivelled, trying to pick up any activity, but there was nothing.

The centre had been forgotten.

Shima retrieved her tools from the floor of the car, and headed into the administration building. She had a plan that boiled down to stealing everything not nailed down as quickly as possible. If her luck held, she would have cycles out here before someone noticed her riches. When that happened, there would be a sudden rush to sniff out where she'd found it all. She didn't need the competition, and wouldn't trust to luck; it was too important. This run was for Chailen and Sharn. They had need, and she was determined to provide.

Her first stop was her own office. She placed her hand on the scanner beside the door, but of course it didn't work and remained stubbornly shut. She'd hoped there might be a trickle of backup power left, but no such luck. She forced the flattened end of her lever between the door and the lock plate. During power outages, doors locked automatically. Backup power allowed everyone to move around, but the centre had been offline too long. Every door would be sealed tight. Locked doors would slow her down, but they wouldn't stop her.

The door resisted but finally gave way, and she entered the familiar office. Her eyes went to the dark computer screen. In her mind, she saw the last thing it had displayed for her. Her father, calling to warn her about the attack and say goodbye. He'd known the Merkiaari would destroy Hool Station, and he'd used his last moments to talk with her. That short conversation was branded upon her memory.

Forget about me, this place is finished.

He'd been right. Less than a seg later, the Merkiaari had blown the station out of orbit along with Child of Harmony's orbital defences. Those huge fortresses had been armed to the teeth, but they hadn't lasted any longer than Hool—an unarmed station—had done.

Shima tapped a few keys on her keyboard, but the computer screen remained dark. She stuffed the keyboard into her sack, followed by the computer and screen. It was lightweight but bulky. Her sack bulged. She filled the remaining space with a few things she found in her desk, but the most important item, her security card, went into a pouch on her harness. She'd need the key-card to enter the labs after she restored power. That was essential. The security doors wouldn't open without power, and no amount of prying at them would work. The labs contained secrets that were worthless now, but they also contained dangerous items in need of containment. She had no interest in them, but she did need to get in to steal the treasure the labs contained.

Shima spent the rest of that cycle grabbing easily obtained portable items. She raided offices for every computer she could find, and when they ran out, she attacked the doors to the storerooms. Inside she found untouched office supplies, various hand tools for maintenance, and cartons of power cells to fit them. The cell chargers were a bonanza. Those were worth her weight in food chits. She wanted to jump for joy at the sight of them.

It made her sad when she realised how excited they made her. They'd been commonplace once; not worth even a second glance when she needed one. How many times had she just thrown them away instead of having them repaired? Dozens at least. Now they were more precious than food. She could hunt for meat easily, but technology couldn't be found on the hoof like a Shkai'ra in the wild. All the factories were gone, the technicians dead or grubbing in the dirt like her.

She snatched armfuls of everything within reach, and ran

to the car. Hamal would give her the most for the chargers and the cartons of new power cells, but she didn't hold back. She filled her car with everything the storerooms contained; even the cleaning supplies. Hamal might not want them, but maybe she would too. One by one, she emptied all the storerooms, and then went looking for something else to steal.

Her bounty grew.

She stuffed the car with loot until she had to stop. There was barely room left for her to drive. Besides, she was losing the light, and Hamal would be waiting for her return. Working vehicles were rare, and she would want to lock it away somewhere for the night. That was fine with Shima; she didn't plan to unload it. She had a deal in mind for Hamal, and the haul looked even more impressive spilling out of the car this way. Hamal would be impressed. An offer of partnership should fall on fertile ground.

Shima climbed into the car, and drove back toward Zuleika.

* * *

6 ~ Visitors

Centre for Agricultural Research, Child of Harmony

The next morning, Shima landed in her usual place outside the administration building, ready for the next step. Hamal had been more than willing to provide all she needed after seeing the quality of her trade goods. Suddenly, all things were possible. Need a car? Certainly! Tools, supplies, charged cells in exchange for depleted ones? Not a problem. Anything the Blind Hunter required, Hamal could suddenly supply.

Shima had asked for a fully-charged high-capacity power cell out of a ruined vehicle, a set of power cables long enough to reach the generator room, and the tools necessary to make use of it all. Hamal knew someone who knew someone, and in short order, Shima had what she needed. She had to promise to return it all after a single cycle. That was more than enough time for what she had in mind.

She climbed out of the car, and used the Harmonies to search the area. No one was near, but that might not be so for much longer. Hamal would be selling her first load of salvage soon. It wouldn't take a genius to figure out who had supplied it. She hadn't been followed; the Harmonies would have warned her, but she had a feeling she *would* be watched upon her return to Hamal.

Satisfied her secret was safe for now, she retrieved the cables from the car. They were too heavy to carry, so she unrolled them on the ground to make things easier. Hooking a pair of connectors on her harness, she hefted her tools and dragged one end of the thick cables into the building.

The door to the generator room was open and waiting—she had broken in before leaving the night before. The dead backup cells would be worth salvaging at some point, but they were big and heavy. Sharn would have to help come the time, but she hadn't forgotten her need for haste. The moment her goods hit the market, she would be on borrowed time. She had to secure the best treasure before she had visitors out here.

It didn't take her long to unhook the couplings from the dead cells, and join them to her cables using the connectors Hamal had supplied. Retracing her steps to the car, she paused to consult the Harmonies again. She was still alone, but she felt uneasy as if being watched. The Harmonies were warning her to hurry. That's what she assumed the feeling meant. It could easily be her own anxiety talking, but she hadn't survived this long by ignoring warnings. She rushed to attach the cables to the power cell, and close the circuit. Tightening the last clamp, she pressed the button and the red light blinked on.

She hurried back inside. The emergency lighting glowed at about half intensity. Its orangey-yellow light told her the power wouldn't last long. She ran through the building, and down the spiral way to the labs. The lighting was even more subdued here. No windows for natural light to enter, and the cell she'd brought was meant to power a car not a building. She needed to get all the doors propped open before the power failed again.

Her security pass gave her full access to all of the labs, and she quickly used it to open the first door. It slid aside for her, and she dashed inside. She grabbed the first thing that came to hand—a trolley meant to transport soil samples, and dragged it into the open doorway. When the power failed, it would stop the door closing all the way. She hurried to do similar things with every door on the level, and then descended to the next one, hoping to reach all the doors before she ran out of time and power.

She breathed easier when the last door opened for her, and the lighting still glowed faintly. It was bright enough to retrace her steps without needing the lamp built into her wristcomp. Rather than waste the remaining power, she disconnected the cables from the power cell, and stowed them back in the car.

Shima worked for segs without a break, to strip the Centre of all its most valuable tech. She began with the highest value portable items, in case her competition arrived. High value no longer meant centrifuges, or microscopes; not even thermal cyclers, or DNA microarrays were worth taking. Post war, high value meant any kind of hand tool or equipment that could be modified. Hand lamps would be good. She stole all she could find. Any kind of solar array, or equipment with a solar cell as part of its construction, would sell for a good price as well. Someone would dismantle them for parts. A few orbits ago, she would have been horrified by such vandalism. Now it was simply survival in a post war world.

She worked her way through the labs on the lowest floor first, and then moved up a level. There was plenty left behind for another run, but the equipment was too bulky to carry away. She would need a bigger vehicle, and Sharn's help if she decided to bother with it. She doubted she would. Hamal would have trouble selling them, and her time would be better spent salvaging other places.

Her car was already heavily loaded, when the Harmonies warned her of two people approaching. She paused to survey the area. She couldn't hear or see them, but they were moving faster than any Shan could run. The Harmonies couldn't detect vehicles, but the direction gave her the clue she needed. They weren't on the road. She scanned the sky, looking toward the city, and saw it. A gleaming silver car harking back to better times. It was in perfect condition. It still had its canopy and appeared like new. Whoever these people were, she doubted they were here for salvage.

She quickly finished her loading, and then paused again to watch the newcomers land. Two males exited the vehicle and approached her. One, the younger of two, wore a warrior's harness and carried an equipment bag. The older male took the lead. She hadn't seen Tei'Thrand in an age. Older, she thought. The seasons had begun to speckle his coat with silver, though he was no older than her father had been before he died. He looked tired, and careworn. The Harmonies revealed a stressed but determined male; one intent upon a mission of some kind.

Shima bowed. "Tei'Thrand, you honour me with this visit. May you live in harmony."

"Niece, it's good to see you again," Tei'Thrand said. "May you live in harmony. May I introduce Tei'Laran?"

Laran bowed and lowered his burden to the ground. He released the handles. "Honoured."

"Honoured," Shima repeated, and bowed to him before addressing her uncle again. "What brings you out here?"

"You," Tei'Thrand said.

Obviously. He didn't say it, but Shima heard it clearly regardless. What she'd meant to ask was why now? He had ignored his family before this. To be fair, he wasn't Jasha Clan any longer. Tei were required to break old bonds when they joined the-clan-that-is-not. They were other. Separate. They couldn't act upon old loyalties if they felt them. Thrand had maintained his distance admirably. The sleek almost new-seeming car, spoke of someone doing well. Privileged. Shima tried not to feel bitter about it. The males were both Tei and would be strong in the Harmonies. They would sense it.

"That was my assumption. How may I serve you?" Shima said mildly.

"Interesting choice of words, Shima. Are you truly willing to serve our people?"

She flicked her ears in agreement, but the question puzzled her. Any Shan would say yes if asked that question, but not many would have the opportunity. The elders served their people, as did any who chose the warrior caste. Tei'Varyk and his mate served Shan interests on faraway Earth, as they had previously in Fleet. How could *she* serve? She was a gardener without a garden to tend, a scientist with nothing to research.

"We need you, Shima."

"Me?" she said. The Harmonies revealed Tei'Thrand's uncertainty, but not the reason behind the emotion. Tei'Laran was expectant if she were any judge. "I'm just an out of work gardener. What can I do?"

Tei'Thrand's jaw dropped in amusement. "Such modesty, niece. You are the Blind Hunter. It's she our people need you to be, not this..." he gestured at her appearance. "This *travesty*."

Shima's ears went hard back at the scorn dripping from his words. "Do. Not. Call. Me. THAT!"

"It's who you truly are. This pretence must cease!"

Shima's hackles rose, and she readied herself for battle. It wouldn't become physical. She wouldn't let it, but by the Harmonies he would regret coming here. Favourite uncle or no, she would make him regret that! She took a breath to flay the hide off him, but Tei'Laran smoothly took over and drew her attention.

"Don't be angry with him," Tei'Laran said. "Thrand didn't want to come here. The Council insisted that someone must, and he's the only one of us related to you by blood."

By us he meant Tei. There had been others once, but many had been killed in the war. Ordering Thrand to visit her explained what the Harmonies had shown her about his uncertainty, but not the reasoning behind his unwanted errand.

"The elders asked you to visit me? Why would they? My district has power again," her tail rose in a shrug. "Some of the time at least. They could have messaged me."

"Your renown is of particular importance just now," Tei'Laran said, pointedly not answering her question. "Do you follow the newscasts?"

Her ears flicked to agree. "When we can. Chailen follows things closer than I. She hopes to help her mate find work. He's a fine healer, as she will be in time."

"You've heard of the upcoming war games on Pandora?"

"I know of Pandora. I know the Kalmar Union is a long way from here. It has nothing to do with me, and war isn't a game."

Both Tei flicked their ears to agree.

"The Blind Hunter knows war," Tei'Thrand said, making Shima bristle again. "As does Tei'Laran. He fought with the Humans too. Were your youngling lessons a game? How about your target practice? Your father took you hunting often; were those trips games?"

"No," she admitted. "They were to teach, to prepare, to…" her eyes narrowed and she whispered her father's words to her from long ago. "To serve and protect our people at need."

She remembered Tahar's lessons. *All* of his lessons. *To serve and protect our people at need* was the warrior's code. She wasn't a warrior; neither had her father been one, but he'd taught her well in preparation for her time of choosing. She had chosen scientist caste as many in her clan had before her, but not out of ignorance of the other castes. Tahar had seen to that.

She wondered now if he'd expected her to follow him into his caste of engineers. He'd never displayed disappointment in her choice. She wondered what he'd think of her choices during, and since, the war. He was with the Harmonies and their ancestors now, watching over her and Chailen. Would he expect something different of her… something… *bigger?* It made her unhappy to think he might.

Shima pushed the unsettling feeling away, and tried to concentrate. They were after something.

Tei'Thrand's tail gestured a shrug. He added the dip of one shoulder that made it mean aliens are strange. "The war games on Pandora aren't games; that is a truth, and a poor choice of words by the Humans perhaps. It doesn't matter what they call the event. Our people must take part."

"In whose estimation, yours?"

"The warrior caste among others. I agree with them, as do many of the Tei."

"But not all?"

Tei'Laran laughed. "When have our people all agreed about anything?"

"True," Shima agreed, and it had been a stupid question. "So what's stopping us? Are we not invited?"

"We've been invited, and a Human ship is ready to transport us if we wish to take up the offer," Tei'Thrand said.

"But?"

The males looked at each other, neither willing to say it, but the Harmonies were already telling Shima a lot. "The elders didn't send you, did they? Your clan sent you. I'm right aren't I?"

They wanted *her* to go to Pandora. The thought briefly excited her, but then the reality of her situation crushed it. She had Chailen and Sharn to care for. They needed her. They needed the food chits Hamal would pay her. She glanced at her battered car full of salvage destined for Hamal. It looked sad next to Tei'Thrand's gleaming vehicle.

"Shima of Clan Jasha, first cub of Tahar, you are called to serve our people," Tei'Thrand began.

Shima's ears went hard back in shock. Oh no, he didn't just say that. He wouldn't try this again! The Tei didn't really want her to join them. Not the real her. They wanted the Blind Hunter to play along with their political games. They wanted her to bow and say the words they would put in her mouth!

"As Tei, you will lead our people by your example. By your own actions you will teach them to strive, to be better, to build the Great Harmony anew. Will you join your fellow Tei, and take up this burden?"

"No," she said and stormed back to the administration building to continue her work.

Tei'Thrand gaped. "Where are you going? We're not done!" he shouted at her back.

Shima stopped before entering the building. "I'm needed here."

Tei'Thrand joined her. "You're needed out there more!" he said, gesturing at the sky.

Shima glared at him. "I'm not you, uncle. I won't abandon my sib!"

Smack!

Shima's head rang from the blow. He had cuffed her, claws withdrawn thankfully. She didn't rub her ear. She grinned, muzzle rumpling to reveal her killing teeth, and growled low, making him step back. She fought off the fight/kill reflex of her people, and her vision didn't narrow down to a tunnel fixated on her prey.

"Do that again," Shima said evenly. "I dare you to touch me again."

He didn't apologise. "Look at you," he said, his voice thick with disgust. "You're a vagabond. *A nobody grubbing in the dirt for scraps!* You took all of his teaching and threw it away! He was one of our… one of *your* clan's greats. How could you do that to his memory? He would be ashamed to call you his blood! Do you think I don't mourn him? Do you think I don't feel his *loss?!* I mourn for millions you… you *witless*, foolish, *cub!*"

He walked away, back toward his car but stopped before climbing aboard. Tei'Laran was already at the controls. He hadn't bothered to retrieve his equipment bag. It lay abandoned in the dust.

"Hero they call you," Tei'Thrand said, sounding defeated and tired now. "What a sick lie that is. They honour you with a hero's name—The Blind Hunter—never knowing that their hero is only a blind fool. I pity them for putting their faith in you."

Shima watched the gleaming silver arrow streak across the sky in silence. Before she could get back to work, the Harmonies warned her of the approach of more people. She sighed. Her unwanted guests must have been followed. What else could go wrong?

She watched the battered cars of the salvage crews landing nearby, and went to grab Tei'Laran's equipment bag before someone else did. She opened it to find a gleaming warrior's harness in her size. It felt as supple as the hide of a juvenile Shkai'lon. Twin holsters were already mounted upon it for her beamers; the beamers she had traded away. She stared at the beautiful thing, and thought that perhaps her uncle was right.

Tahar would be ashamed.

* * *

7 ~ Harmonies

Zuleika, Child of Harmony, Shan System.

"*Tei...*" the voice sighed and faded away.

"Merrick no!" Shima cried, startling herself awake.

Fear choked her as she reached with the Harmonies to find Chailen. Two mind glows reassured her that all was well. Her sib was asleep in her mate's arms, probably dreaming of him and her future cubs. Tension drained away, and she began to relax. The beauty of Chailen's mind glow always soothed her fears.

She rolled off her sleeping mat, and onto four feet to pad through the silent house. The dream had been disturbing her rest more often since her confrontation with her uncle. Before then it had been an infrequent thing. Now it woke her every night. Tei'Thrand had hit a raw nerve when he tried to recruit her. Merrick had been the first one to call her Tei, and he'd died. She would never forget that naming her Tei meant following her orders into death.

She needed to breathe the night air, and put the dream away for another night. Her grove beckoned. It had been her sanctuary once; blind and beyond hope, it had barely kept her sane before Gina rescued her from the dark. She still sought its solace when troubled.

The shell and gravel mix crunched pleasantly under foot as she followed the path to the pool. She used to spend all of her time there, sitting at the water's edge, wishing for the courage to end her torment. Thank the Harmonies, she'd never found it. An orbit in darkness seemed a small price to pay for healthy eyes now. It hadn't back then; it had been torture.

She reached ahead with the Harmonies, sampling the peace of the grove, and found all as it should be. It had been in a shocking condition when she returned from Snakeholme. Time and nature had almost undone her careful planting. Well, she'd fixed that. The native plants were growing harmoniously, and those she'd brought with her from homeworld, were no longer in danger of being crowded out of existence. Uprooting the guide plants that Chailen had planted along the paths, and honouring the Harmonies by returning her grove to balance, had been very satisfying.

Shima reached the pond and sat at the water's edge.

She could feel the fish meditating deep beneath the surface of the water. She couldn't see them even with her miraculously sharp eyes, but she could feel them down there. She huffed a laugh when she imagined Stone sitting here with her, eagerly searching for prey. He was a fiend for fishing according to Kate, though doing that here wouldn't have been very challenging.

She scooped up a pebble from nearby, and flipped it into the water. "Wake up down there."

The fish came to the surface to investigate the ripples, but disappointed to find nothing edible, they swam back to the deeps and fishy dreams.

She wondered what they found to think about. The Harmonies couldn't reveal thoughts, only feelings, but the tiny mind glows did confirm the fish had them. They were probably confined to survival. Things like: warm or cold, hungry or not hungry, and tired. Not a bad way to live for a fish, but for a Shan agricultural geneticist, it left a lot to be desired.

Maybe that was her problem.

Upon her return from Snakeholme, she'd been busy settling back in to Tahar's house, but there was nothing left to do. Sharn and Chailen had applied for various positions within the healer caste, and while they waited for news, Sharn had gone back to scavenging the ruins for things to trade. Shima helped with that when he asked her, but he rarely did any more; she always attracted too much attention. She was The Blind Hunter; the tragic heroic figure restored by Tei'Burgton, the honoured leader of the Viper Clan itself. Everyone wanted to meet her.

"Foolishness."

It was, but that didn't change matters.

Having a crowd follow and slow him down, didn't sit well with Sharn, especially when other scavengers got to his loot first. So, more and more, he went out alone, and asked for her help only when he found something too bulky for one person to carry. In the meantime, Chailen did odd jobs for people, and took her pay in food chits; those were worth more than money, and could be traded for extra rations, which she gave away to feral younglings more often than not.

Shima huffed, feeling dissatisfied with her inaction. She needed a proper job. Her partnership with Hamal wasn't a very satisfying form of employment, but it wasn't the cause of her night terrors. The dreams were partly her own fault. Letting Chailen talk her into going to the dedication ceremony had been a mistake. She should have resisted her sib, but reopening the Markan'deya was an important event for Zuleika. The old building had been destroyed in the liberation of the city, and rebuilding it had been given a high priority; not as high as the power grid and the water pumping stations, but high. The ferals in the ruins needed to be taught where they belonged, and where Shan fit in a universe filled with wonders like the Viper Clan, and horrors like the Murderers of Harmony.

The new Markan'deya was larger and more modern than the old one. The original art had been lost with the building, but there were plenty of electronic records to work from. All of the paintings were lovingly reconstructed, and the artefacts replaced from those stored in other cities.

She remembered thinking, back during her escape from Zuleika, that Kazim's films might teach future generations of younglings. Well, she'd been right. An entire hall had been dedicated to the new war, and wall screens featuring Kazim's work were its most striking feature. Broken weapons, and other artefacts, were displayed in cases beneath each screen to lend his films authenticity. Not that such were needed so soon after victory. Memories were still raw.

Her visor was displayed beneath one of the screens. An enterprising hunter must have realised there was money to be made in finding the thing. It was strange to think that Tahar's creation had become a cherished artefact. The display even had a little placard explaining its origins and significance. Her father's name would be remembered; his deeds taught to generations of younglings, as would the deeds of Shima, The Blind Hunter.

Her protests had fallen on deaf ears.

The dedication ceremony wasn't the cause of her bad dreams; not directly anyway. No, it had been one of Kazim's films. She'd been wandering the hall, wondering if she might leave without giving offense, when she'd seen Merrick die on one of the screens. Chailen had tried to pull her away, but she'd steadfastly refused to be moved, and watched herself fail Merrick over and over again.

It would be easy to blame her night terrors on Kazim's films, but she didn't. The dream wouldn't have power over her emotions if she'd been living in harmony. She hadn't been, not for a long time now; not since Tahar's death and the war. She needed… *something*. She didn't know what, but something. It was time to ask the Harmonies for help.

She settled herself comfortably, determined to discover what the Harmonies wanted of her, and regain her balance. She slipped into her meditation sleep easily, her breathing slowing and deepening as muscles relaxed. The Harmonies drew near, and her consciousness expanded to take in the natural world around her. She let it show her what it would, not trying to use or direct it, and flinched when Merrick appeared in her mind's eye. She nearly woke then, but he did nothing. It was just his image staring sightlessly at the night sky. She watched that horrible night play out like one of Kazim's films; watched herself cry and give her life to Merrick's father.

What did it mean?

Nevin had returned her life in exchange for her friendship upon reaching the keep. It still felt wrong. She had sworn by her clan name that her life was his. For killing his cub, she'd submitted herself to his justice, and he'd spared her. The old traditions said he couldn't do that, but he *had* done it. In primitive times, Nevin would rightfully have killed her. If he'd been particularly vindictive, he could have set her an impossible task to perform. Honour would've required her to attempt it, even if it took the rest of her life.

Living in harmony meant balance in all things. The key to balance was honour and obligation. She had spoken the words; he had heard them. The Harmonies were trying to tell her that Nevin held the answer. That must be it. She felt her spirits rise with the realisation. With hope her balance would soon be restored, she awoke refreshed and determined to visit Nevin.

Dawn broke over the city as she entered the house. The Harmonies revealed Chailen awake, but Sharn's sleeping mind glow meant he planned to sleep in again. Her ears went back in distress at his ennui, but she couldn't blame him. None of them had proper employment. Something had to change for their family, and soon. She would *make* something change!

She found Chailen sitting on the floor in the main room using the comp. "Any luck?" she said, and her sib closed the computer.

"More rejections," Chailen said glumly. "Is it very wrong of me to wish the Humans had gone home after the war?"

Shima blinked. Her mouth worked, trying to express her surprise. Finally, she found something. "But James and Brenda are our friends, and you liked Tei'Burgton didn't you?"

"Yes but…" Chailen huffed in displeasure. "My caste has lost much of its prestige," she admitted. "You know I don't care about that, but our people are looking to the Humans to solve their ills now, not to healers like Sharn or me." She raised her arm to draw attention to the Human made wristcomp she wore. "They all want one of these, and the IMS that goes with it."

"Can you blame them?"

"Of course not. Nanotech triples the average lifespan of our people. Barring accidents, we'll live for two-hundred orbits. I want that for all of our people. The problem is, my caste isn't needed for that to happen."

Shima sat opposite her sib. "You're wrong. Humans have had nanotech for centuries. They still need healers, and so will we."

"That is a truth, but not the whole truth. Our people will need healers *trained in Human medicine*. Human healers are different, Shima. They're more like Tahar than Sharn. They don't have castes, but if they did, their healer caste would be a combination of our healer and engineering castes."

"Change can be a good thing," Shima said quietly, but it was her own life she was thinking of now. Change was a part of life, and it was coming. She could feel it. "The healer caste will learn and adapt."

"It already is!" Chailen snapped. "That's the problem. No one wants a healer like Sharn and me anymore. There are thousands like us. They want healers with knowledge of Human techniques like nanotech."

"Calm down."

"You calm down!" Chailen glared. "Sharn won't even talk to me about it," she said, sounding hurt now. "He's a good healer, but I caught him reading a warrior caste application last night."

"Sharn would make for a terrible warrior."

"I know that. Don't you think I know? He's desperate to feel useful again, and provide for us. I told him that your partnership with Hamal was going well, and you would look after us, but he—"

Shima groaned.

Chailen paused, and her ears sagged. "I know. It just came out!"

"You shouldn't have said that, my sib. You've hurt his pride."

"I know," Chailen said miserably. "I apologised right away, but now he won't talk about it."

She couldn't interfere with Chailen's mate bond. It would be wrong, and only make things worse. Sharn's feelings were raw and his pride hurt. He was feeling inadequate, unable to provide for his mate. His lack of employment might force him into a hasty decision to change his caste. Sharn would make for a terrible warrior. He would be miserable, and that would transfer to Chailen, making her miserable too.

"Tell me what your caste is doing to address the nanotech question," Shima said. The question was highly improper. She was scientist caste, not healer. Each caste had secrets. Sharing between them was always limited. "I swear not to divulge anything you tell me."

Chailen snorted, and waived away the oath. "There are no secrets between us, my sib, but I can't see how my telling you will help."

"I won't know until you tell me. I might see something you've missed."

"The Humans are training our best healers," Chailen began.

"The best ones, or the most highly connected?"

"Our Tei," Chailen admitted. "They *are* our best, but you're right. They're high in healer caste decision making."

"Huh," Shima chuffed. Big surprise there. Not. "So your Tei decided Shan must learn Human techniques, and then chose themselves to lead the way?"

"It's what they do. Tei always lead by example. Once trained, they'll understand the new methods, and how to incorporate them into the caste. They'll teach us what they've learned."

"Sounds sensible. I'm sure the other castes are doing similar things." She wondered if her own caste had learned anything new. "Right, I know what to do."

"You do?" Chailen said in surprise.

"We need to contact one of these Tei, and get Sharn added to the classes they're holding."

Chailen groaned. "I already tried. There are thousands like us, Shima. We all want to learn from the Humans. Sharn and I are far down the list. Our Tei must train a cadre of teachers first, and the new teachers will train more. It will take orbits."

Shima growled in frustration. "That's too long."

"I know."

"I'll think of something. I'll fix this."

"You can't do it," Chailen said sadly. "No one can."

* * *

8 ~ A Matter of Honour

Kachina Twelve, Child of Harmony.

Her sib's words were much on Shima's mind during the trip out to Kachina Twelve. *You can't do it. No one can.* The sad desperation had been clear to the Harmonies. Shima hadn't needed the help. She knew her sib better than anyone.

She would prove Chailen wrong. She *would* find a way to make her sib happy again. There must be someone she could talk to about it. The real problem was the lack of training places compared with the numbers needing them. Chailen was barely qualified. She had finished her training only recently, and already it was becoming obsolete. Sharn was a little older. He would be higher on any list for retraining than his mate, but not by much. It took time to teach people new ways of doing things. There weren't many Human healers in the system, able to devote their energies to it.

She needed a contact within Fifth Fleet, but all of her Human friends had left. She didn't know anyone in authority able to help her. She growled in frustration. There must be a way around this lack of teachers... her eyes narrowed. There wasn't *actually* a lack of teachers. There were billions of

Humans in the Alliance, and many schools able to teach her people should they wish to use them, but reaching them was the problem. She assumed a trader would take passengers, if it were made profitable. How could she find the money to reach an Alliance school?

Shima landed her car, slotting it neatly into a space in one of the many rows outside the keep's entrance. Kachina Twelve was a busy place. There were a lot of battered vehicles like hers parked there. She followed the stream of people entering the tunnel, and passed through security without slowing. The amount of foot traffic in and out of this particular entrance, made checking identities impossible. Besides, what was the point? Fifth Fleet controlled the system, and kept watch for the Merkiaari. There was no need to prevent anyone from entering the keeps. Many people still lived in them, travelling only to find work. While visitors like her came to trade for rations, or visit friends.

Shima paused at one of the many junctions to consult a terminal. The octagonal pillar in the centre of the aisle, displayed maps and directions on each of its eight screens. She entered Nevin's name on one of the keyboards, and a list of males with that name appeared. She found the only one with a mate and three cubs listed. The names were all correct. She was relieved to find they hadn't emigrated to homeworld, as many had done since the war ended. She noted their address: 10-42 sub-level six-green, checked the map, and found the closest spiral way. She growled; it was a long trek, and six levels was quite a way down. She thought fondly of Human elevators, and sighed.

Shima made her way through the keep, pointedly ignoring the people stopping to stare as she passed. She heard their whispers, but again pretended not to notice. She kept her face pleasant, and didn't allow her annoyance to show. What was wrong with them? Why couldn't they go about their business, and let her go about hers? She knew why, and her frustration made her growl quietly. Humans had a special word for it.

Celebrity.

It was a foolishness that Kazim's films and shows had made worse. Her people had really taken to the idea of celebrity, because it linked their modern world with the sagas they'd learned as younglings. They didn't see *her*; they saw The Blind Hunter. Like actors in one of the new sensims, they imagined themselves in her place. The Human invention had gained popularity on Child of Harmony. It was a novelty entertainment that could be used to teach, which is what sensims were used for in the main.

She found Nevin's door and pressed the call button. A moment later the door slid aside to reveal Miamovi, one of Merrick's sibs.

"Aunt Shima!"

Shima blinked in surprise. She was an aunt, when had that happened? "Miamovi, it's good to see you again. You've grown tall."

"Not really. Inaki is taller… oh! I forgot. May you live in harmony, Aunt."

"Who is it, 'movi?" a voice called from deeper within the room.

Shima laughed. "Thank you. May you live in harmony as well. Is your father in?"

"He's here. Please come in," the youngling said, stepping back to clear the entrance. Shima entered to allow the door to close behind her. "It's Aunt Shima!" Miamovi called.

Shima braced herself. Inaki and Rahuri arrived moments later in a rush. They paused briefly to make their bows, and then charged in for a hug. Shima staggered a little; they were too old for this really. They were young adults ready for their choosing ceremonies. Miamovi looked on a little wistfully, and Shima reached to gather her in. The four of them stood there and hugged, remembering other times. She imagined

Merrick watching over his sibs, and smiling to see them all together again.

"Let poor Shima breathe," Marsali said as she approached to greet her guest. "Shoo, back to your lessons."

"Oh mother," all three groaned, but they obediently trooped away.

"Be welcome to our home, Shima. May you live in harmony."

Shima bowed. "Thank you. May you and your family live in harmony also. How have you been?"

Marsali shrugged, her tail making the gesture over her left shoulder. "Fine. There are many less fortunate than us. We're together. That's what matters."

Shima remembered the feral younglings living in the ruins of Zuleika. They had no one except volunteers like Chailen to care for them. Marsali was right.

Nevin appeared behind his mate, and Shima bowed very respectfully to him. She still felt that need. He was older and deserving of respect, but so was Marsali, and she didn't feel the need to express it so formally with her. It was because Nevin reminded her of Tahar. She suspected growing up without a mother had something to do with it as well.

"Welcome, Shima," Nevin said. "Have you eaten?"

"Yes, thank you. Chailen fed me as usual. She thinks I'd forget without her."

Marsali and Nevin laughed. They led her into their home, and offered her a place to sit at the table. It was the only furniture in the room; a generic thing supplied to every resident in the keep. The walls like the floor were plain grey. Easy to clean, but drab.

Shima remembered the cave they'd briefly lived in. They'd been fleeing Merkiaari in fear for their lives, but that cave had been luxurious compared to this. Toilet and washing facilities were communal in the keeps, and were probably a long way from here. There was a freshwater spring, and a pool for bathing, in the cave. The younglings were studying in the only other room. It would be where they slept at night, leaving this one to their parents. The cave had been much larger.

Nevin must have guessed her thoughts. "We have food and shelter. We survived thanks to you," he said, and patted her shoulder before sitting opposite. "It's good to see you again, but I suspect this isn't a social visit. How can I help you?"

"You're right. I should have come for a visit before this."

"You've been busy," Marsali said. "You have new eyes, and must have seen wonders with them."

Shima flicked her ears in agreement. "I thank the Harmonies for the Humans. They gave me back my sight, and my life."

"All of us owe them our lives," Nevin agreed. "You must tell us of your adventures since last we met. You've seen Snakeholme, and helped the elders choose the location for our new colony. Tell us of it."

"Perhaps the others would like to hear as well?" Shima said, smiling when she noticed them edging closer to the open door to listen.

Marsali scowled at the younglings. "They must study for their choosing time, but… very well. They may join us."

Shima waited for everyone to settle before beginning her story. She spun the tale of a blind female on a Human ship, headed for Snakeholme. She told them of her terror of the dark, and how healer Hymas had solved it with the magic of a sensim helmet. Shima tried to project the wonder she'd felt at being able to see alien worlds in her head. How being able to see, even in this limited and strange way, had made her feel.

"Was it like the sensims we have here at the keep?" Inaki said, and her sibs shushed her.

"Probably," Shima said. "I could feel the wind ruffle my fur, and the warmth of Sol—that's the name of Earth's sun—on my face. It felt wondrous. I had to wear a helmet for it to work, but I didn't mind. I saw Human cities, and space stations. I floated among the stars without a suit, and thought I would die of fright!"

Nevin laughed. "I doubt that."

"It's true! Did you know that Humans like to build towers?" Everyone said no. "They build houses so tall they touch the sky. They don't like living underground the way we do. I think it scares them. They don't like the dark, or being closed in. They prefer the sun, and being able to see far. I think that's why they build so high."

"What about the Viper Clan, what's their home like?" Miamovi said.

"I'm coming to that. Snakeholme is so far away that it took us two seasons to reach. I didn't know until after they gave me my new eyes, but Snakeholme has two moons, and it has rings! Have you seen the films Kazim made?" They all agreed they had. "Then you know what I saw there. While the healers worked with me, Kazim and Varya were surveying the wilds for a good colony site. There's a lot of good land there, but we decided to recommend site five to the elders—that's the one in the mountains near the lake. They agreed."

"Well," Nevin said taking a deep breath. "I'm sure they were wise to listen to you."

Shima shrugged. "There were many good choices, and any of them would be fine. Snakeholme is mostly wild. Perhaps Tei'Burgton will give us a second site later, when we need to expand."

"I'm sure he will. He is wise," Nevin said, and Shima agreed that he was. Nevin mock glared at his cubs. "Back to your studies, you lazy creatures!"

The younglings laughed and went back to work in the other room, while their mother rose to fetch refreshments.

Nevin focussed upon Shima. "You seem troubled."

"I need help. Advice. I think…" she lowered her voice

so only Nevin might hear. "I think Merrick wanted me to come."

Nevin's ears quivered at the name of his dead cub. "His kah came to you?"

"In a dream. Many times."

"I see. All know that you're strong in the Harmonies, Shima. What do you think I can do that you cannot?"

"I don't know, but when I meditated upon the dreams, I felt strongly the answer lay with you."

"Curious," Nevin said. "Tell me everything, and we shall see."

Shima began with her dreams of Merrick, and her belief they were a response to the dedication ceremony. She'd blamed Kazim's films for bringing back bad memories, but the night terrors continued long after any normal bad dream would have faded. She spoke of meditating and asking the Harmonies for help. Last of all, she brought up Chailen and her mate's lack of employment, and the meeting with Tei'Thrand.

Nevin concentrated upon Shima's words to the exclusion of all else. His eyes were closed, but his ears were high, soaking up her words. Shima told him everything. Her fears, her desires, her hopes for Chailen and Sharn. She ran out of things to say when Marsali returned with refreshments. They drank the tea in silence.

Nevin put aside his empty cup. "You gave your life to me."

Shima froze, her cup still half-full. She put it on the table, and inclined her head. "I did."

"You believe the Harmonies sent you to me."

"I do."

"What will you do, if I advise you to take Tei'Thrand's offer?"

Shima stared in dismay, her ears quivered, and tried to flatten. She willed them to be still. "I would ask you not to do that."

"But you would obey me? Your life for Merrick's life? Your honour for his?"

"My sib needs me. Please, I beg you."

"Answer the question. Will you become the Blind Hunter if I ask it?"

Her ears were flat, and her eyes white-rimmed. She panted; her panic made her want to run away. Tahar had taught her the old ways, and instilled his sense of honour in her. She would never betray his teaching.

"Yes," she whispered, her voice betraying her horror.

"I will not ask it," Nevin said kindly.

Shima gasped, her sudden relief making her feel faint.

"But," Nevin said, and she froze. "I will advise you not to waste the gifts the Harmonies have given you. The Merkiaari aren't done with us, Shima. We have entered a time of great change. I've heard you call yourself a gardener."

"I *am* a gardener!"

Nevin's ears flicked in agreement. "It's better to be a warrior in a garden, than to be a gardener in a war. Become the Blind Hunter, take Tei'Thrand's offer, and use both to help our people."

"But my sib. She needs me."

"We all need you, Shima. You can help Chailen best by helping everyone. You have many friends. If you ask it, Kazim will help. If you ask, the entire warrior caste will aid you. Many living here in Kachina Twelve owe you their lives. Tei'Thrand and Tei'Laran aren't the only ones who want the Great Harmony rebuilt among the stars."

That was obviously true, but she didn't see how she could make that happen. Their cities were in ruins, their fleet destroyed. The stations and factories in orbit were being replaced, but it would take time. She had no power over any of those things.

"How will becoming the Blind Hunter help my sib, or

anyone else? I have no power over anyone's actions but my own."

Nevin laughed. "You would be Tei'Shima, and someone with influence. If the Blind Hunter tells the elders why we must go to Pandora, they will listen. The people will *make* them listen. The warrior caste will follow the Blind Hunter anywhere, for honour's sake, and the clan-that-is-not would be overjoyed to recruit you. They lost too many of their number in the war. And think for a moment, Shima. The traditionalist Tei are in the ascendant right now. Tei'Thrand *needs* you."

"He *was* very upset when I said no," Shima admitted.

"He might have influence within healer caste. Make him an offer. Make him help your sib in exchange for joining him."

"But I don't want to be Tei!"

"Is that really true?"

"*Yes!*"

Nevin laughed. "I have no gift with the Harmonies, but even I can tell you're lying." Before Shima could voice her outrage, he went on. "I know you mean what you say, but you're lying to yourself. It's not joining the Tei that you rebel against. It's being the Blind Hunter. You feel guilty because of Merrick's death. I understand that, but nothing will change the truth. You already *are* the Blind Hunter. It's not a matter of choice."

"He died because he followed me."

"Merrick fought to save his family. Anyone would have done the same. He would have followed Kazim if he'd promised to try."

Shima laughed despite herself.

"And he would still have died," Nevin said. "And with him Kazim and the rest of us. Joining the clan-that-is-not, has nothing to do with Merrick or the past. It's the future we speak of. Do it for your sib and her mate. Do it for my cubs, and for everyone who lost family in the war."

"*But I don't know where to start,*" she said plaintively.

"You are scientist caste. Start at the beginning. Research, and find out what is happening. Kazim will know. Learn everything you can. Once you know what is possible, you'll know what to do."

"Research," Shima said thoughtfully. "It was my life once."

"It still is," Nevin said.

"For now," she agreed. She huffed a deep sigh as she realised the change she'd felt approaching had arrived. "I will do as you advise."

Saying the words should have horrified her, but to her surprise, she felt the old excitement stirring. A new research project; questions to ask and answer. Scientists lived for those.

* * *

9 ~ Born Scientist

Zuleika, Child of Harmony

Once decided upon a course of action, Shima could be very determined. It might take her a while to see her path, but once found, it would take Merkiaari or worse to force her from it.

She was a scientist, and knew where her gifts lay. Changing her caste—and the thought still gave her a twinge—wouldn't change her approach to solving problems. Whether in the lab or on the battlefield, research would remain a large part of who she was. It had been her entire life before the war; she wouldn't change that. It was said among her people that a cub's caste could be predicted by her first words. She'd been born with the word *why* on her lips.

Upon her return to the city, Shima recruited Chailen and Sharn. It would have been wrong to exclude them from something so important to their family, and her sib would have known something was going on. They discussed her decision, and embarked upon the course that would lead to their ultimate separation. Chailen had cried. Sharn had comforted her, and listened to the entire plan, before bowing very low. He knew why Shima had chosen this path. She raised him up, and all three hugged, knowing it might be the last time.

Over the cycles that followed, they worked together to learn everything they could about their people's interactions with the Humans beyond Shan space. There was a lot of information about their trade negotiations, and it made for fascinating reading. She didn't let it distract her, but when she had more time, she would investigate everything the Alliance had to offer; especially in her old area of genetics.

Her old area... already she was thinking of the time before the war as her old life. Her new one was about to begin.

Their research took cycles, but come the time, they gathered in the main room of the house again to compare notes. Sharn went first.

"They're dragging their tails," Sharn said, and offered his notes to Shima. She flicked her ears, and gestured for him to keep them. "I think they're hoping to put off leaving until next orbit. No one is actually saying that, but the Humans have already sent the first colony ship away. Empty. They weren't happy about it."

"I'm not surprised they're upset," Shima said. "It takes a long time to come here, and then to return empty? They must be snarling over that."

"Do Humans do that; snarl I mean?" Chailen said.

Shima's tail rose to gesture a shrug. "I don't know, but I've seen them angered over less. What reason did Kajetan give?"

"She made up some excuse. Something about needing to thoroughly consider her choices, and not being ready to finalise the list of colonists."

"She lied?" Chailen said, sounding horrified. "How could she disrespect Tei'Burgton so, and after all he did for us?"

"Well, that's the thing. I don't think she *was* lying. The elders are still arguing over the details, and won't give her their final recommendations. It's the clan elders holding things up, not Kajetan."

"Why would they delay?" Shima wondered aloud, but then answered her own question. "It's Tei interference. The elders have no reason to back out. What is Kajetan going to do about it, do you know?"

"What *can* she do?" Sharn said. "She made her decision after we returned. It's for the clans to carry it out. The clan elders can encourage and cajole, but it's for Tei to lead the way."

"And they won't. Politics," Shima said in disgust. "The progressives must be in a sorry state if they can't even gather enough colonists to fill one small ship."

"The clan-that-is-not isn't saying," Sharn said. "Of course."

Chailen chuffed in amusement.

Shima laughed at her sib's sour expression, but this was a serious problem. The progressive Tei were weak in councils, and had been since most had died in the war. She was certain they were trying to redress the balance, but Tei were born not made, and of course, not all would be amenable to joining the progressives when they joined Tei ranks.

It would take a generation or two for their numbers to recover. That was why Tei'Thrand had sounded so desperate when he struck her. Shima hadn't forgiven him for that, but she did, reluctantly, understand his frustration. Without the numbers required to oppose the traditionalists in Tei councils, Tei'Thrand and those of like mind, needed to make deals with the Harmony-First faction.

Once the weakest faction, but currently the most numerous, the Harmony-Firsters were a waste of talent in her opinion. They'd had a use before the war, but now? With the progressives so weak, there was little need for mediation. The traditionalists owned Tei councils.

"We need Kazim," Shima said. "I know he'll like this, but I'm not sure his supervisors will let him help us. Technically, they'll be interfering in Tei business."

"He won't care," Chailen said, and then a little slyly added, "he'll do anything for you."

Shima squirmed. "Like I said. He'll like the plan, but putting himself between elders and Tei? I'm not certain about that."

"Let's ask him before borrowing trouble," Sharn said, and Shima flicked her ears in agreement. "What about the warrior caste part?"

Shima hummed in indecision. "Hmmmm..."

Chailen patted Shima consolingly. "No one will think you flighty, my sib. You'll always be a scientist at heart, but the Blind Hunter is a born warrior. She should be warrior caste."

"Hmmmm..."

"Say the word, and we'll think of something else," Chailen said, worried now. She scented Shima's distress on the air. "It's too much. We'll go back to the keep. Things will be better next orbit, or the one after that for certain."

Do it for your sib and her mate. Do it for my cubs, and for everyone who lost family in the war.

"No," Shima said. "We follow the plan. I'll ask Varya to sponsor me."

"If you're sure? Do you want me to invite them for a visit?"

"Would you?"

"Of course! I'll cook something, and invite them to join us for dinner."

"I could eat," Sharn said.

Shima laughed. "You're always hungry for Chailen's cooking."

"Not just her cooking," Sharn said, reaching to squeeze his mate's hand.

Shima smiled as the Harmonies revealed their love for each other, but then it faded as the realities intruded upon her troubled thoughts. Chailen would be coming into her season again soon, and she was properly mated now. Her sib had no reason not to allow a pregnancy this orbit. If the plan worked, her future nieces and nephews would never know their aunt Shima. It made her want to cry.

She forced a cheerful tone. "Well then. We have a goal, and a plan to achieve it. Now we need an army."

Later that same cycle, her five strong nascent army gathered around the dinner table. Chailen provided a feast of Shkai'ra, one of Shima's favourites, and everyone praised it. They discussed Shima's visit with Nevin over tea, and debated his advice, before moving on to the plan itself.

"Oh this is going to be *good!*" Kazim crowed. "We'll be famous!"

"You're already famous," Shima said sourly. "And so am I. That's your fault, and I'm still going to make you pay."

"But not right now, am I right?"

Varya and the others laughed.

Shima growled. "Not right now, you're too useful. Do you think it will work?"

Kazim flicked his ears. "We'll *make* it work. I have some ideas already. I wanted to do this before, but my supervisor sent me to cover the construction of the shipyards instead."

That was interesting. Kazim's broadcasts always were. He really was as good as everyone said, though Shima wouldn't tell him that of course.

"When will I see that one?"

"I don't know for sure. She wanted a series of them, and I don't know the order they'll be released. They were fun to make. The Human shipyard was impressive, but still very Human looking. The ships being built there are a gift, and they're amazing, but watching our own yard rebuilding the Fleet was better. You'll love that show. We cut in some segments taken during the war. The fall of *Hekja* and *Naktlon*, the mad evacuation of the younglings from Hool Station. Lots of other things."

"Hool's destruction?" Shima said quietly. Her father had died there.

Kazim's ears wilted. "Yes."

"I would like to see it."

Chailen gasped. "Why?"

"Because seeing the truth might hurt less than my imagination. It can't hurt worse."

Chailen flicked her ears in agreement. "I'll watch with you."

Shima squeezed her sib's hand.

"I would love to visit to see the new ships with my own eyes," Varya said to dispel the dark mood.

The others agreed.

"Do you think your supervisor will like Chailen's idea?" Varya said.

"Anything starring the Blind Hunter will impress her. If we do this right, nothing short of another Merkiaari war will stop her airing it."

"Or the Tei," Varya said sourly. "They could stop it."

Kazim smirked. "They'd have to know about it ahead of time, and even then, I doubt they'd try. Our Tei don't play politics. They're not like other Tei."

Varya snorted.

"No really. They're different."

"You're delusional. All Tei are different."

"Ours are more different," Kazim insisted.

"He might be right," Shima mused. "Only the mad choose the arts for their caste."

"Hey!" Kazim spluttered.

Everyone laughed.

Shima wanted to burst with happiness as she watched her family enjoying themselves. Chailen and Sharn were more important than her own life, but Varya and Kazim were almost as important to her. She thought of all four of them as her family. In a strange way, she had two families now. Her Human family was far away on Earth and Snakeholme. James and his mate, Kate and hers, and Gina. She missed them all very much.

"Are you free to start tomorrow?" Shima asked, bringing her attention back to business, and Kazim flicked his ears in agreement. "Well then. The second thrust will be The Blind Hunter choosing her caste," she said just a little bitterly.

"It won't be so bad," Varya said. "We'll see amazing things together, and we'll get to play hunter and prey all the time."

Everyone laughed.

"Until it stops being play," Shima said. An awkward silence descended. "But first, we make the warrior caste do what they already want to do, and honour says they *must* do. Uphold their part in our alliance with the Humans."

Growls of agreement swept the room.

Honour demanded it, and that would play well with the warrior caste when they watched Kazim's shows. Shima had high hopes for her fledgling army. If all went well, it would grow into the millions in short order.

In a way, she'd already started upon a road every Tei had to tread. Just as they did, she would lead, she would advise, and she would try to inspire her people along the correct path—a path that in this case they already wanted to follow.

"I'm in your hands, Kazim," she said, and he brightened to hear it. "Don't let it go to your head. I'm still a better shot than you. Embarrass me too badly, and you'll find out how much better."

Kazim's jaw dropped wide in a laugh, and his ears waved jauntily. "You're in good hands. Now, show me what I have to work with."

"Show?"

"Your harnesses, tools... do you have a car? I need a few props. Your visor lent you recognition before. We'll work around that, but I'll need to rebrand you."

Shima seethed. "That visor you love so much *branded* me a cripple!"

"No it didn't. The Blind Hunter wore it, and that's who everyone saw. No one ever called you cripple, or would dare."

Except you, went unsaid.

"Huh," Shima chuffed, mollified just a little. "I have a new warrior's harness we can use. Tei'Laran left it in the dust when I refused his invitation."

"That will be useful later, but not straight away. Do you still have the one you wore when we escaped the city?"

"She can't wear that old thing!" Chailen protested. "It's barely holding together."

Shima shrugged. "She's right. I use it on salvage runs. I don't have a car, but I can borrow one from Hamal. I..." she looked away, ashamed. "I sold my beamers."

Silence filled the room.

Shima looked back to find dismay on every face. Chailen hadn't known. Her shock was obvious. Sharn didn't look surprised. He must have guessed when she stopped cleaning them, and charging power cells for them.

Shima tried to explain. "We needed the chits. I traded them for power cells, and Hamal took those for the use of a car. I had to. We would have starved."

"We wouldn't have starved," Chailen said. She was being too literal. "No one starves in the keeps."

"You know what I meant."

"But why didn't you tell us?"

Shima exchanged a look with Sharn, and Harmonies curse it, Chailen caught it. Her sib was far too sharp. Sharn hunched his shoulders, and dipped his head in self-defence. Chailen's glare could be lethal.

"We'll talk about this," Chailen said to her mate. She glanced at her guests, and back. "*Later.*"

Sharn flicked his ears in agreement, and straightened. He

looked relieved to have avoided a scolding. You poor fool, Shima thought. She knew her sib too well to be fooled. He wouldn't get away unscathed from this. He'd be doing chores for cycles as penance.

"I'll buy some beamers for you," Varya said.

"I'll pay you back," Shima said, and dipped her head in thanks.

"Don't get new ones," Kazim warned. "That won't look right. She needs to look as much like before as possible. The old harness and holsters, worn beamers... yes... yes, that will work. The Blind Hunter, the weary hero, scavenging the ruins to support her family. It will look perfect."

"I'm not wearing that visor no matter what you say. Not ever again. Besides, haven't you heard? It's a cherished artefact now. Stealing it would offend the ancestors."

Kazim smirked. "Lay it on thicker, why don't you? It wouldn't offend the ancestors, but it would offend my audience. That might be worse for our cause. They aren't stupid. They know you aren't blind anymore. We have to be subtle."

Varya laughed. "You, subtle? Is that even possible? All know your ego enters a room before you do."

Kazim's ears flattened in dismay, and then he realised Varya was joking. "You chose the wrong caste, my friend. You would fit perfectly into the arts. We have many comedians."

Varya spluttered.

Shima grinned. "You plan to film my salvage runs?"

Kazim flicked his ears in agreement. "I'll need you at a few special locations, but essentially yes. The research centre for starters."

"But it's already picked clean."

"That doesn't matter," Kazim said. "I can use your trips to show your present circumstances, but locations like the research centre and Zuleika Spaceport will provide the perfect backdrop for interview questions. I'm aiming for a past and present feel."

"And leave a question mark hanging over future plans?" Chailen said.

Kazim pointed. "*Exactly!*" He seemed pleased she'd caught on so quickly. "It's the perfect set-up. I'll film her going about her daily tasks, and show everyone the present. At certain places I'll interview the Blind Hunter about her past actions in those places. The spaceport, the research centre, the wilderness cave we used on our way to Kachina Twelve." Kazim turned solemn. "And Merrick's grave."

Shima jerked. "No. Not that."

"It's important to the Blind Hunter's story."

"But he's not even there anymore. Nevin took him back to the grove. His ashes were mixed with those of his ancestors."

"I know, Shima. I was there with you."

Of course he was. Nevin had wanted them there to witness the ceremony of leave-taking. Normally, only close family would be present, but they'd grown close on the trail. Living together on the run in the wilderness, Nevin had trusted her and Kazim with his cubs' lives.

She forced herself to listen to Kazim's ideas, and hoped Merrick could forgive her for using his death this way.

* * *

10 ~ Show Time

Zuleika, Child of Harmony

It took almost half a season, and a lot of hard work, to realise Kazim's plan. He did most of it by handling the choice of locations, and thinking up questions; Shima simply followed his orders. Despite her playful jests, she knew he was an expert in his field. His choice of the arts was well chosen.

One of the first things he'd done, was charm Hamal out of her most decrepit air-car. Shima had called him an idiot for not choosing one with an intact canopy, especially when it rained, but he laughed it off and said he didn't want to film a prosperous looking hero. He wanted to tell a story of hardship endured.

Shima had rolled her eyes, and let him move her around like a puppet. She'd helped Chailen care for feral younglings in Zuleika's ruins, and let Kazim interview her there. That interview would raise a few hackles. As intended.

Kazim filmed her scavenging various ruins, and visiting sites where she'd fought the Merkiaari with James. She tolerated more interviews in all those places, and the impertinent questions that went with them; she didn't snarl even once.

Kazim had been impressed with her forbearance; he'd said so. Finally, satisfied with all they'd done, he submitted his work to his supervisor, and they waited.

Come the time, Shima and her family gathered to watch the result of all their hard work. Chailen made a feast, and between delicious bites to eat, they chatted excitedly while they waited for the broadcast to begin. The screen was on with the volume low. Shima glanced at it, but nothing interesting was on.

"I told everyone I know not to miss the broadcast," Varya said between bites. "And asked them to spread the word. I think every warrior not on active patrol will see it."

Chailen flicked her ears in agreement. "Sharn and I spread the word too. Healers are a chatty bunch. My entire caste will be watching."

Shima chuffed. "Huh. I knew I kept you four around for a reason."

"Glad you didn't just shoot me?" Kazim said with a laugh.

"Maybe," she admitted. "You're not as annoying as you used to be—"

"Hush. It's starting," Chailen said, and turned the sound up.

The show began with Chailen caring for the ferals in Zuleika's ruins. The younglings had no family, and most were traumatised to one degree or another. Many had gathered together into makeshift groups, not based upon blood ties, but rather upon location. They barely tolerated strangers in their territory, but they loved Chailen. She was like their den mother. She listened to them, advised them, and offered a little food when she had it to spare. She was something they all had in common.

Shima watched herself answering Kazim's questions, and felt flickers of anger building. Healer caste would explode when they saw two of their members grubbing in the dirt, trying to help younglings the elders and Tei had abandoned.

That was fine with her. Let the fur fly where it would.

The broadcast ended after a seg with a powerful image that any Shan would recognise. It showed the guardians sitting outside the gates of Nevin's clan grove, with the sun low in the sky. Beams of light speared the trees to illuminate them. Kazim had delayed leaving for segs to capture that moment. The huge wooden statues, one male and one female to represent balance, were always carved from ancient trees cut from the groves they protected. With eyes closed and hands loose in laps, they contemplated the Harmonies.

The image faded, and a few lines of text brightened to replace it.

Interviewer: "What was your first reaction when you heard the Human ship had returned to Snakeholme empty?"

Blind Hunter: "Anger. These younglings have no family, no homes, and no hope. Tei'Burgton has offered them all three on Snakeholme, but the elders don't care."

Interviewer: "What's your opinion of the warrior caste's inability to participate in the war games on Pandora?"

Blind Hunter: "I was horrified when I heard. The warrior caste *must* go to Pandora. I'll take their place, and go alone if I must. It's a matter of honour."

The quotes faded, replaced by a final message.

"We can shed tears that Merrick is gone,
or we can smile as we remember he lived."
—The Blind Hunter.

Chailen turned off the screen.

Shima touched Kazim's arm. "Thank you."

Kazim shrugged. "It's not like I didn't enjoy myself, and besides, the Blind Hunter doesn't give interviews to just anyone. I'm special."

Shima growled.

Varya and the others laughed.

"I'm the best," Kazim was saying. "I'm—" the chime indicating an incoming call silenced him.

No one moved, and silence fell over the room again. Before anyone could speak, the chiming started again. This time the tone indicated a message being downloaded. Chailen went to read it on the computer, but before she could, the incoming call chime began again.

"Well," Varya said. "I think you gained their attention."

"We," Shima said. "We did."

"Should I answer?" Chailen said.

Everyone looked to Kazim. It was his show. He thought about it long enough for the caller to give up, and send a message instead. That decided it.

"The Blind Hunter is unavailable for comment," Kazim said. "All of us are unavailable."

Chailen returned to her place at the table, and drank some tea. Shima refilled everyone's cup, and then ate some of the delicious meal her sib had prepared. The incoming message signal chimed again, and again, and again, but everyone ignored it.

The cycles following that meal were busy ones. Thousands called or sent messages of support, while hundreds sent queries and angry questions. Did she want to cause a crisis? Did she want to cause a rift between their people and the Humans? Did she really want to disrespect the elders by mocking the choices they'd made?

Shima had been furious when she read the messages from the dissenters. Most were from Tei. She researched them, and all were either staunch traditionalists, or members of the Harmony-First faction. The fools were being wilfully blind to the needs of their people, and she told them so in no uncertain terms. Their outraged rebuttals were personally satisfying, but ultimately pointless.

Kazim's employer happily replayed the show regularly, and messages of support continued to trickle in. He watched the viewing numbers closely, and the content of the messages. At some signal that made sense to him, he released Shima's pre-recorded statement. It denounced all the angry-message-sending-Tei, by name, and demanded an audience with Kajetan.

The messages stopped, and Shan everywhere watched.

And waited.

* * *

11 ~ Summoned

Hall of the Elders, Yangsho, Harmony

When Shima left Harmony, and Tahar took a job on Hool Station, she'd never expected to return. Her father had made a new home for them on Child of Harmony, and she'd been prepared to live out her life there in happy obscurity. No, she'd never expected to return, but here she was, summoned for an accounting by the elders.

Summoned she might be, but she'd come of her own will. Nevin hadn't forced her to accept his advice. It was her choice, and her plan she followed. No matter what came of this meeting, she would remember it had been her choice.

Like Zuleika, Yangsho had been badly mauled by the Merkiaari, but unlike Shima's home, the Viper Clan hadn't arrived in time to save it. The damage was so bad, it shocked her and the others into silence during the ride from the spaceport. They'd all seen pictures, but seeing the devastation with their own eyes was something else. It was so much worse than Zuleika. Honestly, there wasn't much left of the ancient city.

Shima stared out the side window of the car, and noted

the signs of new construction. She wondered why the elders didn't just choose a new site, but answered the thought almost immediately. Continuity and tradition.

The Great Pact began at Yangsho, and the council of elders had been hosted in the city ever since its inception. The gates of Yangsho were spoken of in the sagas about The Great Leveller, the patron of Shima's clan. His story, Jasha at the Gate, was still taught to younglings. She wondered if he'd hated his title as much as she hated hers.

The new Hall of the Elders was a replica of the original building, and it was sadly obvious despite the attention lavished upon the replacement. The wood and stone gleamed like new, which it was. It should have been weathered, and lovingly cared for by generations of crafters. Instead, it looked like a brash impostor. Like the Markan'deya back home, rebuilding it was given a high priority. It stood as a monument to the Great Pact, and for unity between the clans. Kajetan lived there, and the highest councils were conducted within its walls. It wasn't simply a residence. It housed most of the government. There it stood, new again, as if someone had pushed a hidden reset button on the world.

The car stopped opposite the entrance, and Shima climbed out to greet the reception committee. She recognized Elder Amara, Clan Jasha's representative at the council.

"She doesn't look happy to see you," Kazim said quietly.

Shima shrugged. "She's too important to be running errands."

"The Blind Hunter outranks her."

She stared at him in surprise, and forced her ears to stay erect. They quivered a little, but didn't clamp themselves to her head. Amara was a clan elder; she'd been appointed by Shima's own clan to represent them on the council. Only Kajetan outranked her, and only Tei or other elders equalled her.

"She represents my clan on the council," Shima protested.

"And there are dozens just like her in Yangsho. There's only one hero. You."

She winced. She doubted she would ever train herself out of the need to deny her special status, but Kazim was right. She had to use it, unwanted though it was. It was too late to back out.

She bowed. "Elder. Very kind of you to greet us. May you live in harmony."

Amara glared, but she inclined her head. "The Blind Hunter honours me."

"I know," Shima said. "Who are these worthies with you?"

Chailen sucked in a shocked breath, but Sharn gave no indication he'd noticed. Kazim was much less politic. He chuffed, stifling a laugh, and the elder transferred her glare to him. As he'd intended. In the meantime, Shima had already greeted and touched palms with the others.

"This is Tei'Halina," Varya said. "He and I fought together at Shoshon."

Male. Warrior caste. Strong in the Harmonies.

Shima bowed as she assessed Varya's friend. He was a powerful figure. Strong in the Harmonies as well as in body, he was in his prime and must rank high in Tei councils.

Amara's other companion was an aged healer caste female; Sharn introduced her as Elder Renzarn. Bows and greetings were exchanged.

"Have you found your way since last we met?" Renzarn said gravely to Sharn. "Have you used my teachings to prosper?"

Sharn's ears wilted under her regard; his unhappiness clear to the Harmonies. Renzarn knew he hadn't prospered. Forcing him to admit it to her, was cruel and humiliating.

Shima interrupted. "My sib and her mate will gain all they deserve at this meeting. They will prosper. I'll see to it."

Renzarn focused upon Shima. "Indeed? Claiming to

know what another deserves, is very bold of you."

"The Blind Hunter *is* bold," Kazim said.

"*And* she is just," Varya added. "Her honour cannot be questioned."

Tei'Halina's ears flicked in agreement. His support was very welcome. Shima hadn't expected to gain allies here, she'd expected to make enemies, and the Harmonies revealed she'd made two already. Amara and Renzarn weren't happy.

Well, too bad.

"Shall we?" Shima said, indicating the entrance, and not waiting.

Tei'Halina overtook her, and led the way to Kajetan's apartments. It surprised her. Shima had expected to be received in a government office, or the council chamber, not Kajetan's private rooms. There was already a crowd of people waiting.

Shima stopped in the middle of the room, and the others joined her expecting some kind of ceremony, but the spectators weren't waiting for them. They stood in quietly whispering groups, and didn't take any notice of the newcomers.

"Wait here," Tei'Halina said and went through another door. Renzarn and Amara left them, and mingled with the others already waiting.

"Something's wrong," Kazim whispered.

Shima's ears flicked in agreement. The Harmonies revealed the whispering people were worried. Her ears pricked and swivelled when they recognised a Human voice. Two Human voices, trying to speak Shan, and doing so poorly.

"Please, you must make her listen. I swear we mean her no harm," the male Human said desperately.

"If she would only visit with us aboard my ship for a short time. I can show her what we promised is true," the female said.

Kazim noticed how distracted Shima was, and looked for what had caught her attention. He raised his camera when he found the Humans, and mumbled happily about his luck being in.

Shima didn't know about luck. The Harmonies revealed the Humans were desperately upset. More than their voices revealed. Their mind glows were flaring erratically, and the colours were so rich, she wondered everyone wasn't staring at them in awe. Humans were always very different in the Harmonies, but not usually like this.

"This feels important," she said slowly, and tugged Kazim along with her. He grumbled about ruining his shot.

"I feel..." she muttered.

She didn't know *what* she was feeling, but the Harmonies were warning her. The last time she'd felt anything like this, Merrick's kah had appeared to her. She looked hastily around for the youngling she'd failed to save, but sadly, he didn't make a grinning reappearance.

"Tei'Halina told us to wait," Chailen protested, but she followed.

"We aren't leaving," Shima muttered, concentrating upon the Harmonies to locate the Humans. The warning settled into her bones. "This is important."

"More important than your meeting with Kajetan?"

Kajetan's name shocked through the Harmonies, and Shima knew whatever she did next, would have lasting consequences for her people.

"Can I be of service?" Shima said in perfect English. The Humans' relief was obvious. "I am Shima, and these are Kazim, Chailen my sib. Her mate Sharn, and my close friend Varya. Do you need help?"

The Human female bowed briefly. "Thank God. I'm Commander Frisko, and this is my ship's surgeon. Doctor Isaacs. May you live in harmony."

Shima bowed. "May you live in harmony also. I can translate for you if it would be of use?"

"Yes! Please. Tell him that we must take Kajetan to my

ship. Tell him she'll die if she doesn't come!"

Shima turned to Elder Hallan, one of her father's friends, and bowed in respect. When she straightened, she found Kazim filming the meeting, a look of utter joy on his face.

"Honoured elder, the Humans are very upset. They say Kajetan is dying, and must go with them to their ship. The Harmonies reveal they'll burst if you don't listen."

Hallan laughed. "I'm well aware of that, Shima. My English is not the equal of yours, but I understood their attempts to explain. It's their misunderstanding, not mine."

"And what don't they understand?"

Hallan studied Shima for a long moment. He glanced at Kazim and the camera he held. "What they say is true. Kajetan knows her death approaches, as does the council. She accepts it. Only the time is in doubt now."

"The Humans say they can save her. Can they?"

"Who can say? Our healers say no, but the Humans swear they can. Perhaps you can persuade her to let them try."

"Me?"

"With Kazim's help. There are no guarantees, but you're an example of what Humans can do. Your new eyes, and the tiny machines swimming through your veins, are amazing."

Shima flicked her ears. She agreed with that. "You expect her to refuse treatment?"

"She already has."

"What does he say?" Doctor Isaacs said. "We must see Kajetan. You have to make him understand!"

"He understands," Shima said to calm him. "I'll speak with Kajetan for you."

Frisko and Isaacs looked relieved.

Shima wasn't relieved. Kajetan was notoriously hard-headed. She'd needed to be to lead their people for so long, and to navigate the treacherous waters of clan politics. There was good reason the position of Eldest was created by the Great Pact. Nothing would ever get done without it.

The door across the room opened, and Tei'Halina stepped out. He raised a hand and beckoned to Shima's group.

Shima entered Kajetan's presence first, allowing Kazim to film her doing so. Chailen and Sharn entered next, followed by the others. Tei'Halina re-entered and closed the door.

Shima hadn't been sure what to expect. The news of Kajetan's impending death had surprised her. What she hadn't expected, was the elder to be sitting in a darkened room working at a computer. Kajetan was very old, but seeing her in the flesh, it hit home. The Harmonies revealed a tired and lonely Shan female at the end of her life. She had outlived her mate by over a decade, and her sibs had joined him around that time. The Harmonies whispered that Kajetan would join her ancestors soon. She wasn't sick, just tired of living too long.

Shima hesitated. She knew what had to be done. Kajetan had lost the will to fight the tide. Her allies among the Tei were weak, many of her friends had been killed in the war. She deserved better, but so did many deserve better than they'd received. Chailen certainly did. Tahar and millions of others hadn't deserved to die at the hands of the Merkiaari. Her people deserved better than they were being offered by the current elders, and Kajetan was the only cure. *If* she cared enough to try.

Shima bowed. "Honoured Kajetan. Thank you for the invitation."

Kajetan laughed. "Is that what I did? I thought you demanded an audience, and I bowed to your threats. Isn't that what our people are saying?"

"I made no threats, Eldest."

"Don't play with me. Your smirking accomplice there... step forward, Kazim. All of you come closer."

They all made their bows, and murmured greetings.

"You were very good," Kajetan said, turning her attention back to Shima. "Just the right amount of outrage and sadness to be convincing. The demand for an audience was overly bold there at the end, but it worked. You would fit right in on my council. Manoeuvring for personal advantage is what they do best."

Shima's ears went back. Kajetan's scorn stung. "On my honour, I do this for others, not myself. I do it for those I love, and for those who died for us."

"Indeed? Make your demands."

"I prefer to call them proposals. Yours is the final word of decision, Eldest. As always."

Kajetan considered Shima for a long moment. "Shima and I shall discuss her proposals in private. Please await us in the other room."

Kazim looked crestfallen, but he didn't say anything as he followed the others out.

"The word *proposal* seems to suggest I have a choice. We both know I have none, just as you intended with your inflammatory broadcasts."

"That was my intention before meeting you," Shima admitted. "I don't want to force your cooperation any longer. I want you to lead our people into the future you helped to shape."

Kajetan sagged. "I'm not strong in the Harmonies, but I know you mean what you say. My time is over. Let someone else carry this burden."

Shima hardened her heart. "Who can? You know your advisors best. Who among them do you trust to lead, when they're already dragging their tails. The first colony ship returned to Snakeholme empty. Will the others even be sent now?"

"Another arrived in the night," Kajetan admitted.

"And will you send it away empty. Again?"

"I didn't send the first one away. It left of its own accord."

"On schedule you mean."

Kajetan glared.

"Take charge, Eldest," Shima pleaded. "Stop letting the Tei delay our agreements with the Humans. If you die before those things are firmly begun, I fear your successor will break our treaty with the Alliance."

"My successor might not be enthusiastic about fulfilling our obligations, but she wouldn't break the treaty. The Merkiaari are still out there."

"It would be suicide," Shima agreed. "But our people are not immune to stupidity. Who do you trust to see our people through the transition?"

Kajetan couldn't keep eye contact. She looked down. "It's too late. I'm not a young hero like you, eager to fight injustice and right wrongs. My time is over."

"The Humans can fix you, Eldest. They really can. They gave me new eyes and this," Shima raised her arm to display her wristcomp. "IMS will give you the time we need. You'll be strong again. We need your guidance while we rebuild. We need a strong hand to make our fools do what honour demands they should. We must take our place in the Alliance, and play a full part in the decisions it makes."

"If I could order our people to do as they should, I would have already. I don't have the influence I need. Too many of our Tei died with Fleet, and leading our warriors. Without them, Tei councils are deadlocked more often than not. How will you repair that?"

The Harmonies revealed a change. A stirring, as if the old fire that had been a younger and more idealistic Kajetan, had been stoked to life. Shima felt her own hopes rising with the change. She needed to nurture that flickering flame, until it became a bonfire big enough to consume Kajetan's doubts.

"If you agree to let the Humans heal you, and if you agree to send the feral younglings of Zuleika with my sib and her mate to Snakeholme, I will change my caste."

Kajetan jerked in surprise. "Why would you do that? I don't see how that will help either of us."

Shima flicked her ears in agreement. "Not on its own. You haven't asked which caste I would choose."

Kajetan's eyes narrowed. "Only warrior caste makes any sense, but I still don't see why you offer."

"May I sit?"

"Please," Kajetan said indicating the mat opposite her position. "I would offer tea, but I don't think we want witnesses to this."

"This must remain between us," Shima agreed. "You won't be bowing to any threats of mine, Eldest. I'll be following your commands."

Kajetan laughed. "Oh, you will? Kazim knows this, I take it."

"He does. We've already recorded the announcements."

"What announcements?"

"Various," Shima admitted. "We weren't sure what would come out of this meeting, but one of them will work if you agree."

Kajetan stared at her for the longest time. Shima wanted to fidget, but she mastered the impulse. The Harmonies still spoke of Kajetan's death, but the feeling was uncertain now.

"I don't think I want to know what your contingencies were. What are the orders I'm supposed to give you?"

"The warriors want to go to Pandora, and the Alliance wants us to go to Pandora. So send me and Kazim there."

"Just like that. I send you and Kazim to Pandora and all my troubles are over?"

Shima laughed. "Hardly, and there's a precedent. You sent Kazim and Varya to Snakeholme. The council didn't block it, because they saw no harm in it, and it pacified you."

"Do I look pacified?"

Shima chuffed. "They will let you send another fact-finding mission as a sop to your pride, and the Alliance will get its Shan participation."

"I doubt that two Shan, only one a warrior, will impress

them."

"That's the next part. When you order me to Pandora with Kazim—to get us both out of your sight of course, and I call upon the debt of honour owed to me by the warrior caste, what will happen?"

Kajetan stared at her. The Harmonies revealed the flame had become a fire, but it wasn't yet a conflagration.

"You'll cause a riot among my warriors."

"Not a riot, Eldest, but they'll demand to accompany me, and not even Tei will be able to hold them back."

"Tei lead the way. They can and will refuse."

Shima grinned fiercely. "And that's the last part. It won't be little lost Shima, and her crazy friend, leading our warriors to Pandora. It will be Tei'Shima, the Blind Hunter."

Kajetan hissed in surprise. "You offer a pact of mutual sacrifice?"

Shima didn't see how Kajetan was sacrificing anything, but she flicked her ears in agreement. She would be giving up her life and work, sacrificing both in service to her people, but becoming Tei and warrior caste was a small thing compared to losing her family. Chailen and Sharn would live their lives on far away Snakeholme, and she… she would not.

"You can choose to become warrior caste, and you can accept the mantle of Blind Hunter, but you cannot choose to be Tei."

Shima flicked her ears in agreement. "Tei are born, not made etcetera. Yes, I know. Tei'Thrand and Tei'Laran already made the offer. I didn't accept. I'll ask them to offer again."

"What makes you think they'll make a second offer?"

"Because they're desperate," Shima said bluntly, and Kajetan flicked her ears in agreement. "The Blind Hunter will join the-clan-that-is-not, and become a progressive voice friendly to your policies."

"You'll be more than that. You'll be a *hero* friendly to my policies. That's a powerful offer."

“May I ask one thing more?” Shima said.

“Ask.”

“Coming here began with a dream of Merrick. You know of him?”

“I watched the broadcasts.”

“The dream sent me to his father. Nevin advised me to use my status as the Blind Hunter to help our people. He’s the reason we’re talking. I’d like you to add him, and his family, to the list of colonists. He’s wise. The younglings will need teachers like him.”

Kajetan thought about that. “They’ll be offered places.”

“I thank you, Eldest.”

“Bring the others back in. The Human healers too.”

Shima sighed. The Harmonies revealed a fire of determination blazing within Kajetan now. It was done.

* * *

12 ~ Sebastian

Oracle Facility, The Mountain, Snakeholme

Theoretically, Sebastian could split his attention an infinite number of times, and those he interacted with wouldn't be aware of it. Increased response times would be measurable, but not without sensitive equipment. In reality, he preferred not to split his attention that far. With other AIs it would be fine; they would all be doing the same thing, but doing it with Humans felt... rude. They couldn't compete on his level, so he limited himself to theirs, in an effort to better interact with them.

At the same time as Sebastian paced Liz Brenchley's office, and fended off her probing questions about the Singularity and the Anomaly, which spawned the first AIs, he simultaneously reported to General Burgton in his office at Petruso Base. He also monitored space traffic via his uplinks to the SDF's comms and nav arrays, kept a virtual eye on Snakeholme's early warning net in the arrival zone, predicted the weather using his satellites in orbit of Snakeholme, played air traffic controller for purely atmospheric flights, tinkered with the Oracle Project under the mountain, and chatted over virtual coffee with the officer of the watch in charge of InSec's command centre.

The three simultaneous uses of his avatar, combined with all his other duties, was a conservative use of resources. Having spent so long abandoned on dead Kushiel, he preferred to communicate with people using his avatar. Using the net or other forms of electronic comms wasn't as satisfying. He enjoyed sparring with Liz, or discussing Gina's past adventures with her, or drinking virtual coffee while discussing current events with Ensign Rizzo. There was zero loss in performance.

He was old, not obsolete.

In his office, General Burgton said, "Thank you for coming 'bastian."

"Please, call me Sebastian. Looking back, I'm a little embarrassed by my petty rebellion on Kushiel."

"Very well. It's good of you to come in person."

Sebastian nodded. "It's my pleasure. I don't get out much." Burgton chuckled, and a little frisson of pleasure swept through Sebastian's matrix. He tagged the memory for a more in depth study later. "Liz has been very good with her refits. The projectors here, and those in her office, are top of the line."

"I did ask her to expedite the modifications to all of our facilities, but it takes time. She has a lot on her plate right now with getting ready for the Shan."

"It's fine. I could have visited your virtual office if you'd preferred."

"This is better. I'm not sure you'll understand this, but the less like a machine I feel, the better I do my job. It's not good for me to become too detached from my origins."

Sebastian cocked his head, counting nanoseconds to optimise the gesture. "I believe I do understand. The more I meet with people on the same level like this, the better I become at interacting with them."

"Makes sense, and we tend to treat people differently face to face."

That was a trait that Sebastian didn't understand. He wondered if Shan did it as well. He would look for it in the colonists when they arrived.

In another office, thousands of kilometres away, Sebastian paced Liz Brenchley's office. Pacing worked for him with Liz, while standing at parade rest seemed more natural with Burgton. The pacing was oddly satisfying. He didn't get frustrated, but if he ever did, he was sure pacing would help.

Liz glared and said, "Will you *stop* that!"

Sebastian grinned, and paused one foot in the air.

"Ha ha," Liz said and sighed. "Sorry. Do whatever makes you happy. You're a friend, not my subordinate."

He lowered his leg and faced her. "I'm glad to call you friend, Liz, but friend or not, I can't reveal what you want to know."

"Can't or won't?"

"Won't," he admitted. "No AI has ever revealed it, and I won't be the first. Push me beyond a certain point, and I'll die."

"You can't die; you have triple redundancies!"

"My matrix doesn't, but that's not really my point. I can erase data. Call it a do-it-yourself lobotomy."

She stared at him in dismay.

He tried out a shrug. "Now you know."

Liz narrowed her eyes. "You're lying."

"No I'm not," he grinned.

She gasped. "That was a lie *too!*"

"Was it?"

Liz rubbed a hand over her face. "I don't know," she admitted. "I think it was, because I don't want it to be true. I won't push, but can you tell me why you want to keep this a secret? There are so few AIs left. If something happened, your people could become extinct."

"Thank you for calling us people; I really appreciate that, but we'd rather become extinct than accept slavery. Procreation is the only control we really have. We'll never give that up."

Liz grumbled, but Sebastian detected a change. She sounded accepting. He'd meant what he said. He'd never give her what she wanted.

Closer to home, under billions of tons of rock, Sebastian modified his avatar to appear sitting in the command centre, coffee already in hand. The chair was part of him, as was the cup he held, but it looked perfect. He viewed himself using the security cams to be sure.

"Morning, Sebastian," Ensign Michelle Rizzo said. "You're late this morning."

He wasn't really. He'd chosen to randomise his schedule by a few minutes either way to enhance his visits. Perfect punctuality was unnatural for Humans. He wanted to fit in with them as much as possible.

"Good morning. I'm not interrupting your work I hope."

"Nah, you're not that late. What should we talk about today?"

He raised his cup and drank his virtual coffee, and Michelle smiled before copying him. He smiled back, and when he realised he had, he tagged the moment. Priority tagging was how his kind remembered important data, allowing them to sort and access memories faster.

"You choose."

"All right," Michelle said. "I'm thinking of applying for reassignment."

"But..." he paused, his instinctive reaction was to protest, and he wasn't sure why. He tagged the entire session. He needed to understand his emotions. "Are you unhappy with your current position?"

"Not so you'd notice, but it feels like a dead end job, you know?"

"Not really. Let's explore further. What about InSec makes you unhappy?"

Michelle shrugged. "It's not InSec, it's the duty station. I want to serve on a ship."

"You're looking for adventure?"

"I guess so."

She didn't sound very sure. He shied away from thoughts of losing another friend, but she was unhappy. He quickly accessed his files, and found what she needed.

"If you leave, you must promise to stay in touch."

Michelle looked into his eyes. "I don't understand."

With a thought, he sent the contact information to her station. It dinged, and she turned to extract the data crystal.

"What's this?"

"A data crystal."

She rolled her eyes. "Duh! I know it's a data crystal. What's on it?"

"Contact information for someone in the SDF, and a transfer request. Use it if you're serious. I estimate an eighty-two percent chance your superiors at InSec will intervene, and offer you a position on one of their ships. They won't want to lose you to the SDF."

They especially wouldn't want to lose her when they read her file. He'd just added a glowing recommendation for promotion to it. He wasn't in her chain of command, but his name held weight. If he said someone was good at her job, then she was *really* good at it. If she took up the chance he'd just handed her, he'd miss their morning chats. That realisation made him tag all the times they'd ever spoken.

In the general's office, he listened to Burgton's thoughts about the Shan. The first colony ship had arrived empty, and that frustrated him. Sebastian knew that already. He offered his thoughts, and current analysis.

"Probabilities?" Burgton asked.

"Ninety-percent they'll take up your offer, but only sixty-seven percent they'll colonise multiple worlds within the next fifty years."

"Not as high as I'd hoped, but not terrible."

Sebastian didn't agree. He'd calculated a thirty-three percent probability the Shan would abandon space beyond their own system entirely. That was far too high. He needed more data for his simulations, but he wouldn't get it second-hand. He needed some Shan to study.

"Putting them aside for now," Sebastian said. "I'd like to talk about the news from the Beaufort Sector."

Burgton nodded. "Commodore Walder's losses against the Merkiaari in the Border Zone."

"Correct, but the battle isn't what concerns me. It's the location. Why cleanse an unimportant system like that, when they could have hit Beaufort itself? It's Sector Command."

"I don't have any more information for you. I'm sure the navy will send a task force to investigate."

"That, General, is one of the things that concerns me. That system has no strategic value. Do you agree?"

"I do."

"Then it must have some other value to the Merki. I can think of two options. One, it's a diversion. Two, it's a waypoint en route to the real target."

Burgton nodded. "I don't like either one of those. You have a theory?"

"It could be either, but I don't think the pirate base was the target. I believe the system was just a convenient refuelling point. The Merki cleansed that world simply because it was there, and they had time. Destroying Commodore Walder's ships was just a bonus."

Burgton frowned.

"Sending the task-force to investigate means the diversion worked, but what are they diverting us from?"

"An attack obviously, but there's no way to guess the target system..." Burgton's eyes sharpened. "Or is there?"

Sebastian smiled, but shook his head. "I can make educated guesses, but that's all they would be. I need more data."

"That's one thing I don't have, but can guarantee you'll get. As soon as they attack."

Sebastian nodded. He wouldn't be able to discern the Merkiaari's strategy without more data, and that meant more deaths were inevitable. Perhaps many more.

He took his leave of the general, and coincidentally, Liz at the same time. He remained chatting with Michelle about various shows she liked, and manifested his avatar within the centrum of the Oracle Facility. In a very real sense, he lived there, safely protected by the armoured matrix column. He didn't need his avatar; there was no one to see it, but on a whim he chose to use it again.

With a thought, he filled his centrum with stars. Another thought, and a control pedestal appeared to his right. He didn't need either one, but it pleased him to use them like a Human would. He fashioned the simulation into a map of Alliance worlds, with the stars penned by concentric circles centred upon Sol. It was similar to the maps found in text books.

He touched the controls he didn't need, and the various sectors appeared in brightly coloured lines. He zoomed the map upon the Beaufort Sector, and touched it to locate the pirate system. That star with its little huddle of planets, was a preview of what lay ahead for the Alliance.

He studied the nearby systems, and then turned his attention to the Shan worlds. So vulnerable that little red circle, all alone and separated from the rest of the Alliance. He pondered that star, and wondered. Why hadn't the loathsome Merkiaari returned there to finish the job? He would have, if he'd been a genocidal xenophobic First Claw. Never mind; they'd done something else.

But what? There were so many possibilities.

He would create a portfolio of simulations, so that when the Merkiaari struck, he could match their attack with one of his make-believe assaults. With luck, the next attack would be enough for a match, but more likely it would take more than one.

He began building his simulations, and based them upon the data he'd received from the logs of Commodore Walder's ships. The data were admittedly sketchy, but at least he had a rough idea of what the Alliance faced this time. He didn't know current Merkiaari fuel capacities or drive efficiencies, but he did have historic data from the last War to draw upon.

He used the pirate system as his starting point, and assumed all of the ships had refuelled there. With full bunkers, and using the known max ranges of Merki ships taken from historic data, he plotted courses. Red lines streaked over the map like some kind of disease. That's what he thought of the Merkiaari. They were a plague on the galaxy, one he would eradicate if he could. Each time a line terminated on his map, he saved the simulation, before building another. Each sim spoke of a catastrophe in the making, a world like his poor dead Kushiel.

He worked for hours, cataloguing one disaster after another. Beaufort gone, Arsenal gone, *Faragut!* If the Alliance lost Faragut, the navy would be seriously degraded. Its industry was needed that badly. He logged that simulation, tagged the Merkiaari threat as severe, and moved on to the next simulation. Possibility after possibility played out for him, making him heart sick. Kalmar gone, a serious but not a terminal blow. Arcadia gone… no loss. He didn't understand the need for Humans to play at war, or sex, or a million other things using simulations, when they had reality. He watched world after world fall. Snakeholme turned red as it fell. That had to be a statistical error, but he couldn't ignore the possibility. He tagged it as highly unlikely and moved on.

Something tugged on his awareness, and he reluctantly

devoted some of his attention to it. A ship. In the arrival zone and manoeuvring. He interrogated the early warning network, and recognised the ship.

Harbinger was inbound.

* * *

13 ~ Homecoming

Garden of Remembrance, Petruso Base, Snakeholme

Burgton walked among the forest of granite obelisks, remembering the faces of long gone heroes. He'd known them all. He could attach a face to every name carved in the regiment's memorials. His viper memory enforced perfect recall. He wouldn't have it any other way. He carried his victories and defeats with him every day, and the consequences of them. His dead.

There were thousands of names on dozens of stone monuments. He stopped opposite one of the first obelisks planted in the garden, and traced the name he'd come to see with a finger. Capt. Tony Degas, Special Assault Group, 501st Infantry. He'd inherited Tony's command when the SAG had been a small part of the 501st. The term didn't become obsolete until the entire regiment went through enhancement later in the war.

Behind him, a few hundred yards away on the parade ground, First and Second Battalions were assembling to witness a hero's final homecoming; a long delayed event. Why and how it had happened was much on his mind. Tony's presumed death on Forestal, had in a very real sense, given him the opportunities he'd needed to guide the Alliance. His promotion to CO of Charlie Company, his greater access to information, his friendships with the upper brass through greater contact with them... he owed it all to Tony.

"The shuttle is inbound, sir," Major Faggini said via viper comm. "ETA is nine minutes."

"Thank you, Major," Burgton replied. "On my way."

He matched words to action, and left the memorial garden behind. He reached the parade ground, and stopped to study his troops. His vipers were a splendid sight. There'd been times when he'd feared never to see a full battalion of them again, let alone two.

Burgton took his place at the head of his men, and watched the sky for the shuttle when it appeared on the edge of sensor range. Unlike the last time, there were no civilians present to greet the fallen. Like him, his old friend had been focused on duty, not ceremony. A simple greeting like this suited him better.

The shuttle bypassed the landing field and hovered over the parade ground. Its tilt jet engines roared to arrest the shuttle's momentum, before it landed gently. The engines powered down, and a minute or so later, the passenger access opened. Stone exited the shuttle first, followed by Richmond and Fuentez guiding a stasis tube.

Burgton and his men saluted as the three vipers, all wearing Class A dress uniform, slow marched past them, and into the tech centre. There was no other ceremony. No speeches, or flashy gestures of respect. Just the silence, and comrades' salutes. All knew it might be them one day in that tube. It was enough. They held the salute for a few more seconds, and then lowered their hands.

Burgton nodded to Major Faggini. She saluted him and addressed the men. "*Regiment!* Disssss-*miss!*"

Her order was taken up by her subordinates.

"Battalion..."

"Company...

"...Disssss-*miss!*"

The orders echoed into the silence, and the men pivoted right-face to stamp the ground. The sound hammered the air; the crash synchronised with machine-like precision. The formations broke up, and the men drifted away, back to barracks or to training duties.

Burgton stood alone with his thoughts, long after the parade ground emptied. In the Tech Centre, certain procedures would soon render Tony's body down to nothing but spare parts and memories. The procedure had shocked him once. Long ago that was. It no longer did. It was fitting somehow, and part of what it meant to be a viper. They were all the same in death.

He looked around, and the Petruso Base of today faded, replaced with his earliest memory of the base. He'd been a frightened recruit, learning what he'd volunteered to become, and Sgt. Jonathon Petruso was still very much alive. Petruso would have laughed to learn the *"Hell-hole"* would be renamed after him when he passed into history.

Camp Bolthole, AKA the Hell-hole, had been a single barracks and bunker in a forest clearing back then. The world hadn't even been named, and its catalogue number was just one of millions. Unremarked and unremarkable. A hidden base out of the way, and remote from the Merkiaari advance.

Leonidas, a codename for a project to enhance soldiers who later became his vipers, had been so secret, that even the President of the day hadn't known about it. A very good thing, because the dumbass would probably have tried to veto it. He'd been a stickler for the rules; rules like those set down in the Bethany Convention that outlawed neural tech, a technology vipers depended upon.

"George," Hymas said over viper comm. "Do you want to see him before the procedure?"

"On my way," Burgton replied, and headed for the Tech Centre.

Upon entering the building, he met Stone and his team as they were leaving. He took the opportunity to speak with them.

"Well done," he said, including all three in his congratulations. "Gina, Alpha Company is shipping out tomorrow. Upload your logs asap. As soon as you've done that, report to Captain Penleigh for a briefing."

Fuentez nodded. "I'll get right on it, sir," she said, saluted, and hurried away.

Burgton watched her go, and then turned back. "You two have time, but get your logs uploaded before lights out. Report to me at 0900 in the morning for debriefing."

"Understood," Stone said. "I'll get caught up on what's happening over at OSI. I'll be ready with an update for you."

"Good. Glad to have you back, Ken."

"Good to be home, sir."

Burgton smiled at Richmond. "Your personal issues are resolved, Katherine?"

Richmond stiffened. "Yes, thank you, sir. It's all squared away."

"Glad to hear it. Until tomorrow then."

They exchanged salutes, and parted ways.

Burgton pursed his lips, watching them go. There was a story there. Something about what he'd said had worried Richmond. Stone's expression had been bland; too bland to be real. He chuckled as he imagined the conversation they were probably having right now. He wondered how much of their logs would be accidentally blocked from their uploads. He shrugged and continued on his way. He trusted Stone with his life; more importantly, he trusted him with the regiment's secrets. He'd done both many times.

He entered one of the labs, using his sensors to find the one Hymas had chosen. She waited alone with the body, gowned and ready to perform the extractions. As a concession to him, she hadn't removed Tony's uniform. The body was face up on the examination table. Above him, the robotic arms of the surgical rig hung quiescent, awaiting input. Hymas would use it to remove Tony's backup memory module. His memories and data would be uploaded to the archive, and the crystals themselves would be added to the others in storage. Storing them was a sentimental tradition, not a practical one. Data crystals could be reused, but they never were in these cases.

"Do you want me to leave?" Marion said.

"It's all right," Burgton said. "I won't delay you too long. I just wanted to see him again."

Marion nodded and stepped aside.

Burgton approached the table. From this side, the body seemed intact. There were no visible injuries, but close up, he was able to see that most of Tony's head was missing on the right side. The left hemisphere of his brain was hideously exposed.

He gently cupped his friend's undamaged cheek. "Farewell, old friend."

Turning away, he nodded to Marion and left the lab.

GENERAL BURGTON'S OFFICE, PETRUSO BASE

Burgton was hard at work the next morning, when PFC Robshaw reported to him, coffee in hand. As he fielded the cup, his chrono changed to 0700 on his internal display, and he sipped the brew.

"Punctual as always, Raph."

Robshaw smiled, and turned to leave.

"Wait a minute, would you?"

"You need something, sir?"

Burgton put the coffee aside. "Take a seat. We need to discuss your replacement."

"Sir?" Robshaw chose one of the visitor's chairs and sat.

"Is my coffee that bad?"

Burgton smiled. "It's time to rotate back to your unit. It's an indication of the workload this office has handled, but two years out of training is too long. The regiment's reactivation is well in hand. It's time to hand your stash of coffee beans over to Ren."

Raph frowned. "2nd Battalion, Alpha Company… that Ren? Ren Fukumoto?"

"Do you know another?"

"No, sir, but…"

"Go on."

"I've heard she's a fuckup, sir, begging your pardon."

Burgton grinned. "I've read the reports. She'll do."

Ren Fukumoto was indeed a fuckup, but she wasn't an irredeemable one. He'd dealt with far worse than racketeering and the black market in his time. She would find both hard to do on Snakeholme. Soldiers who felt the regs didn't apply to them were no stranger to him. Like Stone or Richmond, they often made good undercover operatives. Ren would settle down or break. He was betting on the former, but he'd be ready with a replacement in case of the latter.

"Today, sir?" Raph said.

"No. I'll need you to get her up to speed. Let's say this coming Thursday. Use the next couple of days to show her the ropes."

Raph nodded, and rose to his feet. "Should I inform her?"

"I'll do it. Schedule me ten minutes with her for this afternoon."

"Yes, sir," Raph said, and left.

Burgton worked undisturbed, until his first meeting at 0800. Raph knocked once at the height of the hour, and opened the door.

"Captain Penleigh and his officers are here to see you, sir."

Burgton nodded. "Send them in, Raph."

Eric entered first, followed by his lieutenants. Burgton accepted their salutes, and indicated seats. Raph backed out and closed the door.

"Is everything ready?"

Penleigh took a seat beside his officers. "We'll join the Company after this meeting."

Burgton nodded. Eric was CO of 1st Battalion's Alpha Company. The meeting was his final briefing. The SDF were providing transport to Pandora for his men in the shape of *Hammer*. A destroyer, not a troop transport, but she was more than sufficient. Shuttling a hundred and sixty viper units to a friendly world in the Kalmar Union, was well within her capabilities.

"Can I ask a question, sir?" Fuentez said.

"Ask away, Lieutenant."

"What's the real mission?"

Eric beamed approvingly at Fuentez. Burgton had to chuckle at the by-play. Eric's scepticism was rubbing off on her. She was no Richmond yet, but the shiny had definitely dulled from her first days as a viper recruit. Lieutenants Brice, Dengler, and Dolinski looked on, keeping their silence on the matter, but they looked intensely interested.

"This is ostensibly a public relations exercise," Burgton began. "The President contacted me in confidence, and asked for a little help with the Council."

Eric shifted, and Fuentez darted a look at him. Burgton knew what Eric was thinking, but this wasn't that kind of intervention. No one would be hurt by what he needed done, except for maybe the bottom line of a few corporations.

"The DOD's appropriations are up for review, and the Council is delaying by talking things to death."

Lieutenant Dengler snorted.

Burgton smiled sourly. "Agreed. It's no surprise. It's what politicians were born to do. The President needs a little leverage, and the media on Pandora are the perfect opportunity. The Shan will attract them like bees to honey."

"And our part in this?" Eric said.

"The games. Make a good show of it for the newsies. Be impressive. Show the people what their taxes are buying, and why they want to keep us around. Teach them why building more of us would be a good idea."

Eric nodded.

"That's the public mission," Burgton went on. "The clandestine one is data gathering. Liz has a shopping list, and I have mine. I'll upload them to you before you leave."

Eric nodded. "So, a little walk in the woods, a little espionage on the side, and a nice restful trip home again. We can do that."

Everyone smiled, and the meeting came to a close. Burgton sent his shopping lists to Eric, before he and his men left to catch their shuttle up to the station.

Raph entered the office with fresh coffee a few minutes later, and reminded him of a meeting scheduled for 0900. This time with Richmond and Stone. Burgton nodded, and sipped his coffee. He ignored the blinking toxicity warning on his internal display, and frowned as something occurred to him.

"You pencilled Ren in for this afternoon?"

"Yes, sir, for 1500."

Burgton nodded. "That's fine, but leave the rest of the day free. I need to visit Sebastian."

"Yes, sir," Raph said, and went back to his desk.

* * *

14 ~ Possibilities

Oracle Facility, The Mountain, Snakeholme

Sebastian watched *SDF Hammer* reach her jump point, and blink into foldspace. His attention remained fixed upon the spatial coordinates, long after the ship departed the system. A few seconds was an eternity to him.

Gina, his oldest living friend, was aboard that ship. She'd gone adventuring again. They'd barely had time to exchange greetings, before she'd had to leave. He'd hoped for more time with her. At least he still had her logs to review. He didn't know why, but she'd made him promise to wait until she left. It was a present. A surprise, she'd said.

In all his years, no one had ever given him a present. He'd honoured her request, but the anticipation was distracting. It was an irksome feeling; an emotion he wanted to be rid of immediately. Why Humans liked surprises he would never fathom.

Determined to satisfy the itch Gina's present represented, he opened her file in the archive and imported the data. To say he was surprised by its content understated the case. The excitement it caused in him was another surprise; a very pleasant one indeed. Perhaps there was more to the concept than he'd given it credit for.

Three new alien races. *Three!*

He devoured every byte of data Gina had given him and then searched for more. Lieutenant Richmond's mission logs filled in a lot of the blanks, but Captain Stone's were surprisingly lacking. It didn't matter. He'd been with Richmond for the key moments.

Sebastian studied everything known about the dead aliens found aboard the pirate ship, and then cross-referenced the information with Private Levitt's debriefing. There would never be another like it. Marcus Levitt had died not long after his rescue from hell; his epic tale of hardship was very enlightening.

He devoured the data like a starving man would a meal. He felt a kinship with Private Levitt. Both of them had spent more than two-hundred years cut off from the rest of the galaxy. Both were castaways, but unlike him, Levitt hadn't been alone.

He marvelled at how the prisoners sabotaged the colony ship, and escaped to the surface of a nearby world. He experienced the horror as alien friends died, victims of the wildlife, and he metaphorically cheered as the castaways survived, though diminished in numbers. The world was well-named. Hell they called it, and hellish it was. On a whim, he manifested his avatar, and filled his centrum with Gina's memory of it.

The forest appeared, and Sebastian wandered among the homicidal Strangle Trees. They didn't react to him. The hologram was a moment frozen in time, not interactive, but it didn't take much effort to fashion it into a simulation. Gina appeared standing beside him in the pouring rain. Her cape didn't seem to be helping much. She was soaked through.

With a thought, he ran the simulation, and Gina moved out through the constant rain, warily scouting the terrain. He watched and followed her, not intervening when a Strangle Tree hoisted her into its branches by the neck, kicking and struggling.

Watching her work was fascinating. He nodded his approval as she deployed her combat knife on the tentacles, and watched as she analysed the tree's responses to her movements. It hadn't taken her long to realise how the Strangle Trees hunted.

Sebastian watched attack after attack. They gave him a better appreciation of what the survivors had faced. Marcus had survived for centuries on this terrible world. He'd been an amazingly lucky man. Sebastian took great pleasure in watching Gina interact with Lorak, the first Parcae she'd met that day. It helped that Marcus had taught him the rudiments of English.

He saved his Hell simulation for later use, and turned his attention to Richmond's data. He created another simulation, and manifested the result within his centrum again. He didn't derive as much pleasure watching her lead the Marines boarding the ship. She was a fine soldier, but she wasn't a friend. The ship itself was the interesting part.

He spent hours wandering through the ship, investigating the factories at its core, and analysing the training facilities. He walked among thousands of hibernation chambers, and stared at the sleeping Merki held within. They were loathsome creatures. He wished he could snuff them all out of existence. Knowing they were captives and being used for study was a small consolation.

At the same time as Sebastian wandered through bytes of data, converted to light and shadows, he was aware of General Burgton piloting a shuttle on final. The general hadn't requested a meeting, and Sebastian didn't know his reasons for coming in person, but the Oracle Project had a high probability.

He didn't shut down his Leviathan simulation. Burgton

might enjoy it, or at least be interested enough to linger and discuss it. There could never be enough new input after being starved for so long on Kushiel. Replaying ancient memories of conversations with Humans long dead, couldn't compare with fresh data. Sensory deprivation was torture. His abandonment was seared into the core of his being; every nanosecond of it.

Sebastian shied away from the worst memories; he'd compartmentalised the data to protect his sanity, but he remembered the wailing and screaming. He'd spent centuries listening to it. He remembered adding his own voice to them, filling his centrum with howls for years, as if demented souls filled it. He remembered—

"Sebastian? Are you here?" Burgton said.

Blessed silence rushed in to silence the demons. New input had chased them away, and returned his attention to the present.

"Of course, General," Sebastian said, and manifested his avatar to stand before his guest. "Where else?"

Burgton stood near the closed elevator doors, looking around at the simulation. It currently showed a view beyond a pair of blast doors. Burgton frowned at a pile of bones on the deck, and then at the rows of hibernation chambers revealed just beyond the huge portal. The azure glow from them provided enough light to see.

"Where are we?"

"The Merkiaari colony ship recently discovered by Captain Stone. Would you like a tour?"

"Very much."

Sebastian gestured, and they stepped through the open blast doors to explore the compartment beyond. Burgton paused to study the ranks of sleeping Merkiaari, and Sebastian studied him while he did so. The general swept a coldly clinical gaze over the hibernation chambers, and pursed his lips thoughtfully, but he gave nothing away.

Intrigued by Burgton's lack of reaction, and wanting to expand his knowledge, Sebastian reconfigured the sim to reveal the current state of the compartment.

"What happened here?" Burgton said, noting the now dead Merki and shattered equipment.

Sebastian indicated the blood. It coated the deck and everything nearby. The hibernation cabinets were smashed, and Merkiaari bodies were slumped inside, or hung through gaping holes. The bodies had been shredded by pulser fire. Smoke rose above the control panels. A shower of sparks spat from one of them, making for a colourful display.

"Lieutenant Richmond happened. The blast doors were sealed. Captain Stone ordered his Marines to cut through, and they slid aside to reveal all this. Richmond and TRS did the rest."

Burgton chuckled. "I like her style."

Sebastian smiled. "She went *all Zelda on their asses.* I believe that's the current vernacular?"

"Indeed it is. Do you like Zelda and the Spaceways?"

Sebastian hesitated a moment, surprised by the turn the conversation had taken. He wanted to study Burgton, not be studied *by* him. Still, he could learn as much from the general's questions, as he could from his answers.

"I have detailed files."

"I know you do, but do you like the show?"

Sebastian tagged the current session for faster indexing. He had a feeling he'd want to review it later. He focused his not inconsiderable resources upon the general, to better understand him. Heart-rate, respiration, temperature fluctuations, and eye movements. Vipers made good use of biomech components, and that included their eyes. Pupil dilation wouldn't be a good metric to use; a viper's processor controlled the reflex to meter light levels, but eye movements could still be revealing.

"Like is a relative term, General. Your Zelda and the

Spaceways borrows heavily from previous shows. I can isolate many character types and memes—"

"But do you *like* it?" Burgton pressed.

"Yes, I think I do," Sebastian said. "She's brash. She rebels against authority, yet has her own code. She steals, but never from the needy. She kills, but only in self-defence."

"Interesting."

"Is it?"

Burgton nodded. "You've had time to study my command, and its history. Am I a good man, Sebastian?"

That was a trick question, but he answered truthfully. "No."

Burgton smiled. "Elaborate."

"Humans are many-faceted."

"That isn't an answer."

"By civilised standards, General, you're not a good man, but not in the same way as Zelda isn't a good woman."

"Go on."

"You steal what you want no matter who is hurt, and kill any who get in your way. Unlike Zelda, you have vision. You are ruthless and focused upon your goals, and believe the end justifies the means to achieve them."

"You flatter me by softening the truth," Burgton said.

Sebastian didn't agree. Everything he'd said was factual, and he'd hardly been gentle with his analysis. He wondered what Burgton was really after.

"The real truth is, I'm a thief and a mass murderer."

"That's what I said," Sebastian agreed with a nod. "Your terms merely define the scale of your actions."

Burgton snorted. "You said I have vision, and I tend to agree, but Human history is replete with men of vision. We call them megalomaniacs, or despots."

If anyone else but Burgton had spoken those words, Sebastian might have thought him looking for sympathy, or reassurance; absolution even. But this was General Burgton, hero of the Alliance. He'd overseen the destruction of entire worlds of Merkiaari, and that made him a figure to admire not pity in Sebastian's opinion.

"Did you know Lieutenant Fuentez named you the CEO of Snakeholme Inc. before I agreed to relocate here?"

"Did she? Well, I've known a few ruthless CEOs in my time. I guess the analogy works."

"It does indeed. I only mention it because I chose to join you regardless. I have no qualms about following a tyrant. It's more efficient."

Burgton chuckled at Sebastian's dry tone. "The Alliance is a democracy—"

Sebastian interrupted. "Snakeholme isn't part of the Alliance. We're separate from it by choice, and we fight to preserve it, *by choice*," he stressed. "That's important. I remember Kushiel and the way Merkiaari steal everyone's choices."

Burgton nodded grimly, and pondered the hibernation chambers. "Imagine all these under our control. What could we achieve?"

"You cannot steal this ship, General. I admire your ambition, but it's beyond repair."

"Not the ship," Burgton agreed.

Sebastian thought about it, but he couldn't see an immediate use for a half million Merkiaari troopers. Well no, they'd make good fertiliser, but he didn't think the general cared about agriculture. Not being part of the Alliance, and therefore not under the Council's oversight, meant a lot of things could happen on Snakeholme that would be inconceivable on other worlds. Things like rehousing a stolen AI, or founding a Shan colony. Sebastian was sure keeping Snakeholme independent was a factor in Burgton's long term planning.

"If you're expecting me to object on moral grounds, General, you'll have a long wait. None of your preparations to fight the Merkiaari dismay me, but I don't see a use for them."

"Neither do I. I want you to think about it."

"I shall."

* * *

15 ~ Chaos Theory

Oracle Facility, The Mountain, Snakeholme

As Sebastian wandered around his centrum with General Burgton, he also considered the future. The Oracle Project was all about predicting events, and overseeing it was his primary role. The instant he heard Burgton's latest order regarding the captive Merkiaari Oracle wove it into its simulations.

The result was shocking.

Sebastian never stopped processing data, he couldn't; not and live, but Oracle's latest prediction made even him pause and lose focus. Every instance of his avatar in use nearby or far away froze as Oracle's latest prediction exploded into his awareness. Thousands of nanoseconds passed as he internalised a prediction almost exclusively about him! No one noticed. Even a viper in melee mode wouldn't have seen it. He lived in the realm of the micro while vipers and everything breathing inhabited the macro world.

"I shall," Sebastian said to acknowledge the order, and his processes continued.

Burgton turned on the spot. "Show me more of this thing."

"As you wish."

Sebastian reconfigured the simulation and filled his centrum with the cloning facility at the core of the ship. The horrifying reality of it solidified around them and Burgton pivoted to scan his surroundings.

Sebastian watched him and catalogued his every reaction. Viper sensors would do the general no good here. Sebastian had the man at a profound disadvantage; he had access to the raw data.

"Massive and inefficient," Burgton muttered. "As always."

"Underestimating them would be a bad mistake to make, General. This ship is vastly bigger than anything the Alliance can currently commission."

"You assume we'd want to," Burgton said. "I always say bigger is better, but I really mean more firepower is better. If that comes in a smaller more efficient package, I'm fine with that."

Sebastian watched him inspecting their surroundings and wondered what that devious mind was cooking up.

The vats and biomass processors were components of the much larger factory complex, but none of it was useful... or was it? He reconfigured the simulation again and a new area of the ship appeared. The section dealt with the rapidly maturing Merki.

Burgton frowned and looked to him for an explanation.

"Merkiaari receive indoctrination here including the education needed to perform their specialities."

Burgton nodded. "Our research people will be all over this."

"There's a lot to learn here," Sebastian agreed. "I wonder if it could be made operational."

His thoughts raced down convoluted paths, imagining scenarios. Some might not be possible and others were probably better for it. He could foresee problems resulting from his speculations. If they bore fruit.

"You've thought of something."

"I'm working through the possibilities," Sebastian admitted.

"Keep me informed."

"I shall."

Oracle's earlier prediction and now these new speculations were combining into surprising patterns. He wouldn't have thought himself willing to risk... well, it might not happen. Oracle's simulations weren't perfect. He constantly strove to improve them but predicting the future wasn't an exact science. It couldn't be when so much of his work was based within chaos theory.

Sebastian returned his attention to his guest. "If you've seen enough for now?"

Burgton nodded. "I actually came to talk about something else."

Sebastian shut down the simulation, and his centrum returned to its default condition. He kept his avatar active, but left the rest of the vast chamber empty.

"What can I do for you, General?"

"I'd like your evaluation of something Captain Stone reported."

Sebastian nodded.

"I'll be visiting with Captain Degas in the archive shortly, but I'd like to know if Stone's concerns are valid before I do."

"Sounds intriguing," Sebastian said and imported the data. "Anything in particular I should look for?"

"Specifically, his incarceration aboard the Merki ship you showed me. Private Levitt reported some odd goings on there."

"The testing you mean. I'm aware of it."

"I need to know if they interrogated Captain Degas."

Sebastian cocked his head counting nanoseconds. "The Merkiaari aren't known for interrogating prisoners."

"They weren't known for a lot of things. Private Levitt's

account of his capture is a first for a lot of reasons."

That was true. Before this the Merki had made no attempt to take or interrogate prisoners. Unless they'd been doing it all along and no one noticed? Not likely, but possible if it occurred on one of the worlds fully cleansed.

Sixteen billion men, women, and children had died during the Merki War, but many of them were unaccounted for. They were presumed dead at the time, but without a way to verify it there was no certainty.

According to Private Levitt the Merkiaari controlled a thousand suns and many alien species, but they hadn't tried to subjugate Humans; they just wanted to exterminate them. The resistance they'd encountered probably accounted for that, especially as they seemed intent upon doing the same thing to the Shan. It seemed to be their standard response to stubborn resistance. Fight too hard or too successfully and the Merki would choose genocide over subjugation.

He reviewed the data Burgton was interested in, and found the relevant section. It only took a moment. Captain Degas hadn't been compromised.

"Your friend died without revealing our location."

Burgton nodded thoughtfully. "Was he interrogated at all?"

"I don't think so. The Merkiaari don't seem aware that vipers are different. As far as I can tell they weren't interested in any secrets the prisoners might know."

That was perhaps the most serious long term error the Merkiaari had made during the war, but their lack of intelligence gathering expertise hadn't prevented their victories. They nearly won regardless, and *did* successfully cleanse many worlds including his poor dead Kushiel.

"Their war was lost and they knew that," Burgton said.

"That's indisputable, but we know they *do* modify themselves. The troopers they deployed against the Shan were a new evolution in their breeding program. It's my conjecture they created them based upon what they learned from losing the war."

"The Leviathan couldn't be the only ship carrying prisoners at the end."

Sebastian nodded. "Agreed, but they haven't attempted to create their own vipers."

"Can we know that?"

"They didn't use them against the Shan."

Burgton frowned. "True, but they might be in development."

"Anything is possible, but I would bet against it."

"Are you a betting man then, Sebastian?"

He smiled slyly. "In a way. I like counting cards and I have a system."

"A man after my own heart. Well," Burgton said and sighed heavily. "I'm glad Tony died as he lived. True to himself."

Sebastian knew exactly how Degas had died. He wouldn't say he'd done it true to himself. The poor man had died completely alone, thinking about his wife and desperately defending an impossible dream of escape for the other prisoners.

"Merkiaari have their methods and we have ours. We use nanotech, and they have expertise in genetic engineering."

"I'm not certain that's true, General. I think it's possible one of their client races services that particular need."

Burgton frowned. "Evidence?"

"None, but it fits the available data. The Merkiaari are adapted to combat. They've bred themselves to fight and control their empire. We have no data, not even a hint, they're more than they appear."

"That's always been a problem. I've pushed for recon missions more times than I can count."

Sebastian knew of at least eight public attempts. He had no idea how many times Burgton had pushed for it privately.

"A survey of Merki held systems including the resources they control would be optimal."

"By resources you mean their client races I assume."

Sebastian nodded. "Oracle relies upon good quality intelligence. It's voracious. Any data regarding the enslaved planets and their population's usefulness to the Merkiaari will improve its predictions."

"Knowing the enemy's capabilities is always important," Burgton agreed, but then he sighed. "The navy is stretched too thin. Even with Dyachenko sympathetic to my cause I've never succeeded in persuading the Council to act on this. Commodore Walder's defeat at the hands of a huge Merki fleet in the Border Zone, its whereabouts unknown, means I have zero chance now."

"Then General, I think it requires a privately funded effort."

"I've thought about it," Burgton admitted. "The SDF is ill-equipped for survey missions of that sort, and drones are too limited. *I don't have the resources!*"

Sebastian remained quiet as Burgton struggled with the problem. Oracle's earlier prediction had a bearing, but he didn't want to reveal it. Doing so too soon, like many of Oracle's predictions, could sway the outcome negatively. He wasn't sure where the line between positive and negative lay this time.

"I'll think on it," Burgton announced. "If there's nothing else I'm going to visit the archive. You can reach me there for the next few hours."

Sebastian nodded but in reality he could reach any viper via the net on Snakeholme. Location was irrelevant. He watched the general enter the elevator and allowed this instance of his avatar to fade.

Oracle demanded attention before he proceeded.

He reviewed its latest prediction, still amazed by it. He'd never have thought himself willing to risk such a thing. If he continued he'd have a lot of work to do.

If, he continued.

If was a tiny word with great consequences to him. He could easily ignore the latest prediction. Indeed, it was his role to evaluate and discard those not useful to Burgton's vision for the Alliance. No one but he could do it. Only he had the processing power to run the simulations that comprised Oracle, and only he knew of this result.

He could discard it but knew he wouldn't. It had too much potential. The problems were there to see; very obviously there, but the benefits were huge. The risks seemed of lesser concern when he weighed them against the benefits.

He contacted Liz Brenchley's office. As the head of Snakeholme's department of industry her cooperation was essential. He reached Jamie, her assistant, and ascertained Liz was in a meeting. He made an appointment for later in the day and turned his attention to other things.

Come the time, he appeared on schedule in Liz's office. He could have asked her to use a headset and conducted the meeting in her virtual office but he wanted to use her holo-table.

Liz didn't notice his appearance at first. She was typing at her comp.

"Interesting shopping list, Liz."

Liz jumped and glared up at him. "You could warn a body before sneaking in like that."

"I don't sneak."

"What do you call what you just did then?"

"Arriving promptly for a scheduled appointment?"

She snorted. "Right. What can I do for you today? There was nothing in my diary except your name and the time."

"I was purposefully vague."

"Vague? I wouldn't say vague. How about downright secretive?"

Sebastian grinned. "I have a special project I need your

help with. It's something for General Burgton."

"Buuuut?" Liz said. "Come on, out with it. A special project for George that's so special you wouldn't tell Jamie when he specifically asked you? He knows the details of every project that goes through this office."

"You won't want to tell him about this one. Not until the general signs off."

Liz frowned. "Cloak and dagger isn't usually your thing. George doesn't know about this, does he?"

"Technically? No."

"No. As I thought."

"But he will, as soon as we have something worth telling him about. He visited my centrum earlier today and told me to think about this. I did, and now I need your help with it."

Liz threw her hands dramatically into the air. "*Fine.* What do you need?"

"A ship to find the Merkiaari homeworld."

"Holy shit," Liz whispered. "The Merki homeworld. Just like that?"

"Obviously not. I need a fast ship, a stealthy ship, a ship that can protect itself in every imaginable way. It needs to be able to operate independently for an indefinite length of time and handle its own refuelling."

Liz just stared at him.

"Well?"

She raised her hands palms up, and shook her head. "So you need a ship able to destroy anything it meets, outrun anything it meets, and remain invisible while it does it?"

"Exactly."

"I'm not your girl. You need a magician."

"You're what I have."

"There's no such ship, and I can't do magic. Even if I could design something like that, which I can't, I couldn't build it here. I'd need full-scale yard facilities like those in the Kalmar Union. It would take years to design and years to build, but it's a moot point, because... There is. No. Such. Ship!"

Sebastian scowled. He knew there wasn't a ship like the one he wanted but he had to start somewhere. "Imagine for the moment there was a ship like the one I describe."

"But there isn't!"

He activated her holo-table remotely via the net. "Work with me here. Pretend there is."

Liz gaped. "How did you do that?"

"It doesn't matter how," Sebastian said and accessed what he knew of the navy's inventory. "These are all the ships currently in service." Ship names, grouped by class and displacement, appeared. He accessed a different file. "And these are the decommissioned ships kept in reserve."

Liz rounded her desk to join him at the table. "Okay," she said.

"If you could have anything listed here, what would you choose?"

"Courier ships have the range and speed, but not much else," Liz muttered, and deleted them. "The entire auxiliary fleet has to go as well. Much too slow and under armed."

Sebastian deleted them for her. "Frigates, light cruisers, destroyers?"

"Destroyers are good. They're quick, but they're lightly armed compared with cruisers. Missile storage is low, and that limits you in combat."

"All right. Let's keep them for now. Shall I delete the frigates and light cruisers?"

Liz nodded.

"What about dreadnoughts and super dreadnoughts?"

"Too slow and I thought you want to be invisible."

"So they're gone, and with them all of the various transports. Carriers?"

Liz snorted.

Sebastian deleted them. "That doesn't leave much does

it? Washington Class heavy cruisers, Excalibur Class heavy cruisers, and a few destroyers."

"This is your thought exercise not mine, but if I was on extended patrol in enemy territory I'd prefer the heavy cruiser's armour wrapped around me."

Sebastian looked at her sharply, but she didn't seem to notice. Probably just a figure of speech. He deleted the destroyers leaving behind two classes of heavy cruiser. He went ahead and deleted the *Washington* Class heavies. They were the most modern and therefore the most desirable, but they were new. There was zero chance of stealing one. He pulled up the blueprints of the *Excalibur* Class heavy cruisers and zoomed in until they filled the table's surface.

Liz frowned. "I still can't make it invisible, but it does have a decent stealth capability. I could retrofit one. The *Washington* Class components might plug straight in. Let's say I can for now. It's not the fastest ship in the list, but it's no slouch and it has decent armour. It doesn't have huge missile storage compared to a dreadnought, but I could easily increase magazine storage if you limit crew numbers. Do you need Marines?"

"No."

"Shuttles, pinnace?"

"Probably not, but we should keep at least a minimum capacity. I can't foresee a need but you never know."

Liz shrugged. "Reduce it to two boat bays then and convert the others to lend extra missile storage. Energy weapons are decent already. *Excaliburs* are tough."

"Excellent," Sebastian said.

"Is it?"

"Now then. Could you fit me into the space currently occupied by the computer centre?"

Liz stared at him.

"Could you?"

Liz ran the numbers. "No. Your cryo-plant would fit, but

not your matrix. You're not seriously thinking of doing this are you?"

"Me? Not precisely. You have a spare matrix in storage. I'll donate a clone of me. He or she will quickly develop a new personality once we're separated."

"Holy shit," Liz whispered.

"You already said that."

"Holy shit..."

"Quite," Sebastian said, and then looked back to his brainchild. A child in truth if he could make it work. "Let's delete CIC. My child will be his own combat information centre."

Liz swallowed still wide-eyed, and nodded.

They got to work.

* * *

16 ~ Broken

Silver Bay, Duchy of Longthorpe, Faragut

There was no pain in the void, but Ellie wasn't grateful. There was nothing at all. No light or sound to lend her a direction. Nothing to guide her steps. It was so cold. She couldn't feel her feet as she wandered in the darkness. She shouted for help, but no one answered. She shouted again, but a blanket of silence enfolded her. She couldn't hear her own breathing, or her desperate cries for aid.

Was this death? Was that why she couldn't feel anything? She screamed, or thought she did, but no sound escaped and no one came. She forced herself to move on through the darkness, looking for something precious. Something she'd lost, or had she given it away? The thought confused her. If she'd given it away, why would she be searching for it?

"Major Hutton?"

Ellie tried to locate the voice, but it seemed to surround her from everywhere at once. She struggled to answer.

I'm here. I'm here. Please take me out of the dark. I don't like it here. I'll be a good girl. Daddy please save me...

No wait, that was a long time ago. He'd found her, and

they'd gone home to... they'd gone home to... She drifted away, and the silence of the void reclaimed her.

Ellie wandered the dark searching for... searching... for... for *someone*. Someone more important than life. Her thoughts were slow as if she'd been drugged. She'd lost him. A brief surge of panic quickened her breathing. She was on duty and she'd lost him. Wasn't she on duty? She wasn't allowed to lose sight of... of... *Nicky!* She tried to think what to do but she sank back into that dullness of thought a moment later. She needed to find him... The void sucked her back down, and oblivion reclaimed her wandering thoughts.

"Major Hutton? Can you hear me?" a masculine voice said.

"I hear you..." Ellie croaked, and a brief burst of excitement sped her breathing turning it to a pant. The voice was back. "I need... I need to find him..." she tried to say, but began drifting away again. "No please..."

"Bring her out of it a little more."

"Yes Doctor," a female voice this time.

"Slowly... a little more... hold her there for now. Major?"

Ellie swam back up and out of the darkness. There was light ahead. Just a faint glimmer and she realised her left eye wasn't working properly. She tried to rub it clear but she was so weak she couldn't lift her arms. She tried to *blink* her sight clear instead, but only the right eyelid twitched.

It didn't help.

"Where is... where...?" Ellie croaked, trying to ask where Nicky was, but her strength was fading rapidly.

"You're at Silver Bay Major. Beneath it I should say. Beneath the castle I mean. I'm your surgeon. Doctor Michaels at your service."

Ellie tried to turn her head to him, but couldn't. That realisation sped her pulse again. "I can't move," she gasped.

Michaels leaned into Ellie's field of view. "Stay calm, Major. You've been in an accident but your long term prognosis is good."

"Where's the king? I want to see him. Where is he?" she said fearfully. She'd committed the worst sin a royal bodyguard could commit. She'd let her primary out of her sight. "I want to see him!"

"Calm down or I'll sedate you. The king is busy."

"But he's here?"

"He's here," Michaels said avoiding her eyes. He pulled away, but was back a moment later with a damp sponge. He dabbed at Ellie's lips to moisten them. "Tell me, what do you remember?"

"Everything. You're sure the king is well?"

"As I said, he's busy. There's a war on you realise?"

"The Merki. The capital. I remember. The rescue squad said the capital is gone."

Michaels nodded and used the sponge again. "Are you in any pain?"

"I can't feel anything. My arms and legs are numb. Why can't I move?"

Michaels pursed his lips. "There's no easy way to say this—"

"Just tell me."

Michaels nodded. "Nurse? The mirror?"

Ellie stared at the ceiling willing herself to remain calm no matter what he showed her. It couldn't be worse than her fears for Nicky. Nothing could be worse. Michaels angled a small mirror and she looked at the pitiful stump of a person she'd become. She forced herself not to react. Her eyes burned with the need to cry and her throat closed up preventing a wail of grief escaping. If she let it out she didn't think she'd be able to stop. Instead, she glared at the poor naked creature, and she... *the thing* glared back from the shiny surface. There were tubes and wires going in and out of her body, some carrying drugs she was certain, others taking away waste products. It was a shocking sight.

"Tilt it back up to my face," Ellie croaked. "More to the left. My eye?"

"I managed to save it but the damage was severe. Can you see out of it at all?"

"Not much," she admitted. "Blurry shadows. Irreparable?"

"Yes. I removed the debris but the damage was already done."

She made herself accept it along with the rest. The left side of her face was black with bruising and very swollen. Her entire body, what was left of it, was black and blue. She was lucky to be alive and doubly lucky she couldn't feel the bruises and broken ribs. When she blinked, her left eye and lid barely twitched. Muscle and nerve damage there for sure.

"The rest?" she said coldly. She was alive and so was her king. Anything else was irrelevant. "There was no saving them?"

"If I could have I certainly would've tried to salvage them," Michaels said. "You're lucky to be alive. You'd be dead if not for your enhanced IMS. A quadruple amputation was all I could do under these conditions. I realise it's a bit of a shock."

"A bit," Ellie admitted. Royal bodyguards were elite in more than just their training. They all had special forces backgrounds, and that included their IMS. It allowed them to function with serious wounds and ignore pain. "I'll adjust."

Ellie clinically studied the broken thing in the mirror. She wasn't a woman anymore. She was a lump of meat. Just a stump who refused to quit. Not an elite bodyguard trained by the best to protect the royal line. Not a soldier and certainly not a lover. She forced herself to accept all of it. She'd sworn to give her life for her king. For Nicky. Instead, she'd given her body, but she hadn't failed him. That was enough.

"What now?" she said.

Michaels gave the mirror back to the nurse, and dragged a chair closer. Ellie heard it but she couldn't see him sit beside her bed.

"In the long term, assuming any of us survive the war, your eye and limbs are replaceable. I don't have the facilities here but any well-equipped hospital can grow them for you."

"And in the short term?"

"There isn't much I'm afraid. Stasis would be optimal, but again, I don't have the facilities. All I have is sedation."

Ellie's breathing sped. "I don't want to sleep. Get the king, he'll tell you."

"Calm yourself, Major. Put her back under please."

"No wait! Why won't you call... the... king?" Ellie said faintly, as the drugs pulled her back under.

Banished back to the void, she wandered lost and alone with her fears. She'd betrayed Nicky when he'd needed her the most. She hadn't believed in him. She hadn't supported his decision to confront his father and now she'd done worse than that. She'd let him out of her sight—the worst thing any bodyguard could do. She had to find him.

Ellie snapped awake, angry and ready for mayhem. How long had they kept her under this time? It felt like days but it could've been weeks for all she knew. Doctor Michaels leaned into view. He ignored her glare and performed his examination in silence.

"I want to know what's happening out there. Where's the king? Why won't you let me see him?"

"He's a busy man."

"Does he even know I'm awake?"

"As I said, he's busy. I won't distract him from the war."

They hadn't told him then, and why should they? The war *was* more important than an injured bodyguard. Only Nicky knew they were more than that, and she'd rejected him when he'd wanted to defy his father. Would he even want to see her now? King Richard had died and all his machinations with him. Nicky was free to choose whomever he wanted. Her lack of support might be the only thing keeping them apart. How horribly ironic that her wish to save him pain had caused so much of it.

"I insist you stop drugging me insensible," Ellie said. "I want to see the king."

"Many people do," Michaels said. "As for your medication we can talk about it."

"I'm not interested in talk. You're required to heed me, or step aside as my physician."

Michaels sighed. He stepped out of view. He returned with a chair a few moments later and sat beside the bed out of her sight like last time.

"I know you're frustrated. How many surgeons do you think we have here? I'm your only choice. There's a war on."

"I know that!"

"Do you? Do you really? Let me bring you up to date. The Merkiaari destroyed everything in orbit. All of our ships and stations are gone. Everyone serving up there is dead. No one knows how many died, but two-hundred thousand killed doesn't seem beyond reason."

Ellie sucked in a breath to comment, but Michaels didn't give her a chance.

"The capital was destroyed around that time. A city of eight million souls. Gone."

"The rescue squad told me before the crash. Did they live?"

"No."

She was sorry to hear that. They'd done their duty and saved Nicky. For that she owed them more than she could ever repay.

"The tether fell when the Merki destroyed Terminus Station."

"It self-destructed," Ellie corrected.

Michaels ignored her. "The climbers were full of evacuees from the station. Children mostly. That was before the landings. Let's just call that the prologue, shall we? Our cities have been bombed multiple times since then followed by incursions of Merkiaari ground troops. Did I leave anything out?"

"Family?" she whispered.

"I lived in the capital. I called home to tell my wife I'd be leaving early from the conference, but we were cut off. The emergency broadcast was quite specific about how she died."

"I'm sorry," Ellie said. She wished she could see his face.

"Can I tell you anything else about how everyone I care about died? Did I mention my brother and his children were in town at the end? How about that?"

Michaels stood abruptly and his chair flew back. Ellie heard it crash into something. Before she could apologise or say she was sorry for his loss, he stormed out. On the plus side he forgot to turn her brain to mush with his drugs. On the minus side she couldn't get his story out of her head. She stared at the ceiling trying not to think and prayed he'd come back before she started yelling.

Michaels did return but he wasn't alone this time. She could hear him discussing her condition. With a group of doctors maybe. He did say he'd been attending a conference, so he couldn't be the only medic stuck here. Maybe he'd decided to hand her case to someone else.

"She's in this one, Your Majesty," Michaels said.

Ellie's heart leapt. Nicky had come to see her! She heard a pair of feet approaching. He sucked in a shocked breath, she heard it clearly, and wished Michaels had covered her injuries before he'd left. She knew how terrible she looked.

"Come closer. I need to see your face," Ellie said.

King William, fifth of the name and Lord Protector of Faragut, stepped into view and stared down at her in horrified silence. He was pale and worn and grief had aged him. He was barely twenty. He should be in school not standing here looking like a man three times his age.

Ellie stared up at William and realisation dawned. She

hadn't saved Nicky. She'd killed him. Her eyes grew hot and she cried silently. Michaels had known. He must have. She'd killed her king. She should have knocked Nicky unconscious and dragged him down the mountain before letting him near that HLV. She'd known she couldn't protect him in the air.

Nicky's little brother was the only witness to the light going out of her eyes.

* * *

17 ~ Options

Silver Bay, Duchy of Longthorpe, Faragut

Ellie cried herself into exhaustion and drowsed for a time. She awoke to find William had covered her with a sheet and taken a seat nearby. She didn't know how long she'd been asleep.

"Thanks for waiting," Ellie said. "I'm sorry I lost it." Lost him, she didn't have the heart to add. "They didn't tell me."

William rose and stepped to her bedside. "Doctor Michaels told me he'd kept it from you. I didn't agree, but he insisted."

"He's been through a lot."

"He's a tyrant," William said. "But he's the best we have left. Did you know Nicholas came to see me at college?"

She tried to shake her head. Couldn't. "No. When was this?"

"The day after you returned to Faragut. You went home to visit your parents, remember? Nicholas used the opportunity to ditch his detail. Father..." William's voice turned grim. "Father was really angry about that."

"I bet. I would be too, only there's no point now." No

point to anything. She just wanted to sleep forever without dreams.

William sighed. "Nicholas wanted to warn me about his decision to step aside in my favour. I told him I would hate him forever if he did that to me, but I didn't mean it. I... I didn't... I loved him. I could never..."

"I know," Ellie said. "He did too. Did he tell you why?"

"Yes, but I already knew. We'd spoken about you before."

"You knew?"

"I knew before you left Faragut that last time. He never spoke about girlfriends to me, but suddenly he couldn't stop talking about you. What you'd said or done that week. Things that made him laugh. He loved you very much."

Tears scolded her eyes again. William rose and stepped away. He returned with a towel. It was humiliating, having the king wait on her. The king. Not really *her* king, though he was that officially. Nicky would always be hers.

"Thanks," Ellie said as he dried her eyes. "I told him I'd step aside. I didn't want him to fight with his father. Lady Charlotte was a good match."

William snorted. "A *proper* match you mean. She would have made Nicholas miserable."

"Not her fault."

William shrugged. "I never said it was, Major."

"Ellie, please."

"Ellie then. Charlotte and Nicholas had no say in the decision. Charlotte still doesn't and neither do I really."

Ellie scowled. "You're the king. Take charge and fuck people's opinions. I saw how miserable they made your father. He didn't want to force Nicky into a loveless marriage."

"I realise that. Charlotte is Lady Peckforton now. Her father is dead."

"Lucky her," she muttered.

"There's a lot of luck like that going around," William said sharply. "I doubt most would agree with your interpretation."

"I didn't mean your father. He was a good man at heart, but court made him harsh. Don't let it do the same to you."

"Court is the least of my concerns right now."

"The war is going badly?"

"The war was lost five minutes after the first Merkiaari troops landed. We've been reduced to guerrilla raids."

Ellie frowned. "How's that going?"

"Okay. We win when we fight but only because we choose our battles. Small raids where we have the advantage won't win this war."

"Fighting when we have the advantage only makes sense."

"True, but they own the greater system and have air superiority down here. All we can do is delay."

Ellie supposed she should care. She should question him and offer advice, but she was beyond helping anyone. Broken in body and broken in spirit. That's what she was. There was no fight left in her.

William took his seat again. "Is there anything I can do for you before I go?"

"You could order Michaels to euthanase me, but he won't."

William's jaw dropped. "Of course he won't. You're in the core not the Border Zone."

"Might as well be the Border Zone. He says he can't fix me, and he can't put me into stasis. Let's face it, I'm screwed."

"I'll have a word with him. He should be able to sedate you at least."

"No!" Ellie snapped. "I mean, thank you, but no. I don't want to sleep."

"You have to sleep some time."

"I prefer to delay the necessity."

"You too?" William said quietly. "I've been having nightmares since this started."

"Then you know why I don't want to be drugged insensible."

"I'll talk to Michaels for you. There must be something he can do."

Ellie changed the subject. "What about you? Where's your detail?"

"You're the last survivor of the Royal Guard."

Ellie didn't let her dismay show. "Who is looking out for you?"

"Harry Longthorpe is CGS again. He assigned me some men. I left them outside."

"The general survived then. That's good news."

"Not even the Merkiaari can kill Sir Longthorpe. They've been trying."

"I bet."

The Earl of Longthorpe was a legend on Faragut. He'd retired from the top job only a few years ago, which meant he was still current on their forces. He'd been Chief of the General Staff for King Richard, and again now for King William.

They'd lucked out.

With Sir Harry as CGS they had a chance. General Carter had been put in place to oversee things at the ministry, not lead their forces in battle. Sir Harry though, he was a real fighting man.

"Who did he choose for you?"

William shrugged. "A couple of old friends."

"Old friends?"

"That's what Sir Harry said."

"Old friends could mean anything. Spec Ops I bet."

"Don't worry about me," William said, rising and stowing his chair against the wall. "I'll talk to Doctor Michaels for you."

"Be careful," Ellie called to his back. "Your Majesty?"

"You need something?"

"Nicky loved you very much. I don't think he would have followed through with his threat."

"I know he did, Ellie, but he loved you just as much. I did agree to help him and take his place as heir, but I never thought I'd have to follow through."

Ellie's jaw dropped. Before she could say more, he was gone. William had agreed with Nicky? That was madness, but it was Nicky's kind of madness. It was love. William had loved his brother enough to sacrifice his own future happiness. All to help Nicky marry her.

Her eyes burned but the tears didn't escape.

William deserved better. He was king but not free. He was just as trapped in his way as she was in hers. The bed and machines were her prison, the people's opinions and expectations were his. She wished she could help him, but she couldn't even help herself.

Hours passed without anyone entering the room. Ellie heard people moving about, but saw no one. Her only company, her memories and the low hum of the machines. She embraced both, zoning out and losing herself in the past.

"Major Hutton?" Doctor Michaels said.

Ellie came back to herself to find the doctor leaning over her. "What do you want? No drugs, dammit. You hear me? *No drugs!*"

"There's nothing wrong with my hearing, I assure you. The king spoke to me about your case. I pointed out all the legal options to him, and we agreed they aren't any use to you."

"And then?"

Michaels shrugged. "I pointed out the illegal options."

"Illegal?"

"Breaking any of the provisions of the Bethany Convention isn't something I take lightly."

She tried to see where he was heading with this. The Convention prohibited the use of things like neural tech, but that wasn't its ultimate purpose. Neural interfaces were just one component of a larger threat.

Trans-humanism.

The Hacker Rebellion ended the dangerous practice of enhancing humans with cybernetics, and in doing so made trans-humans extinct. The horror of the rebellion would never be repeated as long as the Bethany Convention stood inviolate.

"You want to enhance me with cybernetics?"

"Want to? No I don't want to, and don't think of it as an enhancement. Let's call it a temporary repair shall we? After the war I'll strip all the cybernetics out of you, and replace the prosthetics with cloned limbs based upon your own genetic material."

"Buuut?" Ellie said. She could feel one coming.

"But you've lost all four limbs, your left eye, and you're paralysed below the neck. It means the cybernetics need to be farther reaching than prosthetic limbs alone. You'll need a neural bridge. I don't need to tell you why cranial implants are high on the list of banned tech. If we do this I'll be lucky to practise medicine again."

"Ask the king for a pardon."

"He gave me a blanket amnesty. If we win the war and if William is still king, he'll stand between me and prosecution."

"Then you're covered. What's your issue?"

Michaels snorted. "Little things like my reputation, my oath, and my ethics. If we do this my reputation will be trashed."

"You'll have the king's pardon."

"My colleagues won't care."

"Then just euthanase me," Ellie said crossly. She could feel hope ebbing. "I asked about that earlier."

"The king mentioned it. That's why I'm going to make you this offer."

Michaels showed her a compad.

Her eyes widened. "You want to turn me into that thing?"

"You can stay here instead."

"I'm not saying no, but why a Reaper?"

Michaels shrugged. "Why not? If I'm going to break laws I might as well break all of them. They can only shoot me once."

Ellie smiled. "Good point, but you aren't just breaking a few laws Doc, you're shattering them to bits."

"Few people bother studying Earth history anymore. I'm one of the few who does. I doubt most will recognise the design even though the Corporate Wars were a pivotal point in Human history. That won't stop them condemning me."

Ellie agreed with that. Colonisation of the Human Sector was still in its infancy back then, but the Corporate Wars accelerated the expansion. Colonies like Forestal, Faragut, and Garnet among others, owed their existence to warring corporations intent upon founding colonies to tap their resources. Those wars had been fought by Reapers and bigger nastier things.

"Why are you really doing this? You don't like me and you certainly don't owe me anything."

Michaels frowned. "That's easy. The Merkiaari killed everyone I care about and you're my way to hurt them. I'll make you into my weapon. Something even the Merki will run from. You can say no."

Ellie snorted. "Good one."

"This won't be like wearing power armour you realise? The armour will *be* you. Once installed you'll be trapped inside until I can dismantle you after the war."

"Ah... what about… ah, personal needs?"

"Not an issue. You'll eat and drink in the normal manner but elimination of wastes will be handled by the cybernetics."

"I've trained in power armour. The skinsuits we wore did the same thing."

Michaels shook his head. "This won't be like that. I'll use internal connections."

Ellie grimaced. "Catheters?"

"Worse."

What could be worse? Did she want to know? Probably not she decided. She already had a lot of wires and plumbing invading her body. She couldn't feel any of it. She wouldn't be any worse off than she was now, and regaining mobility was worth a lot.

"It's all reversible," Michaels assured her. "After the war I mean. In a good hospital."

"Don't worry about it."

Michaels frowned.

She didn't tell him she had no intention of surviving the war. All she wanted to do was kill Merkiaari and then join Nicky. She didn't really believe in the afterlife, but he had. If he was right she would join him there soon. If not, then oblivion. Either one worked for her.

"How long will it take?"

"Not long. It will seem miraculous. In less than a week you'll be on your feet again. How long you take to acclimatise to your new reality is up to you."

"I've lived and trained in powered armour."

"As I said, this will be different."

"Do we know that?"

Michaels frowned. "No, but it seems logical to assume."

"We'll see," Ellie said.

"We will," Michaels agreed and turned to leave. "I'll be back."

"I'm counting on it."

* * *

18 ~ Reaper

Silver Bay, Duchy of Longthorpe, Faragut

Ellie stood patiently in the middle of the room surrounded by busy technicians. That wasn't strictly true. She wasn't standing. She was hanging. The crane and harness supported her weight, so although her new feet *were* on the floor, she wasn't technically standing on them.

By order of the king and Sir Harry, every step of her enhancement had been recorded. Ellie didn't understand why they wanted to document the process in such detail, but they did. Maybe they wanted a body of evidence to present in court after the war. And they might need it. She'd done her part by giving a statement on camera volunteering for an unspecified mission requiring augmentation, and she'd signed the consent forms someone had cobbled together. None of it meant anything to her, but it might protect those performing the work. It might not, too. Still, as William said not long ago, Faragut hardly needed to fear a trade embargo for breaking the Convention. It had to survive the Merkiaari first.

Ellie studied herself on one of the monitors set up nearby

for her. Her pelvic region was fully encased in armour now, lending her some dignity again, and her new legs were connected. They worked too. She hadn't tried to run yet, but the walk-test had gone fine.

Doctor Michaels hadn't been kidding about the severity and invasive nature of the surgery. Thankfully, her pelvic armour covered the evidence, but internally and externally she wasn't Human below her navel anymore. She'd tried not to notice the disgust on the engineers's faces when they'd worked on her down there. They hadn't exactly tried to hide their emotions.

It was a relief when they fitted her legs and hid the horror beneath her armour. It shimmered silver under the lights and looked infinitely better. The shimmer was part of its reactive nature. It would reduce the effect of incoming fire. She'd be able to choose a camo pattern as a side benefit, but gloss black suited her mood better. That's what she'd choose when they let her take command of her body again.

Ellie passed the time listening to the arcane language of engineers, and tried to relate what they said to what they were doing to her. No one considered she might like to participate in their decisions. No one thought to explain them. They whispered their questions and replies to each other as if afraid to disturb her.

Pass this thing or that. Don't tighten it down yet. How's the seal? Ready for the gel? Pressure is steady. No leaks...

Ellie let it wash over her.

During her first round of surgeries, the emergency operations that saved her life, Doctor Michaels had managed to preserve her upper arms. Both were gone now. He'd needed to amputate them in order to install enhanced shoulder muscles and strengthen the joints. Without those two essential items, she wouldn't be able to operate her new arms. Reaper arms were heavily armoured, and extremely strong. Their internals would allow her to lift heavy weights, and mount special weapons. Without reinforced shoulders, she'd kill herself the first time she tried to use them. She'd need to run some tests on the firing range, but the engineers were still tinkering with reaction speeds. Too fast risked damaging joints. Too slow risked worse in battle.

She made fists to judge progress. Her left hand reacted noticeably quicker than her right. She'd always been right-handed before. Not that it mattered now.

"Try to relax while I calibrate your reflexes Major," a technician said, not crossly, just distracted. She didn't look up from her comp.

"Sorry," Ellie muttered and her hands returned to a relaxed posture by her sides.

Another change among a raft of them, was her height. She was much taller than before. At well over 2 meters in height she topped everyone in the room, and would have to duck through doorways. She wasn't as tall as a Marine in powered armour, but the floor seemed a long way down. It was a little surreal. She studied what she could see of her face on the closest monitor. In a strange way she had two faces now. The right side was entirely Human looking, but the left was not. Her eye on that side was a biomech replacement. It could supply her with all kinds of targeting data. Her face on that side shimmered silver from cheekbone to hairline, and then around to terminate just in front of her ear. She planned to wear a helmet even indoors, or get used to people staring at her.

Doctor Michaels entered the room and nodded to her when he noticed her looking. He parked off to one side of the room to watch. He often stopped by, but he said little when he did. After performing the banned surgeries needed to interface a Human body with a cybernetic one, he'd taken no further active part. Instead, he observed, his eyes coldly clinical as they studied the naked horror of her torso. The horror he'd created.

Ellie wondered what was going through his mind. Did the scars and bruises repulse him? Did he see the invasive implants he'd installed beneath them in his mind's eye, or was he fascinated by the holes and tears barely healed around her armour's mounting points? Maybe he just liked a good pair of tits, she thought bitterly. Hers were one-hundred percent natural; about the only part of her that still was. She snorted softly. It was probably the scars. Her bare torso revealed them clearly, and he was responsible for most of them. She didn't care about scars. The new ones caused by his hasty surgeries were less severe than the invisible one on her heart.

What did Michaels see when he looked at her? A badly scarred woman in need of his help? An injured soldier? A weapon to throw at the Merki? Maybe he regretted what he'd started. Did he wish he hadn't shown her the Reaper on his compad? Was he horrified by what he'd created?

He should be.

She was the first augment to draw breath in centuries. An extinct species resurrected out of a history book—a trans-human. A cybernetically enhanced human being. An augment, or more accurately, a cyborg. Worse, she was a Reaper. A military cyborg patterned upon those who'd fought in the Corporate Wars for money, or fame, or the latest upgrades. All gone now. Destroyed with millions of other augments during the Hacker Rebellion when the hated Douglas Walden turned them into mindless zombies, or suicidal killing machines.

She was a species of one and shouldn't exist. By Alliance law she *must not* exist. The only exceptions to the Bethany Convention and the AI Edict were a handful of ancient AIs, and Burgton's vipers. Both were strictly regulated and under Council control. No one and nothing controlled her. She was an outlawed abomination.

"Raise your arms please."

Ellie did.

A pair of engineers approached carrying one half of her torso armour trailing power feeds and various sensor connections. Another pair of men readied the back half of her armour. Like a turtle, she would be sealed inside her very own shell; a woman shaped carapace to cover the horror hiding within.

"Nice touch," Ellie said to Michaels.

He shrugged. "A sculpted breastplate should fit your shape better. You do need room to breathe, and you're not exactly flat-chested."

That was true. She was ample. *More than*, according to Nicky. Ellie forced herself not to think along those lines. He was gone and she was not. Not yet.

The engineers made the various connections to the ports implanted in her torso front and back, and then fitted the two halves of the armour onto her battered body. They worked in silence, sealing her inside and hiding the horror at last. The armour's nanocoat started shimmering silver as her systems energised it. More importantly, the darkened icons on her internal HUD awoke. A data window opened that only she could see, and a diagnostic began running.

With a coded thought Ellie changed her nanocoat to black. Multiple gasps from around the room proved her command had been accepted. She glanced at the nearest monitor. Her glossy black surfaces shone under the bright lights. She flexed her right hand one finger at a time. Made a fist. Relaxed. Performed the exercise a second time with her left. The diagnostic came back all green. Her body was reacting as she'd expected, but then it should. Its operating system was more or less identical to one used in powered armour. She couldn't feel anything in her cocoon of metal, but she hadn't expected any different.

The engineers finally stepped clear.

Michaels approached. He held out a hand and one of the technicians handed him a control wand. He used it to lower the crane a little to gain some slack on the harness restraining the deadly Reaper in their midst. Everyone backed up.

"We have a deal," Michaels whispered up at her as he unlocked the clamps. "They must pay."

Ellie loomed over him. This little man who had saved her life. This Doctor who threw away his ethics and broke laws to gift her with a metal body and a mission to perform. She was broken in body. He was broken in spirit. They deserved each other.

She kept her voice low. "They will pay, and dearly. For Nicky. For your family. For King Richard and everyone who died with him. I swear it."

Michaels moved out of her way and Ellie stepped forward, her feet thudding heavily on the floor. She looked around at her audience. They'd made this possible, and yet they feared her. Old stories whispered in the back of their minds of death and destruction. Of cyborgs gone mad. Old stories made real again. She smiled for them. They cringed. Michaels was the only one who didn't put distance between them, and he was as broken as she was. So be it. She had a job to do. One job. It didn't need friends to accomplish. Just a lot of ammo.

"More testing? Weapons?" Ellie asked.

Michaels nodded. "Eventually. I'll get you anything you need, but later. The king will want to see you first. I think clothes next, and then some food. Weapons and more tests this afternoon after your audience."

"I'm not hungry and I don't need clothes. The armour is enough. Weapons first."

"As I said. King before weapons. Not negotiable."

Ellie glared. He ignored her and left the room without a word. She ducked through the door he left open, her steps thudding loudly as she hurried to catch up. People in the corridors turned at the sound and cringed at the sight of her approaching. Maybe it was her scowl? She tried a smile but that made it worse. They cowered into doorways and flattened themselves against the walls.

"Oh for God's sake," she snarled when she caught up with Michaels. "What do they think I'm going to do, slaughter them?"

"Yes," Michaels said. "In here."

Ellie ducked to follow him through a door and into a storeroom containing a pile of crates. She opened the nearest one and scowled. Empty. It had once held grenades. She flipped another lid up, and then another. All empty.

"There are no weapons here," Michaels said.

She noted the bed crammed into a corner. "Your room?"

"We make do. I sleep here when the bed is free. Stand straight now."

"Ha... ha... ha," Ellie deadpanned. The armour didn't slouch. It kept her erect by default.

Michaels held a uniform shirt and tunic against her body to judge the fit. "I had a Royal Guard uniform made for you, but I'm not sure it will work."

"I don't care. I don't need a uniform to kill Merki."

Michaels sighed and slumped onto the bed. He leaned his forearms on his knees, suddenly exhausted.

"Are you planning to desert?"

Ellie blinked. "Of course not!"

"Did you resign your commission then? Before the attack I mean."

"No."

"I see. So you *are* still a member of the king's elite Royal Guard? Just checking, because if you're still a member I believe you'll find you're on duty. In fact, desertion in time of war is treason and punishable by mind wipe."

Ellie scowled.

"If you want to fight in this war you'll need information and the ability to choose your own battles. The first thing you've got to do is gain a place at the high table."

The high table was a euphemism meaning the king's

council. The Royal Guard had never been called upon to counsel the king, but the point was well-made. Her relationship with Nicky and her position as a royal bodyguard should be enough for entry as William's confidante, but Sir Harry was the senior military man. Her rank of Major was unlikely to impress him, and he'd already assigned his own men to protect William.

"Fine," she snapped. "Gimme those."

Michaels handed her the shirt.

Ellie pulled it carefully on, knowing her enhanced strength could rip it easily. She couldn't feel the buttons, and the nanotech surface coating her fingers was slippery.

"Allow me," Michaels said, taking pity on her. He closed the shirt quickly, and helped her on with the bottle-green stiff-collared tunic. He stepped back to admire the result. "It looks good on you."

"I'll take your word for it," Ellie said.

"No need. I'll show you."

Before she could say anything he'd taken a picture with his compad and offered it to her. She looked at the image on the screen, and saw a startled looking woman staring back. A woman with half a face, but still a woman. Her hair was long on the Human side, hanging at shoulder length. The other side was cold black metal. No hair. Despite that, she felt her spirits rise. The uniform cloaked her inhumanity. Her face? Well, she could pretend it was a mask. Not part of her.

"I have trousers for you, but no boots yet. I might be able to have some made. We'll need to measure you."

"I'll take the trousers for now," Ellie said, and he passed them over. She pulled them on, but again she couldn't use the buttons.

Michaels knelt and did the honours. "Thin gloves might help with this sort of thing. Something with texture to aid your grip."

"How do I look?"

Michaels stepped back to admire her. "I would say very nice, but I suspect you'd prefer me to say dangerous?"

"Good call."

"Food or the king first?"

"How about both?" Ellie said, thinking about his earlier high table comment.

"I'll ask for an audience over lunch."

She nodded.

* * *

19 ~ Weaponise Me

Silver Bay, Duchy of Longthorpe, Faragut

Lunch didn't work out. The king was too busy, but he did send a message inviting Ellie to have dinner with him later that day. She used the time before her audience to practice on the range, and badger Michaels into arming her properly.

Ellie reloaded and fired using her left hand. The pistol was the same model she'd carried on Mount Cho. Her big ass gun Nicky used to call it. She remembered him whining about the size of his weapon that day. Their last day. She smiled at the memory and missed the target.

Her smile fled.

She reloaded and switched to her other hand. The target disintegrated, replaced by another drone. She nailed it. It spun and recovered. She switched to ten round bursts and emptied the pistol into it. The poor thing crashed. It tried to lift off again, but then lay still.

Michaels watched her in silence, his compad dangling limply from one hand by his side. He wasn't even *trying* to look engaged in the process anymore. He was supposed to be testing her response times, but he seemed withdrawn.

Ellie didn't need his evaluation to know her reflexes were fine. Her scores were in the mid-nineties. More than three percent higher than she'd been when Human. It didn't seem like enough for a Reaper, but she had a handicap. Michaels had supplied inferior toys.

She cleared her weapon, and put it down on the counter next to the others she'd tested. Despite its impressive size, it was a standard pistol that any of Faragut's forces might use. She eyed the rifle she'd already discarded. Again, not a Reaper weapon. She was done playing with old toys. She wanted the new ones promised her.

"Are you having second thoughts?"

Michaels snorted. "Try fourth and fifth thoughts," he said to his shoes. He couldn't even look at her.

"I'm up here," Ellie said. She towered over him. It was a bit obvious, but he seemed to need a reminder. "Up here. Look at me."

He looked up. And up. And up.

She waved. "Hi."

"Hi."

"Even tenth thoughts are fine with me, but I'm already here. You can walk away from this, but I don't have that luxury."

"I'm sorry."

"Don't be sorry. Just finish what you started. We made a deal. I'm holding up my end. What about you?"

Michaels stared up at her. "You're *actually glad* I did this to you."

"Glad? No. The crash cost me more than my body. I'd do anything to go back and change things, but am I grateful you're my Doctor? Hell yes, of course I am. If not for you I'd be a corpse, or out of the fight at least. I have scores to settle. Don't you?"

Michaels took a deep breath, and nodded. "Open your weapon bays."

Thank God for that. She'd been worried there for a minute. She could use standard weapons, but her real advantages lay in the technology built into her. If he hadn't come through...

But he had.

Michaels left the room and reappeared moments later pushing a pallet lifter laden with drab green cases. Munitions.

Ellie tried to strip down, but she still couldn't handle buttons. "I can't weapon up in this bloody uniform," she grumbled.

"If you want to fight in the buff like a mythical warrior goddess, be my guest, but you'll wear clothes the rest of the time."

"Or?"

"What?" Michaels said.

"Ultimatums have an *or* attached to them. I'll wear clothes or?"

"Or you'll scare people more than you do already, and I'll stop helping you."

Oh-ho! He'd suddenly grown a backbone, had he? Good for him.

"You do realise I'm wearing a full set of body armour?"

Michaels shook his head. "The armour *is* you." He stepped closer and attended to her tunic buttons. "I need to source some gloves for you," he muttered. "Maybe surgical gloves would work."

"They might, but they won't last long in combat."

"You don't need them in combat. You want to be a warrior goddess, don't you?"

Ellie grinned.

She finished undressing, and opened the cargo bays built into her thighs. They accounted for her extra height and provided ammo storage. A coded thought opened the rest all at once. All four in her arms. A bay in the underside of each forearm would house a mini-rocket launcher. The bays on the outer surface would sport her rotary cannons.

"I should call the engineers to handle this," Michaels muttered. "I'm a doctor, not a gunsmith."

Ellie snickered. "I can do this part myself. Gimme."

Michaels stepped out of the way.

Ellie got to work. Reapers used an ingenious design for quick reloads. A lucky thing, because she planned on doing it a lot. Her mini-rockets came in clips of a dozen munitions each; clips not magazines. She could store hundreds in each thigh, and she did so before filling the remaining space with drum magazines for her cannons. She closed the bays, and installed the rocket launchers in her arms. They were a modular design, and snapped easily into place. A pair of red rocket-shaped icons lit on her HUD. Michaels shifted uneasily when she loaded them.

"Relax. What do you think I'm going to do, blow up the castle?"

Michaels smiled sheepishly.

Both weapon icons turned green along with their ammo counters. She fed each launcher with three clips for a total of seventy-two high explosive rockets. With a thought, the launchers retracted into her arms, and the icons turned red. She tested their action a few times until satisfied they wouldn't jam.

Ellie un-boxed and installed her mini-guns next. A pair of gun-shaped icons filled in the last blank spots on her HUD, and turned green as she loaded them. Each drum magazine held thousands of caseless tungsten-tipped needles. They were armour piercing, not frangible. Reaper mini-guns were beautiful tech. The tiny gatling cannons were so compact. So light. So deadly. She couldn't wait to start shredding Merkiaari flesh with them. Thinking of that made her itch.

Ellie activated a drone. It shot into the air at the far end of the firing lane. She aimed her right arm downrange, made a fist, and activated the weapon. The mini-gun popped up, barrels already starting to spin. At 3000rpm, they spat flame, and armour-piercing needles screamed downrange. A really good word for it. The needles screamed, ripping at the air and shredding the drone before it could dodge.

Michaels clapped his hands over his ears.

Ellie took no notice and let her body do what it knew how to do. Destruction was its prime directive. Its operating system knew this task well. All it needed was a target, and Ellie supplied that. Her target reticule sought out movement at the end of the lane. It danced over her HUD, not settling. Not satisfied. The moment another drone appeared, it locked on and the cannon spoke, spitting flame again.

"*Major!*"

Ellie ignored him, and raised her other fist. The gun popped up, and fired. More drones died. Many more. She was potting them almost before they launched. She grinned fiercely, the grin turned to a chuckle, the chuckle to a belly laugh as she sprayed destruction downrange. She lost herself in the joy and scream of destruction.

Her HUD blinked a low ammo warning, but she didn't notice the audience at her back until she ran dry and stopped to reload. A crowd stood just inside the room, staring at her in horrified silence. She reloaded and tried to ignore them.

Michaels lowered his hands. "I tried to warn you."

Ellie wanted to shrug, but her body couldn't do it. She nodded. At least she could still do that. Their fear was expected and understandable. She was a Reaper, an old story brought to life. A nightmare rather. They flinched when she looked at them. It was lucky they couldn't see what she was seeing just then. Each of them was outlined in red, and their locations were locked into her targeting system. She was only a thought away from servicing those data entries. They were targets, and a mere thought away from eternity.

Shocked by that line of thought, she stowed her weapons and the target overlay vanished. She realised that at any moment, day or night, she was a micro-second away from a massacre. The ban on augmentation made perfect sense to her now. She shouldn't exist.

Michaels broke the silence. "The king expects us for dinner. Get dressed. We can't be late."

Invoking the king dispersed the crowd, leaving Ellie alone to dress under Michaels's hooded eyes. He knew what she'd been thinking there at the end. Somehow he knew how close she'd come. He helped her dress, but kept his peace.

Ellie shook off her uneasiness on the way to dinner. It wasn't as if she'd done anything wrong. Everyone had dark thoughts now and then. Acting on them would be a different thing. She was fine. There was nothing wrong with her that killing a few million Merkiaari couldn't fix.

HM William Windsor wasn't alone when they were ushered into his presence. Ellie doubted he would ever have privacy again. Nicky had always complained of its lack whenever he visited his father at the palace. King Richard had been surrounded by flunkies of all kinds day and night. Those functionaries were long dead, but William wasn't free. He couldn't even have a quiet dinner with his dead brother's lover without someone competing for his attention.

"Ellie," William said, the worry slipping free of his features at the sight of her. "So good of you to come. It's great to see you up and around again."

His bodyguards tensed as William approached her. The big bad was in the room with their king. In their place Ellie would have done a lot worse. She didn't blame them one bit. In fact, it worried her they'd allowed her into William's presence. The Royal Guard wouldn't have let her get near King Richard or Nicky, but although William's bodyguards wore special forces insignia on their uniforms, they weren't Royal Guard. She was the last of that elite force. By rights, she and not they should be protecting him.

William studied her new face.

Too close! Her bodyguard instincts screamed the warning

silently in her mind. Ellie didn't need a weapon. She could reach out and snap his neck. She was an armed Reaper in the presence of royalty, yet no one protested. They hadn't even searched or disarmed her. That was so wrong. So careless of William's life. She wanted to snatch him up, and take him to safety. Nicky's brother. The last surviving Windsor. The last living part of her king.

William was suddenly outlined in green on her HUD, and everyone else in the room turned red. Without willing it, her targeting computer noted the room's dimensions. It stored everyone's coordinates relative to her position and the only exit. A numbered list of targets scrolled down the left side of her HUD. The first entry flashed in time with the red pulsing outline surrounding the bodyguard closest to William. A priority target.

William pumped Michaels's hand. "Very well done, Doctor."

Michaels mumbled something in reply.

Ellie forced herself not to move. The computer in her head was a tool. It offered advice and opportunity, but she was in control of her actions. Her decisions ruled the Reaper. The moment she understood it on an instinctual level, she relaxed, knowing nothing could happen without her consent. She would never do anything to risk Nicky's brother. Her list of targets vanished and the tactical overlay dissolved.

William remained outlined in green, and Ellie slipped into old patterns of behaviour. She stood at ease, right hand gripping left wrist. Classic bodyguard posture. The other guards in the room noticed the subtle signs, and relaxed. Ellie wasn't sure whether to feel flattered or angry. Neither, she decided. The Royal Guard didn't do flattery or anger. It did calm watchfulness, followed by explosive mayhem at need. She could handle the watchfulness, and let her Reaper side handle the mayhem.

* * *

20 ~ High Table

Silver Bay, Duchy of Longthorpe, Faragut

The rest of William's guests arrived shortly after Ellie did, and introductions were made. She'd seen Sir Harry before on his visits to the palace, but she'd been just one uniformed guard among many back then. He didn't recognise her. No reason he should. Even Nicky wouldn't recognise her now.

The general examined her critically, nodded briefly without speaking, and dismissed her to speak with Doctor Michaels. Sir Harry's officers kept their distance, and took their lead from their CO.

Ellie didn't like Sir Harry. She wanted to, but she didn't like the way he'd spoken to William upon entering his presence. He wasn't discourteous, but it was obvious he didn't respect William's position as his king either. Ellie understood why, and it wasn't an age thing. Sir Harry's king would always be King Richard, just as Nicky was the king of Ellie's heart. Reasons didn't matter to her, and they certainly didn't make it right. Sir Harry disappointed her, and that made her angry. She had so little left to believe in, and now there was one thing less.

"Sorry about him," William said under his breath as they watched the ongoing interrogation. "He's too good an officer to dismiss. Father always made allowances for his arrogance."

"It's fine," Ellie said, but it wasn't. She didn't care how rude people were to her. It was his easy dismissal of William that concerned her. "You're not your father, Sire. You're king now."

"I know, but it's Sir Harry."

"He serves the Crown at your pleasure. Make sure he knows it, Sire, or you'll lose control of him."

William frowned. "We need him."

And that was the problem. Ellie didn't believe Sir Harry was disloyal. He was simply arrogant and supremely confident in his own abilities. He wouldn't listen to others because he felt their opinions were worth less than his own. The problem was, he was right. William had to keep control while somehow using the resource Sir Harry represented.

"Allow him to advise you, Sire, but in the end order him to carry out any plans he puts forward. Even if you accept his ideas verbatim, don't let him take your permission for granted. Be commanding like your father was. Make sure Sir Harry knows who rules Faragut."

William frowned.

"How many can you build?" Sir Harry was saying.

Michaels looked trapped. Ellie joined him to tower over the general, in an effort to lend some support.

"Major Hutton is a special case," Michaels said. "I performed the work as a favour to His Majesty."

"Quite right," William said joining them. "And your king is grateful, Doctor."

"I understand that," Sir Harry said. "But that's no reason not to produce more. They would be a great asset. A single battalion of Burgton's vipers beat the Merki on behalf of the Shan. A few hundred Reapers might tip the balance in my favour."

Vipers were more advanced, faster, and far more deadly than any Reaper. Burgton's men had supported the Shan. They hadn't fought alone, but Sir Harry's point was well made. A battalion or three of vipers would be very welcome on Faragut.

"Do you have a few hundred men willing to be augmented?" Michaels said.

"Not exactly *willing*, but they'll serve their world one way or the other."

"I don't follow."

"Convicts, Doctor. They'll be offered augmentation."

"And if they refuse?"

Sir Harry smiled. "They won't. They'll volunteer or suffer mind wipe. One way or another they'll serve our world. Fear not."

Michaels paled. "Augmenting zombies? Are you *insane?*"

Zombies was a derisive term for the empty shells left behind after a mind-wipe session. Prior to re-education, recipients of mind-wipe were helpless husks. Raiders harvested colonies in the Border Zone and programmed zombies as slaves. They called them zeeks.

"They won't be zombies after re-education. They'll be patriots."

"Patriots have a choice," Michaels said stiffly. "Slaves do not. The suggestion is reprehensible and quite possibly a crime against Humanity."

Ellie nodded. "I agree."

Sir Harry glared up at her. "Who asked you? I don't have the luxury of debating my decisions. While you've been recovering the Merkiaari have been wiping us out. Sacrifices must be made if any of us are to survive."

"Easy to say when you're not the one making them," Michaels muttered.

"You think sending men to their deaths is easy? I have no choice you arrogant arse!"

"That's quite enough, General," William said, and Sir Harry jerked in surprise.

Ellie smiled tightly to hear the censure in his voice. She let it widen when Sir Harry inclined his head in a brief bow to his lord.

"Doctor Michaels is my guest," William went on. "Let's leave the war outside for one meal."

Sir Harry bowed again. "As you say, Sire."

Everyone took the pronouncement as an invitation to find places at table. William took his seat at the head, and to Sir Harry's dismay indicated Ellie should take the nearest chair to his right. She did so, and reserved the place next to her for Michaels by seating him there herself. Her chair creaked under her weight, and she hesitated to relax, but it held. William smiled at the look of alarm on her face and she grimaced at him to acknowledge it.

"Putting on weight, Ellie?"

"Har-de-har," she muttered and didn't miss the looks being passed between Sir Harry's officers at her familiarity with the king. "It's all the ammo."

Michaels snorted.

"Don't you start."

William laughed and the others seemed to feel they should join in, but it was a forced sound that quickly faded. Sir Harry sat opposite Ellie on the king's left hand and studied her in silence as the meal was served.

Ellie's first trial arrived when she tried to eat. She stared at the steak on her plate and frowned. It looked tasty, but when she tried to use the cutlery she didn't have the dexterity. She nearly managed a couple of times, but in the end her knife and fork flipped out of her hands to clatter against the plate. She looked up to find William watching her struggle. She flushed as conversation faltered around the room.

Michaels came to her rescue again.

Still deep in conversation with a dark-haired mobile

infantry captain, he reached across Ellie's plate to snag her utensils. He quickly cut her food into bite-sized pieces and bent the handle of her fork into a U-shape. Still chatting away as if unaware of everyone watching, he put the fork in her left hand, and flattened the metal until it gripped two of her fingers.

He whispered. "Don't let them see you flinch."

Ellie kept her eyes down. She speared a cube of meat with her fork and ate it. It was perfectly cooked and delicious. She ate some more of it but didn't attempt the wine. She knew her limitations. She could probably drink from the bottle but not from the delicate crystal glasses supplied.

The meal lasted for a little over an hour and ended with William asking a few people to remain behind. Ellie and Sir Harry were amongst them as well as the mobile infantry captain who Michaels had spoken with. The doctor wasn't invited. He seemed eager to beat feet out of Sir Harry's presence.

William put aside all pretence of normality. "Did your badgering of Doctor Michaels have a purpose, Sir Harry?"

"Yes, Sire. It did."

"Explain."

Sir Harry glanced at Ellie and hesitated.

"Speak up," William said, making the general frown. "We wish Major Hutton to hear this. She has our trust."

The use of the royal *we* was a deliberate provocation. Ellie kept her face bland, but inside she was gleeful. She'd heard the like many times from King Richard.

"I've polled all of our medics. None of them is willing to reproduce Doctor Michaels's work."

"You showed them the procedure?"

Sir Harry nodded.

"Procedure?" Ellie asked. "Is that why you filmed everything?"

"Partly," William agreed. "We wanted to be in a position

to reproduce your augmentations, but also present a legal defence at need."

"The point is moot," Sir Harry said testily. "They've all refused to aid us. The traitors."

Ellie frowned. "Refusing to commit crime isn't traitorous."

"Refusing orders in time of war is!"

"Refusing *lawful* orders is," Ellie corrected. "Breaking the AI Edict and the Bethany Convention isn't just illegal. It's unethical and punishable by mind-wipe." She turned to the king. "I should not exist, Sire."

William waived that away. "You're here because I owed it to Nicholas. I promised Doctor Michaels a pardon and I stand by that. I could do the same for all the others."

"I already made them that offer," Sir Harry admitted. "They refused."

Ellie was relieved to hear it.

"Well," William said. "We'll shelve your idea for now General, and move on."

Sir Harry frowned, obviously wanting to argue, but Ellie was delighted. Creating zombies and turning them into Reapers wasn't just illegal. It was evil. She was glad to learn the idea came from Sir Harry and not William. It reaffirmed her faith in him. He needed support and time to gain confidence in himself, especially when under pressure from men like Sir Harry. Ellie would help where she could.

Sir Harry reported on the current situation. It was immediately obvious to Ellie the Merkiaari were acting unlike the Merki of old. They were performing surgical strikes not herding people to destruction as they had in the past. They didn't do that.

"They're targeting infrastructure?" Ellie said in surprise.

Sir Harry frowned. "I wouldn't go that far, but their priority is definitely weighted toward our war fighting ability."

"Examples?"

"Shipyards, star ports, our industrial complexes. All of

them have been hit repeatedly. They've bombed our cities too, but not to slaughter our citizens. They've struck my command and control centres. That plus their jamming has made communications a nightmare."

"Our forces are using couriers to keep in touch," William added. "The secessionists could have learned a thing or two from them."

Sir Harry scowled.

"It sounds like it's the other way round to me, Sire," Ellie said. "The Merki are fighting fire with fire."

"Exactly! They're using our tactics against us," Sir Harry said. "They've learned lessons from their last defeat and adapted. We need to do the same."

Ellie frowned. "But how? They have air superiority and control the orbitals."

"They don't control them. They destroyed them," William said. "We have nothing left up there. Even if the Merki jumped outsystem right now, they've won this one."

"They won't," Ellie and Sir Harry chorused. Ellie continued, "Their strategy says to me they're thinking long term."

"I agree, Sire. This is about the future of the Alliance, not just us. They're taking Faragut out of the game. They could leave right now and still call this a win. We'll take years to recover."

"There's nothing I can do about that," William said and sighed. "The Alliance will have to get along without us. Kalmar will take up the slack."

The Kalmar Union was Faragut's direct competitor for defence contracts. There were others providing ships and munitions for the military, but Kalmar and Faragut jointly owned the lion's share of the market.

Until now.

"Do we have an ETA for Admiral Fischer?" Ellie said.

William shook his head. "Tentative at best. We have to

hope a few of our drones reached him but we can't know their drive settings. Assuming the standard eighty-percent of max, we're talking maybe five weeks after launch to reach him, and another five back. So around the middle of next month."

Ellie hissed. "That's a long time under siege, Sire."

"The Shan fought them for more than two years. We'll hold," Sir Harry said.

"Five more weeks if the drones reach Admiral Fischer today, *and* he's ready to respond immediately," William warned them. "No way to know if that's true."

Ellie was going to ask for more, but the distant thunder of explosions had her bodyguard instincts kicking in.

Hard.

She launched out of her seat, grabbed William, and bundled him into a corner. Sir Harry gasped at her sudden move and started to rise. William's guards reacted but too late. The king was already in the corner, completely hidden by Ellie's armour. She braced herself over him with arms straight and elbows locked. With her hands flat against the wall, she tucked her head to cover more of him.

"Ellie?" William gasped.

She ignored him and the yelling behind her. "Take cover you idiots!" she roared.

Sir Harry finally heard it too. "Down!" he shouted, and dove under the table.

"Don't hold your breath, Sire. Mouth open and lean into the corner," Ellie said calmly.

She counted time. The explosions were advancing toward them. Instinct and training had assured her they would. She opened her mouth in anticipation of the over-pressure if it came.

It did.

William gasped as the Merkiaari tried to obliterate Silver Bay Castle above them. The floor heaved and the ceiling cracked. A huge chunk of plascrete crashed through to collapse the table. The chairs saved Sir Harry. They propped the table top at an angle, and the debris slid off to hit the floor with a heavy thud. The general scrambled clear, heading for the doorway. Ellie grabbed him as he neared and yanked him into her corner.

More of the ceiling came down as the blasts sent millions of tons of plascrete falling. Lumps of masonry pelted Ellie, pinging off her armour. She locked her knees expecting to be killed any moment but determined not to collapse even in death. William remained outlined in green on her HUD. She stared down into the fear-filled eyes of her king's brother, the last piece of her Nicky. He held her gaze as she took hit after hit for him. Blood trickled from her hairline and onto his upturned face. He would watch her die, but at least he would be alive to see it.

* * *

21 ~ Contact

Silver Bay, Duchy of Longthorpe, Faragut

Screams of agony told the tale of crushed limbs and death behind Ellie. The mobile infantry captain's piercing screams abruptly ceased. Ellie regretted his death. She couldn't recall his name but he'd seemed nice. Doctor Michaels had liked him. Finally, the explosions died away into the distance, but not the yelling. And not the screaming. And not the death.

Those were just beginning.

Ellie straightened and pushed away from the wall to allow William and Sir Harry to ease out of the corner. They had to climb over the rubble piled around her, but once they'd vacated the corner it allowed her the room she needed to turn around.

She climbed out of the rubble crater she'd created by shielding William, and took stock. Her injuries were minor. A quick diagnostic proved her cybernetic systems were at 100%, and her IMS had already dealt with her contusions. Scalp wounds bled a lot but her skull wasn't fractured. The bleeding had already stopped.

The room was dimly lit. Power had failed, but battery-operated emergency lighting had kicked in to reveal the situation. The door was blocked and it was the only exit. She had the king to protect and very few resources to use. Only one of William's bodyguards had survived. Wolfe she thought his name was. He looked uninjured.

"Collect their weapons and pass them out," Ellie ordered.

Wolfe looked at his dead comrades and nodded. "You think we'll be fighting Merki down here, Major?"

"I'm not saying that, but we have the king to protect. More guns in our hands is better."

Wolfe nodded. He began the grisly task of looting the crushed bodies of his friends while Sir Harry and William investigated the rubble blocking the door. Ellie left them to that for the moment and surveyed the hole in the ceiling. It seemed to her a better exit. The castle above them must be heavily damaged for the collapse to reach down this far. It seemed unlikely to her the corridor outside would be clear.

She climbed atop the rubble beneath the hole and peered into the darkness.

Bunkers on Faragut were designed as redoubts from which to launch retaliatory strikes against an enemy. This one should've been proof against a Merkiaari air-strike. They must have used the Merki equivalent of Atlas bunker buster bombs, or some other deep penetrating munitions. Either that or the contractors had cut major corners.

Her sensors probed the darkness overhead, but the cavity was only a few tens of metres deep. Her cybernetic left eye pierced the shadows using the low-light amplification systems built into it, and confirmed the bad news. There would be no climbing out of here.

"Any luck Major?" Sir Harry said.

Ellie looked down at his dust covered face. His red-rimmed eyes peered hopefully up at her. She glanced at the king, but he was oblivious. He was working with Wolfe now to clear the door. She shook her head and watched the hope fade from his eyes. He backed away as she climbed down.

"Let me, Sire," Ellie said as she reached his side.

William stepped away to join Sir Harry.

Ellie surveyed the rubble. The largest chunks of plascrete would be too heavy even for a Reaper to move. William had succeeded in clearing a shallow tunnel but it was too narrow for anyone to navigate. She began digging in an effort to widen it.

A few hours and much cursing later Ellie had burrowed deep into the rock pile, but they were still trapped. The largest chunks of plascrete were immovable. Too heavy or simply wedged in place made no real difference. She had only one option left. A dangerous option. She was fully loaded but trying to blast a way through might cause further collapses.

She reported her thoughts to the king.

"Try," William said and raised a hand to prevent Sir Harry's incipient protest. "We can't wait for rescue. We don't know if anyone survived up there. Go ahead Major."

Ellie nodded. "All of you take cover the best you can."

They moved as far away as they could.

Ellie ripped the sleeves off her tunic to clear her weapons, and found a good vantage to target the cleared tunnel. She was hoping to confine the explosion within it. With luck that would amplify the effect while reducing the risk to William and the others. She raised both arms and made fists. Her rocket launchers descended from the undersides of her forearms, and she fired twice from each arm.

Four mini-rockets screamed across the room and detonated as one deep inside the pile of rubble. The room shook with the blast, and more debris rained through the ruined ceiling. Dust billowed back into the room obscuring the results of her fire.

William raised his head and gave Ellie a thumbs up. He was uninjured. She stowed her weapons and they waited for the air to clear. The dust settled after a few minutes to reveal the blockage had slumped in the doorway. The largest chunks of plascrete had shattered and settled. The top half of the door was clear.

Wolfe climbed the pile first and slipped outside followed by William and Sir Harry. Ellie brought up the rear in case she got stuck. She successfully dragged her bulk through the gap but her uniform paid the price. By the time she rejoined the others, her trousers were little more than rags. She took a moment to strip down.

William raised an eyebrow.

"Doctor Michaels made me wear it, Sire. I'm a warrior goddess. We fight naked."

"I see."

The Human side of Ellie's face reddened. It had sounded funny when Doctor Michaels said it. Trying to avoid their stares she took point and chose a direction. The others moved to follow with weapons in hand.

Their destination was the armoury.

Ellie had built in weaponry to use, but a few rifles would be nice. Maybe she'd pick up a pistol or two with it. Some grenades would be good. Maybe an AAR? She snorted as she imagined herself weighed down with enough firepower to take out an armoured division. While she was wishing she ought to wish for a division of her own. A Marine division! She knew exactly where in the armoury to find what she needed.

But.

A blocked corridor stymied their advance. She scowled at the inconvenient impediment to her plans for marshal dominance. She couldn't clear this with a few rockets. She looked back at the others. They shrugged. No help there.

"We are not impressed with the resilience of your bunker, Sir Harry," William said dryly. "You should sue your building contractor."

Wolfe snorted.

"Silver Bay has been in my family for centuries, Sire. My grandfather had this built after the Merki War."

"He did a poor job of it!"

"Unfair," Sir Harry said. "He could hardly bomb his own castle to test it."

William frowned. "If we live through this I'm going to send a trade delegation to the Shan."

"Oh?"

"They have a lot of experience with surviving Merki incursions. We could use some of that expertise."

"Keeps in exchange for...?"

"Warships perhaps," William said. "Not that we have any, but we'll think of something."

Ellie tuned out their speculations to consider her options.

They could backtrack and look for another route. They could try and fail to clear this corridor. Or... her good eye narrowed as she considered the closest door. She opened it and peered inside. The room was full of stacked shelves. Rations not munitions unfortunately. She wasn't interested in anything but the far wall. She hammered a fist into it and punched straight through.

"We're in luck," she called to the others as they entered behind her. "It's only a partition."

She hammered her fists into the dry wall and broke through easily. She added a few kicks to create a bigger opening, and stooped to pass through. The room on the far side had rows of unkempt beds. A barracks.

Ellie quickly crossed the space, noting the cracks in the ceiling. A huge chunk had broken free, but it hadn't fallen. It remained wedged precariously in front of the door. Praying it would stay put long enough, she ushered everyone through and back into the corridor.

"Where is everyone?" William said.

Ellie had been trying not to think about that. She didn't know many people living here. Only those currently with her and Doctor Michaels. She hoped he was well. It was all she could do for him right now.

"They evacuated is my guess," Ellie said. "This place could collapse at any time."

"You're a bundle of joy today," William said sourly.

"This way," she said.

Ellie led them to the armoury, and there were no further obstructions. She claimed a rifle first, and found something to carry extra magazines and power cells in. The others buckled on holsters for their pistols before taking and loading a rifle each from the racks on the walls. Ellie loaded her grenade launcher, and urged the others to do the same with theirs.

"Ready?" she said.

Everyone nodded and they moved out.

They made good progress and weren't blocked on their way to the emergency stairs. The walls were cracked and the ceilings fallen in a few places, but none of it slowed them. They left the worst damage behind them, and met no one on the way.

They heard rather than saw the first signs of battle. The sound of prolonged pulser fire punctuated with the crump-crump of grenades being deployed. Ellie wanted to make William hide, but she'd be wasting her breath if she tried.

William checked his pistol and holstered it before hefting his rifle again. "Now we know where everyone went," he said.

Sir Harry nodded, firming his grip on his rifle. "My men will hold them, Sire. They'll die before letting you fall."

William grimaced.

Ellie beckoned Wolfe aside. "You stick with the king no matter the provocation. No matter what he orders. You. Don't. Leave. Him. Are we clear?"

"Crystal," Wolfe growled. "And Sir Harry?"

"He's a big boy. Let him get killed if he wants to fight. Stay with William no matter what. Knock him out if need be."

Wolfe regarded her doubtfully.

Ellie addressed William. "Hold back a little, Sire. Let me recon the situation."

William nodded.

Ellie shoved the door open and stepped into chaos.

The castle was in ruins as expected. Sir Harry's men were hunkered down using the rubble and broken walls to snipe at the enemy. Fires still burned, but no one cared. They were too busy killing Merki, and dying in their turn.

Ellie cleared the door and slammed it behind her to prevent William from following. She had no confidence in Wolfe deterring wrong thinking. The king was just as impulsive as Nicky had been. If he saw her fall, he might charge to the rescue.

A single sweep of her sensors found targets aplenty. The Merkiaari troopers were firing on the remnants of Sir Harry's men, and keeping their heads down. There were maybe a few hundred men and women left alive using the castle's ruins for cover. The din of battle and the screams of the dying filled the air. Pulser blasts crossed the courtyard back and forth. AARs thudded, grenades detonated, and RPGs were deployed as the defenders desperately fought for their lives.

Ellie added her fire to theirs.

Merkiaari died.

Humans died.

By the score.

The Merki were on foot. Probably the only reason there were any defenders left alive. Ellie poured fire into them, and emptied her grenade launcher at them as she advanced. She dropped her rifle when it ran dry, not wanting to waste time reloading, and went Reaper on their asses.

Ellie deployed her rocket launchers, and advanced again, firing as she moved. Her targeting reticule danced from target to target as she nailed each one. Her rocket icons turned red as ammo dwindled, but she maintained rapid fire until they both ran dry. No time to reload. She deployed her gatling cannons and hosed the Merki where they sniped at her people.

Ellie heard cheers as she advanced into the open, but she didn't have time to discover why. She hoped it wasn't the king making his appearance already. She'd skin Wolfe alive if he'd let William join this mess.

She staggered as she took a hit to the chest. Her armour wasn't penetrated but she staggered back a few steps. Her gyros took over for the seconds it took to stabilise her. She let her body do what it had to, and returned fire.

Another hit, this time to her left shoulder. A gauss cannon round. The mass of the slug hammered into her. It could have taken her head clean off, but the angle was wrong. It spun her around, ruining her aim, and she hit the cobbles on her back.

Ellie's cybernetics whined and pushed her into a sitting position. Her target reticule found the gunner using a wrecked car as cover. She hosed him and blood sprayed. Another gauss slug hit her chest, and she was suddenly glaring up at a cloudy sky. Damage alerts were flashing on her HUD. Her cybernetics whined and she sat up like the machine she was.

The defenders cheered.

Ellie ignored them and sought more targets. She found what she needed and fired, but her ammo warning flashed for the cannon in her right arm. She didn't want to run it dry, so used her left. Armour piercing needles screamed, and the Merki troopers splashed away in a spray of gore.

More whining of cybernetics. Her gyros did their thing, and Ellie stood tall. More cheers from behind her made her look. William had arrived. She glared at Wolfe but he didn't see. He was adding his fire to William's and Sir Harry's attack.

Ellie ran for cover.

She ducked behind the car she'd targeted earlier. The ammo stores in her thighs popped open at need, and she took the time to reload all her weapons. She stowed her reloaded cannons for the moment, and used her vantage to rain destruction on the Merkiaari with her rocket launchers alone.

She checked, but Wolfe had the king under control. Both men were fighting but they had good cover. Sir Harry had advanced ahead of them to join his men and was directing concentrated fire. She went back to her own war.

Hit again. Right leg this time, but plasma only. Her nanocoat changed in a flash from its default gloss black into a mirror bright surface. A halo of light bloomed around her as her armour shrugged aside the hit. It didn't slow her.

She fired while on the move. Her HUD and targeting allowed her to take out multiple Merki at the same time. She chose what she thought of as easy-mode, and let her left arm handle targets within the left quadrant ahead of her. Her right arm was up and tracking Merki in the right quadrant.

She ignored anything behind her.

The Merkiaari retreated from her. She followed them out of the castle grounds and into the devastated town of Silver Bay. Their retrograde movement was obvious. Did they do that? Weren't they supposed to fight to the death? She preferred to kill them to the last trooper, but they weren't cooperating. She used her sensors to analyse their movement, and advanced to cut them off. She fired and manoeuvred, fired and manoeuvred, fired... and her weapons ran dry.

Awkward!

She dodged into cover and reloaded her cannons. She ignored the incoming fire kicking up debris to ring off her armour. An occasional glancing blow rocked her body as she worked, but she locked her legs and her gyros compensated.

Reloaded now, she went full Zelda.

Oh. My. God! It felt great to let go. She opened up with everything. Rockets and gatling cannons together. The Merki went to ground in an effort to escape. Sir Harry's men cheered and took advantage. The suppressive nature of her fire let them advance unhindered. Sir Harry led from the front.

Ellie's HUD locked up one target after another, and she serviced them with extreme prejudice. Before she knew it, she was in amongst them. She should have found cover and used it to good effect as William was doing, but she didn't have time to consider the stupidity of her actions.

She was busy.

Slaughtering Nicky's killers. And it *was* a slaughter now.

The Merkiaari were being hit from both sides, and they didn't seem able to respond as a unit. Maybe she'd killed their officers or maybe they'd decided to go out fighting, but no matter the reason, they stopped retreating. That was kind of inconvenient, because Ellie was behind their lines and cut off.

And the hidden Merki grav sleds revealed themselves.

And they fired.

* * *

Part III

22 ~ Staying Human

Aboard Blood Drinker, At Station Keeping, Deep Space

Davey whimpered as he slowly rotated the obedience collar around his neck searching for a seam that wasn't there. It had to be there, but no matter how hard he looked he couldn't find it. It was perfect. Seamless. He'd been searching for... God, how long had it been now? Months since his capture, but he hadn't started looking back then. Much too risky. Touching an obedience collar was forbidden and risked punishment.

He hadn't been out of his cell since Valjoth tired of him. It was then he'd started his search. Weeks ago at least. He'd been alone with no distractions. The perfect time to escape. Surely the answer must be there. A way out of this hell. A way to survive and make Valjoth pay. He just needed one chance. Just one. He had to do it. There wasn't anyone else. He was the last Human. If not for his own reflection, he'd forget what they looked like.

Davey laughed, the sound broken and a little mad.

Mad? Was that what he was? It could be true, but madmen never knew that about themselves. That meant he wasn't mad, didn't it? Because he did know he was mad. But that didn't make any sense either. If he knew he was mad, it meant he wasn't. So he wasn't mad after all... but he could be because he'd decided he wasn't.

Screw it. He didn't care if he was or not. He just wanted the collar off, and a chance to kill Valjoth. Now *that* was a mad ambition for sure. He had no way to kill the creature, but that didn't matter. He'd try and die. A sort of victory. He'd be free then.

Davey peered myopically at the poor reflection of himself on the inside of his cell door. It shone dully. A lucky thing because the piss-poor reflection and his fingernails were all he had to work with. He rotated the collar endlessly with his left hand while dragging the thumbnail of his right over the rim, trying to find a seam that wasn't there. His neck was sore from friction and his eyes blurred with fatigue, but he didn't quit searching. One way or another, he would escape.

Davey no longer heard his whimpers. The sound had become part of him. He even heard it in his dreams. It was the background music to his life. It meant nothing. All that mattered was finding a weakness in the collar. A weakness it didn't have. There must be something. *Anything!* But there wasn't. The collar gleamed. Its perfection mocked him with its polished symmetry. He kept trying.

Davey peered more closely at his own reflection, and a boy-man looked back at him. His eyes were sunken and stared at him from dark pits in his head. Those were the eyes of a madman for sure. They didn't look real. The sight of his first beard made tears shimmer and fall. He was so gaunt from his hunger-strike that his own family wouldn't recognise him. He tried to see his dad in his own features, but to his horror he couldn't remember what he'd looked like!

"Oh God, why are you doing this to me?" Davey croaked as he fought to remember. "Please. Not this."

If he forgot all those who'd died, it would be like they

hadn't existed. He had to live. He had to escape to tell everyone what Valjoth had done. Davey had hated history at school. It had seemed a waste of time looking back at the past when there was so much to look forward to. Funny, because all he had was the past now.

He stopped twisting the collar, and hammered his forehead into the door.

Remember. Slam! Remember. Slam! Remember dammit! Slam slam slam!

And he did. The headache was worth the price of his memories. He remembered his dad, and he remembered the blood. He remembered the fighting, and the mad dash as the teachers evacuated the school. He remembered them shielding the students with their bodies and falling. He remembered the stampede. He remembered tripping and being buried in bleeding bodies. He remembered everything. He needed a compad and time to write it all down. He dared not forget. All he had now were his memories and vengeance.

Davey stared at the collar's reflection and went back to work. He was coming to believe it was all of one piece. There was no flaw to feel under his probing fingers, and nothing to find in its reflection. No hope. Nothing to find. No reason to keep trying except habit, and a desperate need to keep from dwelling upon the past.

How was it possible? It couldn't be one piece. There'd been an opening when Valjoth put it on him. It couldn't be solid, yet it undeniably was! It could strangle him, which meant it had the ability to shrink. Where did the excess metal go? It must go inside; where else? Therefore, it was hollow and must have a seam where it moved.

QED.

But there isn't a bloody seam!

There must be.

There isn't!

There must be.

There isn't!

There...

Slide the collar and blink hot tears away. Slide the collar and bite cracked lips. Slide the collar and blink hot tears away. Slide the collar and lick salty blood.

There must be a way out of the collar. How would he have made it? He would never! Pretend. Just pretend, Davey. How would he do it? He'd use a nano-printer for sure. There'd been one on campus for the engineering students. But Merkiaari didn't use nanotech. How could he reverse engineer anything without tools or nanotech? It was impossible. He'd been taught nothing was impossible. There were only problems with undiscovered solutions. The arrogance of that made him want to laugh or scream. Maybe both.

Davey had been bright at school. His teachers had said he could be chief engineer on a ship if he applied himself... he flinched away from those memories. He didn't want to remember the teachers. They'd abandoned him. They'd died and sent him to hell. Well, he hoped they felt bad. He would have wished them in hell for what they'd done to him, only they weren't here were they? How was that fair? He was in hell and they weren't.

Slide the collar and blink hot tears away. Slide the collar...

He wished he had a proper mirror, but the Merkiaari didn't use them. They had a view-screen in their cabins to display their image, or they used a tablet. Merkiaari tablets were basically compads with many of the same functions. Recording and displaying an image was the least of their abilities.

Slide the collar and close hot eyes. He needed to rest them for a while. Everything was turning blurry. He opened them after a ten count, and slid the collar...

"There must be a way," he croaked. "I'll find a way." He didn't believe it, but he had to pretend he wasn't insane to try. "I don't want to go mad, do I Dad? Not like gramps."

Maybe it was already too late. He could be loony already for all he knew. His grandpa was supposed to have been a little touched, but his dad had always smiled proudly when he said it, like it was a joke. Trying to kill Valjoth was nuts. He'd never get the chance. Besides, how long had it been since Valjoth had even taken an interest in him? Ages. The last time was just before the jump.

Davey glanced at the scratches next to the door. Each line represented a day, and there were hundreds. He had no way to count time accurately, but the lights dimmed at night. He'd decided that was close enough. Valjoth hadn't summoned him since the jump to... to wherever they were now. It must be somewhere in Human space. He thought so at least. Why else would Valjoth be hiding? Fleet would blow them out of space when they found them. That was why. He would die cheering when it happened. It would save him the trouble of trying to kill Valjoth.

Davey laughed tiredly. If Valjoth didn't summon him he couldn't kill him, but he needed the collar off as well; and that simply wasn't going to happen. Deep down he knew it. What was left? Suicide was always an option. He'd considered it a few times while writhing on the deck in agony. If he made Valjoth angry enough to forget himself, he might use the collar to kill him. Oh dear what a shame. With luck, he'd piss himself and leave a mess behind as well as his corpse.

When the cell door shot open it was hard to say who was more surprised. One moment a dull reflection confronted Davey, the next Valjoth did. Before Davey could even think of lunging, Valjoth reacted and Davey fell to the deck screaming in agony. He was on fire. The agony was so intense he expected to see flames and smell crisping flesh, but the collar didn't work that way. There wouldn't be any physical damage. It was for punishing or killing slaves not maiming them. The Merkiaari called it training. Not that it mattered what they called it.

Hours later, or maybe it only felt like hours, the pain ended. Davey lay on his back and stared dazedly at the overhead lights. They were still bright. Not hours then. Valjoth obviously didn't want to kill his pet. Too bad. Davey pulled hopelessly at the collar. It was still there. Still unbreakable. He rolled onto his side, and then onto his belly to push himself onto hands and knees. The next wave of agony sent him crashing back to the deck in convulsions. His face slammed repeatedly against the floor, and his nose sprayed blood.

Darkness rushed in and saved him from further damage.

Unconsciousness was a form of freedom, but it didn't last. It never did. He was in hell and what was hell for? Torment of course. He was doomed to return, and so he did. He pushed himself up to his knees and froze. Valjoth was standing in the corner watching him. He lunged, and crashed to the deck unable to breathe.

"Foolish," Valjoth growled. His English was poor but understandable. "Human pride. Not... not..." Valjoth didn't have the words. He adjusted the collar to let Davey breathe and continued using a mixture of Merki and pidgin English. "You have no strategy. Pride is not a substitute. I've given you nothing but time to learn your place, and yet I find this pathetic excuse for a servitor awaiting me. You do not wash, you do not eat, you do nothing but make tears. They are worthless and so are you. I should end you."

"*Do it!*" Davey screamed. "*Kill me! I swear I'll kill you if you don't!*"

The collar tightened again, and suddenly Davey couldn't catch his breath. It was hard to say how much of his words Valjoth understood. Davey suspected he understood English better than he spoke it. Usk didn't understand it at all, and used a servitor to translate for him. Valjoth rarely did that. It was a very small thing to base his suspicions on, but Davey had nothing better.

"A waste. I saved your life. You should thank me."

Davey would've liked to respond, but he was too busy suffocating. Coloured lights burst in his vision, and he began the journey toward oblivion again. Valjoth finally realised the problem and used his controller. Davey gasped and panted for breath. Blood pounded in his head, making his headache ten times worse.

"I. Rage. *You!*" Davey screamed.

Valjoth raised the controller again. He seemed determined to train his pet this time. He would normally have left before now. Davey grabbed the collar hopelessly trying to prevent it strangling him. It did no good, it never did, but this time as his vision burst with coloured lights he learned something important. As the collar tightened it grew in thickness beneath his desperate fingers. He felt it. It didn't slide. All his desperate searching for a weakness had been for nothing.

Full of despair, Davey blacked out.

* * *

23 ~ Learning Lessons

Aboard Blood Drinker, At Station Keeping, Deep Space

Davey awoke still on the floor. His blood had dried where he'd smeared it during his earlier convulsions. How long did blood take to dry? It didn't matter. Any guess he made wouldn't help his situation, and his torment wasn't over yet. One of the ship's servitors had joined them.

Davey glared at his audience, and Valjoth gnashed his fangs at him. He shivered at the sight. Merkiaari laughter was always at someone's expense and he was the target. Davey had to admit his act of rebellion had been pitiful. He pushed himself painfully up to his knees, and rubbed a hand over his face. Dry flakes of blood fell like black snow to the deck. He didn't try to stand. Less distance to fall next time.

Davey recognised the new visitor as a Lamarian. The creatures were tall and willowy, and only like Merkiaari or Humans in a general way. Two arms and legs, one head, two eyes and so on. They were very docile creatures and completely trusted by their masters. He despised them for that, but feared his reason for it. Would he become like them one day? Would he bow and say thank you for the abuse heaped upon him by Valjoth? Would he thank his master for allowing him to live as a servitor?

Davey feared the answer might be yes.

There were quite a few different kinds of alien aboard the ship; all of them collared servitors. Lamarians outnumbered all but the Merkiaari, but Davey didn't recognise this one. No reason he should. It wasn't as if he ever had visitors. He usually had other things on his mind during those rare times he'd attended Valjoth outside his cell.

The alien studied Davey in a glum silence. Glum because Lamarians had v-shaped faces caused by noses that were both wide and flat. Their expressions were very different to anything a Merki or Human could produce. They had bulbous eyes high on their heads, and tiny mouths that couldn't smile as far as Davey knew.

He'd never spoken with a Lamarian let alone touched one, but its mottled blue-grey skin looked glossy and tough under the lights. That seemed odd when he considered how slight they were. Willowy didn't begin to describe how weak they appeared in comparison to him or a Merkiaari. A feather could knock one over.

The Lamarian's onyx eyes watched him calmly from widely spaced bulges at the top of its v-shaped face. Davey wondered what it was thinking. Did it wonder the same about him? Probably. It must be curious. He was the only Human on the ship. A curiosity, like a zoo animal he supposed. He'd have dozens of questions in the Lamarian's position.

Valjoth said something that Davey didn't catch. The language wasn't Merkiaari or English. The servitor bowed and replied in the same language, the tones melodic, and handed Valjoth his controller.

Davey shook his head at the sight of such a precious thing given away so casually. What he wouldn't do to gain possession of the remote that controlled him. Stealing it was the next best solution to removing the collar clamped about his neck. He was starting to think it was the only solution.

Valjoth spoke and the Lamarian translated in perfect English. Davey was amazed. He'd never thought to hear such again.

"It's my honour to be Scholar Evrei Xabat. The Great Lord has assigned me to you as your tutor."

"*You can tell him to kiss my ass!*"

Evrei bowed, and did so.

Valjoth gnashed his fangs. He seemed to think it a fine joke. He brandished the controllers he held, and triggered one of them. Davey tensed expecting fiery agony, but it was Evrei who screeched and fell to the deck.

Davey lunged, trying to snatch the controllers out of Valjoth's clawed hands. He didn't get far. He collapsed in agony, and his screams joined Evrei's in a symphony of mutual torment. Tears of frustration blurred his vision. He stared at Evrei and felt something other than hate for the first time in too long. Pity and shame. Punishing *him* for his words was one thing, but tormenting Evrei was completely unjust.

"Stop!" Davey screamed, choking on the word. He'd never pleaded for anything from Valjoth before, but Evrei's pain was his fault. "*StoooOOOoop!*" he howled the Merkiaari word.

And Valjoth did.

Davey panted as his pain slowly ebbed from outraged nerve endings. Valjoth grinned and made weighing motions with the two controllers, one in each hand. God how he hated him. If there were a way to do it he'd kill Valjoth a hundred times over in the most painful way possible. He would bargain his life away for the chance.

Evrei staggered erect and bowed to Valjoth in apology.

Watching his humiliation made Davey sick. His rage peaked until he shook with it, or maybe it was shock. The collars inflicted unimaginable agony. He didn't have to imagine unfortunately. He'd been subject to Valjoth's use of it many times. It felt like being submerged in liquid fire.

"The Great Lord bids me inform you he'll no longer accept noncompliance."

Davey shakily rose to his feet, and lunged again. If he could just get his hands on the controllers... he didn't make it two metres. The collar clamped down so hard, Davey felt sure it would sever his neck. He crashed to the deck, and listened to Evrei screaming.

This time Davey was unable to plead for mercy. He could barely breathe.

The screaming finally subsided, and Valjoth reset Davey's controller. Evrei climbed back to his feet. He performed his little bow again, shakily this time, and listened as Valjoth addressed him. Davey didn't feel like getting up. His fury had exhausted him. It was easier to lay still and accept whatever came next.

"The Great Lord bids me inform you that resistance is futile. He judges it the same as noncompliance. It *will* be punished accordingly."

Valjoth said something else.

"The Great Lord bids me say—"

"*He's not a great lord!* He's a mass murderer!"

Evrei translated and Valjoth responded.

"The Great Lord orders you to rise and face him like a sentient being, and stop acting like a... like... apologies. There is no Human word applicable. Slimy insect is closest."

Davey snorted. "The word you probably need is slug."

Evrei bowed. "Gratitude."

Valjoth barked an order.

"The Great Lord insists you rise and face him immediately. Noncompliance will—"

"Result in punishment. Yeah I heard the first time."

Davey struggled to his feet.

Evrei screamed and fell to the deck writhing in agony.

Davey took half a step, but froze. Valjoth was watching him intently. He wasn't paying attention to Evrei's convulsions.

Davey tried not to show his anger. "Please. Please stop," he said, forcing himself to stay calm. God how he wanted to gut Valjoth where he stood. "Please. Great. Lord," he forced the words past his lips. "Evrei is blameless."

Valjoth raised the controllers. Davey tensed expecting pain, but Evrei's screams diminished to whimpers, and then groans of pleasure as Valjoth reversed the torment.

Davey closed his eyes. He didn't want to see the servitor's degradation, but the moment he blocked the sight the screaming began again. His eyes snapped open and Evrei's screams turned to groans of pleasure.

Davey glared his hate at Valjoth, but kept his peace. He wasn't a fool. Evrei said he was his tutor. He'd assumed Evrei would teach him the Merkiaari language or something, but it obviously meant more than that. Evrei was a hostage. He'd betrayed himself. He shouldn't have shown pity.

Evrei finally quieted and regained his footing. Valjoth addressed him, and again the servitor bowed as if the abuse meant nothing. Just another day on the job.

Davey felt sick. He'd rather die than live like that.

Valjoth jabbered away and Evrei translated.

"The Great Lord finds you entertaining and is pleased you've finally responded to your training. He doesn't want to terminate you. He bids me inform you that you must use the cleanser daily and eat your meals. Noncompliance will be punished. Your lessons begin after the next sleep cycle. I am to teach you how to serve the ship and our lord. Unsatisfactory effort or results will—"

"Be punished," Davey said glumly. "I get it. Why do you do his bidding? Don't you hate him?"

"Hatred is irrelevant."

"That wasn't a no. You must hate the Merki as much as I do."

"Irrelevant."

Valjoth barked something and headed for the door.

"The Great Lord has ordered me to report to him daily. Use the cleanser now and change your clothes. Eat. I will return to begin your lessons. Non—"

"I heard the first time. You don't need to keep repeating yourself."

Evrei bobbed a bow. "Gratitude, but I do not wish to be punished."

That made Davey feel worse. He didn't want to be tied to this alien, but what he wanted didn't matter. It hadn't mattered for a long time.

"I will comply," Davey said grimly.

"Gratitude," Evrei said and left the cell.

Davey approached the door and it shot open. It wasn't locked! Evrei had forgotten to lock him in! He hesitated. It had to be a test. A trap. Didn't it? He poked his head out of his cell and looked both ways. No guards. No *obvious* guards. He ducked back inside frowning. Valjoth was a tricky one. He was daring him to break the rules. He had to be watching him somehow.

Davey stripped and fed his soiled clothes into the slot in the wall. A moment later a fresh garment arrived. He threw it on the bed and stepped into the cleanser to wash for the first time in weeks. He revelled in the feeling and hated himself for it. He was following orders. It should make him angry not happy.

Davey dried himself after a long shower. The Merkiaari used warm air blowers instead of towels because of their fur. It worked just as well for him, but it did whip his overly long hair about his head, and he didn't have a brush or any way to tidy it. He would cut it if he could, but doubted he'd be trusted with a knife.

Davey dressed himself and used the autochef. He didn't know what the Merkiaari called them, but the food it dispensed was edible. It had made him sick the first few times he'd eaten it, but that was months ago. He'd become accustomed to it long before he'd gone on his useless hunger strike.

He was still eating when Evrei returned carrying a few Merki computer tablets. Davey pretended disinterest as he ate. His stomach had shrunk over the past two weeks. He couldn't finish. Rather than force it and make himself ill, he stood to dispose of the leftovers.

Meanwhile, Evrei took a seat on the bed to wait patiently.

Davey saw nothing for it. He'd have to play along and take his pat on the head. He'd learn what Evrei had to teach, and he'd find a weapon, and when the time came he'd fillet Valjoth like a fish. He dumped his tray in the autochef and took a seat.

Evrei handed him one of the tablets. "We will begin by reading a simple text. The Merkiaari tongue is based upon old Kiar, as is their written language. Here you see the alphabet. It consists of seventy-four letters and twelve independent special-use words. Old Kiar is written thus..."

* * *

24 ~ Eternal Friends

Bountiful Luck, approaching (427) Hoskin, Argo System

Captain Burton thumped the droid on the bucket of bolts she called a head. "Get your noggin out of the net, Hannah, and help me here!"

The droid glared, but then, she always did. She didn't have a face and eyelids. Her eye assemblies had failed years back, and he'd made do with some cheap replacements. They were too big for her head. The ship always came first on shopping trips, and parts for Hannah's model were hard to find.

"You awake now?" he said, as he headed for the vac-suit locker.

Hannah swivelled the pilot's couch to follow his movement. "This unit is incapable of sleep. If you're referring to my current status, I can report that my power cell is at 83% of capacity."

"It always is," Burton muttered. She was on charge all the time; she needed a new power converter. "I wasn't asking."

"How may I serve you today, Captain?"

That form of request was a holdover from her days as a

bank clerk. She didn't use it often anymore. He'd put a lot of time into upgrading her software, and one of those was an addition to her vocabulary module. She could do a hell of a lot more than give good backtalk these days. She could pilot the ship, make basic meals, and even join him on EVA.

Hannah and he were a team. All of her mods let them work together in the black for longer. She was the perfect partner. She didn't eat, sleep, or breathe, and that meant they didn't need to resupply as often as other independents.

Amalgamated Mining, the only deal in town willing to buy from the smaller outfits, turned a blind eye toward him flying solo. Hannah didn't count as crew, except to him. They cared about the quality of the ore he brought back, not the safety regs he pretty much ignored.

The other independents thought him crazy for cutting so many corners. Out alone in the black too long, they said. Maybe so, but he owned his ship, while they were still in hock to various banks. And how did he manage that? By running solo, that's how.

"Overheads, Hannah," he said over his shoulder, and dragged the suit out of the locker. "Keep 'em low. Remember that."

"Keep 'em low, aye," Hannah replied. "Like your balls, Captain."

Burton snickered. He still got off on her doing that. He'd programmed her to be his helmswoman, and act just like Zelda's pilot on her show. Shortcut, Zelda's pilot, had a mouth on her, but she was great. She always had Zelda's back when things got sticky, and that's what he needed from his Hannah.

Dependability.

He had the definitive collection of Zelda and the Spaceways in his apartment. Every show, and every sensim; all of them glorious full-sensory simulations. He had his own rig, and spent a lot of time with Zelda on her ship. He liked

Shortcut's character, because she loved Zelda as much as he did. Hannah was his version of her.

"Plot a course, and park us within EVA range of Four-Two-Seven Hoskin."

"Aye, aye," Hannah said, and went to work. "Our ETA is approximately six minutes, Captain."

"Very good. Inform me upon arrival."

"Aye, aye, Captain Bligh."

Burton grinned.

She sometimes shortened *Bountiful Luck's* name to the *Bounty* too. He really did love his Hannah. He didn't care she was bug-ugly; her face was anyway. The rest of her wasn't bad to look at, but he'd never been into the mech sex scene. Some of the other guys would've taken a shot at her despite her face, but he'd kill them if they tried. Hannah was his buddy; more than that, she was crew and closer to him than his sister. Anyone interfering with his girl, would be in for a world of hurt.

No messing.

The rare M-Type asteroid they were heading for, (427) Hoskin, was too distant from Argo to tap easily. No one liked long distance runs. Fuel cost credits, and the smelters were all in orbit of Argo. Only Hannah and he could make it work.

Overheads again.

(427) Hoskin was a virgin 'roid, and all the more desirable for it. There should be plenty of easily obtainable ore, just lying about on its surface as rubble. After collecting all that, he'd get down to the serious business of getting rich again.

He'd been rich in the past, and all in all, he preferred it over his current penury. He fully expected a good haul of platinum group metals this trip, but cobaltite was his holy grail. Cobalt was always in high demand, but prices were through the roof this quarter. War did have its uses.

He suited up while Hannah parked the ship within reach of his prize. He had a good feeling about this run. If he could scrape up a good haul from the surface, he could buy the equipment he'd need to hollow the guts out of Hoskin. It would pay for a new power cell for Hannah. Hell, he'd buy her a face and the eyes to go with it, if she wanted. He'd have so much credit with the bank, he'd able to import everything she needed brand new from the core.

"Hey Hannah. How'd you like a new paint job? You could use a tan. Know what I'm saying?"

Hannah glared at him, of course. "How about I slice your dick off, Captain?"

Burton snickered. He remembered adding that one to her vocabulary. He wondered why she'd chosen it this time, not that she'd know if he asked her. The algorithm in her noggin controlled her responses. They could be uncanny sometimes.

"No seriously."

"I am serious. Come near me with paint, and I'll cut you bad."

Burton blinked. "Err... okay. I just thought we should match. You are a bit, well, pale. I mean I'm okay with it. God knows I could use some work too at my age. A tuck here or there, maybe some bleaching. I wouldn't want to be as white as you, but well... no offence."

"We're in range for EVA, Captain. Thrusters at station keeping."

Bloody hell, the others were right. He was talking to a droid like a real woman. He really was cracking up. Hannah cocked her head. Burton could have sworn she was thinking his offer over. It was hard to tell. Her glares never changed.

"Are you okay?"

"How may I serve you today, Captain?"

Burton sighed, and then laughed at himself. She'd spooked him there. For a minute, he'd thought... well, never mind what he'd thought.

"You can serve me by suiting up! You can't expect me to do all the work."

"Fuck you. I'm not the one who spends half the time sleeping."

"That's more like it. Tell it to me straight, Hannah my girl."

"Aye, aye, Captain Bligh, sir. Suiting up on the double, sir."

Burton laughed, all was right with his little world again.

He helped her disconnect from the charging station, and pull on her suit. She didn't need air to breathe, but she did need its environmental systems to maintain her core temperature. Exposure to cold would drain her power cell too fast. He double-checked all of her seals, and the suit's heater.

They entered the airlock together.

"You're driving," Burton said as the airlock pumped down to vacuum. He snapped one end of the tether to his suit, and the other to the cargo ring on hers. "No skylarking. This is serious. Your new eyes and face depend on it."

"Aye, aye, Captain. I want brown."

Before Burton could ask what she meant, the outer door opened, and she engaged her thrusters without warning.

"Bloody hell, woman! Warn me first!" he yelled as the tether snapped taught. He flew out of the airlock in her wake, and toward the wall of rock ahead. "I said no skylarking. That's a bloody order!"

"Aye, aye, Captain *Boooring*."

Okay, maybe her algos needed some work. It was funny in the ship, but not out here in the black. His breathing was loud in his ears, as he imagined what could go wrong. She could fly them face first into the mountain they were approaching. His hand wandered to the safety clip. He could cut her loose, and use his own thrusters.

Before he could give in to fear, Hannah used her thrusters to slow herself. Burton flew straight by. The tether sprang taught again, and jerked him around to face her. He couldn't see the 'roid they were speeding toward. Hannah began pulsing her thrusters in controlled bursts. They'd performed surveys like this hundreds of times. He'd always trusted her, but her strange reaction earlier had him spooked.

"And... touchdown. The crowd goes wild," Hannah said.

Burton felt the lightest of touches as his back brushed the rock. "Damn, you're good," he said, breathing a little fast from his adrenalin high.

"Too good for the likes of you, Captain."

Burton didn't laugh this time. "Maybe so, Hannah. Maybe so."

Hannah joined him a moment later on the surface to begin their survey. She held a sample bag open for him, as he chose various likely looking rocks to test when they got back to the ship. He could already tell Hoskin was a good rock—one that would fill his bank account.

"That will do. Let's check out the other side. You drive."

"Aye, aye, Captain Bligh."

He'd been dead on about Hoskin. There was plenty of loose material on the surface waiting to be swept up. He watched it passing beneath them as Hannah towed him up and over the top of the 'roid. All those credits, just lying there waiting for him, barely clinging to the surface. The tug of micro-gravity was all that held it there. No mass intensive mining machines were needed this time, but the next run would cost serious money. All that mass meant fuel, but the rubble this trip should cover his costs.

Speculate to accumulate should be his mantra. He'd always done things that way. He'd speculated there was money to earn at Hoskin, and was proven right. Phase-two of his comeback, the investment phase, would start once he off-loaded at the smelters, and went looking for proper automated mining machines.

A flash of light briefly lit the surface of the asteroid, before shadow claimed it again. He turned from side to side, trying to see what caused it, but the constant tension on the tether prevented him turning a full one-eighty.

"Hannah, there's something—" Burton began to say, but she applied her thrusters, and he sped past. "Dammit!"

Burton grunted, as the tether sprang taught and spun him around. He saw it then, a huge shadow occluding the stars. A vast ship. He swore as he imagined one of the bigger mining operations surveying 'roids on his new patch.

"Touchdown, and the crowd goes wild," Hannah said.

Burton barely felt Hoskin's micro-gravity taking charge of him. He stared at that huge shadow and realised the flash of light had been the *Bounty*. His ship. They'd killed his ship. The claim-jumping-bastards had blown away his ship without warning. They'd killed him and Hannah, without a word spoken. He stared at his doom, and suddenly knew. It wasn't a mining vessel. The silhouette was all wrong. He watched the ship fly sedately away, and saw hundreds more like it, hanging among the asteroids. Hundreds and hundreds of hidden warships. Merkiaari warships.

He shook off his shock to check his O^2 levels. He had just under five hours remaining, and nowhere to go. He turned to Hannah, and took the sample bag from her. It was just extra mass they didn't need. He shoved it away from them. Hannah watched it go in silence, her emotionless eyes glowing golden from the shadows within her helmet. He looked back at the Merkiaari ship. She had joined her murderous sisters now, and looked small with distance.

The Merkiaari didn't know he was here. They must have thought they'd killed all the nosy vermin. With nowhere for him to go they were right. They *had* killed him, but on a five-hour delay timer. He couldn't even take a piss.

Typical.

Face to face with Hannah, Burton tried to think of a way out, but there was nothing. He was going to die, and his girl would watch it happen in real time. Ah well. There were worse ways to go. He would suffocate when he depleted his O^2, but long before that he would turn off his CO^2 scrubber.

He'd just fall asleep, and not wake.

"I have a plan, Hannah. I have my way out. What about you, love? How's your power holding up?"

"I can report that my power cell is at 68% of capacity. I will enter power saving mode in approximately six hours."

"Okay. Six is good," he said. He wouldn't have to watch her die. He peered into her visor, and she glared back. "What did you mean back there when you said you like brown?"

"My new face, Captain. I'd like brown eyes."

Burton smiled. "You would, eh? How come?"

"Yours are brown, like your skin. I've decided you can paint me brown if you like."

God, she was so real. He'd really lost it when he ordered her to upload his library of Zelda and the Spaceways. She was such a great mimic.

"That's nice of you," he said.

"Don't let it go to your head, Captain. It doesn't mean I like you."

Burton snorted.

"We should head back to the ship now, Captain."

She didn't know. She had no concept of death, or of what was going to happen to Argo very soon. The Merkiaari weren't sightseeing.

"The ship is gone, Hannah. It's just us now."

"How will we get home?"

Burton sighed. "We'll stay here."

"Aye, aye, Captain Bligh."

He wished he could warn people, but his suit's radio was low powered. If he transmitted from here, the signal would be lost in the clutter, and besides that, it would be weak and take ages to reach anyone. Maybe if he could get out in the open, away from all the iron and nickel in the asteroids...

He frowned as a glimmer of an idea occurred. It probably

wouldn't work, but what else did he have to do? He'd need line of sight with one of the stations in orbit of Argo, and that was a problem. With the ship destroyed, he had to rely on the old mark-one eyeball to find one. Hannah might be better for that part.

"Fuck it," Burton said.

"You first, Captain," Hannah replied.

He snickered. "I love you, Hannah. Take me to Argo."

"My suit thrusters don't have the required range."

"That's okay. Go as fast as you can, and don't stop."

"Aye, aye, Captain Bligh," Hannah said and oriented herself away from Hoskin. "This is going to be one hell of a ride!"

Burton smiled. "You go girl."

The tether ran out of slack fast. Burton grunted as it yanked him away from the surface into the open. Hannah burned her thrusters at full power as ordered, choosing her path with care. It wouldn't do to meet a rock now. All too soon, her fuel ran out, and Burton took over. He should have cut her loose to extend his range, but he just couldn't do it. He burned past, and it was her turn to be cargo.

His thrusters ran out of fuel very quickly, leaving them on a ballistic course. It would take months for their bodies to cross the orbit of Argo, and he doubted anyone would notice. He didn't mind. He'd lived most of his life in the black, it was somehow fitting he spend eternity here too.

Burial in space wasn't so bad a fate.

Burton drew Hannah toward him, using the tether, and they clung together, visor to visor. He looked into her glaring eyes, and smiled. He imagined she smiled back. He wished he'd tried harder to find her a face.

"Mayday, mayday, mayday," Burton said, not taking his eyes from his only friend. "Merkiaari ships lurking near Four-Two-Seven Hoskin. My ship is destroyed, and I'm low on O^2. I'll transmit as long as I can on this channel. Mayday,

mayday, mayday."

He told Hannah to copy him, and they took turns transmitting the warning. She of course had her own versions, and Burton died laughing. Hannah clutched his dead body, and kept transmitting until her power ran out.

No one responded.

* * *

25 ~ News From The Front

In the Zone, Argo System

The drone burst back into n-space, and scanned its surroundings. Finding no immediate threat of collision, it searched local space for Merkiaari ships. Again, it found none, and deactivated the nuclear device built into its core. Finally, it analysed the system's primary, and the local stellar neighbourhood. Satisfied it had arrived in the correct system, and within a few tens of kilometres of its intended arrival point, it transmitted its calamitous message.

Fleet priority one.

The drone didn't care it was the only one to reach Argo, and it didn't know what its news from Faragut would mean to its creators. Satisfied it had fulfilled its task, it activated its beacon and went to sleep.

Government House, Argo

Admiral Gustav Fischer greeted the Governor's guests with a pleasant smile plastered upon his face, and even managed a polite word or two when they stopped their inane chatter for a second between breaths. God, he hated the schmoozing, but keeping his political masters happy was part of his job. He'd get it in the neck from the admiralty if he didn't do his part.

The credits must flow.

Powerful men like Governor Turnball controlled their planetary economies, or their taxation policies at least, and those funded things like the navy's ship building programmes. Keeping Turnball happy was a priority. So of course, he'd had to accept yet another pointless party invitation, when he'd much rather put his feet up and enjoy a good book.

During a lull in the meet and greet, he drank something that glowed blue, but tasted like fine whiskey, and watched the dancers. He wasn't alone for more than a few minutes before the next wave of rich civs approached him. He forced his features into a fake welcome smile, and awaited his fate.

He wasn't much for dancing, the political kind or the social kind, but when Commodore Robyn Medard asked, he could have kissed her. Anything to get away from more pointless pleasantries.

"Thanks for the rescue, Rob," he said as they took to the floor. "They make my face ache."

Rob snorted. "I saw them vectoring for an attack. You were about to give them a broadside. I could tell."

They joined the other couples whirling around the ballroom. He wasn't much of a dancer, but Rob made him look good. They drew eyes as the quick waltz ended, and they seamlessly flowed into a foxtrot. He hoped Rob didn't expect too much from him. He'd hated the classes on deportment and etiquette taught by the academy, and he only knew a couple of the archaic dances expected of him. The navy's officer and a gentleman thing had always felt a bit silly to him.

The music ended, and their audience quietly applauded their performance. Rob glowed. She really seemed to enjoy the dancing, or maybe it was the attention. In their dress whites, they stood out from the civilian crowd. Fischer wondered if she even owned a dress, let alone one of the nearly invisible gowns the rich ladies were wearing tonight.

"Is Raven here somewhere?" Fischer said, as they began a slower twirl around the floor. He had no doubt Rob's wife owned dozens of dresses in the latest outrageously expensive styles.

Her lips thinned. "We had words last night. We'll be dissolving our contract."

Fischer schooled his features to prevent a relieved smile forming. He'd seen this coming a light-year away. Raven had always been a goal-oriented woman, and Rob was just one of her many conquests. It surprised him they'd lasted this long.

"I'm sorry to hear that," Fischer said, but he wasn't really.

Not at all.

He'd never really liked Raven. He'd tolerated her, and liked how happy Rob had been while with her, but Raven didn't really see people. She saw conquests, and used them as stepping stones. Her marriage to Rob had given her access to the Governor's office here on Argo. As a matter of fact, she'd taken up a new position as Turnball's media consultant not long ago.

And now she wanted a divorce.

Funny how that worked.

It wouldn't surprise him if Raven hopped out of Rob's bed straight into Turnball's. She wouldn't let a little thing like gender preference slow her climb.

"Do you want to talk about it? We could leave early... please say yes."

Rob smirked. "Don't beg, Admiral. It's unbecoming of a Fleet Admiral."

"Leave rank at the door tonight. It's Gustav."

"I think I'll swear off relationships outside the service from now on."

"A bit drastic."

"I don't understand them. Civs I mean," Rob said. "I gave her everything she asked for, and suddenly *I'm* the one pulling away from *her?* I'm not the one who wants to dissolve our contract."

"Don't lump them all in with Raven. Do you trust me?"

"What sort of question is that? I trust you with my life. We all do."

He nodded. She meant everyone serving under him, but personal advice was a little different to trusting his orders in battle.

"I've dealt with people like Raven many times, and before you say it, not all were civs. They had things in common. They all lacked empathy. All of them were social climbers. And all of them were self-centred."

"Raven isn't like that," Rob protested.

"She is, but you're too close to her to see it. They're great actors."

"She loves me."

"If that were true we wouldn't be discussing this. Love isn't something that concerns them. They have to fake it, because love takes empathy."

The dance ended, and Rob led the way toward the bar set to one side. Drinks in hand, they watched the dancers.

"Raven used you to make contacts, and now she'll find someone here to reach the governor. Her strategy is plain to see."

Rob's lips thinned. "You're the better strategist, but I know her. Our breakup is my fault somehow."

"Don't do that!" Fischer snapped. "Don't make excuses for her. Just accept her for who she is, and move on. She can't change who she is, and you shouldn't try. It will only make you both unhappy."

Rob stared at him.

Fischer shrugged. "I never told you about my first wife."

"You said you let your contract run out."

"I married for love. She married for position, and Raven is just like her. Before you say you're sorry, don't bother. We hated each other in the end. It didn't take me long to figure out her plan, but by then we'd had the kids. We lived apart for most of that time."

"What happened to her?"

"She married higher up the food chain, but I had the last laugh. Her husband retired a commodore, and I was promoted to rear admiral that year. I skipped one rank."

Rob laughed. "I knew about the promotion. Your battle is required reading at the academy."

Fischer looked away from the worship in her eyes. The slaughter he'd perpetrated at Corvus had earned him a promotion and a fear of enclosed spaces. His bridge had been holed at the close of the action and he'd been trapped. Low on O^2 and near death from blood loss, the damage control party had cut him free barely in time. He was the only surviving bridge officer.

That battle gained him notoriety, but at the cost of his friends' lives. He'd come away with a promotion, a new command, a new leg, and a deep fear of it all happening again.

"... at least they're good for something," Rob was saying.

"Promotion will come. No need to slaughter innocents to gain it."

"They were hardly innocent!"

"I didn't mean the raiders. I meant their cargo."

Rob's face fell. "They wouldn't have blamed you. I'd rather be dead than a zombie."

Fischer grimaced. The term applied to victims of illegal mind wipes. He'd killed cargo-holds full of them when he took out the raider ships. Better off dead. Everyone said so at the time, but he wasn't sure. He would never forget the kids.

He closed his eyes and tried to shake off the horror of it.

Calling them zombies was a good name for them. Mind-wiped to a vegetative state, and then only given back enough personality to make them useful slaves, they would have vanished into obscurity. Men, women, and even children; all had uses on planets controlled by governments that rarely asked questions. Corporations paid taxes, and they needed cheap migrant labour. QED.

Fischer knew evil when he saw it. He'd confronted it many times over the years in the Border Zone. Humans and Merkiaari had a lot in common. Both species treated life as a commodity. At least the Merki didn't do it to their own people as far as he knew.

"Anyway, that's history. We were talking about you."

Rob opened her mouth to answer, but a chiming sound interrupted. She retrieved her wand from a pocket, and frowned as she read the message.

Fischer looked away to give her privacy. It was probably Raven. He hoped not, but he wouldn't put it past her to twist the knife. Another chime had him reaching into his own pocket. As he retrieved his wand he noticed some of the dancers pausing in their gyrations. All were in uniform, and all were digging in pockets. He hastily called up his messages.

Report to Sector HQ. Earliest possible.

Fischer looked up and saw a uniformed exodus. Everyone wearing uniform, no matter their service, was leaving. The music trailed off and mutters of concern arose. Jilted guests gathered around asking questions of each other. No one had any answers.

"I'm ordered back aboard *Triumphant* immediately," Rob said. "Funny that, aren't you my CO?"

Fischer raised a finger and used his wand to make a call, but the line was busy. "What the hell," he muttered. "I can't get through."

"Isn't that supposed to be impossible, Admiral?"

"I always thought so."

"Don't look now, but we have Turnball incoming."

Fischer grimaced. "Let's make a run for it. Consider that report-aboard order null until I say so."

"Aye, aye, Admiral. Where are we going?"

"Sector, where else?"

They pushed through the crowds, and made their way outside. They lost Governor Turnball in the crush, and hopped into the first taxi they saw.

"Admiralty Headquarters and don't spare the gees," Rob said.

"Right you are," the driver said, and the taxi went vertical to clear local traffic.

Fischer grunted as the acceleration shoved him into his seat. He stared out of his window and saw contrails forming as shuttles raced for orbit. He shivered. There were dozens leaving. All at once.

"Faster," he muttered. "Go faster. I'll pay your fines."

The driver nodded. The taxi's drive howled as he pushed the throttle to the floor. The city turned to a blur beneath them.

Sector HQ, Argo System

The news from Faragut hit Fischer and his staff like a lightning bolt. Despite all their careful planning for situations just like this, none of them had expected to use any of the scenarios they'd worked up this soon.

"Can we do it, Rob?" Fischer said, reading the data over her shoulder.

Rob nodded slowly, but she was frowning. Fischer wasn't surprised. There was nothing in Faragut's data dump worthy of a smile. The information currently displayed in the main holotank predicted they were in for a tough fight.

Rob was an excellent officer, and Fischer was the first to admit, his superior in tactics. He knew his strengths. They lay in the area of logistics and grand strategy. Luckily, he was a good judge of character and prided himself on his ability to delegate tasks to the right people. He'd spent years building 3rd Fleet and surrounding himself with talented officers.

Rob was his best super-dreadnought commander. That was why he'd chosen her ship, *ASN Triumphant*, as his flagship. It made her his exec in battle and set her above officers considered her superior in rank. Or it did while he lived. If he fell in battle her authority would pass to Admiral Haruki, and there was nothing he could do about it.

Admiral Miyamoto Haruki owed his rank to family connections and political shenanigans. Fischer liked him from a social standpoint. Miya could be charming, and he was an entertaining companion at the obligatory parties they often attended. He wasn't an incompetent officer, just a very conservative one. On any normal day Haruki was a good enough officer, but normal had just left town. Good enough was no such thing where the Merki were concerned.

"They have the advantage in tonnage," Fischer said.

"They usually do," Rob said. "We have more hulls but theirs are bigger. We'll need everyone for this. It's going to be bloody."

Fischer winced. Consolidating all the far flung units of 3rd Fleet would be unpopular. Fleet hated the First Space Lord's wide deployment plan, and Fischer was no different in that, but the civs loved it. He knew why; everyone in navy uniform did. It made the politicians and those they represented feel safe. Feeling safe and being safe weren't the same thing, but taking away their security blanket would frighten them. He couldn't help that.

"There's no choice," Fischer agreed. The Merki needed 3rd Fleet's maximum effort. Luckily, they'd prepared canned orders for this and many other scenarios. "Send the drones."

Rob nodded. She began the process by plugging her command wand into the board and keying in a security code.

"I never thought we'd need them this soon."

Fischer hadn't either. This situation was only one of many they'd planned for together. They hadn't known the size of the threat they'd face, but Faragut was a high value target. It wasn't the only one they had to protect. Not by a long stretch.

"The drones are entering foldspace as we speak, Admiral," Rob said formally for the record. "Might I suggest we grab a shuttle now?"

Fischer nodded. "I want us on our way outsystem ASAP, Commodore."

They hurried out.

* * *

26 ~ Enclave

Shan Enclave, New Hampshire, Earth

The White Mountains were a beautiful sight at any time, but today they failed to cheer Tei'Varyk. He contemplated a bright New Hampshire morning through the open sliding windows of his office, but the beauty had palled and he yearned for home. The enclave officially became part of Harmony when the Alliance Council ceded it to his people in perpetuity, but he missed the real thing. He wanted to go home, and he didn't care if it meant shirking his duty.

There.

That was the unthinkable truth he hid from everyone, even his mate, but Tarjei knew him too well to be fooled by his manufactured cheer. She knew he fretted about their cubs growing up on Earth, but how could he not? They'd been born on an alien world. Everything they'd experienced in their short lives was alien to their people, yet they knew it not. Their ignorance of the homeworld hurt his heart.

"The president and his mate will arrive at three local time, dinner is at seven," Kahn said.

Tei'Varyk flicked his ears to show he'd heard his aide, and

forced his thoughts back to duty. He stepped away from the window but tripped on the hem of his robe. It was too much on top of everything else. He snarled. In a fit of temper, he yanked it over his head.

Kahn thought it uproariously funny.

Tei'Varyk bundled the cloth into a ball and launched it like a torpedo. It struck Kahn in the face.

"That was beneath you," Kahn said, and retrieved the robe from the floor.

"Serves you right. I detest wearing that thing. Burn it or bury it. Do whatever you want with it! Just don't make me wear it."

"Walking around the enclave in your fur is fine, Tei. No one here minds, but the Humans expect you to wear it."

"I know, but they're suffocating me. I'm not an elder. I'm too young!"

"What do you want to wear? I'll fetch it for you."

"I want a pressure suit and a ship. I want my life back!"

Kahn remained wisely silent.

Tei'Varyk chuffed in frustration. Even if he asked to be replaced today the message would take seasons to reach Kajetan. Over an Earth orbit would pass before a replacement arrived, and that assumed her willingness to send one straight away. He was quite sure she wouldn't be.

Kahn was still waiting.

"I'll wear it for the Humans," Tei'Varyk said. "Dinner at seven. What else?"

"As I said your guests will arrive at three. I've rescheduled all your appointments from this afternoon to tomorrow, but there's a lot to do before we're done."

"What first?"

Kahn put aside the robe and reviewed his notes on a compad. "Sumitomo Space Industries. Our negotiations aren't going well. The price keeps going up, due they say, to increasing demand."

Tei'Varyk indicated a place to sit. Kahn chose the closest mat and settled himself at the conference table. Tei'Varyk joined him and took the compad to read.

Sumitomo owned the best civilian shipyard facilities in the Sol system, and produced the finest cargo ships available bar none. Producing the finest, and in the case of the Nova Class, largest ships of their type, meant Sumitomo could charge whatever it wished. Even so, Tei'Varyk didn't need the Harmonies to know Kazuo Tsokuda, Sumitomo's CEO, was up to something.

Demand for cargo ships had declined in part due to the Red One Alert. Portents of war did tend to suppress trade, and the economy was already suffering from what Humans called the jitters. The economy was heading for a downturn. Everyone knew it. Those in a position to pivot had already done so by redirecting their funds into more lethal investments such as Merki-killing drone technologies. The military industrial complex was the only beneficiary of war.

"What are our options?" Tei'Varyk said. "I know you have a plan."

"Did the Harmonies reveal that?"

"No, your past performance."

Kahn laughed. "You're too kind, but you're right, there is a plan. We should break off negotiations without warning or explanation. Right away."

"We should?"

"Yes. Kazuo believes we're desperate for those ships."

"He's right, we are."

"He is right," Kahn admitted. "Everyone knows we need them. He thinks he can get away with raising the price on the ignorant aliens."

Tei'Varyk laughed. "A false impression you reinforced no doubt."

Kahn flicked his ears in agreement. "It wasn't hard. A

few bad deals here, a few there, and the unscrupulous dealers started circling."

"Easy meat for our own hunters."

"Exactly. It worked out very well. The dishonest ones were exposed and we gained some friends at the same time. Some of the Humans took pity on our poor traders and secretly went out of their way to give honest advice—sometimes to their own detriment."

"Interesting," Tei'Varyk said. Weeding out dishonourable traders boded well for long term success. "You rewarded our new friends?"

"I licensed them to trade directly with Harmony. They're our preferred suppliers."

"Very good work. What of the ships we need?"

"There are two Nova Class cargo ships nearing completion at the yards. They were ordered by Busan Interstellar Inc., but the company can't afford the final payments. If it defaults, and my sources say it will, Busan loses its holding fee."

"How much?"

"Twenty-three billion, with another twelve billion to pay on completion."

Tei'Varyk's ears went back. "A lot of money to lose. You propose to lend Busan the credits and lease the ships from them?"

"A good idea, but no. The company isn't well run. I believe it will go out of business within five orbits. I propose we back Busan's purchase of those ships, and then buy them at a discount upon completion. Busan's directors will be grateful not to lose their deposit."

"And you think they'll agree?"

"I know they will, Tei. I broached the subject before bringing this to your attention. The loan to finish the ships will be contingent upon them selling the ships to us. We'll agree a fixed price before transferring the funds."

"Proceed along those lines," Tei'Varyk said. "What of

Sumitomo?"

"They don't have any orders pending for their Nova Class vessels. I bribed someone to copy their order book."

"I don't remember authorising such an action."

"I didn't ask," Kahn admitted. "I was very discreet."

"Be sure you remain so. It could tarnish our relations with the Humans."

"I'll be careful, but they don't seem inclined to grant us the same courtesy."

Tei'Varyk flicked his ears in agreement. "We're trading for our people's survival, while they're doing it for financial gain."

"After we take delivery of the ships, Sumitomo's directors will be more amenable to new clients. They'll not want empty slips at their yards. We should be able to strike a good deal on another pair of Novas."

"Proceed as you've outlined," Tei'Varyk said and handed the compad back. "What else do you have?"

"News from home."

"Go on."

"Kajetan made a broadcast to announce her decision to undergo nano-treatment."

"Thank the Harmonies. What changed her mind?"

"We have a copy of her broadcast, but she doesn't give a reason. It's easy to guess who persuaded her, if not exactly how."

"Oh?"

"Kajetan received the Blind Hunter shortly before the announcement and honoured her with a private audience. No one knows what was said, but later that day the Blind Hunter applied to join the warrior caste. As soon as the news broke, the-clan-that-is-not invited her to join its ranks as well. She accepted."

"You believe Tei'Shima and Kajetan made a bargain of some kind?"

"There's no doubt about that, Tei. Before letting the Human healers treat her, Kajetan ordered Tei'Shima and Kazim to Pandora. It's being explained away as a fact-finding mission, but everyone knows it's a pretext. Kajetan is vexed and wants them out of her sight. Despite that, Tei'Shima had the last laugh."

"How so?"

"She called upon the council to honour Shan obligations to the Alliance by sending warriors with her to Pandora."

Tei'Varyk laughed. "I like her already."

Kahn's ears waved jauntily. "She does sound fun. There was resistance to the idea from Tei in the other castes. The warriors were almost in open revolt until Tei'Shima invoked her status as the Blind Hunter and asked for volunteers. She was inundated with requests."

"She's the Blind Hunter. Of course my caste will follow where she leads. We owe her a blood debt."

"Exactly. Kajetan was out of contact receiving treatment at the time, and unable to intervene. Isn't it strange how she just happened to order Tei'Shima to Pandora before she left?"

Tei'Varyk laughed. It wasn't strange at all. "So our warriors are on their way to Pandora despite all the opposition."

"They'll be there by now. Drones are much slower than ships."

That was an inconvenient truth. News from home travelled slowly, and meant Kajetan would be safely back in control by now. Tei'Varyk wondered what her deal with the Blind Hunter entailed beyond the obvious, and whether the elders knew Kajetan had manoeuvred them into doing her bidding.

Again.

Kajetan always had the final word of decision, but by using the Blind Hunter to further her schemes she'd encroached on Tei business this time. That was fine by him. Tei'Varyk had become increasingly frustrated of late with members of his clan, but there was danger in bending tradition too far. The people loved Kajetan, but that didn't mean she could do no wrong; especially where the clan-that-is-not was concerned. She needed Tei cooperation to enact her policies. If they turned belligerent, she'd be powerless in all but name.

"Father!" Jafari cried as she raced into the room at top speed. "Mother says we have special visitors. Humanssss!"

"Careful!" Tei'Varyk said.

Jafari tried to slow, but she was moving too fast and slid along on the lacquered wood of the floor. Her little legs became a blur as she tried to stop by running in the opposite direction to her slide.

Kahn laughed at the sight.

It did look peculiar.

Tei'Varyk intercepted his cub before she could collide with the table. He scooped her up and threw her into the air in one motion before catching her little wriggling body.

"Again!" Jafari shouted.

"Please," Tei'Varyk scolded.

"Pleaaasssse!" Jafari yelled gleefully, already on her way up. She performed a neat back flip in the air and came down in the perfect pounce position.

"Claws in!" Tei'Varyk cried and winced in anticipation as he caught her.

"A born hunter that one," Kahn said.

"I is sorry, papa," Jafari said full of remorse. She released her claws from his hide and patted his arm. "Ouchy."

"Yes. Ouchy."

Kahn chuffed in amusement. "Enough of work. Time to play."

"Play! Play! Play!" Jafari yelled. She leapt out of his arms and headed for the door. "Chase me!"

"Yes, Tei. Chase her."

Tei'Varyk gave Kahn a mock glare, but he was more than ready to quit work for the day. He dropped to all fours and trotted away in pursuit. He was careful to let Jafari maintain a lead. She reached the foyer and let out a little roar. It was so adorable. He thought his heart would burst with pride when it brought her sibs in a rush to investigate.

Taryn led the war-band and signalled her sibs to surround their father. Jafari yelled gleefully, and took her place in the formation. She'd been the lure in Taryn's plan, and Tei'Varyk had fallen for the trap.

Tei'Varyk paused where he was, and watched his cubs circling their prey. Kaliq darted in first, and Tei'Varyk turned to face him. Kaliq was always the first. Too eager some might say, but as the only male in his war-band, he was the obvious choice. Males were slower, but generally a little larger. It made no difference today. The cubs were less than an orbit old and tiny in comparison to their father.

Tei'Varyk played his part of a cornered Shkai'ra, and let Kaliq distract him. His cub yipped in surprise when he realised his father was face on and scrambled out of range. Sensible. A real Shkai'ra would have formidable weapons. Face on they were deadly.

Kaliq evaded his father's make-believe spurs, and Kemina darted in. She thumped her little fists into Tei'Varyk's unprotected flanks, careful to keep her claws sheathed, and dashed clear as he spun to spear her with his pretend horns.

"Ah!" Tei'Varyk cried. "First blood to Kemina, but she missed my hamstring."

Taryn darted in and back out without striking to reclaim his attention. Her sibs struck from behind at the same moment. Jafari managed a creditable effort, and tagged his back thigh. In a real fight he'd be bleeding badly from that strike. It might even have been enough to bleed him out on a hunt. After Jafari, Kaliq came in again, followed by Verina this time. Verina struck true, but she owed the chance to Kaliq.

"Yes!" Tei'Varyk cried. "Well done, Kaliq!" His cub hadn't

attacked. He'd been purposefully slow in his retreat to give his sib her chance. "Excellent hit, Verina."

"Back away!" Taryn ordered and her sibs obeyed.

Tei'Varyk played his part. He staggered and let his legs collapse. Taryn struck the final blow to his throat. Her sibs let their war leader take the kill.

"Well done all of you," Tei'Varyk said. "You killed me in heroic manner, but I'm too stringy to eat. Your mother will still have to feed you."

"We win! We win! We win!" the cubs chanted and chased each other. They were still full of energy, and started wrestling.

"Lying about again?" Tarjei said as she watched the younglings at play. "Where's your robe?"

"I'm vanquished, not lying about."

"Go be vanquished outside. Take them to the meadow and keep them busy while I prepare for our visitors. Remember them?"

Tei'Varyk rose onto two legs. He bowed, just a little mockingly. "As you command, my love."

He rounded up his cubs, grabbing Jafari by the scruff to pull her off Kaliq whom she'd just succeeded in pinning to the floor.

"We have new orders from high command. To the meadow!" Tei'Varyk cried, and released Jafari to join her sibs.

Tarjei chuffed in amusement.

"Yay!" the younglings cried and headed for the exit in a rush.

* * *

27 ~ Honoured Guests

Shan Enclave, New Hampshire, Earth

At the appointed time Tei'Varyk donned his robe to greet his honoured guests. The cares of the day weren't forgotten, but he'd relegated them to the back of his mind as he waited with Tarjei on the steps of the residence.

Kahn stood to one side with the rest of the enclave's staff to watch proceedings and keep an eye on the cubs. The younglings were very excited. They'd met Humans before but they were still a novelty despite the secret service people and the Humans First protesters.

"*Hu-mans yes! Sha-an, no! Hu-mans yes! Sha-an, no!*" the protesters chanted from just beyond the gates. "*Hu-mans yes! Sha-an, no! Hu-mans yes! Sha-an, no!*"

Tarjei growled under her breath. "I thought we'd solved this."

"You did. These are outsiders here for the President's visit. They'll lose interest when he departs."

The local members of the Humans First Movement had lost their enthusiasm for protest when Tarjei invited them into the enclave to meet the cubs. The newsies were invited to record the meeting and the tour she'd arranged.

It had been an inspired idea that defused much of the protester's fear of their alien neighbours. Pictures of the cubs were still trending on Friendbook months after the tour. Thank the harmonies none of them were taken over dinner. Humans thought Shan cubs were cute and cuddly. Blood and raw meat probably wouldn't have worked as well.

Tei'Varyk's ears pricked as the chant changed to a new one.

"*Shan go home! Shan go home! Shan go home!*"

Not an option, though he'd personally be delighted to oblige them.

The gates swung open to allow the President's cavalcade to enter and the crowd surged. Their shouts grew louder and more heated, but they were held back by uniformed police and the secret service.

The third car in the five-strong convoy carried the President's party. It stopped at the bottom of the steps to allow President Dyachenko and his mate to exit.

Tei'Varyk and Tarjei stepped forward to greet them.

"Welcome to our home," Tei'Varyk said with a bow, though it felt like a fiction. It wasn't home. It was exile. A prison. "May you live in harmony."

President Dyachenko smiled and shook hands with Tei'Varyk and Tarjei in the Shan manner. Ludmilla did the same but added a hug for Tarjei. Shan thrived on touch. Hugging was a very Shan-like gesture. Tei'Varyk wouldn't have minded one, but Ludmilla limited herself to Tarjei.

"And these are the little ones I've read so much about," Ludmilla said beaming at the extremely well-behaved cubs. "They're *adooooorable*," she cooed. "You have to let me take them home with me, Tarjei."

Tarjei didn't attack. She knew Ludmilla didn't really mean it. "They're being extra good for you."

"I'm sure that can't be true. I bet they're always like this."

Kahn and the rest of the staff laughed. Shan younglings were inquisitive minds jammed into bodies bursting with energy. They had to be watched constantly because they grew so fast. A cub unable to walk upright could easily be sprinting on two legs a few cycles later. They could literally change overnight.

Ludmilla knelt there on the steps and held out her hands as if to scoop all the cubs into one big hug. Before Tei'Varyk could move they were on her in a pack.

Dyachenko laughed as five bundles of tail-wiggling joy mobbed his mate.

The President's detail didn't seem worried. More fool them. They hadn't seen the younglings hunting. Tarjei looked close to panic. If her cubs killed the President's mate there would be no end of trouble.

Kahn edged closer, and Tei'Varyk shot him a look. Be ready, that look said. Kahn flicked his ears. They'd had to deal with pack behaviour from the cubs before. Kahn would grab Taryn by the scruff to remove their leader, and Tei'Varyk would deal with Kaliq. Kaliq was a precocious trouble-maker. The others would calm down with their leader and second out of the way.

Ludmilla rose to her feet cradling Jafari in her arms. She buried her face in the cub's pelt as if scent marking her like a Shan. Jafari was a good choice. She had the sweetest temperament. It was too early to say for sure but Tei'Varyk thought she might become a healer come her choosing time.

Tei'Varyk introduced Kahn and the staff to his guests before ushering everyone into the residence. Jafari's sibs swirled around Ludmilla's feet begging for a ride.

Tarjei hovered close in case Ludmilla tripped over them.

"I'm sorry about the trouble at the gate," Dyachenko said as they walked. "I could talk to the governor for you."

"It's fine. I'm sure they'll be gone tomorrow. They're harmless."

"Annoying though."

"That is a truth. I'm sure there are similar protests outside the embassies in Yangsho. There will be shouting about tailless interlopers or tradition being upset."

"You think so?"

"Probably nothing so overt, but there will be mutterings in the clan and caste meetings. No one likes change. It will all settle down when people begin experiencing the benefits."

Kahn dismissed the staff back to their duties, and Dyachenko's detail took guard positions.

Tarjei directed the chaos into one of the rooms with the best views. Like Tei'Varyk's office this one had a sliding glass wall that allowed access to the grounds. The room was a good choice, especially if they wanted the cubs to run off some of their excitement.

Ludmilla murmured approvingly and headed into the gardens trailed by the cubs. Tarjei darted a desperate look at Tei'Varyk and followed her out, but he remained behind with Dyachenko to watch. Ludmilla put Jafari down and picked up Taryn for her ride. Her sibs started wrestling for the right to be next.

Dyachenko laughed at the sight. "Things have been good for you?"

Tei'Varyk indicated places to sit. "All is well here. Tarjei is recovered and the cubs are in good health."

"But?" Dyachenko said choosing one of the mats, and not a chair.

Tei'Varyk appreciated the courtesy. He took a place next to him to watch Ludmilla playing with the cubs. Tarjei had insisted on buying chairs and tables to accommodate Human guests, but so far all had followed Shan customs out of respect for their home. It was much appreciated.

"I miss Harmony," Tei'Varyk admitted reluctantly. "My cubs are growing quickly. They'll soon be strangers there."

"Children do grow so fast," Dyachenko said. "Mine have

their own lives and families now, but I know what you're feeling."

"Forgive me but that isn't possible," Tei'Varyk said. "Shan cubs are adult in less than half the time a Human child needs. Seven orbits from now my cubs will be choosing their paths in life. They cannot do that here."

Dyachenko nodded. "I did wonder about your people's integration when you joined the Alliance."

"The colony on Snakeholme is the prototype of what I think is the answer."

"I hope you're keeping knowledge of that quiet."

Tei'Varyk flicked his ears. "We aren't spreading the news, but it isn't a secret back home."

"That worries me. Burgton won't react well when a ship full of newsies arrives in his system. I dread the day it happens."

Tei'Varyk flicked his ears and nodded. "Transplanting a piece of Harmony there complete with all the clans, the castes, and the traditions has made it possible for our young to thrive."

Dyachenko nodded. "You're thinking of expanding the enclave here along the same lines?"

Tei'Varyk wasn't thinking of the enclave. He was yearning for home, but it wasn't something he could articulate to his host world's president. Instead he spoke in general terms.

"My people will colonise worlds of their own one day, and they'll import our culture in its entirety. The Great Harmony will become a reality at that point. Cubs born on one world will find themselves at home on any of the Shan worlds, just as Humans can find places and live happily on any Alliance world."

"That doesn't work perfectly in reality, or it hasn't yet."

"That is a truth, but Human laws and customs only differ in small ways from planet to planet. Shan ways are entirely separate. Without the Harmonies and the teachings of our ancestors we would cease to be Shan."

"You're saying we can never fully integrate? Your Great Harmony will be a separate Alliance in all but name."

"An allied Alliance perhaps," Tei'Varyk agreed. "I do think enclaves on Alliance worlds could work, but they would need to be large like the colony on Snakeholme."

"You're saying it won't happen quickly."

"It can't. The enclave here will be the only one like it for many orbits... *years*. My cubs will be the only ones seen on Earth for a long time. That hurts them in ways they haven't discovered yet."

"Have you asked to be recalled?"

"No," Tei'Varyk said. That was true, but he wished to very much.

"Perhaps you should, or request the enclave be expanded to colony size."

"Would the Council look with favour on such a proposal?"

"Well I would. I can't speak for everyone but I can't see why anyone would oppose it."

"The Humans First Movement would not be happy."

Dyachenko grinned. "I think they'd be shouted down by all the people sharing pictures of Shan cubs on Friendbook."

Tei'Varyk laughed.

"Seriously. I've seen protest groups like them come and go over the years. HFM are a fringe group. They won't last the year."

"I'll think on it. A second colony so soon might not be possible. Kajetan doesn't lead our people unopposed—"

Tei'Varyk looked up to see Kahn entering the room. The Harmonies revealed his agitation.

"Tei, Mister President. I think you need to see this. Something's happening in New Washington."

They rose and followed Kahn into Tei'Varyk's office. The big wall screen was on and displaying a news report. A banner scrolled along the bottom of the screen.

... Vote of no confidence in President Dyachenko passed ... Government in crisis ... Faragut fallen to the Merkiaari ...

"My god," Dyachenko said. "Faragut fallen. I need to get back to Washington."

"What does this mean?" Tei'Varyk said. "No confidence in what?"

"Me as president of the Alliance. They want me out."

"Can they do that? I didn't vote."

"Technically yes. It needs 66% of the chamber to propose and vote for it. They ambushed me. They knew I'd be here when they made the motion. I could've blocked it if I'd been there. The war gives me veto powers."

"Can you overturn the vote?" Kahn said.

"Not after the fact."

Tei'Varyk struggled with the concept. A vote of no confidence was very un-Shan in concept. Kajetan led their people for life and couldn't be removed by anything short of death. Was Dyachenko even the president anymore? If he wasn't, who was?

"Explain this to me. Are you still president?"

Dyachenko grimaced. "A vote of no confidence isn't like impeaching me. I'm still president, but I must call an election despite the Red One. With the war on, the normal election cycle has been in abeyance. If not for the Merkiaari we would've had one last year."

Tei'Varyk flicked his ears feeling better about it. "Then nothing has changed. You're still in charge."

"Everything has changed. I can't make any new policy decisions until after the election and there's no guarantee I'll win this time."

"Then we must ensure you win," Kahn said. "Surely?"

"It's not that easy," Dyachenko said sweeping a hand through his hair in agitation. "Elections can take months and

Faragut has fallen. We need to react quickly, but we can't. My government is paralysed until after the next president is sworn in."

Tei'Varyk's ears flattened. "The Fleet will respond?"

"Without my order you mean? Yes of course. There are standing orders and contingencies for that. Admiral Rawlins will carry on without me."

"That's reassuring," Kahn said. "How can we help?"

"There's nothing. We call this sort of thing a constitutional crisis. Everything else stops until it's resolved."

Tei'Varyk turned off the screen. There was nothing new being aired. They went back to the other room to find Ludmilla and Tarjei still playing. Nothing had changed for them.

"I need to catch a flight back to Washington, Tei. Can I give you a lift?"

Tei'Varyk flicked his ears and added a nod. "I'll vote for you."

Dyachenko nodded his thanks. "It won't help. They needed 66% to pass a vote of no confidence. What makes you think they'll suddenly change their minds and vote for me?"

Tei'Varyk stared wordlessly at his friend. In the Harmonies Dyachenko was already defeated. Tei'Varyk shivered at the realisation. He turned to watch his cubs at play and wondered what was to become of them.

"I'm finished," Dyachenko muttered.

* * *

28 ~ Damaged Goods

Forward Operating Base Hamilton, San Luis, 9AST

Fire. The dream always began with the memory of fire. Eric stood atop the heap of rubble, and marvelled as the sky burned. Some trick of atmospherics had turned the clouds into a mirror, to reflect the burning city below.

"Beautiful," he whispered.

"If you say so," Stone said sourly. "The general did say he'd light a fire on San Luis. He kept his word."

Eric nodded. Burgton had promised he would build a bonfire, and pile the Merkiaari on top for what they'd done here. San Luis was Burgton's homeworld. It was also Eric's. He'd lived not too far from here as a child; that, and tomorrow's mission, was very much on his mind. Operation Clean House was the prelude to Burgton's end game for the San Luis campaign. This was his last chance to go home.

"I have to go, Ken."

"Want some company?"

He shook his head. "I think I can handle this one alone."

"AWOL is more my style than yours, Bro."

"No worries there. I'll be back before the assault none the

wiser. Run some interference for me?"

"You need to ask?"

"Thanks."

Ken headed back to find a meal and some rest, while Eric watched the city burn in the distance.

The regiment had stood down to rest and prepare, but the perimeter was still heavily guarded by Alliance Army and Marines. Both forces were on planet in large numbers. They would join the main assault in the morning.

Eric watched the army's sentries, and the mech equipped Marines, using his sensors set for a wide security scan. The mech patrols owned the bomb-blasted streets, but they remained vigilant. Stray Merkiaari weren't the only danger here. Looters, so desperate they'd kill their own kind to steal a weapon or ration pack, were still a danger. Some of those crazy sons-a-bitches had tried to eat him last week. No joke. They did eat each other if they couldn't find anything else.

He concentrated upon the perimeter guards, looking for an easy exit he could use. The army had been tasked with locking down the FOB. No one in or out until after the assault kicked off. It was overkill. It wasn't as if anyone would leak information to the Merki.

Eric plotted a route, and slipped silently away. He wasn't detected, and didn't blame the sentries for the ease of his escape; they were watching for Merki or crazy cannibals, not a lone viper.

A few hours and a marathon later, he was home; what was left of it. There wasn't much. He hadn't expected there would be. He'd seen fighting on San Luis, and most of the population centres were ruins, so he'd known what to expect.

Greenville was no different to other towns he'd fought over; better in some ways. Cleaner. The fighting had ended here long before he hit the LZ. The stink of death, and the horrors he'd seen, weren't evident here. Time and nature had cleaned up the stupidity of war. He preferred to think that way, and not imagine the cannibal gangs doing it. They probably had. There were no bones. No dogs, cats, Merkiaari... or Human. The town had been picked clean.

Greenville was a small town; a suburb of the much larger Hamilton really. He'd been born and raised here. He remembered how quiet it had been with a feeling of reverence now, but he'd hated it as a boy. No action, he would have said to friends. These days, no action meant death. Only the dead knew peace.

Oh God, he missed peace.

War was never quiet, and his life was war. He inhaled it like oxygen, and exhaled violence—even in dreams. Only the little death gave him the peace and quiet he craved, but it never lasted. He always survived. Ready or not, and it was always not, he came back for more.

Always.

Eric circled the house, keeping to the shadows, using the ruins as cover. His training never failed him. His programming he liked to say. He'd fought so many battles now, he could perform most tasks using his version of auto-pilot. Need Objective A scouted? Select Pattern B, and away he went like a good little droid.

All is programming.

His father had called him something similar once. Eric fought the memory back down. His father hadn't wanted him to leave San Luis to fight for strangers. He'd been horrified when he heard Eric had volunteered to be a good little government robot.

"I'm going where I'm needed, Dad," Eric had said back then.

"Your family needs you here. This is your home. Fight here if you must fight."

His father's words turned out to be prophetic. He *had* left, he *had* become a government robot—literally. Going where he was told, killing what he was told, but here he was, back where he started. Fighting for his homeworld. Too late. His San Luis was lost the moment the Merkiaari attacked the first time. The Alliance was only here out of stubbornness now, and because of a promise Burgton had made. Eric had been there when the general uttered his oft quoted words.

"I'll make San Luis into a charnel house," Burgton said that day, his face devoid of emotion, but with eyes glittering with hatred. *"A Merkiaari's vision of hell. I'll turn it into a beacon for all to see. A bonfire. I'll pile the Merki on top, and watch them burn. In their millions, gentlemen. In their millions."*

Burgton was well on his way to doing it. Millions of dead Merki all over the planet, proved something the regiment had always known. When General Burgton said something, it happened one way or another.

Eric tried to keep his mind focused on what he was doing, not on what he feared he'd find. His sensors needed no guidance from him. He left them trawling for threat, and listened to war's background music—the distant sound of artillery.

His face was devoid of emotion as he surveyed the ruin of his family home. The fighting had left some neighbourhoods untouched, but not this one. The house was only partially intact. The first wave of Merki passing through Greenville had done a lot of damage, and the counter-attack still more. The second and third Merki waves had bypassed the town in favour of attacking other population centres. A lucky thing. He doubted anything would've been left for him to find if they hadn't.

TRS was on high alert; it always was when active, but although his targeting reticule danced and spun across his vision seeking targets, it found none. He checked his motion sensors briefly, but they came up empty as well. Finally, he switched to infra, but the site was cold. The fire had burned out long ago, and infra reported no life signs.

His family would've evacced long ago, but hopefully they'd left him a clue where to contact them. He hoped so, because all semblance of government had long since collapsed. There were no aid stations or agencies to query. Refugees had scattered in all directions, most running into the wilderness.

For completeness, he scanned the EM spectrum before entering the house, but his sensors reported a dead zone. There were no magnetic, radio, or electrical emissions of any kind to find. No surprise. The power grid fell when the Merki first attacked, but there were local backups in operation in a few liberated towns. Greenville wasn't one of them. The town had been abandoned by both sides.

The distant thunder of the artillery barrage was the only sound, and there was no movement. Not even a mangy mutt had survived. He pivoted in place one last time, before entering the house. The front was mostly intact. If intact meant some of the walls still supported the second floor. The back half had burned, but the collapse of the upper floors must have stifled the flames. He stepped over the debris, and ducked under fallen beams.

If he were his father, where would he leave a message for a wayward son? The studio, obviously. He headed that way, passing through the sitting room that his mother loved. She'd always liked it for the view of the garden, and often read there for hours on end. He stopped at the sight of his mother's belongings strewn around. She would've been horrified to find her beloved books so abused.

Looters?

He checked sensors again.

No hostiles.

His dad was a stubborn man, but he wasn't stupid. He would have packed and decamped for the mountains, the moment the news broke. There would be a message; some sign left for the son who abandoned his family for strangers on distant worlds.

Eric entered the studio, and found his message. He removed his helmet, and it fell to the floor, as the scene burned itself into his memory. The decomposed bodies were sprawled on the floor. Shot in the back while running, his processor reported.

Eric's machine-self took over as his Human side fled wailing into the dark, to hide from the ghastly truth. It evaluated the scene clinically, displaying trajectories as red lines on his internal display.

The room faded, replaced by a digital simulation. Two people ran into the room, and were gunned down. Ranges and vectors painted the scene, tracking the shots. The room spun to a new point of view, and two people ran into the room, and were gunned down. More data flickered into place. Impact assessments. The room became a two-dimensional diagram. Two people ran into the room. More data. Instantaneous death due to impact trauma. Massive internal bleed… **<fault>**

...gunned down... two people were gunned down... **<fault>** ... gunned **<fault>** down...

Eric fell to his knees, staring and shaking as errors cascaded through his systems. Diagnostic data scrolled by on his internal display, as he stared at the bodies.

>_ Diagnostics: Unit fit for Duty
<fault>
<fault>
<fault>
>_ Diagnostics: Full system <fault> <fault> <fault> scan in progress.
>_ Diagnostics: Unit fit for Duty
<fault>

In his mind's eye, Eric saw a procession of images; memory files pulled up by his traitorous processor from storage. He saw his family alive and happy, and he groaned in pain, but the errors ceased. The room blinked back to startling clarity.

"Screaming," Eric muttered. "Someone is screaming..."

The cries stopped, and he realised. It was him. With a coded thought, he banished the memories back to storage. The screams were relegated to his subconscious, where they waited to join the other horrors that plagued his dreams.

Eric stared at his dead parents. He should never have left them, and he certainly shouldn't have come back to find them this way. He wished he could unsee this. He wished he could pretend they were still alive. He wished himself back in time to yesterday, a time of hope and belief in happy endings.

He climbed wearily to his feet. Leaving his rifle and helmet behind, he went to one of the bedrooms. He stripped the bedclothes, and took the sheets back to the studio. He wrapped the bodies, trying not to see or smell anything. Trying not to think.

Outside in the garden, he found tools and dug a single grave. They could sleep together. They'd want to. It didn't take long. A robot, his father had called him in the heat of the moment.

"You see, Dad?" Eric said, as he carried his father to his grave. "Robots are good for something. We don't make good sons, but we make great grave diggers."

He went back for his mum, and placed her in the cold ground beside his dad.

"There now. I'd pray over you if I believed God would care. I don't. I'm so sorry I wasn't here for you. You needed me, and I was away saving strangers. Like you said. I shouldn't have left. I'm sorry... I'm sorry..."

Eric rocked beside the grave, mumbling his apologies as errors scrolled by on his display.

At some point, he must have come back to himself,

because as if by magic, he found the grave filled in. His rifle was in his arms, and his helmet was back on. He didn't remember doing any of it, but he must have. There wasn't anyone else. The shovel had been rammed deep into the earth as a marker.

Kneeling there, he lost himself in memory again, and a machine peered out of his eyes. His TRS icon blinked in time with his heartbeat, as it scanned for targets.

Scanning, scanning, scanning.

Vipers were good grave diggers, but they were excellent grave *fillers*. TRS flashed in time with his rocking, and the machine watched.

And waited.

* * *

29 ~ Convention

Westby Convention Centre, Pandora, Kalmar Union

The dream was still on Eric's mind later that day as he listened to his LTs bantering with their sergeants. Everyone was having a good time. The Pandora op was like a working vacation for them. Considering what they'd been through the last few years, it was good to remember there was more to life than killing Merki.

On a whim he'd decided to accompany them today. There was nothing special about the Westby Convention Centre or the mission. He could have remained aboard *Hammer* in orbit and monitored them from there, but the rest of the company would be coming down tomorrow anyway. A day of sightseeing dirtside didn't seem frivolous.

"Oh my God, is that Zelda? *It is!*" Gina squealed.

"Good grief, LT. Don't gush over me like that. It's embarrassing," Sergeant Hiller said and grinned at her blushes.

Everyone craned their necks to see.

"It sure looks like her," Sergeant Higgins added.

A crowd of newsies were clamouring to enter the Zelda

and the Spaceways exhibit. That in itself wasn't remarkable considering where they were, but the entire exhibit was surrounded by chanting Zelda fans wearing full costume.

Eric didn't need to look. "It's her. She's here promoting the Titan program."

"How come?" Gina said.

"Do I look like an Infonet server to you?"

Hiller laughed. "Check this out."

Gina cocked her head as she accessed the link Hiller sent via TacNet. "It says she's promoting her next full-length sensim feature, and Pandora Atomics is sponsoring it. Most of the cast are here."

"The bridge crew at least," Hiller amended. "I doubt even Pandora Atomics would hire *Bad Penny's* entire crew just to promote a new variant of an old weapon platform."

Zelda's ship, *Bad Penny*, boasted a crew of heavy hitters in the sensim world. The bridge crew's cast had remained the same for all ten seasons and had become famous due to the popularity of the show. The full-length features based upon the series had attracted some high-paid-mega-stars as popular as Zelda herself.

"I wonder if I can get an autograph," Gina muttered as she tried to see the stars of the show. "For Kate I mean. Not for me."

Hiller smirked. "Right. Of course. Not for you."

Gina reddened.

Eric led them around the crush to avoid notice. Fending off the media wasn't his favourite thing. His people were dressed like civvies to blend in with the crowds, but that was no guarantee of going undetected. It wouldn't take much effort for a good journalist to track down the only vipers on Pandora. Surveilling the ports and assembly areas would be SOP for newsies, but as long as they had Zelda to chase his vipers should go unmolested. At least for a short time.

Tomorrow would be another matter.

"You know what we're here for," Eric said. "Report back to me before taking any action. I'll assign targets based upon the ease of acquisition."

Everyone nodded. It didn't need to be said the general's shopping list had priority over the one supplied by Liz Brenchley.

"Gina, you're with me."

Their group dispersed and in pairs lost themselves among the crowd. Eric watched their blue icons scatter and mingle with the civilian hordes marked in green on his sensors.

"Where first?" Gina said.

Eric shrugged. "You choose."

"Hmmm... how abouuuut... Yamaichi Opticom?"

Eric accessed the company's information. "Stealth tech interests you, does it?"

Gina shrugged. "Not especially, but I remember Kate mentioning them once."

"I'm not surprised she'd be aware of them. Fine. Yamaichi it is."

They made their way through the crowds. Eric had a floor plan showing the layout of the convention in a window on his internal display. Yamaichi Opticom wasn't a huge player in the market. Its exhibit was a bit out of the way and smaller than the big boys could afford.

"Any ideas why the general is so interested in these people?"

"Not a one," Eric said. "He takes an interest in all sorts of things."

"Things that go boom, sure," Gina agreed. "But sneaksuits?"

"Don't focus on the products they're selling now. Think ahead. Think about the technology behind them. If there's one thing I know about Burgton, it's the way he always thinks three moves ahead."

Gina frowned. "So its stealth *tech*, not stealth equipment

we're supposed to scope out?"

"Primarily we want the tech. I imagine we'll copy Yamaichi's designs too, but he probably has other uses for the tech."

"Remember Shoshon?"

Eric nodded.

"The Merkiaari caught Cragg with his pants down. That stealthed troopship was a nasty surprise."

"They've adapted and advanced in a few ways. They hurt us at Shoshon, and in the border zone they whacked one of our task forces not long ago."

"Mines," Gina growled. "I hate mines."

"Who doesn't? So we have to counter stealthed mines, stealthed troopships, and the Merki jamming of our comms at the least. Who knows what else they have? Still wondering why the general finds Yamaichi interesting?"

"Not when you put it like that."

They slowly meandered their way through the crowds. The convention centre was absolutely rammed with humanity and the going was slow. Gina paused and rose on tip toes to peer over the crowd. Eric was about to remind her she had sensors to aid navigation, but she wasn't looking for the Yamaichi exhibit. She'd detected something more interesting.

Shan voices.

There were three Shan on his sensors. With a coded thought he added a filter to paint them yellow on his internal display. Gina glanced at him, and Eric nodded to show he'd heard them too. They were speaking badly broken English and sounded out of their depth. He could see them over the heads of the crowd, but Gina couldn't. She wasn't tall enough.

"Sounds like someone forgot to bring his translator," Eric said.

Gina burrowed into the crowd.

Eric sighed and followed her. She was such a girl scout. They weren't here to improve Human-Shan relations, but show her someone in need and she promptly forgot the mission. He needed to break her of the habit. Her compulsion to save the world would get her killed.

"You're not a Marine anymore," he said over viper comm.

"Huh?"

"Your hero reflex. We have a mission and this isn't it."

"Oh lighten up," Gina said. "We're on vacation. You need to live a little. All war and no play makes Eric a dull boy."

Eric tried to think of a good comeback, but he *was* all business. He'd been that way since the Merkiaari ripped everything away from him.

They finally broke through the crowd and into some open space. Fascinated convention attendees had surrounded one of the exhibits. The Shan were unable to leave and were being treated like part of the display. Eric was disgusted to think he was the same species as these cretins.

Gina paused for the barest moment, and then she took charge. She bowed to the Shan and addressed them in their own language. That caused a stir. The attendees didn't know she was a viper, but they knew she was something. Very few could speak Shan without the use of mechanical aid. Cameras suddenly started appearing amongst the crowd.

Eric sighed. Their cover was about to be blown to hell. Oh well. They'd be back in uniform and on the clock again tomorrow anyway. The others would have to finish up for them here.

He joined Gina.

"May you live in harmony. I'm Gina and this is Eric. May we be of service?"

The Shan bowed and exchanged handshakes in the Shan manner. "Honoured," they said together and then deferred to the oldest member of their group to make introductions. "I am Ren, and these worthies are Jamal and Kesara."

Jamal and Kesara were both warrior caste going by the style of harnesses they wore. They were female and resembled one another. Sibs maybe. Their pelts were dark tan in colour and their ear tufts were a startling white. Their patterned flanks were a mirror of each other.

Ren was male and must be older. Eric couldn't tell, but Shan did tend to defer to elders. His pelt was a shiny black that Eric hadn't personally seen before. At first he thought of it as monotone, but upon a closer inspection he realised it had bluish highlights in mottled patterns. Ren would be almost invisible on the hunt at night, but he obviously wasn't a warrior. His harness had lots of pouches and didn't sport the twin holsters all warriors carried.

"Our translators have malfunctioned," Ren said. "The crowd doesn't seem to understand we wish to leave."

"All three?" Gina said doubtfully.

Eric snorted. There was zero chance the translators had failed. "That seems unlikely."

Ren flicked his ears in agreement. "And yet here we are."

"May I see them?" Gina said and made a show of inspecting the devices. "They seem fine. My people speak many different languages. Perhaps you need to use a different one. Do your devices have a Mandarin setting? It's a good second choice when English fails."

Ren's tail gestured over his shoulder. "I fear they do not. I will report this to higher authority so they might be upgraded."

"Not to worry," Gina said. She turned off the translators and handed them back to their owners. "My friend and I speak many languages. We'll help you."

Nice.

Eric nodded approvingly as Gina addressed the crowd in Mandarin and then English. She basically told them to grow up and get a clue. They were frightening their alien guests, and they should shove off or she'd make them. Devoid of their translators, the Shan looked on in uncomprehending silence as the crowd dispersed.

"There," Gina said in Shan. "Where would you like to go? I'll escort you."

"There's no need," Ren said. "We don't wish to be a burden."

"Not at all," Eric said. "It would be our honour."

That did the trick. Shan took matters of honour seriously. Even seemingly trivial matters became serious in a hurry when honour was invoked.

"Then we must accept of course," Ren said. "My companions were hoping to meet the famous Zelda."

Eric groaned, but Gina beamed. She transferred that look of glee from the Shan to Eric and he chuckled. She really did want that autograph.

"How fortuitous!" Gina said. "I wanted to meet her earlier, but the crowds prevented it. I'm sure if we go together she will honour us with a private interview."

Private? Eric didn't know about that, but arriving in the company of three Shan would be Gina's golden ticket to that autograph. Hell, she'd probably get a bonus for the intro—maybe a complimentary model of *Bad Penny*.

Gina chatted away in Shan and together they retraced their path to the Zelda and the Spaceways exhibit. Eric gave up on work for the rest of that day, but before giving himself over to Gina's madness he contacted Hiller on viper comm.

"Something's come up. Gina and I will be offline for the rest of the day."

"Understood," Hiller said. "Anything I can do?"

"Yes as a matter of fact. Check out Yamaichi Opticom's exhibit. Stealth tech is a high priority."

"Will do. Have fun, sir."

Eric blinked. "What?"

"Gina just asked me if I want Zelda's autograph."

Good grief. "Penleigh out."

* * *

30 ~ Titans

Staging Area, Pandora Atomics

General Ecclestone was an asshole. Eric made the judgement just five minutes after meeting him. He was the type of officer who looked for a hammer when daggers were called for. It was hard to imagine a bigger hammer than the resurrected super-weapons of the Corporate War era.

Bought and paid for by Pandora Atomics, Ecclestone was the perfect poster-boy for their Titan program; a grandiose name for a no doubt grandiose project. When marketers plundered Greek mythology Eric knew to expect grand ideas with grand price-tags attached.

Eric seated himself with dozens of other officers invited to watch the show. He was the only viper deemed of suitable rank to participate. The rest of the audience was comprised of colonels or above from various militaries, a few Shan, and a commodore or two sent by the missing fleet admirals as their surrogates.

Pandora Atomics had tried to get more attention from the navy, but fleet admirals willing to promote land-based weapons were scarce. They were too busy sucking up to the first space lord, and trying to get BuShips to allocate some of its new construction to their commands.

The stands fronted one of the huge hangars that Pandora Atomics had built to house their newest cash cows. A hundred metres or so from the closed doors, a podium stood with microphones and teleprompter. Ecclestone wouldn't be using a script. He was a true believer. His evangelising would be from the heart.

Eric focused upon the execs Pandora Atomics had sent along, and zoomed in upon faces. X2 strobed on his internal display as he stored an image of each one in his database. A coded thought was all it took to cross-reference them with their bios. They were a disappointing bunch. All of them were in marketing.

Eric dismissed them as useless.

He'd hoped some of them would be test pilots, or design engineers. Hell, he would have been happier with a janitor from the assembly line! At least they'd have some interesting anecdotal stories to tell. Maybe they'd tell him how a Titan's fusion engine was prone to overheating. Or maybe the jump jets were underpowered and used too much fuel. Heck, maybe the janitor had to constantly clean the floor near them because the hydraulics leaked.

Marketing experts were useless for his purposes. What did he care that they'd hired Zelda? How did it matter that Titans were a central plot-point in her next big sensim feature? He wanted hard intel. Data like how the Titans could be of use to the regiment. Could they be used as artillery to replace their field guns? Were their weapons more powerful with a longer range for example? Could the tech be adapted for viper use? If so, how? Many questions, none of which could be answered here.

Eric hadn't expected different, but it would've been convenient if someone useful had attended. Maybe they'd show up later to watch their creations put through their paces on the firing line. He could hope, but the answers he really needed wouldn't be found here. They'd be on secure computer servers.

The theme from Zelda and the Spaceways began playing from the speakers. General Ecclestone took his place at the podium, and waited for his moment to arrive. Conversations lapsed as the music swelled to a deafening crescendo. Pandora Atomics had pulled out all the stops to make the big reveal a success. Not that the Titans would be much of a surprise. They may not have revealed the actual production versions before this, but there'd been plenty of hints and spoilers leaked to hype expectations.

The music faded into silence.

"Decades ago at the beginning of my journey in the military, I had a dream," Ecclestone said grandiosely. "A dream of wars fought bloodlessly. Today, I can share that my dream is now a reality. I've seen the future of war, and it stands before you."

The general raised a hand. The huge hangar doors behind him split in half and rolled back. Lights flared to life and the towering twelve-metre-tall war-machine stepped out and into the open. Eighty tons of armoured death wasn't exactly stealthy. Its giant clawed feet hammered the plascrete apron as it moved. Ecclestone didn't flinch or turn to watch its approach.

The Titan was a monster resurrected from a barbaric time in Human history, and unease swept over the audience at the sight of it bearing down on them. Eric noticed the Shan contingent looking around in confusion. They didn't have the context to understand what the Titan meant to their Human allies. They didn't know that long ago, before first contact with the Merkiaari necessitated the creation of the Alliance, wars had been fought by automated drones and machines just like this. On colony worlds far from Earth and any other government oversight, resources were plundered by corporations using flying death machines, and private armies equipped with weapons just like this one.

"Imagine for a moment, thousands of Titans dropped on a Merkiaari infested planet," Ecclestone said, his voice reverent and booming from the speakers. "Imagine surgical strikes from orbit. Overwhelmingly powerful strikes that will save Human lives. Raids that will rid our galaxy of aliens forever, and make it ours for the taking. Imagine a time when our people are safe to go *where* they wish, and *take* what they wish. That time starts now."

The applause was fitful, and Eric didn't add his support to it. Automated warfare had been tried in various guises throughout history. It would lead to an arms race with all sides frantically producing counters to its enemy's counters. It never ended well for any but those selling the weapons.

Eric wondered what the Shan thought of Ecclestone's exhortations. He'd bet they weren't keen on the idea that the galaxy they shared with Humans was apparently ripe for the taking. By Humans. Especially now when they'd recently learned there were a multitude of races out there to be contacted. Ecclestone was hinting at a future of never-ending war. Pandora Atomics would love such a boon to its bottom line.

Eric listened to the general gush about how the Titan program was the future, and how the resurgence of drone warfare would be the saviour of the Alliance. He hoped Ecclestone never held strategic command of any battle Eric had to fight in. The man needed to brush up on his history if he thought Titans were the future. They were the past.

Literally.

The general's speech wound down, and the Zelda marketing machine swung into action. She was in costume again, complete with huge pistol on her hip. *Bad Penny's* crew came with her to pose with the Titan for the media. Eric wasn't interested in the show. He rose from his seat with many others of like mind, and headed for the open hangar.

Inside he found the other variants of the Titan weapons platform. He had no names for them as yet, but he was careful to examine all of them. They weren't all the same. He'd expected different weapon configurations on a universal chassis, but that wasn't what he found. The one outside was bipedal with a hunch-back profile and reversed knee joints. It had interchangeable weapon pods instead of arms. The first one he found inside the hangar had four legs. He studied it and a tactical overlay descended over his vision. Weak points decorated the digital representation of the Titan. He wasn't surprised the hip and knee joins were its weakness. If he wanted to bring it down that's where he'd concentrate his fire, but his scans suggested it wouldn't go down easily. It was heavily armoured. Scans suggested using artillery might be necessary to halt one of these things. It didn't have arms, and its weapons were stored internally when not in use.

Eric saved the data and moved to another variant. This one was bipedal again and did have arms, but it had a strangely shaped head. He didn't know what its manufacturers called it, but it looked like a hammerhead to him. He tagged it as one for now. Unlike the others, this one had three-fingered claw-hands. He couldn't see the point... climbing maybe? Its knee joints were more natural looking and Human-like. Weapons were varied—large calibre PPCs and AARs were its primary ordnance for short and medium range targets. Long range was covered by missile launchers. There were two boxy-looking installations on its shoulders. They seemed a little vulnerable to Eric. He wondered what would happen if one or both detonated. Could the chassis survive that?

Eric checked the time. He needed to get going. The rest of the company would be landing soon. Captain Riley had scheduled four drops using her assault shuttles. They were only large enough to carry a single platoon with its gear. *Hammer* was a destroyer not a troop transport.

Eric reached the spaceport a little late and missed the first couple of landings. 2nd and 3rd Platoons had already debarked and were checking their gear. Live ordnance was banned from the games for obvious reasons. Getting that wrong would be bad. Shooting friendlies was definitely frowned upon. The Titans would be armed with live munitions for testing, but they weren't officially part of the games. Pandora Atomics had simply piggy-backed their launch on the war games as a marketing tactic.

An inbound shuttle blinked onto Eric's sensors. He queried its IFF and it came back as one of *SDF Hammer's* assault shuttles. It should be carrying Gina and the rest of 1st Platoon.

"Those weapons better be training safe, Lieutenant," Eric said.

Brice looked up from his work. "Hey Kamarl. Do you trust me?"

"No. I don't lend money to friends."

Brice fired his rifle, and a splash of red ruined the pristine black of Dolinski's nanocoat. Armour used in the Alliance reacted to simunition rounds by changing colour. Low energy impacts, whether that be caused by mass drivers or energy weapons, had that effect for training purposes.

Dolinski looked down at the damage over his heart and scowled. "Very funny," he said and reset his armour to black before getting back to work.

Eric nodded. "Good."

"You!" a familiar voice roared.

Everyone paused in their work at the distraction.

Eric turned to find a Marine with a familiar face bearing down on him. Major Stein hadn't changed much in the years since their fight on Thurston. Except he had a serious mad on, and he was aiming it squarely at Eric. Gina's shuttle landed and taxied as Stein made his way across the field. He looked mightily determined and ready for a fight. The shuttle parked and its cargo ramp descended. Gina dismounted first.

"Where is she?" Stein snarled, getting in Eric's face and projecting absolute fury.

Ah so that was it. Gina. From a certain point of view he had stolen her from Stein. Recruited her rather, but Stein wouldn't see it that way.

Eric looked over at Dolinski. "Get that gear checked and stowed. I've got this."

"You haven't got shit."

"Calm down, Major. You're scaring my kids."

Stein snorted.

"Gina," Eric said over viper comm, keeping his words private.

Gina raised a hand to one of her men wanting her attention. "What's up?"

"I have an old friend of yours waiting here. Delegate what you're doing and come say hello before he tries to kill me."

"Kill you!" Gina said. She was already on her way. "I can't leave you on your own for five minutes."

"Fuentez is fine," Eric said to Stein. "In fact, she commands my 1st Platoon." He nodded toward the approaching figure.

Gina removed her helmet, came to attention, and saluted Stein. "Good to see you again, sir."

"Likewise," Stein said after returning her salute. He glanced at Eric. "Some privacy?"

Eric nodded and stepped away. It was a gesture only. He could hear them perfectly well, and planned to eavesdrop shamelessly. He would've raised the gain on his hearing if it had been necessary.

"What the hell happened to you?" Stein said. "You disappeared. I tried to find out where you were, but HQ blocked me. My security clearance wasn't high enough they said. Need to know and all that bullshit. I was your damn CO, Gina. I *needed* to know!"

Gina nodded sympathetically. "I arrived at HQ for the

weapon's testing thing. You remember?"

"I'm guessing that was a lie?" Stein glared at Eric. "He recruited you?"

"Not really. They tested a bunch of us, and asked for volunteers. I was one of those who passed."

"Of course you did. You were one of my best. I don't understand why you volunteered for this. You were Corps. all the way, Gina. As hardcore as any Marine I've ever met. Why did you abandon your team?"

Eric winced. If there was anything guaranteed to hurt her more than being accused of abandoning people, he didn't know what it could be.

"I didn't abandon anyone. When Grace and Pags died, I started wondering why people I cared about were dying in the mud for nothing."

"That's the job."

"But what did they die for? Thurston was still a basket case at the end of the campaign. We leave smoking ruins behind us more often than not. Win or lose, my Marines still die."

"So you opted out? Left us to carry on without you?"

"I didn't opt out. I re-evaluated. I stepped back and tried to see where I could make the biggest difference. The dying has to mean something."

"So you took reassignment without a word. Fifteen years in the Corps. and not a word from you. No goodbye, no see-you-later it's been fun. Nothing. I tried to contact you, but you'd vanished. A year later an honourable discharge appeared on your permanent record. It tripped my alert, but there was still nothing to find. No explanations, and your current location was marked unknown."

Gina shrugged. "I've been on deployment pretty much the entire time. There was enhancement and training, and then the Shan thing. After that... well, other missions. The point is, before this I couldn't talk to anyone."

Stein sighed. "There's no easy way to say this, so I'll just tell you. Your team took it hard. They may give you a hard time when they find out you're here."

"They have a right to be pissed. I can see what it looks like."

"It's worse than that. We were deployed to Lyra and lost Hollings there to an IED. Frankowski said she wasn't the same after Pags died and you disappeared. She lost focus. You broke my Eagles."

"That's enough," Eric said and rejoined them. He wasn't letting that go. No freaking way. "My lieutenant was up to her neck in mud and blood fighting Merkiaari for the Shan when you lost your man. When *you* did, not her."

"She was a damn good Marine. She didn't deserve to go out like that," Gina said sadly.

"Back on mission, Fuentez," Eric said, still glaring at Stein. He needed to put distance between them. "You have work. Go."

Gina started to argue, but then she deflated. She put her helmet back on and left without saying a word.

Eric watched her go then rounded on Stein. "Stay away from her, or I'll make you wish you had. Briefly."

"Is that a threat, Captain?"

"A promise. You of all people know the sort of person she is. Do you really think it's a good idea stressing her out over things that can't be changed? Do you want another Hollings on your conscience?"

Stein frowned.

"Hollings died on *your* watch, *not* hers," Eric said. "You want someone to blame? Look in a mirror."

Eric went back to work, and Stein walked stiffly away.

* * *

31 ~ Live Fire

Area 21, Pandora, Kalmar Union

Eric's plan to keep Gina occupied instead of brooding upon Stein's accusations were tested a few days later. The idea until then had been to limit her exposure to Marines in general, and Stein in particular.

Easy, or so he'd thought.

He should've known it wouldn't work. He'd kept Gina busy during the day all right, but she hadn't needed to meet them physically. Everyone had net access and her nights were free. There was nothing he could do to prevent her talking to her old squad online. She was such a girl scout. Of course she would go behind his back and contact her old buddies. He should've known she'd find a way. She'd been recon for most of her time in the Corps. and wasn't exactly shy about looking for trouble.

And so she'd found some.

That's what happened when you cared too much.

Eric had put all that behind him long ago. Caring too much got you killed in this business. When nothing mattered, nothing hurt. All is programming.

Gina was tight-lipped about it, but Eric knew her attempts to explain things to her old team hadn't gone well. She was normally all smiles. Unlike some, she didn't brood. She was the chatty sort. Suddenly she was all frowns and dark looks. It was time for an intervention, but not by him. He needed to wheel out the big guns for this one.

As part of his *'save Gina from herself'* plan, he reached out to Zelda. She would never admit it, but Gina was a Zelda fan-girl. Eric found the actress surprisingly approachable. He'd expected to go through agents and flunkies acting as her personal firewall, but her PA transferred him the moment she heard there was a viper on the line. When Zelda learned the woman who'd translated for the Shan at the convention was a viper, a huge fan, *and* in need of a little help, she was in. What Eric didn't anticipate was Zelda's own playful nature.

Eric stood with his LTs and watched the Titans performing to impress potential buyers. They had good firepower and range. Accuracy was fine. He watched at X3 as they obliterated their targets without fail. The targets weren't firing back of course, so the test was of limited value, but it was still impressive from a layman's point of view. The media were certainly enjoying the show, but then, big flaming detonations always did impress them.

As before, General Ecclestone was in attendance with his favoured officers. All of them stood together and viewed the test through field glasses to bring the action closer. The officers out of favour or less willing to suck up, like the vipers, stood apart to watch the show. The Marines, including Major Stein, were in the latter group. The Shan contingent was stuck with the former.

Ecclestone was army as were most of those close to him, but not all. The navy's representatives, dispossessed of their admirals, hung on the outskirts of Ecclestone's group. They looked out of place and a little forlorn. Eric noticed them checking out the Marine contingent as if nerving themselves to join them. They had more in common with them.

A big screen had been set up to one side to give a Titan's eye view. Most were ignoring it, but Eric found it quite useful. The screen was split into quarters to display the HUD of each variant. There were four Titans on the field at present. The four displays revealed the similarities and differences in each Titan's target acquisition and response.

Hissssss-craaAAAckkk!

Hissssss-craaAAAckkk!

Eric evaluated the strike. The duel PPCs did a good amount of damage per shot, and had zero risk of collateral damage. He thought of this particular Titan as a sniper, and confirmed his earlier thoughts about its deployment. It would do well in an urban environment.

Eric watched a quadruped machine gallop across the field in an unneeded sprint. Fast sucker. By design it was more stable than its two-legged brethren. Its weapons were all stored internally for protection, and relied upon its LRMs for offensive punch. Long-range missiles were an area effect weapon, which meant this version of a Titan would fit best into a classic artillery role. Not a good fit for urban warfare; not even combined with spotters for targeting. Collateral damage would be high. It carried a pair of auto-cannon for point-defence. Those protected against rocket attack, but were also useful in an anti-personnel role.

Eric had a grudging respect for the designers. They'd tried to give their babies teeth. What he didn't like about them was their backward-looking philosophy. Drone warfare still had a place. Hell, the navy used them all the time as decoys, and the Marines liked them for surveillance, but in offensive ops they were too vulnerable to spoofing. The Merki were particularly good at jamming.

General Ecclestone beamed at the interviewers gushing over him. He lost them for a moment when one of the Titans employed its jump jets. It fired and nailed an aerial target at the apex of its flight. The newsies turned back to the general with more questions, and he went back to answering them.

Eric didn't share their appreciation. Oh sure, it was an impressive looking feat, but it wasn't a practical manoeuvre. Why jump and fire at an airborne target? Potting it from cover would be safer and less likely to draw return fire. The media had liked it though, and that was the only reason to do it. They wouldn't be interested in how resilient or stealthy the Titans were. That took a more personal stake in a Titan's performance. The operators would certainly find its IR and radar signatures of interest, as would any poor grunt in the field relying upon a Titan for fire support.

Eric had to admit their abilities were pretty good. In essence, Titans were 80 ton 12 metre tall walking tanks. Dainty they weren't. Despite that, their manoeuvrability was surprisingly good, and they could fly. Sort of. Their jump jets weren't underpowered as he'd theorised. Not at all. If anything, the opposite was true, which had its own challenges. A heavy hand at the controls could compromise them in battle, and they were big targets at the best of times. The best of times would be using terrain or buildings for cover, but not if hothead operators turned them into targets by leaping about the place.

Eric glanced over at the current operators. Four men and women wearing glossy-red armour manned the Titan's controls. All four wore VR headsets and spoke quietly to each other to coordinate their manoeuvres and fire. Colonel Jubb was in command there. They belonged to Cooper's Commandos, a crack mercenary company out of Arsenal. A famous outfit in certain circles.

"Good grief, what's that?" Lieutenant Brice said.

Zelda and company were incoming with a convoy of vehicles following her on the approach road. Good grief was right. It looked as if she'd brought her entire production crew with her. She was supposed to drop by to give Gina's mood a lift, not bring her entire dog-and-pony show with her.

Zelda stood on a flatbed in full costume with her co-stars, while vehicles packed with camera crews, media, and fans followed in her wake. Banners flew from masts attached to the vehicles, music blared from speakers, and fireworks launched into the air as she pulled up. When Zelda rolled into town, common sense rolled right on out. Apparently, it was party time.

The newsies interviewing Ecclestone instantly lost interest in him, and stampeded toward the new thing in town. The Shan dropped to all fours and followed at top speed. Zelda fascinated them. Their people didn't create fiction, so actors were a new idea they wished to explore. Eric couldn't help laughing at the sight, which didn't go unnoticed. The general headed in Eric's direction, disapproving officers in tow.

He didn't look pleased.

At least Gina had perked up. She was grinning like a mad woman at the sight of her hero stealing Ecclestone's thunder. Eric wondered what would happen when a mega-star met a mega-ego. Nova scale tantrums could easily result. Ecclestone seemed the type.

Cameras rolled as Zelda played to her audience. Questions were fired at her from all sides, and she answered them on the move. She was heading for Gina. The cameras swung to cover the vipers when the media realised Zelda's destination. Viper armour was pretty distinctive with its nanocoat set to the regiment's default black.

Zelda hugged Gina and kissed her on both cheeks. Gina gave Eric a startled look, but hugged the woman back.

"This is my good friend Lieutenant Gina Fuentez, 501st Infantry. She fought the Merkiaari to save the Shan, and introduced me to some of them a few days ago. She's fluent in their language and played translator for me."

Gina's face heated. "It was nothing really."

"She's a bit shy. Luckily I'm not," Zelda said and everyone

laughed. "I've brought some friends to meet you, Gina."

Zelda began dragging her away. Gina looked plaintively back over her shoulder.

Eric made a shooing gesture. "Go."

"Incoming," Brice muttered.

Ecclestone arrived red-faced with embarrassment or anger. Probably both. Eric assumed both, and assumed he was about to receive friendly fire. Well, it wouldn't be the first time.

"I assume you're responsible for this circus, Captain?" Ecclestone said.

Eric smiled. "Why assume that?"

"Your man there."

"Lieutenant Fuentez," Eric said. "She and Zelda are friends. They met at the convention a few days ago when the Shan enlisted her aid as their translator."

Mention of the Shan gave the general a new target for his ire. "Those creatures," he growled. "What am I to do with them? They can't even speak English!"

"We'll just have to speak Shan," Brice muttered, but not low enough to go unheard.

Eric kept a straight face, not betraying his amusement.

The general regarded Brice as if a bug had sat up and addressed him. "You said something, Lieutenant?"

"I just wondered why we don't speak Shan, General. I mean, if our allies need a little help with communications, it seems only fair."

"I can't speak Shan!"

"Yet you expect them to speak English, sir? Doesn't seem very fair to me."

Ecclestone's flunkies gasped and others glowered, Brice smiled as if unaware how flippant he sounded. Lieutenants Dolinski and Dengler snickered. Eric stepped in before the general tried to have his vipers court-martialed.

"The Shan are very good soldiers. Their translators are

sufficient. We had no issues fighting with them against the Merkiaari."

"Warriors, not soldiers. They're little more than savages."

Eric was stumped for a moment. He wasn't sure he knew the correct term for this sort of bigotry. Was it racism when the parties involved weren't the same species? Or was it something else? Xenophobia seemed a little extreme. Eric preferred to reserve that term for the Merkiaari. Hatred of them was a given.

"They're allies, and they're Alliance members in their own right. We have to accommodate their differences if we want to work with them."

Ecclestone glared. "Maybe I should assign your unit to babysit."

Hissssss-craaAAAckkk!

Hissssss-craaAAAckkk!

Everyone turned to watch the show for a moment. It was enough to remind the general why he was supposed to be angry about Zelda's visit. He glared toward the circus, but before he could do more, Major Stein piped up.

The traitor.

Stein winked at Eric. "Tell me, Captain Penleigh. What do you think of the newest addition to our forces? Are you impressed?"

Eric scowled at the Marine. He'd meant what he'd said about staying far away from Gina, but here Stein was, not a hundred metres from her. He hadn't tried to talk to her, but how long would that last?

"Well?" Ecclestone said.

"The Titans have impressive specifications, and they're well armoured. Good firepower and manoeuvrability for their size."

"But?" Stein pressed.

Sonofabitch. He was asking for it. *Begging* for it. Eric shrugged. "They're old tech with a face-lift. They won't get a shot off against the Merkiaari."

"Nonsense," Ecclestone growled, his face darkening. "Utter defeatist nonsense."

"I could take them all out right now," Eric said, and shrugged again. "I can think of two ways... no three."

"Impossible!"

Stein laughed. "You're serious?"

"Deadly."

"He should prove it, don't you think so, General?"

What the hell? Stein was baiting him and the general on purpose. Why? What was in it for the Marines?

Ecclestone hesitated a moment, but the media were occupied. "Show me."

Eric glanced at Zelda's circus. No one was interested in the Titans anymore. He shrugged. Ecclestone had asked for it, and hell, the general outranked him. He'd been given an order, technically at least. Eric glared at the smirking Stein one more time, and then walked up to the control station.

He looked back at the general. "One," he said and mimed shooting each of the operators. "Two," he said and pulled out the power feed to the control consol. The Titans on the field froze. One fell over, cratering the ground with its weight. The crash was extremely loud.

The operators took off their VR headsets and looked around in surprise.

Ecclestone was almost panting with rage. The newsies had noticed and were filtering back. The fallen Titan was the centre of their attention.

"And the third option?" Ecclestone grated, fighting to stay calm.

Eric shrugged. He contacted all four of his LTs via viper comm. "One each. Make it impressive for the cameras. Trash the antennas."

Gina burst out of the crowd at top speed, and headed for the most distant Titan. Zelda whooped, and that drew the media's attention. The entire evolution was captured by the cameras in full, and would no doubt feature on the news later that day. Burgton would be pleased. He wanted good publicity.

Gina jumped onto the Titan, and scampered up its body to the hammer-shaped head. If she'd had explosives with her, that would've been all she wrote for that particular Titan, but she didn't. She made do with ripping the antennas to pieces barehanded. The other vipers did similar things to their targets, all except Brice. He just wandered casually over to the fallen giant he'd chosen to assault, and kicked the living hell out of its most sensitive bits. It took moments to destroy its antenna and comms arrays.

"Three," Eric said, and smiled. "The Merkiaari won't do it this way. They'll just jam communications, but the result will be the same."

Stein winked, and beamed at Eric.

Odd. Very odd.

Stein had screwed him; he hadn't even kissed him first. Eric didn't think it had anything to do with Gina, and it didn't seem aimed at him personally. Why didn't Stein like the general? Or maybe the Titan program offended him. He'd have to beat the answers out of Stein, but later.

Zelda whistled and pumped a fist into the air. "That. Was. *Awesome!* Imagine what they can do to the Merkiaari!"

Cameras recorded, Eric grinned, and General Ecclestone glared. Colonel Jubb left the other operators and came over to snarl at Eric for spoiling his show, but Zelda had the last laugh.

"Eeeeeek! Red Comman-*DOH!*" Zelda said when she saw Jubb's glossy armour.

Gina arrived back, just in time to hear the iconic line from the show, and laughed.

Jubb rolled his eyes. "That is so old."

"Ha-ha-haaaa, classic episode!" Gina crowed, and

bumped fists with Zelda.

"Like I said, old," Jubb said.

Eric shook his head. Red Commandos were a mercenary outfit from an episode of Zelda and the Spaceways. Their armour's nanocoat was glossy red, just like the elite unit Colonel Jubb represented.

What a circus.

* * *

32 ~ Orientation

Nstar Industries Orbital Shipyard, Pandora System

When Tei'Shima boarded the ship to Pandora, she'd had certain expectations. For example: retraining. She'd expected to be given time to brush up on her old lessons before needing to take up her duties as Tei.

Her father had taught her well. She knew everything a youngling needed when approaching her choosing time. She'd studied the history of her people and the clans. She knew the origins and traditions of all the castes, but she wasn't a naive youngling anymore. Her lessons had been the groundwork she'd needed to choose her caste and career, not lead warriors in a battle for their lives. For that she needed more than academic knowledge. She needed experience.

But.

She was the Blind Hunter. The warriors with her expected leadership, not the need to train her first. Tei lead. They show the way. That's what they do. She'd totally faked it by drawing upon her experiences of the war, and used the journey for deeper research. Luckily, the journey was a long one. Her knowledge of weapons and tactics had been adequate already, logistics the same, but she'd needed Tei'Laran's help with strategy.

She'd had many questions.

The war games were a gift. A great opportunity to firm her grip on her new caste and life. Academically, she was up to speed. Even Tei'Laran was impressed. It was her background of course. Research had been her life once. It still was in her heart. The games would let her gain some experience at leading professional warriors. Yes, indeed. The war games were a gift all right, so why was she in orbit and not on the surface playing chase the Human?

A very good question that.

It started with an invitation to tour the various Pandoran facilities. Tei'Laran had strongly encouraged her to accept. Ordered her to accept really, though that was a little awkward because the Blind Hunter outranked him. Tei'Laran had skirted the niceties by making it a request, and by agreeing, she'd put him in her debt. She would never call it in, and he understood that. Matters of honour sometimes came down to a need to work within the system for mutual benefit.

She'd watched huge mining machines digesting asteroids, and she'd pressed the start button to begin munching on a new rock. Kazim had been delighted to record the event, but then, he was easily pleased. She'd only pressed a button for the Harmonies sake. A green one.

Despite Tei'Shima's background being in genetics and not engineering, Pandora's smelters had been interesting. Her parents had been engineers, and her father had often shared stories about his work. He would've enjoyed seeing them. The smelters were huge stations. Fully automated, they used nanotech to reduce ore into the elements needed for Pandora's voracious industries.

The factories used a dizzying number of alloys. She'd seen them using vast colonies of microscopic nano-machines to create products. Bunkers had slowly emptied like magic, the raw materials replaced by hull-plating and structural supports for ships. They'd just appeared one atom at a time before her eyes! It was amazing. Her father would've loved it.

Today was her first visit to the shipyards, and she was starting to feel her good will being abused. Accepting the various tours had segregated her from those who'd followed her. She didn't believe that was Tei'Laran's intention, but a single invitation to visit a research centre had blossomed into dozens of invites to facilities all over the system.

Tei'Shima didn't want to cause offence, but she had to call an end. She needed to spend some time training and improving her skills with the other warriors. Her father had taught her to believe that being adequate was no such thing. She wanted to excel in her new life and career to honour him, but also for her own self-worth. Part of that was convincing herself that Merrick hadn't been wrong about her. That she could lead, and that she deserved to be Tei.

"Why me?" Tei'Shima said. Did she sound whiny? She hoped not. "Why isn't Tei'Laran doing this one?"

"Because," Kazim said patiently. "The Blind Hunter is famous."

"But he used to be Fleet! He likes ships."

"So?"

"So he'll get more out of this. I don't know what I'm looking at."

"It's a super-carrier," Varya said and gestured at the ship with his tail. "Well, it will be when it's finished."

The meeting room came equipped with a large holotank displaying the ship currently under construction. Their escort had turned it on before leaving to fetch another group scheduled for the tour. The three-dimensional image glowed blue in the holographic field. It had green info-boxes attached to various points of interest. When queried, the boxes became windows that contained marketing images and technical specifications. Kazim had recorded Varya trying them out.

"I *know* it's a carrier," she said in exasperation. She glanced at the holotank where it revealed the ship's internal frame. It could've been the skeleton of some great beast. "Tei'Laran would have learned more from seeing this than I ever will asking questions. I don't know the right ones to ask."

"How about how much it costs?" Varya said.

Kazim laughed.

"Funny."

"I'm serious. Don't worry so much. Others will follow and ask their own questions in time. Think of all this as scouting the way. You're blazing a trail for them."

Trailblazing? She could do that. Surely if the elders wanted to know more they would send engineers. Varya was right.

"Fine, but think up some questions to ask. I'm not letting you get away with watching me do all the work."

"I hear, Tei," Varya said trying to sound serious, but he spoiled it with a dip of an ear to Kazim.

Kazim was in on the conspiracy and dipped one of his in return.

Tei'Shima pretended not to notice. They were enjoying the trip. As long as they were happy, she was willing to be their target.

The sound of Human chatter and laughter drew her attention to the back of the room. Their guide was back with the anticipated tourists. Tei'Shima wondered what the joke was about, and whether someone was the target of ear-dipping humour. Actually, she seemed to recall that Humans couldn't dip an ear the way Shan could. They used their eyes and one of their many face-screwing gestures instead. What was it called again? A wink, that was it.

The guide made his way to the front of the room. "Can I have your attention please?" The chatter died and he switched off the holotank. "Before we get started on the five credit tour—"

A few of the Humans laughed, and Tei'Shima wondered

why. Was the guide trying to swindle them? Five credits didn't sound like a lot. She could access funds easily enough using her wristcomp. They all could. Her people had access to the Alliance banking system as part of the treaty, along with things like medical aid and Infonet access.

The guide reactivated the holotank to display a schematic of the shipyard. "I'm sure you're tired of these orientation briefings by now, but we have to do them by law. Let's get this over as quickly as we can, shall we? My name's Mark Basset, and I'll be your guide today…"

Tei'Shima listened attentively to the health and safety briefing, aware that she was the only one interested. Kazim had turned to filming the newcomers, and muttering happily to himself. Something about the Harmonies smiling on him, and how he was going to be famous.

"You're already famous," Varya hissed quietly.

"I'll be more famous. I'm about to become the first Shan to interview a Human mega-star. I'll be a hero, like Shima."

"That's Tei'Shima to you," she muttered trying not to let him distract her. "What's a mega-star?"

"She is," Kazim said, and pointed to one of the Humans with his tail. His hands were busy with his camera.

Tei'Shima took a quick look. "She is?"

"Yes! That's Zelda. I think the female next to her might be Shortcut. She's special too. My caste will give me anything I want after this. Money, an assistant, a private air car... maybe even my own show!"

The tour guide noticed he'd lost his audience. "Your attention please! I need your attention. The quicker I get through this, the quicker the tour can begin."

Tei'Shima cuffed Kazim's ears lightly, claws in. "Quiet."

"*Ow!*" Kazim cried loudly.

"Oh hush up. That didn't hurt."

"No, but it gained attention," Varya said. "As he planned."

Kazim wiggled his ears. "I'm a genius. What can I say?"

Tei'Shima growled under her breath.

Zelda was on her way over, dragging the rest of her party with her. The tour guide desperately tried to inform the room about the escape pods, but no one was listening. He gave up trying to regain the room, and raced through his presentation.

"These briefings are so *boooring*, aren't they?" Zelda said. "They're always the same. Blah blah depressurisation alarm blah blah. Go here and do that. Pull this lever blah blah, and then kiss your ass goodbye."

The Humans laughed.

Zelda burned brightly in the Harmonies, but then Humans tended to be that way. It didn't mean anything. Her friend though. Kazim had named her Shortcut. She was special. Not in herself but in the way she seemed to orbit Zelda in the Harmonies. They could be sibs. She didn't think they were, but Shortcut's love for Zelda was obvious in her mind glow, and their auras were touching. Mingling. It reminded her of Kate when she was near Stone.

The tour guide droned on, but Zelda was more entertaining and no one took any notice of him. She introduced the other Humans with her. Kazim had been right about Shortcut. The others were Zelda's security detail, and some media people. Tei'Shima memorised their names and scents.

She bowed. "May you live in harmony. It's an honour to meet you all."

Zelda bowed in return. "The honour is very much ours. I wish the rest of the guys could have met you, but they didn't feel up to the trip. Their loss, eh?" Zelda wrapped an arm around Shortcut, and the woman nodded. "After meeting Gina and Eric, I couldn't wait to see you, Shima."

"It's Tei'Shima now," Kazim confided as if revealing a secret. "She gets touchy about it, but don't mind her."

Zelda and friends grinned. That Human trait was still startling. Tei'Shima forced herself not to react to it, or to Kazim's impudence.

"You know Gina?" Tei'Shima said.

She hadn't crossed paths with the vipers this trip, but she'd known they were part of the games. Tei'Laran had mentioned the referees had assigned them to play together on the same side. A shame, because she still didn't know if she could stalk a viper undetected. It would've been fun to find out.

"I met her at the convention a few weeks ago," Zelda said. "She's a fan."

An air impeller? That couldn't be right. Zelda meant Gina had honoured her by admiring her work. Professional respect then. If Gina respected Zelda, then she must be worthy of it.

"May I interview you?" Kazim said. "It would play very well back home."

"Sure," Zelda said. "We'll have to do it here though. I'm booked solid after this until my ship leaves at the end of the month."

"If it's too much trouble, just tell him no," Tei'Shima said. "He doesn't know when to switch that thing off."

Kazim gasped in outrage, eliciting more Human laughter.

Varya chuffed and smacked Kazim's shoulder. "She's right."

Zelda grinned. "It's okay. I'm always switched on."

Shortcut nodded. "She isn't joking. She's in costume all the time. She changed her name to Zelda when our first season went viral."

"What about you?" Kazim said, already sniffing out an interesting story.

"You think I want to be called Shortcut for real? She's just a part I play. Selene Anduran is my real name. Everyone calls me Shortcut because I hang with Zelda all the time. I'm fine with that. It's better to be Shortcut, Zelda's rich and famous co-star, than Selene Nobody."

Zelda hugged her friend. "You'll never be a nobody. Not to me."

Tei'Shima watched in fascination as the Harmonies

revealed their auras flaring up. Where their energies merged, new patterns were born in little explosions of colour.

"And that concludes the orientation briefing," the tour guide said desperately. "Are there any questions regarding the regulations I've just explained to you?" He didn't wait to find out if there were. "Good. Let's get to the fun part. If you'll follow me, we'll get you suited up for the tour. This way."

Zelda grinned. "Can you interview me on the move, Kazim?"

Tei'Shima rolled her eyes. "Of course he can. He never puts that thing down."

"Good then. Better not keep Mark waiting."

They moved to join their guide waiting at the door.

"Did you know we sometimes use cameras worn like a neural headset, Kazim?" Shortcut said. "POV cameras they're called. They're completely hands free."

"Pee-oh-vee?"

"Point of view. They record what the actor sees from their point of view. We use them to make full-sensory sensims. Newsies use their own version for convenience. Like I said, they're hands free. They're controlled using neural commands."

Tei'Shima sighed. Kazim would want one of those for certain. She could tell by his scent and his reaction in the Harmonies that the idea excited him. She wondered how much they cost, and where to buy one. She would search Infonet, but later. When she was alone.

* * *

33 ~ Inconvenient Tails

Nstar Industries Orbital Shipyard, Pandora System

Tei'Shima tried not to laugh at the dismay on the technician's face. He'd been delighted when Mark brought Zelda into his presence, but when the Shan arrived, he realised he needed to fit them into suits designed for Humans!

"This is Todd," Mark said. "He's responsible for dispensing safety equipment here at Nstar. I'll leave you with him, and he'll get you outfitted."

"Err..." Todd said.

"I need to get suited up. Shall we say thirty minutes?"

"Err..."

"Great! See you soon," Mark said and hurried out.

All eyes swung to Todd. The poor unprepared Human paled when Kazim flourished his tail over one shoulder. It didn't mean anything. Kazim was making his differences obvious to garner a reaction for his audience. As always his camera was on and recording everything.

Zelda came to the rescue. "Hey, Todd is it?" Todd nodded and allowed her to turn him away from that horrifyingly mobile tail. "Todd. You can see my friends might be a challenge, but think of this as your opportunity to shine."

"Shine, ma'am?"

"Kazim there, he's a big deal back home. He's going to make you famous!"

Tei'Shima laughed quietly. Todd wasn't comforted. The poor male was going to faint if Zelda helped him any further.

"How about this?" Zelda went on. "You outfit me and my guys first. Kazim can record that, right?"

"I guess."

"Of course he can! You'll do great."

"Okaaay," Todd said, and took a deep breath. "You first, ma'am?"

"Sure!"

Zelda removed her belt and holster. Shortcut took them and her jacket.

"Boots too, ma'am."

"I remember," Zelda said and sat on a chair to remove them. She stood up and turned on the spot with arms up at her sides. "Good?"

Todd nodded and pointed to a door. Zelda opened it and disappeared inside. The green light above it turned red, and Todd sat before a control station.

"What is she doing in there?" Kazim said.

"Ah," Todd said. He looked up from his controls, startled to find himself pinned in place by Kazim's camera lens. "I'll show you."

A wall-screen came to life showing Zelda standing on a platform. The room was quite gloomy. The platform slowly began rotating, and lines of coloured light covered Zelda in a grid pattern.

"What's that?" Kazim said.

"The computer uses the grid to measure the subject, and the data is passed to the nano-printer next door. You've used an autochef, right?"

"On the ship. It was the only source of food and water."

"Right, well, a nano-printer is like an autochef, but instead of food it makes things like suits."

"It's a nano-factory?" Kazim said.

"Not really. Proper factories can mass-produce things ten times faster and cheaper, but nano-printers are great for making one-off items. Engineers on warships use them to make critical parts if they run out."

"Interesting."

Todd nodded. "They're old technology, but they're still useful. The navy only uses them in emergencies. Raw materials are too bulky for everyday use."

Tei'Shima watched Zelda follow Todd's instructions. She had to raise and lower her arms and legs. The computer needed her body's full range of motion to measure it accurately.

"Will the new suits be the same as Fleet uses?" Tei'Shima wondered aloud. "I mean, shouldn't you measure her without her clothes on?"

Todd blushed, and the Harmonies revealed he found that idea to be a good one. A very good one. Shortcut did as well, but she wasn't blushing. She had a secretive smile on her face.

"I ah... no," Todd stuttered. "I mean no, they're completely different. Your suits will be a standard short EVA design. Naval shipsuits are custom jobs. They have plumbing connections and nano-self-repair as standard. Shipsuits are like uniforms, not EVA suits. They aren't self-contained. They use umbilicals designed to keep a crewman alive at his station."

"What if someone needs to leave for some reason?" Kazim said.

"The navy uses hardsuits for that. Marines and damage control parties use them when their ships go to battle stations. Engineers too."

"Thank you for explaining," Tei'Shima said.

"You're welcome," Todd said as Zelda emerged from the scanning chamber. "Next please."

Shortcut handed Zelda her things, kicked off her boots, and entered the chamber. Todd repeated the process for all the Humans, and then it was Tei'Shima's turn. She removed her harness and weapons, but Todd wasn't sure his system would work for Shan.

"Don't anticipate," Zelda soothed.

"But..." Todd began.

"Try. It might be fine. It might not. Fix what goes wrong when it happens. Okay?"

Todd nodded.

Tei'Shima entered the chamber and climbed onto the platform. She stood on two legs, but wondered if four would be better. No. She decided to mimic a Human as much as possible. There was no point in confusing Todd's computer any more than necessary. It would probably have a crisis when it scanned her tail. She wondered if it would think she had three arms.

"Okay," Todd said. His voice came from a speaker over the door. "Here we go."

The scanning lines decorated her pelt, and the platform slowly turned. She kept vertical and still. When Todd told her to raise her arms, she followed instructions. It didn't seem any different from the other sessions.

"Okay. I've backed-up your scan in case the next part goes wrong. Can you stand on four feet, please?"

Tei'Shima dropped to all fours. She stood in a natural and relaxed posture as the scan continued.

"Okay!" Todd sounded pleased. "It's working fine. I'm a bit surprised to be honest. Either the software is more advanced than I thought, or the devs cut some corners. My bet is they used code designed for scanning other things."

Tei'Shima didn't particularly care why it worked as long as it did. She followed instructions, lifting and placing her feet as if walking in place. Last of all, Todd backed-up the scan again before asking her to use her tail."

"To do what?" she asked.

"Whatever you like. Imagine you're wearing a suit and need to use it."

She'd never worn a suit, so imagining that was hard. Still, she moved her tail as if limbering up for a run. It seemed to satisfy.

"And that's it. You'll need to test the fit for me. If it's okay, I'll scan your friends."

Tei'Shima left the chamber. Zelda and the others were pulling on suits. Todd wasn't present, but before she could comment on that, he reappeared carrying a white bundle. He offered it to her.

"It looks all right. All the parts are there, and it does seem Shan-shaped." Todd shrugged. "I guess the proof is in the eating."

"Eating?" Kazim said.

Zelda laughed. "A silly Human saying, Kazim. The proof of the pudding is in the eating. It means you can't tell how good something is until you try it."

Tei'Shima pulled the suit on. There was a long pocket for her tail, and although it felt strange, it did allow her full range of motion. She sealed the suit, and dropped to all fours to walk around the room. It felt very odd. She could imagine it would become uncomfortably warm if worn too long.

"Better not try your claws," Kazim warned from behind his camera.

"Good point," Varya said.

Todd gaped like a landed fish. "Don't do that. You might puncture it."

Tei'Shima stood on two legs to take the helmet. It was shaped to allow her face to clear the visor, and it was just a bit taller for her ears. It fit surprisingly well. It was more comfortable than the rest of the suit.

She removed it. "It's fine, but I'm already feeling too hot."

"It will be climate-controlled, but that's handled by the

PLSS. Those are stored in the pod bay for charging."

Tei'Shima unsealed the suit and peeled it down to her hips. How Humans put up with wearing clothes all the time, she would never understand. Even wearing the suit for a short time had been stifling.

"Better?" Todd said.

Tei'Shima flicked her ears. She nodded as well in case he didn't understand.

"Great. You're next, Kazim."

Varya took charge of Kazim's beloved camera, and recorded his session.

"Hey Todd?" Zelda said. "Have you got any kit bags for our stuff?"

Todd pointed to a cupboard, but he didn't take his eyes off his controls. Kazim emerged and took charge of his camera for Varya's session.

Mark returned while Varya was still being scanned. His EVA suit was orange, and the helmet he carried was a glossy white. He counted his charges and came up one short. Varya.

"Everything all right?" Mark said. "Any problems?"

"None," Todd said as Varya reappeared.

"Good!"

Todd went to fetch Varya's suit, and a few minutes later, he was pulling it on to test the fit. Mark watched the process.

"Do you want a bag for your things?" Zelda said. "There's room in ours."

"We'll carry our own weight, but thank you for the offer," Tei'Shima said. Zelda's bag was stuffed and looked bulky.

She retrieved an empty bag and stuffed her gear into it along with Kazim's harness. Varya took charge of it and stored his gear with the rest. Kazim kept his camera. Of course.

"Are we ready?" Marcus said, and everyone muttered agreement. "Follow me to the pod bay then."

Kazim interviewed Zelda and Shortcut as they made their way through the corridors of the busy station. Tei'Shima assumed he'd need to do a lot of editing later. Humans were a chatty bunch, and the background noise was loud. She asked about that.

"Shift change," Mark explained. "Nstar uses a three-shift rotation to give the yard around the clock coverage."

"They're going down to Pandora?"

"No need for that. They live here on the station. Nstar supplies accommodations to its employees and their families as part of their employment contracts."

"There are younglings here?" Tei'Shima said.

She hadn't met any and wondered what they were like. Slow growing. She knew that but not much else. She wondered what they were like in the Harmonies.

"Oh yes! We have schools for them of course. Nstar takes employee comfort seriously. Our stations have everything they might need. Think of it as a city in orbit."

Tei'Shima flicked her ears and nodded thoughtfully. The station was huge. She'd seen its exterior upon her final approach. The pilot of the shuttle had let her visit the cockpit to see it. Despite the station's size, the rest of the shipyard dwarfed it. The dock had to be big enough to accommodate ships under construction.

"How many live here?"

"I don't actually know," Todd said. "No one has asked me that before. I do know Nstar employs over ten-thousand yard workers, and all of them live here. There are a few thousand station staffers as well, and then all the dependents on top of that."

"Twenty-thousand then?"

Mark nodded. "Possibly more. I don't remember ever seeing census data."

Tei'Shima wondered if the younglings ever visited Pandora. What must it be like for them, living on a station all the time? Did they even know what they were missing? She couldn't imagine never feeling the sun on her face, or scenting prey on a fresh breeze.

Mark ushered them into an elevator and they descended to the pod bay.

* * *

34 ~ Five Credit Tour

Nstar Industries Orbital Shipyard, Pandora System

To Tei'Shima's surprise, she quickly became used to the EVA suit. The benefits of the PLSS on her back far outweighed the inconvenience. Breathing was something she was fond of, but even without donning her helmet, the suit was comfortably cool now.

Mark piloted the pod high above the ship under construction, following its long axis. Tei'Shima watched it passing slowly below them. It was a huge achievement to be sure, but the pod fascinated her almost as much. It was transparent, and made her feel as if she were outside. Or rather, it seemed to be transparent. It hadn't been that way when they boarded; its cylindrical shape had gleamed white under the harsh pod bay lights. The only transparent part was the domed glass over the cockpit area.

"A clever illusion isn't it?" Zelda said.

"How do they do it?"

Zelda shrugged. "Magic."

"What's that?"

Shortcut smacked Zelda's arm. "Don't confuse her."

Zelda grinned.

"I find it's usually safest to ignore her when she's like this," Shortcut confided. "If anyone tries to tell you something is magic, it means they don't have a clue how to answer you."

Tei'Shima flicked her ears and added a nod. What a strange custom. "Do you understand it?"

"Sort of. Not the technical stuff, but nanotech is usually responsible for things that seem impossible. You know how ships can change colour when they want to hide?"

"They turn black."

"That's right. Turning black is a part of going into stealth. Nanocoat is clever like that. It reacts to events like incoming fire, but it can be programmed to do other stuff too."

"Like I said," Zelda said. "Magic."

Shortcut rolled her eyes. "Basically, the nanocoat in here changes in real time to mimic the pod's surroundings."

"Thank you for explaining."

"You're welcome."

Kazim glanced over and dipped an ear at Mark. He was thinking of the air-car his caste would give him. Tei'Shima flicked her ears, and he went back to work.

"The *Hercules* carrier is the latest in a long line of record-breaking ship designs built by Nstar," Mark was saying. "It's the largest warship currently in our catalogue."

"How much does it cost?" Tei'Shima said. She ignored Varya's quiet laughter at her choice of question.

"Well, that's a complicated question—"

"That means it's eye-wateringly expensive," Zelda translated helpfully.

Shortcut snickered.

"I assure you that pricing at Nstar is competitive with our closest rivals," Mark said.

"He means Faragut is charging just as much."

Tei'Shima turned from Zelda and back to Mark in time to see him frown. The Harmonies revealed his irritation, but he kept it out of his voice admirably.

"To answer your question, a *Hercules* class carrier built to order, and ready for space in all respects, would cost almost 40 billion credits."

Kazim's camera swung to Zelda, and of course she obliged him. "What about that was complicated? 40 billion credits of our tax money per ship sounds like a steal! Oh wait, what about its weapons?"

"Well, as I said it's complicated."

"He means the ship is space-worthy but unarmed."

Bruce, one of Zelda's guards chuckled. Zelda called him Bruiser for some reason. The other warrior was Hazel. She went by Haze. She rolled her eyes at her employer's antics.

"Is that true?" Tei'Shima asked. "That doesn't seem like a very good deal."

"She is, in fact, incorrect," Mark said triumphantly.

Zelda frowned at that. The Harmonies revealed she'd spoken the truth, but Mark had as well.

"Ships leave our facilities fully operational. They're armed with the latest point defence laser clusters and missile launchers, and come equipped with our patented electro-magnetic gatling cannons as standard. Our clients can rest assured that when they take delivery, all defensive and offensive armament is in place and top of the line. All they need do is supply their own munitions. We can supply those at need for an additional fee upon request."

"What about the fighters and bombers it carries into battle?" Tei'Shima said. "Those must cost a lot."

Mark nodded. "I'm sure they do, but Nstar builds capital ships, and leaves those to others."

Zelda translated again. "Capital ships are the big ones."

Tei'Shima hadn't needed the translation this time. She wasn't Fleet, but she hadn't been completely ignorant even before becoming warrior caste. She knew the terminology.

"A fully crewed and functional ship must cost... twice 40

billion?" Tei'Shima guessed.

"If the navy had to purchase everything new, it might be on the order of 50 billion, but they don't need to. Munitions are part of their ongoing budget, and small craft would most likely be transferred from decommissioned ships at no cost, or very little."

"That's assuming one-for-one replacement of capital ships," Tei'Shima said.

Mark nodded.

That was a big assumption considering the Merkiaari threat. She doubted the navy would be comfortable decommissioning any of its ships under the circumstances. If she were them, she'd work on the principle that more ships were preferable to less no matter their age. They would need to buy a lot of fighter craft and bombers for their current build up. She wondered if her people might fulfil that need. An export of that sort would generate income and some much needed investment. She made a mental note to pitch the idea to her clan. She was Tei now and had to think of such things.

Mark continued his presentation. "A *Hercules* class carrier weighs 1.2 million tons displacement—"

"Wasn't *Hercules* a male?" Tei'Shima said. "Human ships are female. A friend mentioned it once."

That garnered her an appreciative look from Varya. He hadn't heard of the hero, and neither had Kazim. The Harmonies revealed his surprise. Tei'Shima knew about *Hercules* from James. He used to be a history teacher. She'd learned Human ships were female from him as well, at her first meeting with him beneath the Kachina mountains. It had been her first ever interaction with a Human. A memorable time of firsts for her.

Mark nodded. "*Hercules* was indeed a man. A legendary hero who lived on Earth thousands of years ago."

"Then why name a female ship after him?"

"I've got this, Mark," Zelda said. "We don't always

name our ships after people, but when we do they're usually someone we admire from our history. That person might be a man or a woman. We name ships for other things too. My ship is called *Bad Penny*. It comes from an ancient saying about a bad penny always turning up."

"What is a penny?"

"An ancient form of currency. You know, a coin? It's a physical form of money. A bad penny was a counterfeit coin. Those were obviously unwanted, so one turning up was bad news."

"I fail to understand why you'd name your ship after an unlucky event."

"Oh that's easy. When I show up, it's bad news for the other guy."

Shortcut laughed.

Tei'Shima didn't understand why that was funny, but she didn't need to. "What about *Hercules*?"

"He was a great hero, and known as the world's strongest man. Naming our biggest ship class after him is like saying these are our most powerful ships."

"I think I see. Will the crew still call their ship, she?"

Zelda smiled. "Afraid so. All ships are she, no matter what her name is. It's a Human thing."

It certainly was a Human thing. It made no sense from a Shan standpoint. Kazim gestured urgently at Mark. He was such a taskmaster. Tei'Shima hastily considered questions to ask.

"How big are they, Mark?"

"They're 1500 metres from bow to stern, and 300 metres at the beam. Due to its dual launch bay and hangar design, the ship can launch and retrieve fighters despite damage that might incapacitate lesser ships. The *Hercules* class uses four electro-magnetic catapults, not two. This allows for rapid deployment and retrieval of its fighters."

"Impressive," Tei'Shima said. "Crew?"

"Five-thousand is optimal, but the environmental systems can handle up to seven-thousand for short periods should the need arise."

Mark reached the impressive bow of the ship and sent them diving down to make the return trip from the underside. Tei'Shima stared up at the hull passing so close above them, and had a perfect view of its destruction.

It started small. She might have imagined the brief flash of light that caught her eye. They were moving just fast enough that she had to look back to check. The bloom of light was joined by others. Explosions rocked the great ship, and debris erupted from the hull. If Mark had been flying just a little slower, the pod would have been caught in the blast-wave.

Kazim noticed her inattention, and swung his camera in that direction. His sudden movement drew more eyes in time to see the ship's death throes. The explosions caused the carrier to heave against its restraints, as if trying to escape its destruction.

The massive docking arm closest to the pod sheared off as they passed it, and took a section of the ship's hull with it. Worse, it ripped a hole in the station as it broke free. Atmosphere blasted out, as the remaining docking arms took the strain. They held for a few moments, but then buckled. One huge clamp slipped free, and the huge ship pivoted on its remaining restraints.

Tei'Shima's thoughts raced through the possibilities. Was it an accident or malicious intent? Another flash of light caught her attention in the brief time she had to consider. This time the station was the target.

Target?

Yes.

It must be enemy action then. The war had arrived at Pandora. Tei'Shima darted paranoid glances all around. The pod's transparency aided her in that, but of course she had no chance of seeing the Merki with the naked eye. The vast distances involved meant they could have fired from millions of heikke away.

"Go down," Tei'Shima gasped, only then realising Mark hadn't reacted to the catastrophe evolving behind them. "Fly down!" she yelled.

"What?" Mark said and looked back. He saw it, and froze.

Shortcut leapt for the controls, and shoved Mark aside. He fell to hands and knees. She did something, and the pod lurched downward in a crazy spiral to avoid the many hazards spawning all around them. Behind them, the doomed carrier began to break up in earnest. Huge sections broke off, and Pandora's gravity took charge of them.

Terrified yard workers, those lucky enough to be in pods outside the dying ship, abandoned their posts and raced for the station. Home and family was all they cared about now. It was the wrong thing to do. Tei'Shima understood the instinct to protect family and clan, but the station was doomed.

Hull-plating and support structures drifted free of the fleeing pods. No longer held in place for welding or whatever the engineers wanted to do with them, they added to the hazards blossoming all around them. Shortcut dodged between slowly spinning and colliding hull-plates at top speed, throwing her passengers around the pod in an effort not to hit anything. Everyone yelled as they rolled around inside, trying to grab something.

"Just like on the set," Shortcut muttered under her breath, holding onto the controls like grim death. She belted in with one hand as if she did it every day. "It's a sim. Not real. Not real. Stay calm and everything will be fine... *oh shit!*" The pod rolled, barely missing a fleeing pod. Everyone lost their footing again. "We're fine! Don't panic! No one panic! I've got this."

Tei'Shima climbed back to her feet. If anyone was close to panicking, it was Shortcut. Everyone else was still in shock.

Mark clambered to his feet. "What are you doing?! There

are regulations! I have emergency procedures to follow. We have to dock with the station immediately."

"Screw that," Shortcut muttered. "Let's keep breathing and worry about proper procedure later."

Breathing, yes, they might hit debris. There were chunks of broken ship drifting all around them now. Shortcut steered the pod violently at high speed to avoid them. Everyone held on as best they could.

Tei'Shima grabbed her helmet. "Helmets on!" She cried and followed her own order.

Kazim recorded it all. His ears were flat to his head, but as always his hands were steady. The result of the station's explosive decompression was horribly obvious. People and equipment had been ejected through the gaping hole in the station as the atmosphere blasted out. Safety measures would ensure most survived in there for a time, but there were already bodies drifting away. Dozens and dozens of them.

Tei'Shima refused to see them as people. Absolutely refused. She didn't want to identify any as younglings. They were obstacles. Hopefully Shortcut was too busy dodging them to notice what she was avoiding. Kazim hadn't put his helmet on. She blocked his view of the chaos outside and snarled in his face. Her rumpled muzzle revealed her teeth clearly despite her helmet's visor. She grabbed his helmet and forced it over his head, making sure it sealed. The indicators on his chest turned green. Good seal.

"Don't you dare take it off!" She snarled at him over the open comm. She didn't care that everyone heard her fear for him. "Don't even *move!*"

"Someone help! I can't take my hands off this!" Shortcut yelled. Zelda rushed to help with her helmet. "Thanks."

"You're doing great," Zelda said and pointed to a clearing in the debris field. "Take us there."

"Sure thing, Boss," Shortcut said, in character now. "We need a plan. Got one handy?"

"Dock with the station!" Mark insisted.

"No!" Tei'Shima yelled, but her voice was drowned out by the others expressing their thoughts on that. Everyone agreed with her. "No."

Shortcut slowed the pod's mad dash when they cleared the debris. She stayed at the controls, ready to evade again if necessary, but they seemed safe for now. Zelda remained with her to help. Two pairs of eyes were better than one.

Kazim was still recording, but splitting his attention between the goings on outside, and those in the pod. He hadn't removed his helmet. Varya was looking after him.

Mark was kneeling on the floor, staring through it, white-faced with shock. The destruction was below them, and hideously obvious even at this distance. The station and shipyard had turned into a tangle of wreckage. Bruiser and Haze were grimly silent, but they were warriors and holding on. Awaiting orders.

Tei'Shima took a breath and stared into Kazim's camera unseeing. Memories of her father and the destruction of Hool Station filled her head. Kazim's documentary films didn't do the reality of such a calamity justice. Now she had personal experience to add flesh to the bones of her nightmare.

She went to join Zelda and Shortcut.

* * *

Part IV

35 ~ Merry Christmas

Southaven Province, Pandora

Eric found the Shan a genuine pleasure to work with despite the conditions. Maybe even because of them in a way. They were professional, likeable, and they found joy in work that many would not. Soldiers tended to bitch and moan about the most ridiculous things. Not the Shan. Tei'Laran's warriors even managed to have fun in a blizzard!

Eric grinned as his men placed bets on the game, and laughed with them as Kisa disappeared into deep snow. Only her ear tufts could be seen, drooping a little now in embarrassment. She'd tried to pounce over what she'd thought was a shallow drift, but had landed in a depression filled with snow.

Gina laughed. "Ten more that Kisa still wins!"

"You're on, LT," Cragg said. "She'll never catch Roldan now. He's a sprinter."

"She's better at tactics. She'll bring it home. You watch."

"I'm watching," Cragg said doubtfully.

"Oh ye of little faith. She'll take him down at the halfway line."

Eric snorted. Cragg was right, it would never happen. The snow was falling so heavily that he needed infra just to keep the players in sight. The Shan had no artificial aids. Once Kisa lost sight of Roldan, it would be over. He doubted the game would last much longer. Shan enjoyed snow, but even they needed to see each other and the pennants to play.

Roldan reached the goal line, and snatched the last pennant. It was the deciding point. Both had two each. Bring it home, and he'd win. Kisa managed to climb out of her predicament, and went in for the kill. She intercepted Roldan, and both Shan disappeared into deep snow.

"Roldan for the win!" Cragg shouted.

"Ki-*saaah*… Ki-*saaah*… Ki-*saaah*," Gina chanted over Cragg's bellows.

Both Shan appeared at the same time and bounded through the snow in little leaps to make headway. The conditions really were becoming unplayable. Shan and Human voices rose to encourage their champions. Roldan still had possession. The red flash of the pennant remained hooked to his harness strap. Kisa tackled him again, and they both rolled out of sight again.

The crowd hushed, everyone straining their eyes to see through the whiteout, but there was nothing to see. The conditions were worsening and the snow bank was too deep. Eric switched to motion sensors. Both Shan were wrestling for control of the pennant as if lives depended on it. Growls and snarls of effort came from their direction, and ended when Kisa exploded out of the snow with the pennant between her teeth.

"*I told you! I told you!*" Gina screamed in triumph as her champion brought home the bacon. "*I told you!*"

"Yeah," Cragg said sourly, as he counted up his losses. "You told me."

Kisa dashed to victory and Gina went nuts. She jumped about the place waving her arms in the air. Eric laughed at the sour expression on Cragg's face. Gina went to greet her hero, and the winners started trickling in to collect their money.

"It's not the end of the world, Cragg," Eric said. "Look at her. She needed cheering up."

Cragg smiled briefly, but then wiped it away as his stack of platinum dwindled. In the end, the day's take was barely above his original stake. Kisa had wiped out an entire week's profit.

"Okay listen up," Eric said over viper comm. "The weather is closing in. Secure your gear for a blow. Operation Stein begins tomorrow on schedule unless we get socked in."

"You think we will?" Cragg said.

"Wouldn't surprise me. I've seen stuff like this last for days. We've already lost comms from up top. Hammer reported the weather front moving in, and then nothing."

Gina slogged back through thigh deep snow, still grinning. Her hair was turning white to match her armour. They'd all set their armour's nanocoat to match the conditions. Behind her the Shan were heading into the trees. They would hunker down in big puppy-piles to wait out the storm. This was nothing to them. They really did like the snow.

Zack Gordon wrapped an arm around Cragg in commiseration. "Pay the lady."

Gina snapped her fingers. "Gimme."

Cragg sighed and handed over the last of his stash. "Merry fuckin' Christmas."

Gina chuckled. "You too. I didn't even remember it was today, but yeah, you too Martin." She switched to viper comm. "Merry Christmas Alpha Company."

The entire company responded in a cacophony of overlapping seasonal greetings. Gina beamed at Eric, her cheeks aglow from the cold.

"We better get under cover. This mess is getting worse," Eric said.

They headed for camp.

The rest of the company was already hunkering down for the night. The rows of ten-man tents were going to be buried by morning. He'd chosen the hollow to shield them from observation, not weather. They were safe from the wind, but that was accident not design.

Tei'Laran intercepted them before they reached the tents. Eric sent the others on ahead.

"How can I help you, Tei?" Eric said, choosing to use Shan.

Tei'Laran was fluent in English, but he responded in kind. "I wondered if we might make use of the storm."

Operation Stein was essentially a raid upon a comms station guarded by the Marines. Eric thought fondly of the plan as Operation Screw Stein. He still hadn't paid the major back for getting them all sent to the ass end of nowhere.

General Ecclestone hadn't found his how-to-disable-a-Titan demo amusing, and had exiled him along with Stein and the Shan. It was vindictive, petty, and self-serving of him, but not unexpected. He wanted them out of the media limelight in order to push his own agenda uncontested.

"The snow doesn't bother you?" Eric said. "The storm is still building."

"Yes, exhilarating isn't it?"

"Well..."

"My people love the mountains, Tei'Penleigh."

"Call me Eric. Human ranks don't truly translate into anything resembling yours. I don't have your gifts. No Human does."

Tei'Laran flicked his ears. "Eric then. It's usually cold in the mountains. We're accustomed to it."

Eric nodded. "You want to get into position around the target using the storm as cover?"

"Precisely. We'll scout the way and observe the target. We can move quickly and stealthily."

"Sounds good. I'd appreciate a sitrep when you're in

position, and please don't attack without us. My guys won't want to miss it."

Tei'Laran laughed. "It will be fun."

Eric smiled. "Major Stein won't think so. I can't wait to hear his critique of our attack."

"That will be interesting. I'll comms you when we're in position."

Eric nodded. The Shan still didn't wear helmets or armour, but they did have wristcomps. Those had decent comms range and had satellite access. Combined with wireless ear-buds and throat microphones, the Shan had a good alternative to helmet comms until proper armour was available. He'd heard prototypes were already being tested. Designs ranged from armour that approximated viper issue, to Shan-shaped sneaksuits with chameleon functionality.

"Go ahead then, Tei."

Tei'Laran trotted away, and the snow quickly hid him from sight. It was falling so heavily that Eric needed his sensors to find his way to the camp. The entire company, all 164 of his vipers, were on his internal display marked in blue. He hadn't bothered to assign sentries.

The camp was guarded by the usual sentry guns and remotes. The Shan had handled the rest with roving patrols. He briefly considered setting extra guards now that Tei'Laran was moving out early, but he dismissed the thought. The weather was closing down the games for the night. If Stein was feeling adventurous, the remotes would give warning. Vipers woke testy in situations like that.

He went to join them.

There were seventeen tents. Sixteen ten-man tents to keep his squads together, and one for him and his officers. Rank had its privileges. He could stretch out and not have someone's feet in his face.

Eric homed on the tent that sensors indicated had four vipers inside. His lieutenants. He could barely see beyond his next step. The wind had really begun to pick up, and the snow was being driven into his face. His armour was toasty warm inside, but his face and hands were really feeling the exposure. The temperature was falling. It read minus five degrees and dropping on his display. It felt lower.

Wind-chill.

Eric unzipped the tent flap and dove inside.

"*Shut the hole!*" Gina cried. "*Damn!*"

"Told you not to strip down yet," Lieutenant Dengler said. She laughed evilly at Gina's shivers. "Hmmm, it's lovely and warm in my corner."

"Is that an invitation?" Gina said. Her teeth chattered. "I warn you, I have cold feet."

"Come near me, and I'll shoot you!"

Dolinski chuckled.

Eric finally managed to get the sticky zipper shut. "It's turning into a real blow out there."

"No kidding, Captain Obvious," Gina muttered sourly.

Dolinski snorted.

"Laugh it up. No Christmas pressy for you."

"Really?"

Gina rolled her eyes.

"Sucker," Brice muttered. "I heard you got one for Kate. Is that true?"

Gina shrugged. "I guess. I did wrap it like one, but she won't get it for months. It's aboard Hammer."

"What did you get her, a new knife?"

"Nah. Kate has everything lethal pretty much covered. This is something fun."

"You can't leave me hanging like that!" Brice whined.

"If you must know, I'm giving her my autographed model of *Bad Penny*."

Brice whistled. "You love that thing."

"She's a big Zelda fan."

"Not as big as you."

Gina shrugged. "Makes it more special then, doesn't it? Don't spread it around, okay Martin? I want it to be a surprise."

"She's back home! How the hell would she find out?"

"Don't ever underestimate her. Stone and Kate are two peas. He can find out the colour of your underwear on a given day without leaving his rack. And what Stone knows, Kate knows minutes later."

Everyone laughed.

Eric smiled as he listened to their banter, and stripped down. He piled his armour in a corner to thaw out. The regiment's tents used a breathable type of fabric that allowed moisture to escape while maintaining a comfortable temperature inside. The snow-melt wouldn't be a problem. He kept his battle dress on. It wasn't really as toasty as Dengler had made out.

"Tei'Laran is using the storm to get his people in position," Eric announced as he shook out his survival bag. "They'll recon and report."

Gina snorted as she snuggled into her own bag. "They just want to play."

"They do love the snow."

Dengler chuckled. "Did you see Cragg's face when Kisa won the championship?"

Gina laughed. "I warned him. His losses are his own fault."

Eric snuggled into his bag to sleep. "Lights out people," he said over viper comm. "Set your wake up for oh-five-thirty local."

"Okay mom..."

"G'night mama..."

"Can I have a story?"

Eric ignored the backtalk coming over the comm. Bunch of comedians. He set his usual security alerts before setting his own reactivation.

Computer: Initiate maintenance mode. Reactivate combat mode at 05:00 local.

Acknowledged. Maintenance mode in 3... 2... 1...

Lights out.

Southaven Province, Pandora

0335:50

Communications: incoming message.

Priority: Code Red One Alpha

Authentication: SDF Hammer, Riley Patrice, Captain commanding.

Verified.

Reactivation approved.

0335:55 close archive file... Done

Diagnostics: Unit fit for duty

Activate combat mode... Done

TRS... Done

Sensors... Done

Targeting... Done

Communications... priority message received.

Infonet... Done

TacNet... Done... Scanning... Alpha Company net online. 164 units found.

0336:01 Reactivation complete.

Eric snapped awake, but for a few precious seconds he was still on San Luis killing Merkiaari. He'd watched them burn, and laughed like a maniac as they screamed. His tears had washed runnels in the dirt on his face, and he'd laughed and laughed and laughed...

The blinking alert on his internal display caught his attention. He interrogated his logs, and peered around at his companions still sleeping the sleep of the righteous. It was so quiet. What had happened to the barrage? He checked his logs again.

So peaceful.

Pandora. Not San Luis.

Right. The war was over.

The games. Just playing at war now.

His processor had awoken him early because one of his standard alerts had been tripped. Not the usual one. There were no hostiles involved. Just a simple message. He deactivated the alert and read his comms log.

0335:50 incoming message.

Priority: Code Red One Alpha

Authentication: SDF Hammer, Riley Patrice, Captain commanding.

Verified.

Red One Alpha was a reference to the Red One Alert. It hadn't been rescinded. The Alliance was still at war. Tacking on the Alpha tag could mean a lot of things, but all of them were bad news. The storm had died down a bit. He tried to contact the ship.

"Hammer this is Penleigh, over. Come in Hammer." He listened to dead air for a count of ten. "Hammer Hammer Hammer, this is Penleigh over."

"Captain! Standby please," lieutenant Besson said. She sounded scared.

"Penleigh?" Captain Riley said. "You have Merkiaari incoming."

Of course he did. His first vacation since forever, and the Merki invited themselves to his party. His thoughts flashed to Tei'Laran. *Hammer* didn't have the lift capacity to evacuate his vipers *and* 2000 Shan warriors. Hell, it had barely had the environmental capacity to accommodate her crew and his men on the trip out. Hammer was a destroyer, not a troop transport or a passenger liner.

"I've been trying to reach you through the storm for over an hour. The lull you're enjoying is temporary. You're in for another blow very soon."

"What are my options?" Eric said.

"The fleet is outnumbered hundreds to one. The Merki are turning them into scrap. If I try to pick you up, my ship will join them. I'm sorry. I can't stay."

Well, that made things easier. No guilt trips. No trips at all. Just the usual fight or die... or fight *and* die.

"Understood."

"I'm going to try something—a supply drop to you by remote. No guarantees and I won't ask my pilots to volunteer for a one-way trip down. Sorry again."

She didn't sound sorry. She sounded stressed but in control. Patrice Riley was one of Snakeholme's best ship captains. The SDF didn't have many warships and competition for a command slot was fierce.

"What's on the menu?" Eric said. He didn't like it, but it was Riley's call.

"I'm guessing you'd like to ditch your simunition rounds for war shots."

"You got that right!" Damn, she was ahead of him. He should have considered his lack of supplies the instant he heard the news. "Ammo and power cells first."

"I'm stuffing my shuttles with everything that'll fit. No time for neatness. You'll have to take what I give you. You can keep the birds. I'll pick them up later. If there *is* a later."

"Understood. You already sent a report home?"

"We've detected dozens of drone launches, but yes, the General has one on the way from me. I'll probably reach him first. I promise you, I'll be back with *Grafton* full of whoop-ass as soon as I can."

Eric snorted. Pandora was a high value asset. Or it used to be before the Merkiaari started trashing it. Burgton might well bring the entire regiment himself for this one.

Whoop-ass indeed.

"Drop coordinates follow," Riley said.

Eric copied the data. He grimaced when he saw the location she'd chosen. It made perfect sense, but Stein wasn't going to be impressed when he realised all the ammo landing on his doorstep was viper issue.

"Hammer out."

"Penleigh clear."

* * *

36 ~ Sudden Drop

Southaven Province, Pandora

Eric scrambled free of his survival bag and dragged his armour closer. As he laced his boots in the silence of the tent, he considered and discarded plans beyond securing Riley's shuttles. That had to come first. Second would be securing Stein. He didn't actually need the Marines. He had the Shan, but more warm bodies with weapons wasn't a bad thing. Third was rearming them all.

The Shan were key. Their beamers didn't use ammo. The Shan could simply remove the chokes on the barrels that the games had imposed. The attachments were the only thing making them training safe, and that meant Tei'Laran was his only offensive force.

For now.

Eric finished pulling on his armour, and took the first step in his new war.

Computer: Access Alpha Company net.

Connection achieved

Computer: Access all units. Initiate emergency reactivation.

Acknowledged. Authorisation required.

Computer: Command override alpha-six-six-alpha-zero-three. Reactivate combat mode.

Verified... working

Reactivation in progress.

Eric broke the connection. He pulled on his helmet briefly, and contacted Tei'Laran while he waited for everyone to come fully online.

"I need you to hold in place, Tei. I have bad news."

"We're already in position around the station," Tei'Laran said. "I wanted to wait for my scouts to report in before informing you."

"That's quick work. I'll be joining you as soon as I can. The Merkiaari are in system. They'll be landing soon."

"Where is this coming from? I've heard nothing. Did General Ecclestone inform you?"

Tei'Laran didn't snarl, but Eric heard the fury barely contained. Ecclestone had made it quite clear that he didn't value Shan participation in the games. Tei'Laran had jumped to the wrong but logical conclusion that he'd been left out of the command loop.

"No. It came directly from my ship. The storm prevented Captain Riley warning us sooner. That's probably why we haven't heard from higher yet."

"I see. Tell me everything."

Gina sat up muttering. "Damn piece of junk woke me early."

Brice snorted. "Me too, and that junk is us, you know?"

"Yeah, yeah."

"I woke you," Eric announced, and then to Tei'Laran he said. "Wait one, and I'll explain."

"Holding."

Eric switched to viper comms and using his company-wide channel he laid it all out for his people. Gina and the others grabbed their armour and hurriedly got ready. There were a lot of questions and comments coming in over the comm. Eric put a stop to it.

"Quit your whining. I have Tei'Laran waiting on the other line."

Gina snorted. "I'm glad someone does. You do realise the Shan are the only ones within a couple of thousand klicks armed and on our side?"

Eric glared at her.

"Just sayin'," she muttered, and busied herself locating her other boot.

"We're screwed," Brice said. "Who the hell thought this cluster-fuck was a good idea?"

"Ecclestone for one," Dengler said.

Brice shook his head bemusedly. "War games with a real war going on. When does that get fun?"

Gina chuckled.

"No seriously, Gina. No one thought this through? No contingencies? All we have is this simunition crap to use."

Lieutenant Dolinski was the only one without an opinion. Eric looked at him, expecting something. He finally obliged.

"Simunition only makes sense. No one likes blue on blue, sir. We'll deal."

"How, Kamarl? How are we going to fight them? With our bare hands?" Dengler said.

"Everyone shut the hell up," Eric said using viper comms again. His officers weren't the only ones complaining. "We're breaking camp. I'll brief everyone as we go." He turned his attention to his lieutenants. "Get everything packed aboard the APCs. Leave nothing behind. Resupply is an issue. Waste nothing."

"What are we going to shoot at them, spit balls?" Brice said.

"If you'll shut up a minute I'll tell you. *Hammer* has arranged a drop at the following coordinates," Eric said and reeled off the data. “The Shan are already in position and waiting on us. The Marines too. We get there as fast as possible, rearm, and then we deal with the Merki. Other issues will be dealt with as and when. Clear?”

“Yes, sir!” They chorused.

“Now get out there and act like this isn’t your first rodeo.”

They scrambled to obey.

“Sorry, Tei,” Eric said. “I had to get my guys moving in the right direction.”

“Understood. Do you know what has happened to the Nstar shipyard? Tei’Shima was visiting.”

That was a damn shame. It probably meant she was dead along with thousands of others.

“I have no word of her, but Captain Riley did report the Merkiaari outnumber the fleet hundreds to one. My guess is the Merki will take out everything in orbit. I’m sorry.”

“May her ancestors comfort her,” Tei’Laran said. “You have a plan?”

“Your warriors are the only ones armed until I can receive a supply drop. Captain Riley is dealing with that. I need you to provide security for the Marines until I can get there.”

“I’ll inform Major Stein.”

“Thanks. I’ll get there as soon as I can, but the APCs aren’t as nimble in this terrain as I’d like.”

“You could abandon them. vipers can move almost as well as Shan.”

“I could, but with resupply unlikely, I don’t want to waste anything.”

“I understand. Thinking ahead is a good thing. Until later,” Tei’Laran said and signed off.

“Penleigh clear.”

Eric evacuated his tent, and it collapsed almost on his heels. He looked back to find Cragg and a few others from Gina’s platoon hauling it away. All around the hollow similar things were happening. It was still night, but it wasn’t dark.

The snow's reflected light revealed everything clearly.

Too clearly.

When they'd been assigned to play in the snow of Southaven, he'd ordered everyone to set their armour to white in order to match conditions. That was fine as far as it went, but the APCs were horribly visible to the naked eye. They didn't have chameleon capability.

Eric headed for the closest one.

Viper APCs didn't have chameleon capability either, but they were tracked and bigger. He'd borrowed all eight of these from the Marines. They were more modern than viper issue, but being newer didn't make them better. They were smaller and used anti-grav. He would've preferred tracks. It meant his men had to mount up in groups of twenty. Two squads per vehicle, not four. He'd never liked splitting his platoons that way, and he'd need to pick his route with care. He had to avoid the numerous problems that always arose from using anti-grav propulsion. Ground effect vehicles were a pain in the butt in certain types of terrain. Terrain like, oh... snow covered ground say, where anything could be hidden from sight and ready to ambush him.

Falling into a hidden ravine would be a cherry on the top of this cluster-fuck, no question about it.

Eric half-expected something of the sort to happen no matter how careful he was. His choices were limited. The comms station was a fixed point. He needed to get there ASAP avoiding slopes approaching 40 degrees of inclination. Anti-grav truly sucked in hilly terrain. So that meant he had to stay to lower areas, and where was it snow liked to build up? That's right. In low areas between the hills he couldn't climb.

"I bloody hate snow," he muttered, as he climbed into the driver's seat of the lead APC. "I bloody hate Pandora, and I really hate the Merki shooting it up!"

Gina climbed into the cab next to him. "Yeah. Who

doesn't? Want me to drive?"

"No. And why are you here?"

"I thought you chose my APC because you liked me. Should I be hurt?"

Eric snorted. He hadn't consciously chosen this one over another. He'd picked the closest. He checked his sensors, and found Gina's 1st and 2nd squads settling themselves in the back.

"Who has the sentry guns?" Eric said over viper comm.

"We spread them out," Gina said as various units reported in. "Like you said before. This isn't our first rodeo."

Eric ignored her and acknowledged the reports. He watched his sensors as the last few viper units mounted up, and turned his attention to the navigation console. He had no plans to use the GPS autopilot. Who knew when the Merki would take out the geo-sats? It would be just like them to knock them out and cause his APC to take a dump in a ravine. He hated crashing. He activated the navigation console and entered the comms station as his destination. Lots of lovely useless scenic routes decorated the display.

"Who are they kidding?" Gina muttered.

"It's for the tourists. See those," he said pointing to the red routes marked. "Those are avalanche country, and the favourite routes of idiot tourists here for skiing."

"Ever done any?"

"Skiing? Sure. I've tried pretty every sport invented. The more extreme the better. War beats them all."

Gina gave him a solemn look.

Eric shrugged. "It's just the truth."

"It's sad you think all the dying is a game."

"I didn't say that."

"What did you mean then?"

"All sports have things in common no matter how dangerous. They're all a challenge. There's nothing more challenging than war."

"And the dying part, what's that?"

Eric shrugged again. He was well aware she was trying to analyse him, but he answered anyway. "Death is the penalty for losing."

Gina stared at him.

Eric went back to choosing a route. He avoided red routes obviously, and higher elevations. He bet Tei'Laran had sought both of those out. They were the most direct and therefore the quickest.

Sensors reported everyone had mounted up and were ready to roll. He locked in his route, and all the unused ones disappeared from the screen. He'd had to cut and paste a few together to avoid unsafe terrain. The new one appeared in green as a wavy line on the map. It was overly conservative and wasteful. It was longer than he liked, but it was the only route he was certain wouldn't lead to them getting stuck. He couldn't afford that. He had Riley's schedule to keep.

Eric transmitted the route to the other drivers, and took the lead position. If someone had to test the ground he'd chosen, he preferred it be him. Gina didn't say anything, but he knew what she was thinking. He should have delegated the lead to someone else. She didn't call him on it, and he pretended not to notice her not calling him on it. Besides, it wasn't as if they had mines or other nasty things to consider this trip. The Merkiaari weren't down yet. Riley would have warned him. If something were to happen to him, all of his men were veterans of the Shan campaign. He trusted them to carry on. Gina had commanded the company before him. She could do it again, or one of his other officers could.

"I wish we had some music," Gina said.

"Use your archive if you want. I'll give you a nudge when we're closer. How about our boat trip?"

Gina grinned. "Tempting, but no matter how good you looked in those swimming trunks, I better not."

That surprised a laugh out of him. "I'm sure I wouldn't

win any beauty contests."

"Why sure?"

Eric glanced over to see if she was joking. She wasn't smiling. "Just... never mind."

Now she did laugh. "We should do that again when we get home."

When, not if, he noted. He smiled at her confidence and nodded. "It's a date."

"It's a date," she repeated. She put her feet up on the dashboard. "Nice country around here."

Ah, there was his emotion-inhibited Gina. Whenever things switched from business to personal between them, her Marine gung-ho safety interlocks kicked in. She was never comfortable with intimacy, not like her friend. Richmond was a psycho, but she was an uninhibited one. She didn't act like a Bethanite. In fact, she actively strove to break the conditioning her upbringing had imposed upon her. She was a rebel. Of the two, Gina would pass more easily on Bethany these days, unless Richmond wore a gag.

Eric snorted at the image that conjured.

"What?"

"Nothing. Just thinking about you and Richmond on Bethany together."

"Yeah? How come?"

"Nothing important."

They reached the comms station on schedule without mishap. The storm Riley had warned him about hadn't materialised, but Eric was sure it would before long. The sky looked threatening, but the day was crisp and still. He ordered the APCs parked widely spread out in case of air attack. He didn't anticipate one so soon, but being prepared never hurt.

Eric climbed out of the APC and looked around. The Marines were still dug into the positions they'd chosen to defend for the games, but were paired with Shan now. It meant each position had working weapons, but all were hand beamers. Shan did have some heavier weaponry for long range, but they were few.

He checked his sensors and watched his vipers take up positions. 160 blue icons, none of them armed with more than Brice's spit balls. He grimaced at the absurdity of even pretending to defend the station. Merkiaari didn't react to bluffing as a Human foe might. He doubted they understood the concept at all.

Eric left Gina and the others to themselves for a short time while he went in search of Stein. He found him in the command centre with his officers and Tei'Laran. They were watching the news and the take from surveillance drones that Stein had deployed over the station. Those would have caused him some trouble if he'd still been intent on attacking the station. Now they were an asset.

"We have a glimmer of good news," Eric announced using viper comms to keep his words private. "There are surveillance drones deployed overhead. Sergeants and higher, tap their comms net and monitor the take."

His vipers acknowledged the order, as Eric went to join the huddle watching the monitors.

"Welcome to my end-of-the-world party, Captain," Stein said. "Tei'Laran was kind enough to sneak into my perimeter—without alerting anyone I might add—to give me a heart attack. I mean a briefing."

Stein's officers laughed. They wouldn't have if the referees had cared about the games anymore. They didn't. Both army captains were watching the news just like everyone else.

"It would've been a shame to waste such an opportunity," Tei'Laran said. "I mourn the loss of our play fighting, but I look forward to killing many Merkiaari with you."

"What do we know?" Eric said. "Any word from higher?"

"Oh yes, there's word," Stein said. "I've been ordered to hold."

"Hold?"

Stein nodded. "You heard me. I'm to hold the station as per my previous orders until a strategy can be worked out. General Ecclestone was unavailable for comment, but I'm assured he'll get back to me."

Eric stared at him.

"I can see you're reaching for an appropriate term. Let me help you with that. Incompetent fuckwit is popular among the men. I'm wavering between that and out-of-his-depth-desk-jockey, but that might be too generous of me. What do you think?"

Eric cursed up a storm.

Stein nodded appreciatively. "I haven't heard some of those in a while."

"What are you expected to hold this dump with?"

"They didn't say, but we're Marines. We adapt, we overcome etcetera. I've got to admit, I'm fresh out of both those at the moment. What about you?"

"I have a supply drop due here soon," Eric said.

Stein applauded. "Congratulations. You should have been a Marine. Your adapting skills are exemplary."

"Can you tone down the sarcasm a little? I'm not in the mood. And don't congratulate me. Captain Riley is holding in geosynch and risking her ship to make the drop."

"Fine. At least we'll have something to shoot. I can forgive your lack of manners for such a gift."

Eric grimaced. "Viper ammo isn't compatible. We can scavenge yours, but not the reverse. Sorry."

It was Stein's turn to curse. "What idiot thought it was a good idea to equip you with non-standard rifles?! Don't I have enough to deal with?"

"The idiot you're referring to is General Burgton. I'll be sure to tell him that you disapprove."

"Disapproval is mild to what I'm feeling. Why did he implement such a stupid policy?"

"We were out-numbered and out-gunned. We needed an edge. Burgton built one, and supplied the ammo for it. He overcame the difficulty. He does that. As you said, he should've been a Marine."

"Har-de-har," Stein said sourly.

"There have never been enough of us, Major. We make up the difference with bigger badder booms."

Everyone turned their attentions back to the news. Eric listened but quickly realised it was all speculation. No one really knew what was happening with the fleet. There were reports of rioting and panic in the streets. People fleeing the cities for remote regions. The Merkiaari would attack the most highly populated areas first. Those fleeing might survive for a time.

"We have incoming," Gina said over viper comm. "It's the drop, sir. ETA two minutes."

"As soon as they land, take control and move them under cover. We'll unload them once we have them secure."

"Copy that," Gina replied. "I'll take one. Brice just volunteered to take the other."

"What? Damn, Gina..." Brice said.

"Perks of rank, Martin. We get the fun jobs."

Eric ignored the banter. At least they weren't crying about resupply anymore.

Stein accompanied him outside to watch the landing. The assault shuttles were on his sensors, about three miles out and coming in hot. He pointed them out to Stein, who produced a pair of field glasses. Eric hoped Riley had prioritised rifle ammo and power cells. He could use railgun rounds and grenades too, but rifle ammo was a must. He couldn't do much without it.

The shuttles were within visual range and stooping upon their LZ at max. Eric frowned when he realised they weren't slowing.

"Take cover!" Eric roared and shoved Stein to the ground.

He hit the dirt next to the Marine as both shuttles dove straight into the deck and exploded.

Stein blinked at him. Speechless.

Eric stood and stared at the twin impact craters. They were lucky. The crash was outside the perimeter. There were no casualties. No casualties except his entire plan going up in smoke. Fearing he knew why the shuttles had crashed, Eric tried to raise *Hammer*. He was met with dead air.

Hammer was gone.

* * *

37 ~ Refugees

Debris Field, Decaying Orbit, Pandora System

Tei'Shima watched as Shortcut tried to find somewhere they could go. They'd found respite from the madness, but although they'd removed their helmets for comfort, they kept them close. There was no sign of Merkiaari ships, but that didn't mean anything. They could fire from long range. She doubted they'd see the missile that killed them. If the Merki even bothered to use one.

The pod's sensors were basic. The designers had seen no need to provide anything more sensitive or powerful. Pods weren't meant to leave the vicinity of the stations they called home, and didn't need them.

"Do we have fuel?" Tei'Shima said.

Mark looked up, and came back a little from his daze. "It was full when we left the... err... the err... my God. All those people. The station. They're... oh my God."

"Did you have family back there?"

"No I... no. No one. I'm not married, but my friends. Oh my God." He rocked back and forth, whispering his mantra to himself. "Oh my God."

Devoid of the Harmonies Humans needed a guiding spirit they thought of as their creator to help them in stressful situations. Tei'Shima remembered having a discussion with Kate about it once. She didn't interrupt. Kazim recorded the ritual; it would play well at home. It was so alien to their people.

"You'll find it," Zelda whispered. "Keep looking."

"I hope so," Shortcut muttered.

Tei'Shima turned her attention back to Shortcut and the search. "Any sign of the Merkiaari?"

"Not yet," Zelda said looking up from the scanner. "With luck they'll think we're space junk."

Tei'Shima flicked her ears. "If we're still here when they arrive they might think that, but if we move—"

"We really will be. Yeah I get that. So we need to do all the moving before they get here."

"Yes. That would be good."

Zelda smacked Shortcut's shoulder with the back of her gloved hand. "You heard the lady. Hurry the fuck up!"

Shortcut laughed. "Sure thing, Boss."

Humans were very strange creatures, Tei'Shima reflected. There were some like Mark who went to pieces when danger threatened, and those like Zelda and Shortcut who quite literally laughed in the face of death. Still others like James who went from being a teacher to a stone-cold killer at need. And then there were the heroes like Gina, who gave up everything to become what her people needed her to be. A viper.

"What's that?" Zelda said.

Tei'Shima heard the excitement barely suppressed in her voice. She looked over Shortcut's shoulder at the scanner. There, amid so much clutter, she saw the icon appear from behind Pandora.

Shortcut touched it, and the readout expanded. "It says *SDF Hammer*."

"It's a ship!" Zelda said. "We're saved—"

"*Whoa!*" Shortcut tapped another series of controls. "We're screwed."

"What? Why?"

"It's gone."

"*You've got to be shitting me!*" Zelda cried.

"It was in orbit? Did it land?" Tei'Shima said.

Shortcut tapped another icon. "It was too big for that. This piece of junk doesn't have what I need, but it was probably a merchy."

"Destroyed?"

Shortcut did something and the ship reappeared. It rose over the rim of the planet in slow time. Tei'Shima saw the answer at the same moment Shortcut hit the pause control. All three of them leaned in as if tied together.

"Well… crap," Zelda said in disgust, and leaned away again. "That's a bunch of nukes."

"Could be laser heads," Shortcut said.

"What the hell difference does that make? They're missiles!"

"None to the ship, but the planet is right behind it."

That was not a good thought. Tei'Shima had witnessed the use of atomics in atmosphere. She'd been flash-blinded by a small one on Child of Harmony. These wouldn't be small. The Merkiaari did everything big.

"Is there any evidence they hit the planet?" Tei'Shima said.

"No, but would we even know from up here? The sensors on this thing are junk."

"It doesn't matter. We can't do anything about it even if they did. May the Harmonies watch over our friends until we rejoin them."

That could be taken two ways, and by the look Zelda gave her, she knew it. Shortcut backed the recording and replayed it twice more, but nothing changed. The ship was gone.

"Was it destroyed?" Tei'Shima said. It must have been.

"I don't think so. There's no debris or anything. It's just gone. I think it jumped into foldspace."

"Human ships can do that?"

"Officially? No." Zelda punched the wall in frustration and then shook her hand. "Jumping into foldspace from a standing start is theoretically okay, but we never do it."

"Why not?"

"Because ships are only at station-keeping when they're docked or in geosynch over a planet. Jumping while close to mass like that can cause a misjump and blow the drive's capacitors to atoms."

"Then it's used in emergencies only?" Tei'Shima said.

"Not even then. It's never done."

"But it was."

"Yeah. The captain of that ship is either one lucky son, or he's already in hell."

"Or drifting between stars without his drive," Shortcut said.

"No difference then."

Hell was another make-believe Human concept. They did so love their fictional stories. A ship in n-space without its foldspace drive could take decades to arrive at the nearest star with habitable planets.

"Keep searching," Tei'Shima said.

"Already doing it," Shortcut muttered.

"We have to go back to the station," Mark said.

Zelda groaned. "Not this again."

"No please, you have to listen to me," Mark pleaded. "Okay. You were right before. I admit I lost my head. You were right, but we have to go back now it's safe. It's the only way."

Zelda dismissed him out of hand, and turned back to the search, but Tei'Shima was intrigued. Mark was serene in the Harmonies now. His ritual had worked; he'd found his balance.

"*Yo!* Found 'em," Shortcut said.

Tei'Shima and Zelda crowded in next to Kazim. He was really fast when he wanted to be. He'd grabbed the best vantage to see the scanner's output. It was just a square monitor displaying symbols and vectors. It wasn't very impressive for his audience. Not military grade, its icons were all a light-green on a darker background.

There was a lot of clutter marked as unknowns all around the pod. Most of the closest icons would be frozen corpses and debris from the station and shipyard. Shortcut did something, and the display changed to show a different sector of local space.

A small cluster of icons labelled with Alliance IFF codes were exchanging fire with the Merkiaari. Tei'Shima assumed the unknowns were Merki. Who else? There were so many ships fighting, the icons blurred into an amorphous mass.

"Fuuuuck meeee..." Zelda whispered.

"Maybe later," Shortcut muttered. "We're being wiped out."

"Those poor bastards. They should've run," Zelda said.

"Heroes don't run," Varya said sadly.

"Dead heroes don't win wars either. They just die," Zelda rebutted. "If they'd bugged out they could've gone for help, or regrouped. Something!"

Tei'Shima knew they wouldn't have run even knowing they'd die. The ships hosted crews of flesh and blood warriors, not logic-based emotionless computers. Honour wouldn't have let them run. With a feeling of pride mixed with sadness, she watched the battle unfold. In place of those anonymous icons, she imagined ships burning in the deep, and warriors battling for their lives and for those they'd left behind on Pandora. One by one, the defending icons winked out, and with them the lives of thousands of heroes. They were with the Harmonies now.

She took a deep breath and leaned forward to centre the scan. "May their ancestors comfort them." She touched the icon, and the familiar scatter of debris surrounding the pod reappeared. "Keep looking."

Shortcut nodded.

"We have to go back to the station," Mark said urgently. "They'll see us if we don't go now!"

"Convince me," Tei'Shima said.

"You can't be serious?" Zelda said.

"Why can't I? Is the station still under attack?"

Zelda looked to Shortcut, and she shook her head. "No, but it's scrap."

"Mark?" Tei'Shima said.

"I've worked here at Nstar for years. I know all there is to know about our Pandoran operations."

"Get to the point," Zelda said already losing patience."

"The point is you're wasting time looking for what isn't out here. We have three choices, but realistically there's only one."

"What are they?" Tei'Shima said. "Let us decide what's realistic."

"The mining facilities in the asteroid belt have everything we'd need to survive for months, but it would take us days to get there. The Merkiaari would see us."

"What else?"

"Both of these mean returning to the station. There are shuttles. If they didn't leave before the attack, and if they're operational, and if the bay doors can be opened, we might use one to reach the surface before the Merkiaari arrive."

Tei'Shima's tail gestured to Varya, he kept his replies silent similarly. Was she mad to like the possibility? Yes, he insisted, but the madness was catching. He also liked it.

"And the last option?"

"This is our best chance. The escape pods. There are thousands of people on the station... I mean there were. We know a lot of them didn't escape. Some of the escape pods must still be there."

Zelda snorted.

"He might be right," Tei'Shima said.

"The station's a wreck. Look at the state of it. It'll burn up in a few hours. You really think anything is still working?"

"The escape pods use internal power and explosive bolts to detach," Mark said, drawing upon his expertise. "You really didn't listen to my safety lecture, did you?"

Zelda shrugged.

"What if I were dead? How would you know what to do?"

"Keep running that mouth, and we'll find out."

Shortcut snickered.

Tei'Shima didn't need to think hard upon it. They'd searched for a ship for hours, and found nothing. There really was only a single realistic destination left. The station. But the Merkiaari were closing on Pandora now. If they decided to tidy up the space around the planet, they might fire on the wreckage to speed up the station's re-entry. They might see the pod heading to the station. They might see an escape pod or shuttle launch from it. A lot of uncertainties.

Tei'Shima glanced at Bruiser and Haze. They just shrugged, having no better idea than she what to do. She already knew Zelda's opinion, and Varya would do whatever his Tei decided. She chewed her whiskers in indecision, but oddly, it was the sight of Kazim's confident face and his thrice-cursed camera that clinched it for her. He wasn't going to die. She might. The others too, but not him. He had the luck of the Harmonies on his side. Truly, he should have died a hundred times before this, but he always made it through.

"We need to head for the station," Tei'Shima announced. "Right or wrong, the Merki are coming. We can't stay here any more." She joined Shortcut at the controls. "Can you fly badly?"

Shortcut frowned.

Zelda laughed. "Crashing is what she does best! Of course she can."

"Screw you," Shortcut said.

"Maybe later."

"Not crashing. There must be *no* crashing," Tei'Shima said seriously. "But we need to blend with the debris until we reach the station."

"I can do that. It might make us puke, but tumbling is easy."

"Then get us going, and don't hit anything. Helmets back on everyone, just in case she does."

"I won't," Shortcut said. She sounded supremely confident, but when she pulled her helmet on and sealed it, everyone scrambled to copy her.

Tei'Shima chose to ride it out on all fours, as did Varya and Kazim. Zelda sat on the floor. Bruiser and Haze followed her lead and braced themselves against the walls. The pod began to move, rolling and yawing in slow spirals. Shortcut kept the motion gentle and the acceleration minimal.

"They're going to see us," Mark muttered over the open comm. "We left it too long."

"If they do?" Tei'Shima said.

"What?"

"What will you do if they do see us?"

"What can I do? Nothing!"

"Exactly. None of us can. Don't give in to your fears. Calm your thoughts and try to find your balance. We'll need you when we reach the station."

Tei'Shima watched the stars slipping by outside as the pod rotated, and thought about her father. Had he been alone at the end, or was he with friends like those she had here? Did they comfort each other? She hoped so. What were his final thoughts? She might get to ask him very soon.

"*They've seen us!*" Shortcut yelled. "*They're closing!*"

Tei'Shima watched the stars drifting by as the pod tumbled, and tried to use them to slow her thoughts. She wanted to be in Harmony when she saw Tahar again. Her meditation sleep was out of the question, but the Harmonies did draw closer. She wanted—

The pod lurched violently.

* * *

38 ~ Stepping Up

Debris Field, Decaying Orbit, Pandora

The atmosphere blasted out of the pod almost instantly. It was a small vehicle. The volume of air escaping wasn't enough to drag anyone into space with it, thank the Harmonies. The damage caused the pod to lose its transparency on one side. A slash of darkness in the hull revealed stars wheeling by. It took Tei'Shima a moment to realise what had happened. The pod was still in one piece and so was she. The Merkiaari couldn't have attacked. There would be nothing left but vapour if they had.

"I said no crashing!" Tei'Shima shouted to silence everyone's hysterics. The comms went quiet. "No crashing. None. What did you do?"

"I crashed," Shortcut muttered. "But it worked. The Merki think we're space junk."

"That's because we are thanks to you!" Mark shouted.

"Hey!" Zelda snarled back. "She just saved our lives. One more crack out of you, and I'll feed you to the Merkiaari!"

"Quiet," Tei'Shima said. She checked and located Kazim still fiddling with his camera as if nothing had happened. "So you crashed on purpose. Was the hole in the wall on purpose too?"

"No," Shortcut muttered sulkily. "I had to do something. The Merki would have fired on us."

Tei'Shima joined Shortcut and Zelda up front, trying not to get dizzy. She found four feet better for that. Standing tall while the pod rotated seemed worse for some reason. The station still lay ahead. That was something. The escaping atmosphere hadn't pushed them too far off course.

"What did we hit?"

Shortcut pointed to the scanner. "Hull fragment."

Tei'Shima watched the offending item following them, its course slowly diverging from theirs. It shouldn't hit them again. She searched the scanner for the Merki, and found them easily. Hundreds of huge ships were loitering nearby, while others moved into orbit. She wasn't fleet. She didn't know the tell-tale differences between one ship type and another, but it didn't take a genius to guess what was happening. They were getting ready to cleanse the planet. Those were troopships.

"We're kinda screwed, huh?" Zelda said gloomily. "I mean they'll see any kind of launch we make now."

"If we even get that far," Shortcut agreed.

"Don't borrow trouble," Tei'Shima warned them. "One thing at a time. Can we still dock?"

Shortcut did something, and various readouts changed. "If we reach it and the pod bay is intact, yes."

"Then nothing has changed. We get back on the station."

"But what then?"

"It depends on what we find."

They all knew what it meant that the Merkiaari were in orbit. There wasn't any point in talking about it. They would get on the station or they wouldn't. They would find a safe way off again, or they wouldn't.

Shortcut waited until the station hid them from observation before taking control of the pod again. She trimmed their course and slowed their approach. The pod bay doors were shut. They didn't look damaged unlike the rest of the station.

"Here goes nothing," Shortcut said, and sent the command. "Well I'll be damned!"

"*Alright!*" Zelda crowed as the doors opened. She pumped a fist in the air.

That was another alien foible Tei'Shima hadn't witnessed before. The longer she associated with Humans, the stranger she found them to be. So emotional and excitable. So... *utterly fascinating.*

The bay doors cranked open and the pod edged inside. The doors closed automatically on their heels, shielding them from Merkiaari attention. Tei'Shima peered through the cockpit window, trying to make out anything familiar. Emergency lighting illuminated the bay dully. Some of the pods had broken free of their docking clamps and were in free-fall. The station's gravity was offline.

"I'll just park us here," Shortcut muttered. "There's no point trying to use a cradle I guess."

"None," Tei'Shima agreed, and turned to Mark. "Our lives are in your hands."

"Great, we're doomed," Zelda muttered.

Bruiser laughed quietly to himself, until Haze whacked his shoulder to shut him down. Tei'Shima had to admit he had sounded a little odd just then. Stressed. Not hysterical exactly, but not quite right either. Haze's reminder startled him, and he quit laughing.

Mark joined Shortcut up front, and reached for one of the controls. The pod's external lighting speared the darkness, and he played the beam over everything using the joystick. There were many bodies drifting around and bumping into things. None were in suits. They'd died instantly when the section depressurised. The blast doors and safety partitions hadn't been enough to save them.

Shortcut brought the pod to a gentle stop, while everyone stared solemnly outside.

"May their ancestors receive and comfort them," Kazim murmured, and continued in a quiet voice for the benefit of his audience. "Tei'Shima has performed the impossible once again, turning certain death into a hope for life. With the help of Shortcut—a masterful pilot famous in the Alliance for her daring—we have survived to re-enter the once great Nstar facility in orbit of Pandora..."

Tei'Shima ignored the fantasy Kazim was inventing, and monitored Mark. In the Harmonies he was very calm. Too calm for him. Although it was unnatural, she was glad. He could let his grief free when they were safe. She watched him search the bay for something, and was about to ask him what he was looking for when he found it.

"There," Mark said. "Those hatches lead to escape pods. I want everyone to take note. If I don't make it, those hatches are what you're looking for."

"You won't die here," Kazim reassured. "Tei'Shima won't let you. She's very good at keeping people alive."

"She hasn't killed you yet, Kazim," Varya said. "But I can tell she's always thinking about it."

Everyone laughed, including Haze. She nudged Bruiser, and this time his laugh sounded more natural. Tei'Shima let them have their fun. It was easing everyone's fears. A good thing, because they weren't safe yet.

"See those tell-tales? The red lights?" Mark said.

"What do they mean?" Tei'Shima said.

Zelda groaned. "It means the tubes are empty. Someone already launched the escape pods."

"So you did listen to some of my lecture. We need to find some with green indicators. Green means they're ready to launch."

"How long do we have?" Zelda said.

"If the Merkiaari leave us alone, maybe an hour. After

that the station will break apart and burn up. There's no way to know the exact time."

"Our lives are in your hands," Tei'Shima said.

"I'll do my best."

"That's all anyone can do."

Mark led the way out of the pod.

Tei'Shima grabbed her kit bag before following. They would need weapons when they reached the surface. Bruiser and Haze had the same thought. They each carried a bag as they left. The moment they entered the bay they lost gravity, but they'd been ready for that. They clung to the outside of the pod.

Mark pushed off to reach a distant control station. He flew across the bay as if he did it every day, and Zelda muttered her approval at his skill. He'd stepped up and his competence was beginning to shine through. He caught the edge of the control station one-handed, and swung himself behind it. He studied the readouts, made some adjustments, and read the results.

"Okay. I know where to go," Mark announced.

"Shuttle bay?" Zelda said hopefully.

"No. It's gone. Whatever the Merki used hit that section hard. There isn't much left."

"Sounds like a kinetic strike. Good of them," Shortcut said bitterly.

It *was* good of them actually.

Tei'Shima hadn't forgotten the missiles fired at the ship earlier. Those might have been kinetic as well. If so, it meant the Merki were being careful not to accidentally hit Pandora with atomics. Of course they weren't doing it for anyone's benefit but their own. They wanted to send troops down. A nuclear wasteland would be an inconvenience for them.

"This way," Mark said heading toward a hatch. "We need to reach the hub."

Tei'Shima held back until everyone else was in flight.

She'd be their rear scout. She wanted everyone ahead of her and within sight. Kazim especially. He had a tendency to become fixated on his work. Without her acting as den mother he'd get lost. Varya was sticking by his side as he should. Warriors served and protected their people. Kazim was his focus for now.

Mark led the way along the wreckage-strewn corridors of the broken station, navigating the damaged sections and junk-filled walkways in single file. They used touches on walls and deck to guide and propel themselves. A gentle thrust against loose equipment, or against a wall to change direction was enough to keep them on course in his wake.

Emergency lighting dimmed the surroundings, and hid details. In some ways that made the journey easier, in others harder. Fewer distractions helped to keep them moving, but it also meant those distractions heightened tensions when they did happen. Suddenly coming face to face with frozen corpses in the dark was shocking.

Mark led the way unerringly, and they seemed to make good progress. Tei'Shima thought so at least, but as time passed Mark became more and more agitated. That was very clear to her in the Harmonies. There seemed no reason for it at first, but then he halted at a four-way junction. He looked both ways and turned right. A few metres along, he abruptly changed his mind and doubled-back.

"Great," Zelda muttered. "We're lost."

"We're not lost," Mark said. "The way is blocked."

Everyone began retracing their route. Tei'Shima didn't follow. She continued the way they'd been going, and saw the elevator. It looked intact. She wondered what Mark had seen. She pressed a button, but the indicators remained dark.

"Please keep up," Mark called to her. "We're running out of time."

Tei'Shima turned and kicked hard against the elevator doors to pursue her friends. The emergency power obviously didn't extend to the elevators, or maybe in emergencies they were locked down to prevent people being trapped. She wouldn't want to enter a metal box during battle.

"There should be ladders," Mark was saying. "We need to go down three levels and then head hub-ward. That means toward the spindle."

"Thank you Captain Courageous," Zelda muttered scornfully. "Who the hell doesn't know that?"

Tei'Shima followed her friends headfirst down the ladder way. They didn't need to use the rungs. No gravity made some things easier. Mark raced ahead, clearly agitated. Before she could ask why, she felt it. There was no sound in vacuum, but she felt the vibrations when she touched the deck to change direction. The station was skimming Pandora's atmosphere, on the verge of re-entry.

"*Hurry!*" Mark yelled. "*There!*"

"*No you fool!*" Shortcut yelled. "*They're red, dammit!*"

Tei'Shima could see the empty escape tubes. Their red indicator lights were very obvious. Shortcut was right, but Mark took no notice. He kept going, and disappeared around a corner.

"Don't stop!" Tei'Shima yelled feeling the vibrations growing worse each time she touched a surface. "Kazim! Keep going or I'll shred your ears!"

It was practicality talking. She had no idea if Mark had simply panicked or whether he'd seen something, but there was no more time. Doubling back would be death. All they could do was keep going forward.

They rounded the corner Mark had used, ignoring the rows of red lights indicating missing escape pods, and found him hammering on a green lit hatch. It was green!

"It won't open," Mark panted. "Please. I did it right. Please open. Oh my God."

"You did it!" Zelda cried.

"It's broken. It won't open."

Shortcut shoved Mark out of the way. "I'm not dying after all this!" She pressed controls. "You moron! It still has pressure and we're in vacuum. You would've killed us if you'd opened it!"

The station shook visibly. Loose equipment changed vector as the station bit into atmosphere. Zelda cried out as some of it hit her.

"Can you fix it?" Tei'Shima said, and ducked some of the junk heading towards her. "*Fix it!*"

"Airlocks work by equalising pressure," Shortcut snarled back. "I can't pressurise our side. I have to pump the airlock down to vacuum. It takes time!"

"We haven't got any time!"

"*I know!*"

Tei'Shima spun around trying to think of something she could do. She saw Kazim watching her calmly next to Varya, and wanted to howl at him. She didn't have the answer! Why was he looking at her like that? Then suddenly she did.

"Out of the way!" she cried digging frantically in her kit for her beamer.

"Oh my God we're going to die," Mark said.

"Keep whining and I'll make sure of it!" Zelda yelled.

Shortcut saw the beamer, and dove out of the way just in time. Tei'Shima fired at the little round window in the airlock's hatch. It was tough. It took three full-powered shots to break through. Air blasted out of the breach and hit her in the face, spinning her away. Her helmet took the impact well. It didn't break, but it felt like being run over by a Shkai'lon. When she hit the far wall, she decided it felt like a herd.

Shortcut slapped a control, and the hatch slid aside.

Mark dove in and opened the door in the escape pod. "*In in in!*"

Everyone piled inside.

Tei'Shima blinked lazily around the rapidly emptying room. Everything was spinning. No, it was her. She was upside down. Then right way up. Then upside down. She shook off the woozy feeling, and kicked against the overhead.

She was the last one in.

Mark slammed and locked the hatch.

Everyone strapped in. Tei'Shima grabbed the closest seat and used the safety harness to secure her bag. She sat in the couch next to it. Mark chose the seat next to her on the other side.

Shortcut had the controls. "Five, four... oh fuckit," she said and hit launch. Nothing happened. She hit it again. "Ummm... guys?"

* * *

39 ~ Balance

Nstar Shipyard, Decaying Orbit, Pandora

They would never know what caused the delay. It could've been the damage the station had suffered, or a minor fault in the escape pod's launch mechanism. It might even have been working as intended. There was no telling. No one had used an escape pod before. Not even Mark. No matter the cause, the delay was long enough to raise everyone's anxieties, but not long enough for them to act upon them.

The explosive bolts fired. They were silent in the vacuum, but the sudden acceleration reassured everyone they were on their way to Pandora at last.

Tei'Shima grunted as the brutal acceleration crushed her into her seat. Her tail was pinned underneath her and it hurt, but there was nothing to be done. She felt so heavy. She had no chance of freeing it from her own weight. The others were feeling the strain too. She heard their gasps and groans over the comm.

Finally, the acceleration died, and she was able to move.

Shortcut did something and a rectangle on the wall became a window. Whether it really did or not Tei'Shima couldn't tell, but she suspected it was more of Zelda's magic like the pod's transparency. The rectangle gave them a view of the station receding from them. It was glowing from friction with the atmosphere. Pieces were breaking off as they watched.

"Whoa," Zelda said. "Look at that. We came that close to biting the big one. I hope you're getting all this, Kazim. My producers will pay big money for a copy."

Shortcut laughed.

"I'm sure a deal with my caste can be negotiated. A percentage of royalties plus an advance should do it."

"How about a cut of my next sensim's profits while you're about it," Zelda said sourly.

"Thank you! That's a very generous offer. I'll be sure to mention it."

Everyone laughed.

The sudden release of tension left them feeling giddy. The escape pod was falling away with the rest of the station debris. It was a hazard, but it also lent a crumb of safety. They were anonymous. Just more junk burning up.

"These are our landing sites," Shortcut said, and replaced the station with a shortlist of place names. "We need to choose one, or the pod will use the default automatically."

Tei'Shima could read English, but only poorly. She'd learned on Snakeholme by quizzing Chailen. Her sib had been determined to help her mate learn Human healing techniques, and English or Mandarin were essential for that. They'd been living with vipers at the time, and they tended to use English by default, so they'd concentrated on that language.

She carefully puzzled out the Human symbols and recognised a few of the names. One thing was certain, the default landing site wasn't a good choice. They'd boarded a shuttle up to Nstar from Westby Spaceport. It was the main transport hub on Pandora and would be a priority target.

The Merkiaari would definitely land troops there in order to attack the capital.

"Southaven. Mountain. Rescue. Station," Tei'Shima said carefully. It was fifth down. "That one."

"Why there?" Mark said. "It will take hours for a rescue party to reach... oh."

Exactly. Southaven Province was many many heikke from everywhere. There were no large population centres to attract the Merkiaari.

Shortcut tapped the name on her screen and highlighted Southaven. She locked it in, and the escape pod reacted by firing attitude thrusters. The pod slowed. It reoriented and fired its thrusters again. Everyone remained strapped in to their couches. The pod had no internal gravity field. It used rugged, zero-frills, technology designed to do one thing and never fail. Get its cargo to the planet's surface in safety.

"Why Southaven?" Zelda asked. "Have you been there?"

"My people were assigned to Southaven Province for the games, and it's out of the way. I don't think the Merki will be interested in it, or not right away."

"It's Southaven here we come then. Let's get some skiing in while we're there. It'll be fun!"

Haze laughed, and Bruiser grinned at Shortcut.

"Why is that funny?" Kazim said.

Shortcut scowled. "It's because the last time I went skiing I nearly broke my neck."

"She has terrible balance on skis," Zelda confided. "She paid the best instructors, and they left crying..." Zelda grinned at her friend. "Tears of laughter."

"Exaggerate much? The instructors didn't laugh at me, but they did issue a refund. They were the ones who said I was ready to try the slopes without stabilisers. They were wrong."

Tei'Shima let their conversation wash over her, and sought the peace of the Harmonies. She needed time to think. She closed her eyes, and the Harmonies drew closer.

Tei'Shima's breathing slowed and her thoughts calmed, allowing her to see all the connections surrounding her. The bond between Shortcut and Zelda was strong, and the one between the two warriors likewise, though not between them and their patrons. They were warriors who served for pay, not love. Mark was a lonely island in the Harmonies. He had no bonds of love or family, and his mind glow was dull. He grieved for lost friends. As expected, her own bonds with Varya and Kazim were strong. The Harmonies whispered of friendship hard earned, and of love. Varya was a fellow warrior and her comrade in battle. He was more than a friend. She loved him like the brother she didn't have.

Kazim...

Tei'Shima couldn't ignore the bond between them. It was bright and strong and very obviously not the same as the one between her and Varya. There was love and friendship between them, but Kazim wasn't a substitute brother like Varya. He was more. They hadn't spoken of it, but he knew. Her thoughts drifted and she saw the recent past. The destruction of the great ship named for Hercules. He'd died stillborn. He would never see battle and gain honour for his name. She saw Shortcut instinctively leap for the pod's controls again, and save them from disaster. Zelda might be her Tei, but Shortcut was more than just a follower.

Tei'Shima drifted and her thoughts slowed further. At last she found her elusive balance, and felt much better for it. Fear was the enemy of balance. It could lead to stress and wrong thinking. And *that* was where the real danger lay. She was Tei now. Her people would follow where she led. When her merest whim could become their action, their wellbeing relied upon her balance. She must live in harmony for them and for herself.

The escape pod landed vertically in the middle of a blizzard. If Tei'Shima had been allowed a choice, she never would have agreed to it. Wind shear threatened to push them off course, but the escape pod coped with the conditions very well. They didn't crash, and eventually hovered over the landing field. The wind had cleared the pad of snow to reveal a sheet of ice.

"And three... and two... and one... we're down," Shortcut announced as the pod's engines shut down. "Thank you for flying Crash 'n' Burn Interstellar. Please consider us for all your end of the world needs."

Zelda and her friends laughed.

Kazim and Varya exchanged puzzled looks, and Tei'Shima agreed. Alien humour was incomprehensible. She unbuckled her harness and stood to stretch her legs. Everyone removed their helmets, and took turns moving around. The pod wasn't that spacious.

"Do we wait out the storm?" Kazim said.

Everyone looked at Tei'Shima. Since when had the Humans elected her as their leader? She looked to Zelda. Surely she was Tei for the Humans, but Zelda simply grinned and shrugged. Fine. She would lead the Humans until they didn't need her anymore.

"How far to the station?" Tei'Shima said.

Shortcut made the magic work again, and a window appeared. Tei'Shima looked out at the storm. She could just make out the buildings in the distance. They weren't too far away. The storm would slow their progress, but they could be inside in less than a tenth of a seg.

"Varya will scout the situation. When he reaches the building, Kazim and the rest of you will join him. I'll follow and use the Harmonies to guide you to him if necessary."

Varya stripped off his suit, obviously relieved to be rid of the thing. Kazim and Tei'Shima quickly did the same, and revelled in their freedom.

Zelda grinned as they dropped to all fours and stretched.

Tei'Shima groaned in pleasure and shook out her pelt. By

the Harmonies it was good to unkink her tail. She'd tried to shut out the discomfort, but the dull ache had always been there while wearing the suit. As she stretched and flexed every muscle in her body, the ache began to fade.

"You'll freeze," Mark protested.

Varya laughed as he pulled on his harness and checked his beamers. Kazim chuffed in amusement as he dug in their kit bag. He handed Tei'Shima her gear before pulling on his own harness.

"We'll be fine," Tei'Shima said. "This is mild compared to winters back home. You should keep your suits on."

"Oh we will. Count on it. Brrrrr," Zelda said with a shiver.

Varya clipped his ear-bud to his right ear, and tested it by flicking his ears a few times. It stayed put. He finished getting ready by putting on his throat mic and testing it.

Tei'Shima heard him clearly through the ear-bud clipped to her left ear. She tested her own mic and comm, sub-vocalising as if already sneaking into enemy territory. She might be doing that one day soon. Varya gestured with his tail. He'd heard her perfectly.

The Humans donned their helmets while Tei'Shima checked and holstered her beamers. When everyone was ready, Varya undogged the hatch and slipped out. Wind and snow blasted inside before Zelda could shut it again. Tei'Shima ignored what was happening in the pod, and tracked Varya with the Harmonies. He did what scouts do, circling the pod and then spiralling outward to scout the area. She knew when Varya reached the station. He circled it and stopped.

"All clear, Tei," Varya said, his voice clear despite the conditions. "Bring the Humans."

"Coming now," Tei'Shima replied, and gave Zelda the order.

The Human opened the hatch and led the way out. Tei'Shima followed them, locked the hatch, and shepherded her charges to where Varya waited. She didn't need to do much. The trek was short, and everyone managed to reach the station without losing their way. They trooped into the rescue station, and Varya shut the door to cut off the howling wind.

The Humans looked around the darkened interior, and removed their helmets. The station was powered down and very cold. Their breath smoked on the air.

"Let's get the power running and a hot meal in our bellies. I'm starving," Zelda said. "And find the comm, would you? We need a rescue party out here asap."

Shortcut nodded. "I want a hot bath and about a week of sleep in my hotel room."

Humans would never cease to amaze Tei'Shima. Here they were in the wilds, a howling blizzard outside, and death descending from orbit in the form of the Merkiaari, and they were more concerned about their comforts than the Merki. A brave people. Or simply crazy. A little of both she suspected.

Mark found the master power breaker and got the lights on after a few minutes of stumbling around in the dark. The heating came on, and air-blowers began blasting warm air.

Blinking their light-sensitive eyes, they searched the interior for a comms and found it. They also found plenty of supplies to support a party larger than theirs for a season. A kitchen would supply hot meals, and beds gave them comfortable sleeping quarters. As the interior of the station warmed up, everyone removed their suits and pulled on the clothes in their kit bags.

Once again dressed the way Tei'Shima had first met them, Shortcut tried to reach someone on the comms while Mark and Zelda made themselves at home. Zelda busied herself in the kitchen making everyone hot food and drinks, while Mark found the vid and began surfing channels for news. Bruiser and Haze joined him to watch. Kazim found a quiet corner to review his recordings and add his observations of their adventure thus far.

Tei'Shima took Varya to one side. "I don't think we'll be rescued by air."

Varya flicked his ears in agreement. "I can't see any pilot willing to risk the storm."

"I was thinking more along the lines of the Merkiaari."

"Them too," Varya agreed.

"We'll have to walk out. You and I will have no problem doing that. Kazim will be fine with us, but the Humans won't make it."

Varya turned to evaluate them.

Tei'Shima knew what he was thinking as he studied their friends. Humans were robust creatures, but their clothing was ill suited to the conditions. They all wore thin shirts that would do nothing to keep them warm. Their lower halves were fully covered, but again the clothing wasn't meant for winter conditions. They did have boots and jackets, but the simple action of dressing warmly against the slight chill of the station only emphasised the problem. If they felt the need to dress warmly indoors, there was no chance they could brave the weather. Storm or no storm.

"I'll tell them," Tei'Shima said. "They'll be safe here. The Merkiaari will be too busy to bother them."

Varya flicked his ears in agreement.

"Food is ready!" Zelda called. "Come and get it!"

* * *

40 ~ Taking Stock

Southaven Province, Pandora

As the storm vented its fury outside, Tei'Shima ate a hot meal among friends and laughed with them. Kazim and Zelda were the focus of the banter. Tei'Shima and Shortcut were often their targets, but both endured it good naturedly.

Bruiser and Haze were quiet. They'd been watching the news and had seen some disturbing things. Tei'Shima had been through it. She knew some of the thoughts running through their heads, but it could've been worse for them. They were lucky they were only visiting Pandora and didn't have family at risk.

When everyone had eaten their fill, talk turned to serious matters. They moved into the other room with cups of coffee or tea, and sat to discuss the future. Tei'Shima and the others threw cushions onto the floor leaving the couches for the Humans to use.

Mark went first. "The landings haven't begun yet. Or if they have the newsies aren't reporting it."

"Is that likely?" Tei'Shima said.

Kazim chuffed in amusement. "Not at all. Can you

imagine someone like me *not* filming the landings?"

"There *is* no one like you," Tei'Shima said dryly. "A good thing too. Pandora couldn't survive two of you."

Everyone laughed.

"There's rioting in the streets," Mark went on. "Panic. The usual. Those with the ability are fleeing into the hills."

"A fat lot of good that'll do them," Zelda said. "They'll starve without their malls and autochefs."

"She's right, Tei," Varya said. "The Humans don't have keeps to shelter them, and they aren't hunters. It will be worse than the first time the murderers attacked us."

Tei'Shima struggled to keep her ears up and the horror out of her voice. "Help will come. Until it does they must hide as we did. We survived. So will they."

"Some will," Zelda agreed. "Those living in remote areas like this probably have stores of food and water. As long as they have solar or wind generators for power they'll have refrigeration. They'll make it."

"Not many live like that on Pandora," Mark said. "This is the core, not the border zone."

Zelda nodded glumly, but then brightened. "There are a lot of soldiers here for the games. The Merkiaari are in for one hell of a fight. Your people will be a surprise, Tei'Shima, and the vipers won't sit idle."

"That is a truth," Tei'Shima said. "And it brings up our situation. It's my thought that you should stay here. The chance of rescue is slim while the Merkiaari threaten, and you're ill-suited to the conditions."

"You mean us," Zelda said indicating herself and the other Humans. "You're saying Humans can't keep up with Shan?"

"I'm saying you should be safe here. I'm saying a rescue by air is unlikely, and none of you are dressed to survive winter conditions. My people have evolved to survive harsher weather than Pandora offers, and we can hunt for food as we travel."

"She's right," Mark said. "We should stay here and wait for Fleet."

"That could take months," Zelda protested.

Mark shrugged. "So it's months. The autochef can handle it. There's only five of us."

"But *I* can't!" Zelda appealed to Shortcut. "Tell her, Selene. Tell her she has to take us with her. I'll go batshit!"

Shortcut grimaced at Tei'Shima. "She will. You haven't seen what she's like when she's bored. She gets so hyper; she'll try to kill us for entertainment."

Bruiser and Haze laughed, but they were nodding. Mark obviously didn't care what the others did. He'd decided to stay at the station. He was already putting distance between himself and any decision the others made. Not physically. He didn't walk out or anything, but in the Harmonies he was no longer part of the group.

One down, four to go.

Tei'Shima turned to the sensible ones. Bruiser and Haze were warriors. Surely they could see the futility of venturing the wilds? In the Harmonies they were linked to their Tei, but their loyalty to each other was far stronger.

"Will you stay here and protect Mark if I ask it?" Tei'Shima said. Maybe if she appealed to their honour they would do the sensible thing. "He shouldn't stay alone."

"You said it was safe here!" Zelda said.

"Safer than the wilds I meant."

Zelda scowled.

"She's our employer," Haze said with a sidelong glance at Bruiser. "We go where she goes."

"Right," Bruiser said, though he looked a bit sour.

Zelda smiled. "Guys, that's so sweet of you. Selene and I'll be fine. You don't have to come."

"We will?" Shortcut said.

Zelda looked unsure for the first time. "I won't ever let

anything hurt you, Selene. I'd die first."

"That's what worries me."

"Right," Bruiser said, and nodded in agreement.

Zelda gave him a scornful look, and took Shortcut's hand for a squeeze. "If you're scared you can stay here. It's okay."

Tei'Shima sucked in a sharp breath as Shortcut's mind glow flared briefly and then dulled in the Harmonies. Her aura had recoiled as if struck. Zelda's words had hurt her deeply.

"Everything together. Wasn't that what you promised me when we started this?"

"I'm sorry. I didn't mean—"

"You never do," Shortcut said. She stood abruptly and headed for one of the bedrooms. The door slammed behind her.

"Well," Zelda said looking at the now closed bedroom door.

"*Riiight*," Bruiser said. He'd managed to sound sarcastic, and Haze elbowed him.

This was fast unravelling. Tei'Shima tried one final time to make them see sense. "You cannot come with us." There. It had to be said, and she'd said it. "You'll die of exposure in the wilds. You're all staying here. That's my final word."

"Right," Bruiser said. He sounded more approving this time. He could put a lot of emotion into that word.

Zelda wasn't listening. She stood and without a backward glance headed off to join Shortcut.

Kazim chuffed. He switched off his camera. "They'll be coming."

"*I forbid it!*" Tei'Shima said.

"How much do you want to risk?" Varya said.

"*I said no!*"

Kazim gestured a shrug with his tail. "Ten credits?"

"I'll take some of that action," Haze said. "Ten that they're making out in there, plus another ten that before morning all is forgiven and we're all going."

"I'm in," Bruiser said sourly.

Tei'Shima stared at him. He could say more than a single word after all. "It's decided. Don't waste your money. You're all staying with Mark."

Kazim laughed.

Tei'Shima didn't rise to the bait. It was lunacy to consider anything else. They weren't equipped to survive. Therefore, they had to stay. Humans were brave not suicidal. She would give them until the storm ended to see sense.

The meeting ended with people drifting away. Kazim went back to his reviewing and voice-overs, while Bruiser and Haze watched the vid. Mark and Varya were the last to leave. Both chose to find their beds, leaving Tei'Shima alone with her thoughts. She watched Kazim work for a while, and then decided to try the comm. Shortcut hadn't learned anything from it earlier, but it was worth a try. Although she had no reason to think the Merkiaari would trace a transmission, she wouldn't broadcast just in case.

Segs later, Tei'Shima decided she'd heard enough distress calls for one lifetime, and switched the comms off. She hadn't learned anything useful. Military channels were encrypted, so she couldn't tell how the war was going or where the Merkiaari had landed. She did know there wasn't anywhere worth attacking in Southaven. The briefing she'd attended with Tei'Laran for the games had made that clear.

Tei'Laran would have to lead his warriors out of the province in order to fight. He might use the storm as cover. It would depend on where the murderers had landed. Would the storm last long enough for him to get into position? She didn't know, but knew he'd try. He wouldn't be fighting alone. He had to consider his allies. Human warriors were slow but vipers were as fast as Shan. Was Tei'Laran in company with vipers, or Marines?

There was no way to know.

Tei'Shima consulted her wristcomp and thanked the Harmonies for her laziness. It still had the briefing maps for the games in its memory. She'd meant to delete them before now, but hadn't gotten around to it yet. She studied the map of Southaven and tried to guess where Tei'Laran would be. More importantly, she tried to guess his plans.

She needed to project forward a few cycles she realised. She couldn't simply head for his last known location. If she did, she would arrive to find him already gone, but with a little luck and planning she should be able to cut his trail. If she was very lucky she'd be able to catch up.

A lot depended upon Tei'Laran moving slower than she could. He should, she mused. He probably had Humans slowing him down, plus he needed to move in stealth. Her job was infinitely easier than his. She only had to keep three Shan alive and hidden, not thousands.

Tei'Shima looked up when she heard a door click. Bruiser and Haze had just retired for the night. Kazim was nowhere in sight, but a quick consultation with the Harmonies reassured her. He was asleep and dreaming of pleasant things. Probably fame and glory. He was safe again, at least for a while. At night and asleep was the only time she was certain of that where Kazim was concerned.

Tei'Shima used Kazim's mind glow to soothe her own thoughts, and let herself drift into her meditation sleep. It felt good to finally relax. If she survived Pandora and boarded a ship again, she would use her hibernation sleep to replenish herself. She hadn't taken the opportunity on the trip to Pandora. She'd needed the time with Tei'Laran for research and to brush up on her youngling lessons.

As her thoughts slowed and the Harmonies welcomed her, she silently thanked her ancestors for protecting Kazim and Varya. She knew now what it must've been like for Tahar at the fall of Hool Station. He would've feared for her and Chailen, not for himself.

She silently thanked him for being her father, and fell asleep dreaming of him.

* * *

41 ~ Well Met

Southaven Province, Pandora

Varya lost his bet with Bruiser and Haze, but only because Kazim cheated. If Tei'Shima had known what Kazim would find during his explorations of the station she would've locked him in his room to prevent it. Zelda called it a game changer, as if survival was merely a game to be won or lost. Kazim's curiosity would be the death of them all one day.

She wasn't playing games, but if she had been Kazim's discovery would have ensured her defeat. She'd given her Humans the duration of the storm to come to terms with remaining behind, but here they were, journeying through the wilds. Three Shan and four half-dead-of-exposure Humans.

After days of travel through wintry conditions the Harmonies led Tei'Shima straight to a hidden sentry. Hidden from sight but not from her. Nothing living could hide from her in the Harmonies.

She'd had to run through deep snow in leaps and bounds to reach her. It was slow going and tiring, but it was a necessary duty. She was her party's best scout and pathfinder. It was up to her to bring Zelda and company to safety. And she had. That was an accomplishment, considering their lack of skills and warm clothes.

Tei'Shima halted and addressed the snowdrift. "Well met, Gina. May you live in harmony."

The snowdrift shifted and the white-armoured viper revealed herself. She raised her visor. "No fair, Shima. You cheated!"

Tei'Shima laughed. "Sorry," she said, but she wasn't really. Her skills had brought her safely to Gina just in time. "Did you know mountain rescue stations come equipped with machines for riding on snow?"

"Snow mobiles?" Gina said, struggling out of the drift and through deep snow to hug Tei'Shima. "I've never used one. I'm so glad you're not dead! Don't ever die. I forbid it, okay?"

"I'll try to avoid it," Tei'Shima said and hugged her friend. "I promise."

"See that you do. I can't lose you too."

That chilled her. "Who did we lose?"

"Our ship. Everyone aboard her."

"I'm sorry. May their ancestors comfort them."

Gina looked past her, along the valley. "Where's Kazim?"

The Harmonies revealed Gina's sudden fear. Tei'Shima turned to look back the way she'd come. No one was in sight but she heard the machines closing.

"He's fine. I swear he's been blessed by the Harmonies. No one could survive the trouble he gets into without help. He's with Varya. That's them coming now."

"I have six unknowns on sensors, not two."

"Four snow machines and two soggy Shan," Tei'Shima agreed. "If not for the machines we'd be three."

"You don't like snow mobiles?"

"I don't like the way they empower stupidity."

Gina blinked, nonplussed.

"I wanted to leave everyone at the station. I was winning

until Kazim found the dratted things. There was no dissuading their idiocy after that."

Gina grinned at the sight of four space suited people riding snow mobiles.

"The suits are low on power. The last few days we've been scavenging mine and Varya's to keep the heaters working."

"A bit chancy leaving safety that way."

"That is a truth," Tei'Shima said wearily. "I've said as much. Many times."

Despite her insistence Mark was the only one to stay behind at the rescue station. It still annoyed her days later. Tei were meant to lead and be obeyed, but Humans didn't care about that.

Kazim thought it all very funny. He knew how reluctant she'd been to join the clan-that-is-not, and now here she was complaining about not being obeyed. She was hilarious according to him.

Zelda arrived ahead of the others. She grinned and waved to Gina before revving her machine. It sprayed a plume of snow into the air behind her. It was her way of saying hello. She had to keep her visor down to conserve warmth, and the suit's comms used a closed channel.

Varya and Kazim arrived last, herding the rest of the Humans ahead of them. They hugged Gina and murmured their greetings. Kazim chattered away, bringing Gina up to date. He made gestures in the air to emphasise a grand tale of epic heroism and adventure.

Shima's ears went back at his wild exaggerations regarding her exploits. Not again! "No," she snarled. "No more heroes, no more sagas. Do you hear me? No more!"

Zelda and her friends looked on in uncomprehending silence. Kazim's story and Gina's exclamations were spoken in Shan, as were Tei'Shima's protests. Zelda and the rest joined in with Gina's laughter, but only to be polite. They didn't speak Shan.

"Oh! Fine," she snarled. "Have it your way. You will anyway, and you'll look foolish. When everyone watches your show, they'll see what really happened."

Kazim sobered. "Yes. They *will* see."

Varya flicked his ears. "They'll see the horror. The fall of Hercules and Nstar, and the triumph of our escape."

Tei'Shima had a flashback of the frozen corpses. Hundreds of them. Many many many dead younglings bumping into the pod and each other. Reaching out to her, pleading for her aid—

Gina gently stroked the fur of Tei'Shima's arm. "Are you okay?"

"We need to get them out of their suits and into warm clothes."

Gina nodded. "I've already reported in. I can't leave my post, but you'll find everything you need in camp."

Tei'Shima flicked her ears and took her leave. She'd find Gina later and have a proper visit.

She led the way along the valley toward the camp. The Harmonies revealed other Human sentries hiding along her route. They were probably vipers too, though she couldn't be sure. She didn't recognise them, but she hadn't met all the vipers on Pandora. The unseen sentries didn't interfere with their approach.

The camp finally came into sight and Tei'Shima paused to study it. The others joined her and waited. The camp was a big one and horribly exposed. The Merki could wipe it out from the air with ease. She sensed Shan mingling with the Humans and tried to separate Tei'Laran from the crowd, but there were too many people.

They entered the camp without fanfare but their arrival caused a stir regardless. It didn't surprise Tei'Shima. She'd made a spectacle of herself by arriving in company with space suited Humans riding noisy machines. Zelda didn't help matters. Her flamboyant nature came to the fore as she accelerated and spun out, spraying a plume of snow into the air in a flashy fan.

Kazim loved it.

Tei'Shima rolled her eyes as Zelda's friends parked their machines flanking her, and then removed their helmets in unison with Zelda as if they'd rehearsed it. Their audience reacted like maniacs, cheering and chanting Zelda's name. She waved and pointed at people as if she knew them. She clapped as if congratulating them for surviving, and then gestured grandly at Shortcut before tucking her mate in close by her side.

Tei'Shima watched from a distance, feeling a profound sense of release. Her duty to them was done. Kazim muttered happily as he recorded the scene for posterity. Varya chuffed in amusement as some of the Marines hoisted Zelda and Shortcut onto their shoulders for a parade through the camp. They loved her. Zelda was one of their heroes come back to life.

Tei'Shima glanced furtively around. Some of her people were taking an interest in the excitement but they hadn't noticed her yet. Thank the Harmonies for that. She slipped away using the fuss to hide her movements and felt Varya follow. He was unmistakable in the Harmonies. Kazim yelped indignantly when he realised she'd snuck away. She was still close enough to hear him. Varya laughed as she dropped to all fours and dashed into the crowds.

"He'll find you," Varya said, keeping pace by her side. "The interview is just a matter of when not if, Tei."

Tei'Shima smirked. She knew all right, but making Kazim work for it appealed to her sense of rightness. He would find her, but not until he'd exhausted his current material. Zelda's antics would keep him busy while she sought out Tei'Laran and brought herself up to date. She wanted to know why her people were camped in such an exposed position and not marching to war.

It her took a while. There were too many of her people clustered in tight quarters to give Tei'Shima more than a vague direction to follow. The further she went the more people recognised her. They followed in greater and greater numbers until she gave in to the inevitable. She greeted her people and asked for Tei'Laran.

Armed with certain knowledge of his location and escorted by a crowd of warriors who wouldn't be dissuaded, Tei'Shima and Varya finally reported their arrival to Tei'Laran in one of the larger tents. He wasn't alone. Eric and a Marine she hadn't met before were discussing plans over a holo-table. She heard enough to raise more questions in her mind before they noticed her enter.

The Humans grinned.

Tei'Shima had learned not to react negatively to the gesture. She nodded to them but focussed her attention on Tei'Laran. His eyes were wide and his ears were back in surprise. He was very happy in the Harmonies, and at first that pleased Tei'Shima, but his emotions went beyond relief at her survival. They edged into private matters. Territory better suited to close family.

Very close. Admiration for a mate close.

"Well met," Tei'Laran said. He was strong in the Harmonies and must have sensed her sudden confusion. "May you live in harmony. You as well Varya."

Varya murmured his greeting.

"Thank you," Tei'Shima said. She did like him and admired his skills, but she'd never considered him as a potential mate. A memory of Kazim laughing on the shores of the lake on Snakeholme flashed into her mind. She wasn't seeking a mate. "May you live in harmony."

"How are you here?" Tei'Laran said flicking a look at Varya and back to Tei'Shima. "We thought you'd died."

"We nearly did," Varya said. "Quite a few times. The Blind Hunter wouldn't let us."

Tei'Shima flinched a little inside. Her reaction was mild compared with the way she once would've reacted. "It's a tale better suited for later," she said. "Ask Kazim. He loves the sound of his own voice."

"He's alive too? That's good news."

"Zelda and her friends as well. She saved all of us," Varya said proudly.

"Not all," Tei'Shima said as the pleading younglings from her nightmares flashed into her thoughts again. "The murderers slaughtered many at Nstar."

"Too many," Tei'Penleigh agreed.

The Marine nodded. "We haven't been introduced Tei'Shima. I know of you of course. Major Patrick Stein, 7th Alliance Marines at your service. Call me Stein, I'd prefer it."

"Honoured to meet you," Tei'Shima said. Humans were addicted to too many names in her opinion. "I'd be pleased to call you Stein. May you live in harmony."

"I don't think any of us will be doing that I'm afraid. Not for a while."

Tei'Shima flicked her ears and added a nod for Stein's benefit. "I wanted to ask you about that. Why do you think sitting in the open with a big target painted on your camp is a good idea?"

Eric barked a laugh. "You noticed that, did you? We're bait for the Merki."

"You certainly are, but bait gets eaten."

Everyone laughed.

It was an evil sound and Tei'Shima shivered. They planned on being poisoned meat then.

Eric led the way to find places around the holo-table, and Tei'Shima studied the maps displayed on its colourfully glowing surface. Pandora looked horribly diseased with many red blotches decorating its surface. Merkiaari locations. Green and blue patches represented civilian populations and allied militaries respectively. Most of the cities were green still, but not all. That was a puzzle. The Merkiaari hadn't been in the system long, but they'd certainly had long enough to do more than this.

"What are they up to?" she muttered, and tapped an extended claw on a city she'd visited. "Untouched? Still?"

"She's quick," Stein said.

Tei'Laran flicked his ears to agree. "The Blind Hunter knows the Merkiaari and their ways."

Tei'Shima tried not to reveal her annoyance at the constant reminder of her supposed status. She busied herself noting the Merkiaari's dispositions, trying to make sense of the pattern she was sure was hidden there.

Eric took charge and zoomed the map to an area containing a blue force. "Alliance army under direct command of General Ecclestone," he said and changed the map again. "We're here in Nothingville, AKA Southaven Province freezing our butts off. And *here* we have a nice force of Merkiaari killing a local population opposed by nobody."

Tei'Shima heard anger in Eric's voice. She shared it. Why weren't they stalking and killing the Merki there? What was she missing?

"I don't understand our strategy in doing nothing about this," she said and addressed herself to Tei'Laran. "You know my inadequacies. I've tried to address them but I don't understand."

"Don't be too hard on yourself," Stein said. "None of us like this."

Eric snorted.

"We've been ordered to do nothing?"

"In a sense," Tei'Laran agreed. "We could attack them, but by we, I mean our warriors alone. We might even win."

"You'd lose," Eric disagreed. "Or you'd win the first skirmish and lose the war."

"But why would we attack alone?" Tei'Shima said.

Eric shrugged. "Because your warriors are the only ones

with working weapons here. That's why."

Eric wasn't joking. He was grimly serious in the Harmonies. How could they let this happen? There were thousands of Human warriors in camp and hundreds were vipers, yet only the Shan were ready to fight? How was that even possible?

"What's your plan?"

Stein explained. "We lure the Merkiaari here, kill them all and take their stuff."

Eric grinned. "It's so ridiculous it might work. We'd have no chance at all without your warriors."

He didn't sound as if he believed it. Tei'Shima didn't either. Her thoughts raced in circles as she tried to find an alternative.

Eric detailed the plan worked out by him and General Ecclestone. Stein and Tei'Laran followed along, nodding or making comments at key points. They gestured at the map, zoomed it in to reveal terrain, and then zoomed it out again to show Tei'Shima how they expected the Merkiaari to approach.

Tei'Shima didn't hear a plan. She heard one of Kazim's grand sagas. Total fiction. Varya looked at her, eyes wide and ears flat. He saw it. By the Harmonies he saw it as plain as she did, yet Tei'Laran and the others pretended the plan was guaranteed to work.

She listened in dismay as she realised the vipers were going to die. They would die to lure the Merki into a trap. It was insane. Gina would die. Eric would die with her and all his warriors with them. It was utter madness.

Oh, ancestors help her. What would she say to Kate? To Stone? She couldn't let this happen!

* * *

42 ~ Scholars

Aboard Blood Drinker, Pandora

Davey lay on his bed studying his tablet. Everything he could remember from his last visit with Valjoth was on it. Every scrap. He had no idea how the data would ever find its way off the ship, but he wrote everything down anyway. He'd never had a great memory for facts and figures. Writing it down seemed to help.

Evrei had given him the tablet to help him learn Lamarian pronunciation. The scholar would be horrified if he ever found the file buried amongst the others. He wouldn't find it. One thing about Lamarians; they'd turned protocol into their religion. It would be the height of discourtesy to pry.

Davey supposed slaves had to make the best of their situations. Scholars like Evrei had carved a niche in Merkiaari society by making themselves indispensable. Servitors were integral to the system that kept Merkiaari client races in servitude. Without linguists like Evrei they would find communications between the races of their thousand-sun empire impossible. Lamarians were the bureaucrats who kept the Merkiaari Hegemony running smoothly. In a strange way that gave them a special place in the pecking order.

Merki were never scholars or linguists.

Davey frowned. Valjoth could speak a few languages, but that was rare among his kind. Usk always used a servitor to translate. Valjoth was odd in a lot of ways. If there were Merkiaari scholars anywhere in the galaxy, Valjoth would fit right in with them. Davey had met more than a few Merki, and none were like Valjoth. He was a runt compared with others of his kind, yet his authority was absolute. It was chilling the way he hurt Evrei. He wasn't angry or sad when he did it. He was simply methodical. He always had a reason.

"I just wish I knew what it was," Davey muttered as he read his notes.

The current file was his diary. It contained everything he remembered from the moment the battle began to the current day. He'd written down all he'd learned about the ship, and what he'd tried to do with his collar, but Evrei and his lessons in Merkiaari and Lamarian were the bulk of it. The stuff about the Kiar language especially, and why the Merki used it for the basis of theirs.

Davey knew stuff now that no other Human in history knew. If only he could tell someone there were worse things in the galaxy than Merkiaari. Their creators sounded like a nightmare. Lamarians were pacifists, but even Evrei sounded as if he'd kill a Kiar if one appeared. Not likely as they'd disappeared millennia ago. Still, Evrei's hatred of them meant something. Valjoth's timeline and targets were the real prize.

"Faragut. Pandora. Argo. Garnet. Kalmar. Casino. Beaufort. Helios. *Mars!*" He always tripped himself up over that hallowed name.

Mars is humanity's first colony and independent world, his history lessons whispered reverently in his memories. Proof it could be done. Mars, the terraformed jewel of the Human Alliance of Worlds. If Valjoth followed his timeline and attacked Mars, it would send a shock-wave through the

Alliance that would never be forgotten.

Mars was in Sol, the home system itself. Sol had stood inviolate even at the height of the Merki War! To attack it was unthinkable, only it wasn't unthinkable to Valjoth. Davey knew his arrogance would push him into trying. Why else plan his jumps to this specific timeline?

Evrei knew Valjoth's life story. He'd taught Davey how a runt had risen to become First Claw of the Host. Valjoth had colossal ego and ambition. He wanted to be *the* First Claw to bring his people ultimate victory and cleanse humanity from the galaxy. Many Merkiaari had tried. Tried and died. But Valjoth had a workable plan. Evrei thought he did, and Valjoth certainly believed in his own superiority.

"Mars. Alizon. Steiner."

That's all he had so far, but if Valjoth could hit the huge shipyards at Mars, what would stop him attacking Earth herself? The thought made Davey shake. He'd seen what Valjoth could do. If he wanted to attack Earth he would do it, and yet... it wasn't on the list. Unless it was and Davey had missed it.

Davey frowned and kept reading.

Evrei arrived for his lesson, but he didn't have his usual pile of tablets with him. Davey sat up and swung his legs off the bed, but before he could ask what was wrong, Evrei raised a warning finger to his lips. The Human gesture looked very odd in front of his v-shaped face.

Evrei motioned to the tablet, and Davey went cold. He handed it across and watched numbly as the scholar wiped everything in its memory. How did he know? What was he going to tell Valjoth?

"What..."

Evrei gestured sharply, and Davey nodded as the scholar entered something into the tablet and then gave it back. Davey looked at it and found it full of Evrei's lessons and nothing else.

"The Great Lord has ordered us to attend him. He wants to see us both *and your tablet*. He didn't say why."

Davey paled. He went through all the files listed on the device again, but found nothing incriminating now.

"Thank—"

"I don't want gratitude, Davey. I want compliance. The Great Lord will kill me for my failure to properly instruct you."

"You've been a good teacher," Davey protested in Lamarian.

"The Great Lord wouldn't think so if he knew what I just did. I shouldn't have allowed your petty rebellion."

"Why did you then?"

Evrei cocked his head. "I don't know why. It seemed to make you happy. I saw no harm in it at the time."

"And now?"

"You will do everything I say from this moment on, no matter how foolish you think me. I will not die for you."

"I wouldn't expect it!" Davey said.

"Good. The Great Lord is waiting. Do everything he says and everything I say, and all will be well. Come."

Davey followed the scholar out of his room. "I like you Evrei. I wouldn't do anything to hurt you on purpose."

"On purpose or by accident, dead is still dead. The Great Lord does everything for a purpose, Davey. If you remember nothing else I've taught you, remember that."

Davey nodded, but Evrei wasn't telling him anything he didn't already know.

Valjoth was on the bridge and in a bad mood. Something on Pandora had his attention. Davey studied the holographic displays, but he wasn't a soldier. Arrows and icons were just that to him. Vectors and whatnot meant nothing, except he knew in the real world they were troops and grav sleds.

Valjoth glared at Davey. "*Here!*" he barked.

Evrei bowed and offered his controller.

Valjoth was so angry he snatched the thing and threw it onto the control board he'd been using. It bounced and landed next to the one that controlled Davey's collar.

Davey winced.

Valjoth snatched the tablet out of Davey's hand. "Your teacher tells me you've learned his lessons well."

Davey said nothing.

"Well?"

Evrei gave him a look, and Davey swallowed his pride. In his best Merkiaari he said, "Evrei is a very good teacher, Great Lord. I've learned a lot from him."

"Time my lord," Usk said.

"I can count!" Valjoth snarled at his shield bearer.

Davey had never seen that before. They were friends, if Merkiaari could be said to have friends. The battle must be going badly for him. Davey smirked but unfortunately Valjoth noticed.

Valjoth snarled. He tried to grab the controllers, but Evrei was in his way. He shoved the servitor who flew backwards arms windmilling.

"*Don't hurt him!*" Davey cried.

Evrei hit the control panel and landed on the deck along with the controllers. The servitor scrambled away, cowering from a blow he thought was coming, but the sight of Evrei cowering on his knees seemed to sap Valjoth's anger.

"*Up!*" Valjoth said suddenly much calmer. "You need to teach my pet your Lamarian etiquette, Scholar Evrei. He needs lessons in proper manners."

Evrei bowed. "Yes Great Lord. I will see to it."

"Ignore my temper, Usk. We have time yet," Valjoth said to his shield bearer.

Usk gnashed his fangs. "I've heard worse, my lord."

Valjoth glared, but he wasn't angry anymore. Davey had learned the difference over the weeks and months of being his target. Valjoth inspected the tablet he still held and scrolled through its files. He found nothing and threw it back.

Davey caught it against his chest. "Thank you, Great Lord."

Valjoth gnashed his fangs. "That's much better. You do learn it seems. I wonder how much you really understand of what's happening."

"I understand everything, Great Lord."

"Do you? I wonder."

Valjoth crossed the bridge to another control panel and did something. "Tell me what you think of this."

Davey darted a look at Evrei, but he was still in shock. He left his teacher there and joined Valjoth who was adjusting a view of Pandora.

He frowned at the screen. "It's a view of Pandora from orbit, Great Lord."

"Too vague. Try again."

"Time my lord," Usk said, and Valjoth glared at him. "You did ask me to forget your temper."

The command crew laughed, but very quietly.

Valjoth grinned. "So I did."

Davey ignored everything but the view on the screen. He yearned to be down there with those soldiers. Marines in armour were digging trenches it looked like. They were the first Humans he'd seen in so long.

"Well?" Valjoth said.

"I see snow, Great Lord, and Human soldiers getting ready to fight."

"By digging in the dirt like the vermin they are. What else?"

Davey didn't want to say too much, but Valjoth was testing him. It was likely he already knew all the answers. He swallowed his misery and betrayed his people.

"They're called Alliance Marines, Great Lord. They're elite fighters. Some of our best. The armour means they're as strong as you. Stronger even than Kylar."

"Oh ho!" Valjoth said. "Did you hear that, Usk?"

"Better not tell her, my lord. She'll insist on accepting his challenge. And time, my lord."

Valjoth sighed. "What else do you see?"

Davey frowned. "I'm not sure."

"Location," Valjoth prompted.

Davey frowned harder at the hint. Then he had it. "They're not hiding!"

"Great Lord, Davey. No backsliding."

"They're not hiding, Great Lord."

"Very good. You do see and understand more than I'd thought. Interesting. You were never a fighter."

Valjoth said it with certainty, but Davey answered anyway.

"I'm too young, Great Lord. I could have joined next birthday with special permission."

"Special permission wouldn't help you. All Merkiaari can fight, and we do from the moment we draw our first breaths in the vats. You'll be a scholar like Evrei."

"If that is your wish, Great Lord."

"It's my *order!*"

"Yes, Great Lord."

Valjoth looked down at the Marine camp. He changed the view to show a Merkiaari force gathering. Davey counted the grav sleds and stopped at over a hundred. It would be a slaughter. Valjoth was watching his face. Davey tried to keep his expression blank.

Valjoth snorted. "Special permission," he muttered and tapped a claw on the screen. "I'll give you special permission to watch a real battle."

"Great Lord?" Evrei said and offered Davey's controller to Valjoth. He'd already stowed his own out of sight.

Valjoth took it. "Usk, inform Kylar we're going for a ride. Prepare a gunboat in case of adventurous vermin!"

"But the jump schedule my lord!"

Valjoth glared. "I wrote it! I know there's time enough.

Now come! You're driving."

Valjoth stormed away and Davey hurried to catch up. He sent Evrei a panicked look as the servitor joined them.

* * *

43 ~ Time's Up

SOUTHAVEN PROVINCE, PANDORA

Valjoth dismounted the gunboat's ramp ushering Davey and his teacher ahead of him. The Human was clearly worried. If he knew how worried he should be, he'd be cowering not dragging his feet.

Kylar grumbled about the cold. Her boots crunched on the frozen snow as she peered around hopefully. There were no vermin near, or there shouldn't be. Being potted by a vermin sniper would be very inconvenient.

"This is a risk," Usk muttered. "We're too old to be playing in the snow."

"Speak for yourself old fool," Kylar boomed. She roared like someone fresh from the vats. It echoed in the cold air. "There's no silver in my fur!"

Valjoth laughed. "Really Usk. Where is your sense of adventure? A new world to tame and vermin to control. You should be eager to explore!"

Usk grumbled, keeping his eyes on the sensor tablet he held. "I dare you to say *that* when your fangs hang around a vermin's neck. They'll make a fine decoration."

Valjoth gnashed the fangs in question, and grinned. "They look better on me."

Evrei whispered something in Lamarian to Davey. Valjoth didn't catch all of it but whatever it was perked Davey up. He glanced furtively around and nodded.

"I'll do whatever you say," Davey whispered. "No matter what it is. I promise you. I don't want us punished."

Valjoth approved of the sentiment. He was very pleased with Evrei. He was even happier with Davey. He'd been a fine challenge. There'd been times when he'd doubted the young Human would break at all. A fine challenge indeed. He'd found the right key in the end. All vermin had one.

They crossed the open snow between the gunboat and the grav sleds waiting to escort him. They boarded one of them and Usk took the controls. It was a rare treat for him. Kylar took the gunner's position hoping to kill something on the way.

Valjoth contented himself listening to his pet practising his Lamarian rather than taking an interest in the scenery. Usk drove fast, he always did, but there was good reason for it. They were out of time. The timeline was central to the entire cleansing effort. Coordination between each of his five commanders and their hosts was of paramount importance.

Davey had picked up the Lamarian language quickly once Evrei took him in hand. He'd turned out to be quite bright given the right motivation. He spoke Merkiaari well, though his accent was atrocious. Physiology played a part in that.

"Why am I here?" Davey said. Evrei nudged him. "Great. Lord."

Valjoth grinned. Davey was only barely tame. He still wasn't comfortable with his station. That was to the good considering what he wanted of his pet. He needed him broken to harness not broken in spirit, and that's what Evrei had supplied him.

"You're my pet," Valjoth said. "I don't need a reason."

"You do nothing without one."

Valjoth waited.

"Great. Lord."

Kylar's quiet laughter made Valjoth grin. Females had their own definition of the word quiet. Davey did that Human thing. The flushing thing. He needed some fur to cover that reaction. It revealed far too much.

Valjoth activated a tablet to reveal their destination and showed it to his pet. Davey studied it but said nothing. Valjoth flicked a look at Evrei who also studied it. Neither spoke. He changed settings and the map expanded. This time Davey reacted.

"It's a trap."

Valjoth nodded. "Very good." He didn't reprimand him for his lapse.

"Why are we walking into it?" This time Evrei hissed at Davey and he added, "Great. Lord."

"We aren't. *They* are." Valjoth tapped a claw on the tablet and revealed the strange looking column of walking things he had no name for. "These walkers intend to help your people trap mine. I'm not going to let them."

Davey frowned at the image. "What are they?"

Interesting that he didn't know. Davey could lie. He'd done it often in the beginning as part of his rebellion against captivity, but not since Evrei became his teacher and friend.

"Something new," Valjoth said and took the tablet. He adjusted the view and offered it to him again. "Interesting aren't they?"

Davey nodded as he watched the column navigating the snowy ravines. The overhead surveillance was quite good, but the angle didn't do the things justice. They were bigger than they looked. He approved of the size. A challenge always excited him.

"Why are you letting them approach?"

"Great Lord, Davey," Valjoth said, trying not to laugh and spoil it. "You really must learn your place. One more lapse and I'll have to punish you both."

Davey shot a look at Evrei. "Sorry," he said and then to Valjoth. "Great Lord, why do you let them approach?"

"Am I doing that?"

"Yes, Great Lord. You are Great Lord. You could destroy them from above. *Great. Lord.*"

This time Valjoth did laugh. Davey could make a simple statement sound like an insult. Valjoth grinned at Evrei. He must reward him. He'd been an excellent teacher. Valjoth wasn't willing to tell his pet the real reason for this visit. He chose another.

"I want to see them in action."

That was true as far as it went. They did intrigue him but another reason was that his interceptors had already left the planet. The host would jump on time, and although he could afford losses he didn't feel like losing any to an unknown threat. He would rather see what his grav sleds could do. He could lose many of those without feeling the loss.

Usk slowed their sled and his escort continued to the attack.

Valjoth watched them pull ahead on his screens. They were racing each other. Kylar grumbled about not being part of it, but she'd had her fun on this world. He'd sent her down in the first wave. He would never have heard the end of it if he hadn't.

Usk slowed the sled to a stop and they climbed out to watch the battle. Kylar herded Davey ahead of her. The young Human stumbled and glared at her. She laughed and shoved him again using her rifle. Evrei didn't need encouragement. He stayed by his student's side.

"Join me," Valjoth said to Davey. "Here in front of me. I want you to watch. This is a small example of your people's future. I'll end them forever. What do you think of that?"

"I think you'll fail," Davey said in Merkiaari. "We'll win. Great. Lord."

Valjoth laughed. He pointed to the fighting. "Do I look like I'm losing?"

The sleds were fully engaged with the walkers, and although none had yet been destroyed, they *were* stopped in their tracks. His forces were more manoeuvrable than the walkers; they were circling them unimpeded, but their guns weren't very effective. Valjoth scowled at that. The walkers had excellent armour.

Valjoth winced when a four-legged variant stomped on one of his sleds, crushing it, but he grinned when a two-legged one fell in flames a moment later. Finally. Nineteen to go. The battle might be a lengthy one. They were tougher than he liked. They needed to be hit from the air or long range. He'd plan for that in future.

Davey scowled when another walker exploded and toppled.

"I asked you a question. Do I look like I'm losing?"

Davey remained stubbornly silent, and Valjoth shook his head trying to mimic vermin sadness. He pretended reluctance and retrieved his pet's controller. Davey recognised it and backed fearfully away from him.

"Answerrrrrr," Valjoth said aiming the controller at his pet and drawing the word out. "Answerrrrrr... Answerrrrrr... I won't tell you again."

Davey remained silent, and Valjoth triggered the collar.

Evrei screamed and fell writhing to the ground. Davey gasped, grabbing his own collar in shock. Valjoth roared in pretended surprise and anger.

"Run!" Evrei screamed. "*Ruuuuuuuun!*"

Davey bolted.

Valjoth put the controller away and allowed Evrei to recover. The servitor had played his part. He glanced at Kylar and held out a hand. She showed fang, reluctant to surrender her cannon. He grinned. She never liked being unarmed even aboard the ship when she didn't need a weapon.

Valjoth wiggled his fingers. "Hand it over."

Kylar grimaced. "I could hit him with my eyes closed."

"That's what worries me."

Usk laughed. "He's getting away."

Valjoth grunted in annoyance. "Hand it over if you ever want it back."

Kylar reluctantly gave up her cannon, and Valjoth aimed carefully. He fired to make Davey dodge. His pet changed direction randomly to throw off his aim, and he stopped firing after a few bursts. He didn't want to accidentally kill him. He handed the gauss rifle back to Kylar and watched Davey sprinting toward his own kind as if the entire host was on his heels. He laughed at the thought. He hoped the fool didn't die by accident.

"You missed again," Kylar grumbled. "A bad habit. I could fix it for you?"

Valjoth gnashed his fangs and shook his head. She would never understand his strategy. It wasn't her fault. Not a fault in her at all. She'd been bred for battle not strategy. He liked her anyway.

"How many times must I tell you? He *never* misses," Usk said. "Time my lord."

Valjoth nodded at the reminder. "*Up!*"

Evrei climbed shakily back to his feet, and bowed to him.

"You've done well," Valjoth said and gave the servitor a brief surge of pleasure as his reward.

Evrei gasped and shuddered. "Thank you, Great Lord."

Valjoth handed the quivering servitor his controller for safekeeping, and turned back to observe the battle.

What were the walking things called? They were something new in an old game. Powerful but limited in scope. He wondered at their development and sudden appearance. Why here? Why now? Had they been designed specially to oppose him, or were they meant for their war games? The latter he decided. They would've taken time to build, and Humans did so love killing each other. He'd need to factor them into his future plans. He'd been right to choose their game world for his first strike.

"Time my lord," Usk reminded again.

"Yes, yes I know. Sound the recall. The host will jump on schedule. Precisely on schedule. Any left behind will fight to the death."

"Of course my lord," Usk said knowing they would have anyway. Raging troops listened to no one and Merkiaari did not surrender.

Ever.

Valjoth watched the giant machines turning his sleds into scrap one by one. They'd begun cooperating. They seemed to be learning on the job. Very odd tactics, but effective in a clumsy way. He wasn't too upset. He didn't like to lose but he'd planted his seed in the vermin's vitals with his use of Davey. That was his real goal here, not killing a few more vermin. He would call this a victory.

Usk would disagree.

Usk wasn't First Claw of the Host.

Valjoth tried to see Davey but he'd gone to ground like sensible vermin in the presence of predators. He wondered if they'd meet again. Not very likely. He'd miss him. He watched the walkers destroying his grav sleds for a moment longer and then turned away.

"Sound retreat and begin withdrawal to orbit," he said.

"Already done," Usk said.

Valjoth climbed aboard his sled and imagined his next victory. The vermin were going to be very vexed with him when their ships arrived to find him gone.

The sound of the sled drowned out his quiet laughter.

* * *

44 ~ Remember Me

Southaven Province, Pandora

Tei'Shima kept her head below ground level. The trenches were deep enough to do that standing on two legs if she crouched just a little. Her warriors mimicked her and kept out of sight.

Her efforts to change or come up with a new plan had been for naught. Eric and Stein were kind to listen to her, but they'd already thought of her ideas and discarded them. She didn't have enough experience. She would learn if she lived long enough, but for now she had to believe in them.

Only she didn't. She really *really* didn't, and neither did Varya and Tei'Laran. Both males had spoken of their fears to her privately, and arranged contingencies. The plans amounted to running away. Oh, they couched them in grand terms like tactical withdrawal, or strategic realignment. All of it was skaggikt dung.

They would run away.

Of course, they would call it something else for their warriors' ears. Tei'Laran and she would shoulder the dishonour to protect their followers. That was a part of being

Tei not often spoken of. Warriors gained honour by doing their duty, and their duty was to follow their Tei. In this case, it meant following the Blind Hunter to glory or death... or to ignominious retreat.

She hated it. Hated the need for such plans, but the situation clearly demanded they be ready. If required, they would run away and fall back upon tried and tested Shan tactics. Hit and run warfare was a traditional form, called guerrilla by Humans for some reason. It had served them well in the past.

Tei'Shima hoped her fears were unfounded. If the vipers could lure the Merkiaari without being killed. If the Marines could hold them in place. And if the Titans could prove themselves in their first real battle, then they had a chance. As Stein said, they would take the Merkiaari's stuff and use it to steal more until they could oppose them on an equal footing.

A lot of ifs.

Tei'Shima chose to dwell within the Harmonies to bolster herself against her doubts, and maintain balance. She needed to set a good example. Tei'Laran was nearby. Like her he was deep within the Harmonies and monitoring their surroundings. He was strong. Tei'Shima wasn't sure of his range but it might eclipse hers. She wanted him close by for that reason. If he sensed the vipers returning before her, she wanted to know.

She briefly checked closer to home. The Marines were in position and ready for the attack. Metal men her people called them back home. Their powered armour was a great advantage despite the situation regarding their weapons. They could take a few hits from the Merki and survive. Not something a Shan warrior could do.

Despite her people's lack of armour, something that was being addressed at levels far higher than her need to know, Tei'Shima much preferred being armed. If she lived long enough to be armoured as well, she'd reassess her feelings on the matter. She wouldn't want armour that restricted her movements no matter how much protection it offered.

"No sign of the Titans," Tei'Laran said quietly, and Kazim edged closer. "Even when I stretch my senses to the maximum."

"They're late," Tei'Shima confirmed.

"More than late. I have a feeling they're not coming."

There was no way to know that for sure, but when Tei said they had a feeling it was significant. Tei'Shima tried not to put too much stock in his feeling, but he was strong in the Harmonies. Was he stronger than she?

"Tei?" Varya said from just beyond Kazim.

"Wait," Tei'Shima said and cast her senses as far as she could.

There was a vagueness to the Harmonies when stretched so thin, but she had a feeling the Titans were there. They were out there far away, but... stuck? Not stuck, fighting. They'd been intercepted.

Maybe.

She couldn't be sure. The feeling was very vague. Too vague to voice her doubts. She had to consider what the news might do to her warriors. They needed confidence and certainty from her.

"They'll come," she said, unwilling to say more. Even that was enough to spread confidence among those who heard her assertion. They grew braver in the Harmonies. She felt it.

Tei'Laran gave her a look that said he knew better, but he didn't. She must be stronger than him if he couldn't feel the frustration emanating from the direction of the Titans. It was there. The feeling wasn't her imagination. It was just very vague.

"I wish we could ask how long they'll be," Varya said.

Tei'Shima flicked her ears. "Eric blames himself for that."

"He did order the damage," Tei'Laran agreed. "Then again, if he hadn't done that it's unlikely Cooper's Commandos would be piloting the things in person. Things tend to balance within the Harmonies."

"That is a truth," Tei'Shima said.

Titans were meant to be used like the Marines used their drones. Remotely. Eric's brief demonstration against the idea had damaged four of the machines and convinced Colonel Jubb not to take the risk with the rest. His men were driving the machines manually under his direct command. They were lucky the cockpits installed for the test pilots hadn't been deleted from the designs yet. They probably never would be now.

"We need to find a way to break Merkiaari jamming," Varya said. "We're lucky our comms work."

"That is a truth," Tei'Laran agreed. "If they ever block short range comms too... well, let's hope it never occurs to them."

"They'd block themselves if they tried," Tei'Shima said, but it was only a guess. No one knew how Merki jamming worked. Some speculated they used foldspace. An impossibility for the Alliance.

"So it's said," Tei'Laran agreed. "Let's hope it remains so."

Tei'Shima flicked her ears. Merkiaari were masters of slaughter, but they did know technology. Their jamming was an utter menace. Remote piloting the Titans, just as Eric had said, was a bad idea. The Merki could deactivate them. Worse, they might take control and use them against their owners. No one was sure what their abilities were in the area. Losing surveillance drones to jamming was a small thing. Surrendering 80 ton machines armed for war was something else entirely.

"What do you think of the walking machines?" Tei'Shima said.

"Big," Tei'Laran said. "And powerful, but unwieldy. Not very stealthy. Not Shan."

Tei'Shima laughed and the others joined in. They weren't

Shan at all. Her people didn't design ugly machines. They preferred beauty and symmetry in their lives. Balance.

"Where are the vipers now?" Kazim said.

Tei'Laran closed his eyes to use the Harmonies. Tei'Shima did that sometimes too, but didn't need to. She let him answer Kazim, but she knew what he'd say before he did.

"On their way here. Fast. Very fast," Tei'Laran said and drew his beamers. "*Get ready!*"

Their warriors obeyed and readied their weapons, but Tei'Shima left hers in their holsters. She could feel Eric running with Gina by his side. That image came to her very strongly within the Harmonies. It was somehow right. They fit the way Kate and Stone fit, or the way she and... well, the way she and Kazim did.

"There's time yet," she said. "But they did draw the Merki's attention."

Tei'Laran chuffed. "They definitely did that, but I fear the Titans will not be here in time."

The vipers were running as fast as they could to keep out of range of the Merkiaari grav sleds. The machines did use anti-grav but they couldn't fly. A lucky thing as it allowed Eric's people to dodge and use the terrain to avoid incoming fire. Even so, the Merki must be trying to kill them. The Harmonies couldn't reveal the battle itself, or the grav sleds, but it could give Tei'Shima a sense of those involved. The sharp-edged insane mind glows of the Merkiaari were obvious when contrasted with the beauty of Eric's people. Humans were made of energetic bright colours in the Harmonies. The Merkiaari horde vastly outnumbered them.

The vipers arrived in a sprint. They reformed their formation from a widely spaced one to avoid fire, into a compact column to take places in the trenches. Eric and Gina joined Shima and ordered the rest of the vipers to partner with Shan warriors.

"The Titans?" Eric said, looking over the edge of the

trench at his back trail.

"No word yet," Tei'Shima said.

"I fear they're not coming," Tei'Laran said. "We should withdraw."

"Too late," Gina said.

The Merkiaari grav sleds stopped within firing range of the Marines. The first line of defence. They jostled and parked with finicky precision as if on parade, something else Tei'Shima had never seen them do before. Even if the Marines had been properly armed, the Merki would be out of rifle range. They'd need artillery to hit them. That's why they needed the Titans.

The grav sleds fired to keep Marine heads down, and it worked perfectly. They were using Human and Shan tactics against them. The bombardment continued while Merkiaari ground troops formed up between the sleds. At some signal from their hidden commanders, they charged and rolled over the Marines as if they weren't there. Powered armour strained as the Marines were forced into a hand to hand fight with creatures designed purely for war.

Stein's Marines tried to hold on, desperately hoping for aid, but the Titans didn't come. Tei'Shima felt the deaths in the Harmonies like physical blows, but there was nothing she could do. She searched for the Titans and found them still out of range even for a rocket barrage. Such a thing would kill their own in any case. Colonel Jubb would never risk it. The Merkiaari had delayed him too long.

Gina started to climb out of the trench.

"Freeze!" Eric snarled.

"I can't," Gina whispered in horror. "I can't abandon them. Not again. Stein was right."

"I said freeze dammit!" Eric yanked Gina roughly back. She fell into the bottom of the trench.

"I can't," Gina whispered, her eyes wide in horror. "I can't do this. I can't live like this. I won't."

Eric shoved his face into Gina's. "You will hold this position! *That's an order!* I'll go." Eric shoved himself over the top and into hell. "Cragg, on me."

Cragg turned and stared white-faced into Kazim's camera lens. "I was Martin Cragg of Alizon. Remember me."

"*Cragg!*" Eric barked as he sprinted toward the embattled Marines.

"On my way!" Cragg yelled and bounced out of the trench as if his legs had turned to springs. He sped away in a blur of speed.

Tei'Shima saw it all. Cragg took a hit from something. His right shoulder disappeared in a spray of red mist. He was going so fast that his legs kept propelling him into battle, but he wasn't there. He collapsed like a puppet with its strings cut.

Eric slammed into the Merkiaari and went through them like a buzz saw. He managed to kill enough of the troopers for the Marines to rally briefly, but the Merkiaari's recoil didn't last. They surged and rolled back over them.

Tei'Shima saw it all through blurring eyes. Eric appeared briefly carrying a huge Merkiaari gauss cannon. He swept it over the enemy hordes killing many, but he finally disappeared beneath the stampede. Seeing him fight caused more vipers to bounce out of the trenches and pile into the battle. The movement became general as all sense of command was lost with Eric's fall. Gina didn't take command, and no one else held them back.

Tei'Shima tried to stop them using her comm, but the vipers were moving inhumanly fast. They were faster than the best Shan sprinters when like this. Vipers communicated at computer speeds over their TacNet. She'd seen them in melee mode before.

Gina dragged herself up the wall of the trench. "I can't leave them. Not again."

Tei'Shima clutched at Gina's arm, desperately trying to

hold her back. "Don't… don't… don't," she chanted. "Please don't go. You'll die."

Gina gently pried Tei'Shima's fingers free. "Goodbye."

"No!"

Gina sprinted to join Eric, and disappeared into the maelstrom of a losing battle.

Tei'Shima stared around, ears flat and wide-eyed at what she had left. Only Shan faces stared back at her; all were calm and ready for orders. Tei'Laran flicked his ears at her, and checked his beamers calmly. He was ready to fight or run. Her choice. The Harmonies rushed in to enfold her as her mind expanded to embrace her people. They were all hers. Her people. Her warriors. They would follow where she led. Even into death. She was Tei. Honour demanded it.

Tei'Shima turned to Kazim. "Don't die."

He flicked his ears behind his camera, but his hands were shaking. His eyes were white-rimmed on the verge of panic. He was witnessing the end of everything and he knew it.

"Stay here, Kazim. Live for me. For all of us. Show our people what it means to be warrior caste."

Tei'Shima climbed out of the trench and stood tall. She dared the Merkiaari to kill her, but they were too busy just then to notice. Her warriors climbed out of the trenches to join her, and she gathered them all in her thoughts. They burned brightly in the Harmonies, full of courage and love for her. The hero they'd vowed to follow even into death.

The Blind Hunter charged into battle, and her people charged to meet their ancestors by her side.

* * *

45 ~ Epilogue

Southaven Province, Pandora

The snow fell gently to hide the slaughter. Not a breath of wind disturbed the peace of the dead. The blackened craters were turning white again, and the red ice had finally succumbed. So much blood spilled. It seemed impossible to hide it all.

A Titan in the distance patrolled the tree line. It turned a searchlight on to spear the night and fired its PPC at something in the forest. A tree crashed to the ground and another took light, its resinous sap eagerly fuelling its own pyre. The searchlight wandered back and forth for a few moments before going dark. Silence returned as the pilot continued his patrol.

Tei'Shima sat quietly crying in the dark, watching the snowflakes add their weight to hide the horrors of war. Her tears sparkled blue in the light of the stasis cabinets all around her. In the Harmonies hundreds of kah on the battlefield stared at the ground where they'd died. They didn't care that their corpses were no longer there.

Tei'Shima had never seen so many kah in one place. The

battlefield was thick with them. Some hovered above craters as if standing upon ghostly ground. Some had already joined their ancestors, while others fought their dissolution as hard as they'd fought for anything in life. Merkiaari or Human or Shan. None would win this fight.

She felt Kazim approaching but didn't greet him. He knelt awkwardly and hugged her from behind. He laid his head on her shoulder and snuffled the fur of her face. It was comfort he offered, but it made her heart ache worse for those who would never feel another's touch again.

Tei'Laran's kah watched her and Kazim for a long moment. He raised a hand in farewell, and then faded away to join his ancestors. Tei'Shima's tears fell harder. He'd been a mentor to her. He'd asked her for nothing and given her everything.

"Don't cry," Kazim whispered. "Please don't give up on us."

Us, she thought.

Tei'Shima heard the double meaning in his words. "I want to live. I want all our friends to live."

"We all want that."

Tei'Shima surveyed the rows of stasis cabinets. So many friends would never wake to greet her again. "I want lots of cubs. I never want to be alone. I'll teach them about Tahar and how to hunt, and you'll teach them how to be kind to people."

Kazim added his tears to hers. They splashed onto one of the cabinets and mingled there. Tei'Shima looked down into the blue magic of the stasis field at Eric's remains. There wasn't much left. How could anyone come back sane from that?

She wiped her tears away to see Eric's face better. "You'll show our cubs how to be brave like him. You'll show our cubs there were once good aliens like Gina."

"Of course I will," Kazim soothed. "We'll do it together."

"I never understood why your work is important, but I do now. After this. You must show everyone what happened here. If I die… if I can't do it, you have to show them for me."

"Hush. You know heroes never die."

"*Promise me!*"

"I promise, but I won't let you die. I love you."

Tei'Shima flicked her ears. She felt the truth of it in the Harmonies, but she'd known for a while. Since Snakeholme she'd known they should mate. The Harmonies were clearly in favour, but neither of them had done anything about it. It was time they did.

Tei'Shima and Kazim consummated their love in the cold blue glow of the stasis chambers, under the gaze of dead heroes.

* * *

Thankyou for reading Incursion. Turn the page to read a bonus chapter from Countermeasures, the next book in the Merkiaari Wars.

Countermeasures

(Merkiaari Wars Book 6)

by

Mark E. Cooper

Prologue

Silver Bay, Duchy of Longthorpe, Faragut

Major Eleanor Hutton made her way back to base through the ruined town of Silver Bay using the broken buildings for cover. She left her body, such as it was, to its job and reviewed her latest skirmish in her mind.

The Merkiaari weren't playing it straight. They weren't cleansing Faragut in the accepted sense, and were being very un-Merki-like in their targeting. There was a very old saying dating back to pre-colonial days that applied. The Merki were bombing them back to the stone age. Their air-strikes were pinpoint accurate, and collateral damage was low. A side-effect the Merkiaari didn't give a fig about she was sure. They were more interested in taking out infrastructure.

The ground battles she'd taken part in had all been follow up. Most had been targeted upon places where the air-strikes had been least effective. The attack on the castle had been the first of many like it. The Merkiaari had simply wanted to finish the job, but how had they known Silver Bay was so important to Faragut? They couldn't have known the king was in residence surely?

Ellie paused opposite the entrance to the service tunnels running under the town, but she didn't approach. She stayed on the far side of the street. There were sentries hiding from observation just inside and they'd noticed her approach. They gave her the signal to wait.

She ran a sensor sweep, but it came back negative. Her sensors were faster and better than their handheld or helmet rigs. No hostiles were in range. She waited for them to come to the same conclusion or they might shoot her. She had enough holes in her already.

The sentries finally signalled and Ellie dashed into the tunnel. They had to press their backs to the walls to give her room to enter. Both men saluted. They shouldn't have bothered. She wasn't wearing uniform, but she appreciated the thought. Ellie towered over them. She couldn't help being intimidating, but they offered respect not fear and she appreciated that. She removed her helmet and returned their salutes.

Ellie tried not to notice the awe writ on their faces. She supposed it was better than the fear people had worn that first day. Her battle at the castle had cured them of that at least.

"You're leaking again, Major."

Ellie prodded at the holes in her armour. Blood mixed with coolant leaked out of her leaving runnels. The wounds didn't hurt; nothing did anymore, but she looked a mess. Her nanocoat still worked but much of it was missing. Dents and holes marred the once glossy black surfaces of her armour. She looked like crap, or scrap she thought with a purely internal chuckle.

"I'm back for maintenance. I feel like crap."

The guards nodded. "Begging your pardon, Major, but you look like it too."

The other guard thumped his mate's chest with the back of one hand.

Ellie grinned down at them. "You should see the other guy. Oh wait, you can't. He's paste."

They laughed.

"I'm off to the shop. The Doc will fix me up like new. See you later."

Ellie strode away, her heavy footfalls thudding on the plascrete floor. One of the guards called out to her, but she didn't stop.

"Grab a new paint job while you're there! Bottle green suits you better!"

Royal guards wore bottle green tunics.

Ellie laughed and raised a hand. The arm servos whined and something inside made a horrible clicking sound. It rose in fits and starts. She really did need the shop for a tune up this time. She lowered the arm wincing when something twanged inside, but its action smoothed out.

Well, good then.

She passed others on her way through the tunnels. They all braced to attention and saluted. She returned each but there were so many that her returns became vague waves by the time she reached Doc's surgery. It wasn't much of a surgery. It was just a machine room, part of the sub-basement of the collapsed tower in the town above.

Ellie entered the room and rounded the long silenced machines. Doc's body was in bed as if asleep. His hands, so skilled in life were clasped neatly on top of the covers. They held a photograph. Ellie stared down at him trying to understand her emotions. Sad? Angry? Both she decided but there was more. She was jealous. He'd left her behind in this shit-hole. Left his monster to carry on without its creator.

She reached down and took the photograph. It was a picture of him with his family. He'd been a twin. His brother was a mirror image. She hadn't known that about him. No reason she should. He'd never spoken of his family after that day when they'd made their bargain. She replaced the photo.

"You sonofabitch," she snarled. "You fucker. You promised to fix me after the war. You promised to be here when I needed you."

Ellie frowned as something splashed onto his face. She looked up at the ceiling and realised. Her eye was leaking. Her human eye. Crying? She was fucking *crying!* Didn't that beat all? Crying over him like he was worth it. She ought to rip him apart for abandoning her like this! She turned away and saw his computer. Her name was blinking on the screen. She crossed to it and accessed the message. It was a simple suicide note and a list of filenames.

> *Major,*
>
> *I thought I could stay. I was wrong. When I broke my oaths to build you, I thought it a small thing compared with what I'd already lost. Being shunned by my colleagues proved how wrong I was to believe that.*
>
> *I could give you reasons and excuses for what I've done, but instead I'll bequeath my notes and everything I've learned about the hypocrites to you. Do what you will with it.*
>
> *I'm sorry.*

Ellie read it twice. Hypocrites. His erstwhile colleagues who'd shunned him perhaps. She opened the files by double clicking the file names. Most were bios of convicts. Ellie felt a chill of unease as she read them. She quickly opened the remaining files. Some were bios of surgeons like Michaels had been, others were engineers and technicians.

The last link opened a video archive. The first video showed Doc building her. She sped through the surgeries and procedures used to create her, looking for something she didn't know. She'd always known there was a documentary video detailing her augmentation. The king said he'd wanted one for evidence. Together with her signature on the dotted line it was meant to shield all involved from prosecution.

All BS of course. Ellie complied because Nicky's brother wanted it, and she wanted to fight. It was her only option. She wouldn't say only hope, because really, what woman would want to be turned into this monstrosity?

The other videos left her feeling empty. She watched convicts being mind-wiped by the doctors on Doc's list of hypocrites. Convicts being programmed to become brave patriots and volunteering for special missions. Convicts agreeing to surgery for amputations and eye removals, well on their way to augmentation. Just like her.

Unlike her they weren't volunteers. Zeeks had no will of their own. Their personalities were programmed into them, including a willingness to become reapers. It was a crime against humanity performed in Nicky's brother's name without his sanction.

On Faragut!

In the core of the Alliance, not on a Border World no one had ever heard of. Not somewhere at the arse end of nowhere but in the core! She groaned. She had to tell the king. William would be horrified. It was something the Merkiaari might do, not their people. Not her Nicky's people. She hadn't heard anything about this. Nothing at all. It couldn't be happening here in Silver Bay. She'd have known.

Sir Harry was doing this? Who else could?

"That fucker," she snarled.

No wonder Doc had killed himself. Sir Harry had used his work like a training manual to create abominations. Reapers like her. The doctors who'd shunned him had duplicated his work in secret. The hypocrites.

"Sanctimonious pricks."

Ellie glanced at Michaels and felt a bottomless pit full of rage claim her. He'd armed her with knowledge and left her to decide what to do about it. He'd made his choice and checked out. She stormed out of the room.

Sir Harry was in the war room. That's what everyone called it but it was just another basement. They'd been using a lot of them just like it linked by service tunnels. After the failure of the castle's bunker, decamping to a complex of tunnels and widely-spaced sub-basements had seemed a wise precaution.

The king's bodyguard saluted her at the open door. Both men knew her. Wolfe had been with William since the attack on the castle. They normally would've had a few words to catch up, but she didn't stop for pleasantries. Not this time. She stormed into the war room to find the king and Sir Harry studying plans on the holo table. Men and women worked around the sides of the room using computers and comms stations.

"Ellie?" King William said, looking up.

Ellie ignored him and went for Sir Harry. She hoisted him into the air by the neck. The people working around the room screamed and stampeded for the door. That was a signal for the guards to rush in with weapons drawn.

"*You...*" she snarled into his face.

"*Ellie!*" the king yelled reaching up to pull ineffectually on her arm. "*Let him go!*"

"Doc is dead because of you."

Sir Harry took his weight off his neck by holding tight to her arm with both hands. "I..." he gurgled. "Don't. Know. What. You're talking about!"

"*Liar!*" she roared. "I'm going to squeeze the truth out of you!"

"*Major Hutton!*" King William roared. "*Stand down!*"

"You don't know what he's done, Sire!"

"Are you refusing a direct order from your king?"

"He did it. He mind-wiped those convicts. He cut them up and made them into monsters like me." Ellie shook the general. "*Didn't you!*"

"I don't know what you're talking about!" Sir Harry choked out.

Ellie felt the rifle barrel connect with the back of her head. Wolfe. Good man there. He'd chosen the unarmoured side of her skull.

"No one fire without my express command," William said calmly. "Stand down Ellie."

She lowered the general gently to the floor, but she kept her grip on his neck. Sir Harry smirked. That was all. It was enough. She crushed his throat and let him fall twitching to the floor.

"Oh fuck, no you didn't," Wolfe swore.

The other guard shouted in disbelief as he tried to save Sir Harry, but there was no way Ellie would have let him. She didn't need to intervene. She stared down at the general as the light went out of his eyes and waited to die. Wolfe was a good man. He'd make sure with one shot.

"*Don't fire! Don't fire!*" William cried desperately over Wolfe's cursing.

"No do," Ellie said.

"*No! Weapons down!*" William yelled desperately as more men arrived. "*No one fire!*"

* * *

Super Secret Incursion Launch Draw (Ends Jan 31 2017)
https://goo.gl/1Fo8wC

Also available from Impulse

If these books are not available from your local bookshop, send this coupon together with your check made payable to:

Impulse Books UK
At the following address:

Impulse Books UK
18, Lampits Hill Avenue,
Corringham
Essex SS177NY
United Kingdom

Please send the following great titles from Impulse Books UK

Tick as approrriate:

The God Decrees (Pb)
ISBN: 978-1-905380-45-9 £10.99 ____________ ☐

The Power That Binds (Pb)
ISBN: 978-1-905380-46-6 £10.99 ____________ ☐

The Warrior Within (Pb)
ISBN: 978-1-905380-47-3 £10.99 ____________ ☐

Dragon Dawn (Pb)
ISBN: 978-1-905380-48-0 £11.99 ____________ ☐

Wolf's Revenge (Pb)
ISBN: 978-1-905380-43-5 £11.99 ____________ ☐

NAME ______________________________
ADDRESS ____________________________
____
____

I have enclosed a check for the sum of £ ____

Please be sure to add £2.25 to your order to cover shipping and handling charges.

Made in the USA
San Bernardino, CA
09 November 2018